The Adventures of Argon Bosch

Kirk Nelson

ISBN:1519527063
ISBN-13:9781519527066

DEDICATION

I dedicate this to the two people that were essential to this book
ever coming into being:
My dearest friend Brian who was there at inception and encouraged me to
the end. Argon Bosch simply would not have existed without him.
And my beautiful wife Cheryl who, even after 30 years,
puts up with my own inner Argon.

CONTENTS

ACKNOWLEDGMENTS

No one exists in a vacuum (except those odd creatures thriving in space) so I couldn't have managed this solely on my own. There are countless authors that have inspired me through my reading years from Lester Dent to Edgar Rice Burroughs to Stephen King. Those and all the rest, good and bad, have each left lessons behind as I closed each book.

And then there are those that saw the seed of something within me that I would have missed. These wonderful friends helped to nurse and cultivate whatever talent may present itself here. Thanks to Rich Heinemann, Tom Ray, Gary and Maurice – friends no one should be without, and Kevin Andrews who held up a light for me
to follow.

Finally, a very special acknowledgement to a good friend and Argon's foil, Scott McCauley, who not only voiced Winston in the videos, but really gave him much more life than I ever could.

CHAPTER 1

I woke up not knowing where I was.

I'm not unfamiliar with waking up in strange surroundings, just never very comfortable with that unsettling feeling. This is likely due to the many occasions I've bolted from unconsciousness only to find myself falling, tied up, beaten, or faced with guns or wild animals. And sometimes I would get the special unwanted surprise of rousing to some combination of these unnerving situations. Like the time I snapped awake, blood in my eye, tied, bruised, and staring into the collective firepower of a large contingent of the Tanaki Peacekeeping Force. And *that* happened twice. One would assume that such rude awakenings would give any normal person the desire to avoid any circumstances that would lead to coming to in an unknown place. This was just one of many such lessons I had yet to learn.

To further complicate things my thoughts were fragmented in an unhelpful quagmire. At least it felt that way. Like my brain was a chilled jar of molasses that had dropped and shattered all across the floor of my skull. The pieces were all there but they were connected by the slowest, heaviest, stickiest medium of communication one could imagine. This, combined with the throbbing pain that accompanied every thought and movement, made the explanation of my dilemma quite apparent. I was hungover.

Once that realization ever so slowly bloomed in my mind I sighed a bit of relief. Sure, waking up in a strange place, hungover, might prove to have complications, but this was something that was more frequent and a circumstance where I felt some sense of mastery. I had done it enough that I was confident in my ability to deal with any scenario. Much unlike the times when a misstep or unfortunate turn of luck could have far more dire consequences. But, strange place. Hungover. That I could handle. I thought.

My prone position was comfortable and warm. I smelled jasmine and tellenight flowers lingering over the linens. I was half inclined to simply drift back to sleep but something nestled deep inside my protesting consciousness urged me to discover more. I tested my right arm. It moved freely so I knew it wasn't tied to something. Fragments of my previous evening were slowly oozing back along the broken jar of my sticky memory. My eyes were open but I couldn't see much. The room seemed overly dim and I suddenly realized my goggles were on. Not necessarily unusual but I had the undeniable feeling that I was, with the obvious exception of my clunky eyewear, naked. I reached up and drew my goggles up across my forehead and, yup, there I was...naked. At first I felt the same confusion wash over me seeing my own reflection looking back at me prone on a large bed with a dark colored sheet protecting my modesty. As the fogginess of my mind momentarily cleared I recognized that there was a mirror mounted to the ceiling above the bed. I should have known...brothel.

There was a time in my life when such ribald behavior would have shocked me. But as age marches on and life's experiences harden and dissolve our early ideals, one has a tendency to accept things that might have been outside the innocent boundaries of youth. The life of an interstellar delivery pilot is very often lonely and a man has certain needs. That's all the excuses I am going to make. Judgments judged, assumptions assumed.

I sat up and a half dozen explosions popped throughout my head. My mouth was dry and even I was repelled by the taste. I am sure my breath was fairly unpleasant and could ruin a meal. Now all I was missing was an urgent, painful need to urinate.

And...there it was. As a few more details coalesced in my mind I knew that even without full recollection my piss would be black as deep space. I've been around long enough to recognize an Obsidian Ale hangover. Not my favorite but understandable under the circumstances. Obsidian Ale was my beverage of choice when I felt like losing myself for awhile. A dense, inky looking drink that tasted bad no matter how many I drank but got me into an amnesiac state quicker than anything else. My "favorite" brew of this repulsive beverage was Blackhole. While not the most popular of the several makes, it was the one I could count on to get the desired effect and not actually kill me.

I cast a quick glance around the room. It was sparse but nicely decorated with a large, comfortable bed, a couple of nightstands that were dark stained wood on which stood a small lamp that gave off a welcome glow, a chair that was draped with what I assumed were cast off blankets and clothing, and a large dresser that matched the nightstands. There were two paintings on either side of the bed showcasing grand landscapes of craggy mountains reflected in a dark lake with lazy red clouds stretching across a bright yellow sky. The room was not overly large but the illumination of the lamps only reached just beyond the dresser leaving the rest of the space shadowed and unknown.

So that was almost all the pieces of the puzzle. But one important detail was still absent. Just then something flew out of the shadows and hit me in the face (my clothes) and a voice shouted, "Don't you have someplace you need to be?"

There was the missing piece...my lovely host.

I drug my pants off my head and looked at who was so anxious to get rid of me. I was relieved to see that it was a female (Obsidian Ale, I remind you) and that she was actually quite attractive (again...the ale, remember). This only concerned me in that I knew I was likely not getting any bargain where her services were considered. I'm not normally so flush as to afford the top tier of anything. I just hoped I didn't manage to rack up a huge tab that would set me up to angle for a credit stake and working it off for the next 4 months. Yes, the voice of experience...again. My judgment, drunk or not, can sometimes be known as "sketchy" and impetuous. I just hoped this time it wasn't impulsive enough to wipe out my bank account.

I smiled my best, charismatic smile. "Where else would I have to be than here sharing your lovely company..." I struggled for a name. She was Obarneen and they had a certain naming style based on the level of social awareness. One where you could possibly shoot for a common pet name that might reference a previous familiarity. If she had been Fremforlohl or Neglodite I would have had a good chance as they use only a handful of personal addresses. Lendorcan, on the other hand, would have been impossible since they use a very specific name and number system that not only confuses the rest of the Galaxy but their own race as well. But Obarneen, I had a shot with that race. Or, I would have had I been in my right mind. I felt fortunate given my jumbled brain that I was at least able to identify her race. Well, maybe I shouldn't give so much credit to my observation and deductive powers as her bright yellow coloring and the extra set of breasts were a fairly obvious give away. With my crippled cognitive abilities combined with her being gorgeous and naked, well, I simply let the sentence hang there, incomplete, for far too long. She took notice.

"Shena." Her expression was a stiff mask of annoyance.

"Right! I knew that. Sheva..."

"SheNA!"

"I thought I said that," I lied. Still too damn foggy. Plus my need to take a piss was having an effect I was sure she was not going to be happy to notice given her current state of mind. She glanced down, looked back up at me with a face that was far closer to disgusted than amused, and quickly grabbed a robe from a nearby chair and tossed it on. Show's over.

"That's not what you think."

"Really?" Her eyebrow shot up.

"No, I mean..."

"You need to leave." I wanted to argue, thought better of it, then did it anyway.

"I don't mean to assume but if I remember correctly, I sorta paid for some *special* time with you and..."

"You did," she sighed, obviously regretting money changing hands and agreements made. "But, thankfully, those four days are over."

Holy shit! I had managed to lose 4 days. My mind suddenly lurched forward, adrenaline fueled and breaking free of the haze, the last week crystal clear in my mind. And it was all too obvious now that I had made a really bad mistake. Winston was going to be pissed. And the client may just kill me.

THE CREATURE BUZZED IN through the doorway of the company's reception office to startle Winston from his sleep. Its insect-like appearance gave it a much more alien look than he was used to. Practically immediately it started clattering in some outer rim language that took him a few moments to process.

There have been many times that others have balked at Winston's value as my lone employee at The Jackleg Courier Service, myself included. He regularly insults my clients and puts on an air of disapproving indignation and even hostility to anyone that ventures into my small company to get something delivered. His own self-proclaimed disapproval of me is enough reason for me to send him packing to seek employment God knows where. And more than once he has attempted to kill me (at least that is my belief). But despite all of these and many other shortcomings I still keep him employed. Have I mentioned my poor judgment yet? But, to his credit, I begrudgingly will acknowledge he is the most versatile employee one could ever want when it came to finding out information (legal or otherwise) and synthesizing a translation from whatever bizarre dialect my potential client produces. Such was the case with the insect thing. Within seconds Winston was conversing in the same click-clack, buzz-toned speech as the mandible snapping creature.

"It is imperative I get this package delivered to a remote location immediately!" it demanded as Winston had later explained to me. "If your pilot cannot comply and leave at once I must know so I may seek arrangements elsewhere without delay."

"Calm down, insect. Don't make me break out my giant shoe. Where is that box supposed to be?" questioned Winston.

"It simply *must* be delivered to specific coordinates in the L'Kahs sector within four days!" it buzzed.

A moment later after checking the coordinates Winston revealed, "That's in Imperial space. Nobody likes to deliver there."

"You don't think I know that? Why do you think I came here of all places? Nobody wants to deliver it. I was finally referred to this place," he motioned around the office with one of several skinny, multi-jointed limbs. "I was told a Mr. Bosch would deliver anything anywhere without questions."

"Yes. He does have that rather desperate reputation. Let me call him in and see what he says."

"Yes, yes. Make it quick. If he can't accomplish this I may have to take it there myself...at no small inconvenience."

Winston clicked over to the inter-office comm system. "Argon. Can you come up here a moment? There is a client that needs your clarification on a delivery."

"Uh...sure," I replied.

A few minutes later I walked into the office and gave a small startled jump. "Holy..." The creature was ugly and definitely of some insect evolution. I've encountered a few species that are based on insect evolution, Brilzak children being a sad mistake of recent memory, but this thing was the ugliest I'd come across. It wore clothing which managed to cover up some of its grotesqueness but I would have far preferred a bag of some sort. It was thin, as most of them are, and brown, another characteristic they all seem to share. Its head could have benefited from a hood as those nasty, stiff little hairs that randomly poked out of its head always gave me the willies. While I find the mandibles an unpleasant thing to watch as they talk (or worse yet, eat... Lord!) it is those compound, staring eyes that make me the most uncomfortable. They are so inhuman that you can never shake the feeling that you are looking and talking to a freakishly large bug that cannot relate to you on any common ground.

I tried to gather my wits and be professional. It was business after all.

"Winston, who do we have here?"

"A rather impatient and rude cockroach."

I shot Winston a stern glance and cleared my throat. "Winston," I scolded.

"Fear not, boss. He doesn't understand a word of Common. Not that those clickity-clack snappers could enunciate a single word of proper speech."

"Does it, er...he...or she have a name?"

"I can't even venture a guess as to its gender, nor do I care to. As for its name, it hasn't gotten around to that yet. It is way too concerned with getting its bloody package delivered."

Just then the thing clicked out something that sounded like feet crossing over gravel.

Winston interpreted for me: "It said, 'Well? What have you decided?'"

"About what?" I asked not knowing what they had been discussing.

Winston said something back to the creature that sounded like a cross between smashing a light bulb and eating space-nuts. Even after years of elocution lessons I knew there was no way I would ever be able to conjugate the verb "kltqut'kczksss" so bug-speak was off my list of possible accomplishments. Winston explained to me that the insect alien had asked for us to deliver a package to the Imperial sector.

"Shit," was my best response. The Imperial sector is on the outer rim of the galaxy and is made up of about a hundred systems that seem to think they are a big deal. They are not part of the Galactic Tribunal ruling government and like to be left to do their own thing. Most of the inhabitants of the galaxy leave them alone and give their little "empire" a wide berth. I've heard plenty of tales about the sector and I knew it was full of infighting and strange religions. Lots of drama. I don't like drama so any appeal it has is wasted on me. While the rest of the galaxy is plenty to keep me occupied and has more than enough things to entertain, I've never wanted to consider Imperial Space to be part of my route. I saw no reason to change that now.

"No."

Winston thought for a moment then said to me, "This thing seems very urgent and desperate, a nice little cocktail that usually allows us to squeeze some extra profit. If this is indeed Imperial business the margin for inflating our price could be even higher."

I pondered his point. Yes, this seemed like the perfect storm of over-charging. My own inner greed started to salivate but my more sensible instincts began to alarm. Imperial space was a big, dark hole at the very edge of the galaxy. It was considered by many as practically a whole different galaxy far, far away.

Despite my usual bend toward practical decisions, my greed was rapidly winning out; a trend that continues to get me into unfortunate situations. Just recently I spent weeks floating through black, empty space to hoard a few extra credits to pay for things I shouldn't have been spending my income on anyway. But the chance to make a big score, to get ahead financially for once always pulls me toward the dark side.

"Ask him what he is willing to pay if I agree to do it."

Again, more sounds of bolts shaking in a paper sack and Vanderloon cards slapping against bicycle spokes. "He says he'll pay 3 thousand."

I pondered the sum for a moment. For the distance it would be about half that. "How soon does he need it there?"

"Four days."

It would take me about two days if I really pushed it. I know a couple unauthorized back currents in the gravity-well network that will bypass the known navigation routes. "Let him know that will increase the cost. It is an outer rim delivery."

More unintelligible noise. "He'll pay 5 thousand."

I didn't hesitate, "Eight."

Winston hesitated until I gave him another stern look then made the counter offer.

It let out a squeak sound. Even without understanding the conversation I could tell our *insecty* guest wasn't happy about it. In fact I almost drew my sidearm as it looked like he might get violent. There was a tense exchange and finally Winston said, "He agrees."

I looked at the insect and smiled. At this point I normally shake hands but there was no way I was going to shake this dung beetle's multi-jointed stick that passed for its hand. I nodded then added for Winston to translate, "We'll need the money up front as he is a new client and we don't normally travel to that section of the galaxy." I smiled again like it was normal for me to say that at every transaction. I could tell from the body language that this also wasn't going over well but I had this cricket forced into a corner.

Finally, "It's done," revealed Winston. I nodded toward the bug and told Winston, "You finish up the transaction and I'll ready the Spud."

"OK."

As I turned to leave the office and head into the garage Winston said, "And Argon..."

"Yes?"

"Nice."

It takes a lot for Winston to compliment me. Generally it has to do with money.

I entered the garage and looked at my ship. The Space Spud, an old Hanton Model 11XC-7 Starboat. I christened it such because the shape reminded me of a potato. No big thought process. Just shape. Potato. I may have been drunk at the time. I also painted it brown. It had definitely seen better days. There were rust patches here and there and a lot of pitting from minor impacts. It also had two large plates welded into place where the hull integrity had been punched through. But I can't take all the blame for its sad appearance. It had been around the galaxy a few times before I got her.

I won my ship in a Vanderloon game. I am partial to the diversion and I can play a pretty fair game. It is something about the way my brain works and my ability to see patterns in seemingly random chaos. The same talent also helps me pilot my ship. So I can do well unless I get drunk. Or I play Winston. I suspect he cheats; he always beats me even though he loathes the game. But in this particular instance I was on a streak, sober for a change, and winning everything this guy had. He was a pompous fool and didn't know when to quit. Finally, wiped out, he offered me his ship for a final "winner take all" hand. Sight unseen I agreed. I felt unstoppable. It was one of the best games I had ever played and I won in record time. He accused me of cheating and violence almost broke out except a Regional Marshal had been watching the game and he quickly intervened and made the welcher honor his bet. One of the best stretches of luck I ever had. Of course it came on the heels of possibly the worst one I ever had (but that is another story).

With my own ship at last I was able to go out and secure my place amongst the independent couriers around the galaxy. I just needed a company to get my start. That came a while later after struggling with freelance work for a few years.

So as I looked at my ship I wished that I could afford to fix her up. My bread and butter. She and I had crisscrossed the galaxy more times than I can count. But we never flew into Imperial Space and that was going to change. And with the money I was going make I would hope to get some much needed repairs done. Then I thought ahead and wondered if this might open up a whole new realm of opportunity for me. The "Empire" might want to utilize my services on a much more frequent basis. Yes! Since no one ever seemed to want to go there and the United Space Parcel Syndicate refused to help them seeing as they didn't have Tribunal recognition, it was free space. A place to make a stake. My ship had finally come in. Literally.

The package was about 2 meters square so I tucked it away in the Spud's small cargo hold. It wasn't very heavy and had numerous call-outs in a couple languages across multiple sides proclaiming the box was "URGENT!" I quickly scanned the Bill of Lading and the contract as I waited for the Spud to warm up her engines. The delivery address was a space station located at some designated galactic coordinates. I punched them in and noticed that the space on my contract for the recipient was simply named "Deck Officer." Must be some kind of military satellite, I figured. The Spud gave me green across the instrument panel and I nudged her out of the bay and onto the pad.

"Winston, I'm leaving now. See you in a few days."

"I'm sorry, Argon, I wasn't listening. I'm busy counting money."

"Funny."

"Try not to die." He paused for just a moment to emphasize his real concern. "Or screw this up."

"That's the sendoff I am used to."

"So glad I could meet your expectations."

I engaged the Gravity Drive, hovered up clear of the buildings, and punched the thrusters. Might as well get this out of the way. And if I took the back short-cuts I would make it there in plenty of time. My mind started to picture the route. I could even stop off at a little place I know and get a little R and R. Maybe celebrate my big score a little. Sure. What harm could it do?

AND SO THERE I WAS, two days late to my delivery, burning up my profits for a job that I would not be able to complete according to contract. As with most new clients I got the full payment up front so they couldn't stiff me on the second half when I showed up late. But that didn't mean they wouldn't resent the fact. I could be worried I wouldn't get the promise of future work from their deep pocketed bureaucracy but I was much more in fear of losing my life if they decided to have me executed. Outside of the Tribunal's jurisdiction I didn't have any rights or legal recourse. Given the beetle guy's frantic insistence on 5 days I had a very strong feeling that the military presence on the station wouldn't look favorably on my tardiness thus also breaking Winston's other prophetic farewell.

I wasted no time in beating a hasty retreat from my 4 day love den and getting to my ship. My lovely companion huffed yet another puff of disgust when I didn't leave a tip. I am not normally this cheap but I was pretty assured I wouldn't be passing this way again - if I ever passed anywhere again! Shit.

I jogged across the tarmac and climbed up on the wing of the Spud. I unlocked the cockpit and quickly got inside. It was a private landing bay so there weren't any formalities in getting an "OK" to launch so I got the Spud fired up and screamed out of that city and into the dawn. Moments later the bright sky gave way to the endless black of space and my Nav Computer took over sending me on course to the space station. Now many people might think I would be foolish to even attempt the delivery at this late date and possibly face certain death but something pushed me on to finish the job. If I wasn't being painfully honest I would say it was an unflagging sense of duty and upholding my oath to "Always get it there!" but that wouldn't be exactly true. I was more propelled to see if I might somehow still salvage this whole mess and get some of these easy pickings on this low hanging fruit. I'm not a brave man but Greed seems to trump Death every time. Plus I just didn't want to give Winston the satisfaction of an easy rebuke. Dying suddenly seemed so much more pleasant.

As I approached the coordinates a small ship screamed past and scared the crap out of me. It made a loud screech/roar sound that was both frightening and annoying at the same time. The ship was smaller than the Spud and resembled a softball sandwiched between two fans. It broadcast a generic message to my comm system asking my business. I stated I was a courier ship and that I had an important package for a space station that was suppose to be near this location. There was a momentary pause where I believed I was being scanned. The Space Spud is not outfitted with weapons (a decision I've always meant to remedy) and this was fortuitous as the scan came with a weapons lock alarm that always managed to make my sphincter clench. I've had to dodge, evade, and outrun far too many attacks in my many travels - none of which were *technically* my fault - to not get a tense knot in my gut when that little light chimed on. The pilot must have approved of what he saw as he came back with a message to follow him since the station had moved from this spot. I am not a space logistics engineer but from what I've found, a space station is supposed to be easily located at a specific area not gallivanting around the galaxy on some whim. If you can't find it, it isn't a station. It's a ship. I followed after my weird little escort. Just as well as the weapons lock remained.

We entered a system about an hour later and it seemed like my usher was steering us toward a small moon. As we closed the distance I discovered that it was no moon but an enormous space station. It was quite an impressive feat of design as it was obviously made to resemble a lifeless planetoid. I have seen a lot of moons, visited some, and crashed into a couple so I am intimately familiar with what a moon looks like. First off, it was enormous. The very scope of constructing such a thing was beyond my comprehension. It was a light gray color and pitted with various canals and holes across its expansive surface. Added to this was a large circular indentation that seriously resembled a massive crater. If it was orbiting a planet one wouldn't suspect anything to warrant a closer look. I can only assume this would be the desired effect. Which made me come to the conclusion that it was not just a mobile space station but a weapon of war. I suddenly had a strong desire to toss the whole job and head back to friendlier space as fast as the Spud could fly. Oh yeah, the weapons lock. I continued my tailgating.

My escorting craft led me to a small bay in the side of the station where I passed through a normal air-lock force field and landed amongst a few ships, mostly some short range craft resembling the one that had lead me to the immense station/ship. A few other larger ones that looked like shuttles and scout craft.

I hopped out of the Spud and opened my cargo hatch. I hadn't even unloaded the box when I could hear somebody yelling behind me. I knew without turning around that all of that hostility was directed at me.

"You there! I say, YOU THERE!"

I turned around wearing my most innocent, confused face. I jabbed a finger at my chest and arched an eyebrow. "Me?"

"Yes, YOU!"

My faux-confusion radiated across the entirety of the landing bay; they could probably smell it in the control booth. I was putting it on thick. "What?" I added to the illusion, eyes wide and innocent.

The man was all business. He wore some kind of uniform and

was followed closely by his entourage of minions. There were even a few of them dressed in gleaming white armor that appeared to be made of plastic. I doubted they could withstand a direct shot from one of my pistols or maybe even a well-pitched stone. To ease my mind my hand brushed across my holster just to reassure me it was still nestled securely there and not left on the dash of my cockpit. Ah, the comforting solid bump of hand and grip.

"I was told you would be here with an important delivery...two days ago!"

"Well, about that..."

He frowned that disapproving frown that usually only your father can unveil. I felt bad, just not that bad. I knew I had screwed this up but I would be damned if he was going to nix my chance to salvage this right from the go. I still had some world class lying and bullshitting to pull off before tossing the whole job into the rubbish pile.

"I don't want to hear your excuses, Mr..."

"Bosch. Argon Bosch."

"Mr. Bosch. You were contracted to deliver an item to this station within a mutually agreed time frame to which you were paid a large sum of money. I find you at fault of breaking that agreement and thusly..."

Did he say, *"Thusly?"*

"Right. But I have certain requirements that also must be met; one of which is my safety! Your patron made no mention of this being a strategic *military* space station and that as such my transporting of your cargo puts me at risk." I was surprising even myself with my ad-libbing such an elaborate excuse, false as it was.

His eyes got wide at my accusations and I knew I had him second guessing my ineptness. Now for the coupe de gras.

"And that wouldn't even be that big of a deal except that I was followed and attacked!"

"What? By who?"

"I don't know who they were but a couple ships jumped me around Ekselsier. I had to lose them or I would have led them right to you and I am sure you weren't looking to announce your location to your enemy."

"Who were these individuals? What did their ships look like and how many were there?"

"Hey, I wasn't joy riding and I certainly wasn't taking time to snap some pictures for you. They fired on me and I got the hell out of there! You're lucky I am as good of a pilot as I am. A less experienced one would have either brought them straight to your doorstep or just gone back home. Or quite possibly been destroyed by their weapons' fire. I may charge a lot but I always get my cargo delivered." He was actually silent for a moment so I decided to push it. "Frankly I am kind of upset right now that you take such a judgmental stance with me before you even hear what happened. In fact I should charge you extra for putting me in danger." My righteous indignation was showing, feigned as it was.

He stood for a second or two, mouth working at saying nothing. I had him right where I wanted him.

"Without any actual proof of the alleged attack I consider it mere fabrication." Well, maybe not *right* where I want him. "For all I know you were wasting our time cavorting with prostitutes and lounging in extravagant beds all at our expense." Damn, this guy was clairvoyant. I needed to get the heat off me or this whole thing was going to go south and they just might...

"Throw him in the brig until we can sort out fact from lie." Two of the plastic armored goons pointed rifles at me. He motioned to another couple of his uniformed minions, "Get that cargo unloaded and have maintenance install it immediately. It is a cover for the exhaust port in sector 89-46-C. A retired engineer on the original plans discovered an unforeseen design flaw and sent this out to us before it could be taken advantage of."

They began to lead me away. At this point I was curious what my next move would be. They led me down a few identical nondescript corridors when there was an alarm followed by an announcement over a PA system. "The station is under attack. Report to your emergency battle stations. This is not a drill." It repeated twice more and then was silent. At this point I looked to my would-be guards but they had run off to what I assumed were their "emergency battle stations." There was no one in the corridor with me. I looked around a few more seconds then decided to simply head back to my ship and get the hell out of there. I quickly turned down the passageway I believed led back to the hangar bay when I collided with a giant of a man dressed entirely in black. I bounced off of him and staggered back to look up. He wore some kind of helmet and was flanked by two other men decked out in black armor. The tall wall of a man also wore a cape for some odd reason. I mean, who wears a cape? They serve no purpose on a space station other than to get in the way or get caught on furniture. I guessed he had a flair for the dramatic. He also seemed sickly as his breath rasped loudly through some sort of breathing apparatus. He looked down at me.

"Mind your place."

"Excuse me?"

"Stand aside or feel the power of the dark..."

It should be stated here to clear up any question as to how I might respond in any certain circumstance: I hate being threatened.

"Now just hold on, mouth breather. I was minding my own business, walking down this passage when you and your little sidekicks come racing along with no care as to..."

He raised his hand out as if he might grab me but simply clenched the air in front of me. The gesture again seemed to lend an air of theatricality to his whole countenance but I suddenly felt like my throat was full of cotton making it difficult to breath and impossible to talk further.

One of his wingmen said, "Sir, we must hurry to our ships. The rebels..."

He dropped his arm and my throat returned to normal. They raced off again down the intersecting corridor, around a corner, and out of sight.

"You better get going, you big, black..." I started to call after him but froze as a large menacing shadow crossed the wall of the corridor he had just entered signaling an approach. Luckily it was just two of the white plastic armored soldiers who darted out and down the opposite hallway. I decided it best to just make my way out of there before I encountered some other overly dramatic thespian.

A few more turns and I found the landing bay. My ship was where I left it so I jogged to it and climbed aboard. Within minutes I had the engines fired up and was coasting toward the docking forcefield. I was glad no one had decided to stop me. It appeared everyone was busy with their attention focused on more threatening details.

I flew out of the dock and into space glad to be free of this strange space station. A moon-sized deadly battle ship. A Death Moon.

As I flew away from the fake moon I noticed several other craft had flown into close orbit and were firing at it. What could they possibly hope to do to impact any real damage to this mammoth station? It would take much more fire power to make a dent in its vast surface. What a bloody waste of...

BOOM!

Suddenly the blackness of space was lit up by an enormous flash of light. An explosion that could only be the utter destruction of the entire space station. The resulting shock wave rattled the Spud. I looked back in the distance to see a brilliant light fading into the darkness. Seems the Death Moon was really a dying star in the emptiness of space. That must have been one lucky shot!

I punched in the coordinates for home. It would be good to be back. I thought about maybe taking a couple days off when I returned and travel to Harityko 8. I'd always wanted to go there. Seems like it might be just the right time.

Little did I know that there would be plenty of traveling ahead and no days off for quite some time. And certainly much more peril than the easy life of Harityko 8 would offer. In fact, had I known what was ahead I might just have stayed a while longer in Imperial space.

CHAPTER 2

I woke up not knowing where I was.

Turns out the autopilot had taken me back at the Jackleg Courier Company landing pad and I had fallen asleep some time before entering the system. I hate when that happens. Sometimes it seems like my life is just made up of disorientation with brief moments of clarity.

I left the Spud on the pad and went around to the front of the building to enter. I had been trying to find a way to spin the whole "adventure" into something with a more positive bent but it wasn't working out right in my head. Of course I could always lie but I knew that Winston would figure it out somehow. Why I was even concerned about Winston's reaction didn't cross my mind. I'd been down this road too many times. Even though he is my employee I grow apprehensive due to my familiarity with his usual belittling reaction. I simply hated that.

"So? How'd it go this time?" he asked immediately upon my entering through the front door with no thought of a cordial greeting or concern for any difficulty I might have encountered.

I forced a smile. "It was..."

"...a colossal fuck-up," he finished.

I frowned and already felt that old familiar feeling washing over me. Damn him. "I wouldn't go that far."

"Oh. So it *was* a fuck-up then," seeming to take joy in this revelation.

"We got our damn money!"

"Yes, but at what cost? Will we see some Imperial lawyers dropping by at some point? Or is it even more serious and it will be some police or *knights* or something to place you under arrest for crimes against civilization? Should I set you up with papers to hide out somewhere again?" If he had a mouth I would have expected a satisfied smile plus it would give me a place to aim a punch. He was taking way too much pleasure in this.

Once again I had to tick through my mental checklist on the pros and cons of Winston's continued employment. Why did I keep him on again? For a condescending brain in a jar, I was never one hundred percent confident that he was one of my best decisions.

INTERSTELLAR CARNIVALS WERE NOT my normal haunts and I especially didn't frequent the Midway as the sights available there were often disturbing to my more Terran sensibilities. There were far too many "normal" races and creatures in this newfound galactic expanse that could offer up cheap fodder for nightmares without having to witness the freakish oddities that were gasp-inducing to the already established veterans of interstellar travel. But, for reasons I can no longer recall, I was in Alongago City when I crossed under the large, brightly lettered banner that proclaimed "The Grand Wheastoviac's Cavalcade of Freaks" as if it were welcoming you to the gates of Shangri La. I found myself slowly picking my way along the various colorful trailers and tents that housed these "exquisite oddities" that I might invest a credit or two to refuel the subconscious hodgepodge of horrors that give me chase during my nocturnal sweats. Joy.

But, as I found when I had visited such places on Earth, the garish illustrations on the outside of the trailers rarely accurately portrayed the strange creatures housed within. I recall as a youth begging my dad to let me see the werewolf-boy that was painted snarling and vicious on the trailer only to have spent some of my meager allowance to see a young boy with long dirty hair and fake fangs barking at me from behind a barred wall. My excitement managed to fill in some of the glaring shortcomings of the cheap illusion until he suddenly drew close to the bars, pulled out his fangs, and asked me if I had any candy. Poof. He was just a kid like me, hungry for candy, and needing a bath and a haircut.

So while I saw some things that were cartoonish in their portrayals there were some more friendly sights - a few common animals from Earth that seemed to garner some attention in these far reaches of Space. They had some exhibits of common goldfish that were touted as being "made of metal and yet floated in water!" I saw a few children exit a trailer with terror filled eyes and parents trying their best to qualm their fears only to find they had simply seen live penguins. Then there were other exhibits that scared the shit out of me and there was no way I'd enter those tents or trailers just to cart away future nightmares. It was near the end of this Freakshow that I heard one of the barkers yell out, "He is a mind that can read *your* mind! See the Living Brain! The Incredible Winston!"

It seemed like a typical scam and I don't know why I even turned to look but it ended up changing my life, though it can be debated if it was actually for the better.

The graphic emblazoned across the side of the tent was at least somewhat well designed and executed. Of course the subject was a simple human-type brain of enormous proportion with stark bolts of lightning reaching out from it to ensnare your mind, or at least that was what the bold type exclaimed: "Zantarif Plood presents Winston - The Psychic Brain! He will steal your thoughts!"

A large, roundish man stood in front of a small podium and shouted at the few that had stopped to take advantage of their "rare opportunity" to see this "shocking marvel of mental magnificence!" He was of a race I had not encountered before; roughly human but the nose was doubled and situated on each side of his face and a coloring that could only be referred to as chartreuse. He wore a tall, weathered hat that reflected the same shoddiness of his clothing. Despite his many extraordinary claims of this brain's proficiency in stealing secrets from your mind, finding lost memories, and acute prognostication he had not been able to get this "amazing marvel" to produce enough income to afford a long coat that was absent of holes and loose threads. I listened halfheartedly and was about to leave when I spied a soft glow coming from an open seam in the side of the tent near the back. It appeared to be an opening that was not secured and by simply walking by I might provide myself with a casual glance as to what might be hidden inside. I disengaged myself from the scant crowd in front of the rotund man fighting desperately to capture their attention.

I strolled slowly toward the flap and then, with a quick glimpse back toward the still engaged host, stole a look inside. It was not bright but I could make out the details quite clearly. Trunks lay around the dirt floor, some open to reveal clothing and assorted sundries. Others remained locked as if hoarding some valuable secrets only a carney barker would appreciate. But near the front of the fabric that divided the tent into rooms there stood a large box. It was wooden with large windows on all sides but the one facing me. The light illuminating the space was being generated from inside. My curiosity gripped by both mystery and danger drew me closer. It was this very quality that afflicted customers outside and forced them to part with their money to make the grand journey to discover what unexplainable strangeness awaited them inside.

But I was going to get to see it for free!

I cautiously made my way past the disheveled cases and trunks to look into the brightness. As I neared I could see that the front facing window was against an opening in the fabric. It would seem that through this window those entering the tent from outside would be able to gaze at the reward of their courage and 5 credits. They would be disappointed.

Inside this large display case was a smaller container made of glass with a lid on top that could be opened to access inside. On the outside of the container was an audio speaker and the inside was filled with a clear liquid. Floating rather unceremoniously in this liquid was a brain. And, by the looks of it, a very normal appearing brain that had some tubes and wires connected to it. It didn't even look real. I almost laughed out loud when I saw it. What a rip-off.

Then it spoke.

"Excuse me, sir. Do you have the time?"

What? His voice took me by surprise. How did he know I was there? I immediately suspected a trick and quickly looked around to see if there might be someone watching me from a hidden vantage point or through a remote camera. I didn't see anything obvious but was still wary that some trickery was afoot.

"Wha...Why?" I stuttered.

"I am simply curious what time it is. It isn't an uncommon question and one that doesn't require a genius level IQ to answer. And here I thought you might be at least capable of answering the most simple of questions. Should I then assume that you'd not be able to answer another staggering query if I were to ask for your name?"

His attitude perplexed me. I was fairly sure he was insulting me but why would he do this? "I do know what time it is and I do know my name."

"Oh well then. Let me see if I can ring the Interstellar Press to let them know I've discovered the next recipient of the prized Wollenhiemer Trophy for Outstanding Wisdom."

"Don't be an ass."

"Excuse me, sir-whose-name-I've-yet-to-hear-as-I-assume-you-still-struggle-to-recall-it. Do your eyes work? I am a brain. I cannot also be an ass. The two are quite different parts of the normal anatomy. So, to honor your strange request, I don't intend to be anything other than what I am and that, plainly, is not an ass."

My first inclination was to just turn around and leave. There have been many, many times over the years that I regret I didn't follow my own impulse. "I speak figuratively, of course, though I think you might literally be the biggest ass I have ever met."

He sighed. How a disembodied brain can sigh, I have no idea. "So, am I figuratively or literally an ass? I've already sought to explain one of those choices but I am getting the impression that you spend a lot of time with asses and why that is I can only assume is due to your *impressive* intelligence. Birds of a feather and all that."

"I am growing tired of this."

"Finally! A feeling I can empathize."

"Later, brain." I turned to leave.

"Wait." I hesitated at his call. "Please."

I faced the sarcastic thing once again. "Why?"

"I can get a little testy floating in this cursed jar. You have no idea what this is like."

"On that you are right."

"The reason I asked for the time is I wanted to know how much longer I was going to be subjected to public scorn and ridicule."

"You mean the people outside that Mr. Plood is trying to get to pay to see you?"

"Yes. The man is a conniver, cheat, and rapscallion. He has no concern for anyone but himself and uses me to fleece those poor people out of their hard-earned money. I am but a pawn in his sadistic game of fraud."

His sudden change of attitude took me by surprise but it struck me as sincere. I could understand that such a helpless...individual could be forced to play along in some huckster scheme. "I...I'm sorry..."

"No, no. Don't pity on me...sir. I apologize for the remarks. What is your name, kind sir?"

"It's Argon. Argon Bosch."

"I am pleased to make your acquaintance, Mr. Bosch."

"Argon, please."

"Yes, of course. Argon. My name is..."

"Winston."

"Well, well. You are capable of simple observation after all then."

"Wait. What?"

"Ha. I jest. I just don't want you to get all maudlin over my sad state. You have a life that I hope is much more fulfilling than mine. Take my small jibes with you as you leave and may they offer a smile at a future time. One I hope for your sake is far from here."

"Uh...thanks?" This Winston was one strange character. Again the thought of leaving - quickly - crossed my mind. I *really* need to act on my impulses more. Instead: "Winston, is there some way I can help you?"

"I think not as I fear this situation is my new lot in life. I am sure I deserve it. I am a sad excuse for a person of any stature or form." He sounded genuinely sad and remorseful as if Fate had purposely delivered him to Plood's doorstep. A pitiful figure he was.

"Why do you say that?"

"It is a sad story really."

"What happened?"

"You actually want to know?"

"Uh, sure, I guess." I cast a quick glance toward the front of the tent through the opening in front of Winston's case. I couldn't really see anything but I could clearly hear Plood still trying to generate interest from the thin crowd.

"Have you ever heard of the planet Mofisticar?"

"No."

"It is very far from here and it is the planet I once called home. In fact, I was the ruler there."

"Of the whole planet?"

"Indeed! While we may not have far reaching influence like the Klanx or preside over vast regions of space like the Grantok our home was a peaceful world that was held together by the dedicated and loving people who lived there. I was their ruler though the title seems to carry a more nefarious connotation. On Mofisticar it was a title held in highest esteem and deep fondness. I was loved by my people and in turn I loved them. I made sure that every single one of them was cared for as if they were my own dear family." He seemed to gather himself as if the retelling of the story caused him pain.

"What happened?"

"I...I made a decision that caused the downfall of my entire race."

"Seriously? Holy crap!"

"Yes, serious blessed excrement! Our planet was a jewel in our system but without space flight we were limited as to the reach of our aspirations. We dreamed as a people to further our civilization into the endless expanse of the universe. We had so much to offer and yet no way to deliver it. So, as the beloved ruler of the planet it fell to me to find a solution to my subjects' plight. But I over estimated my own abilities. I became prideful and believed that I alone could solve this problem and bring about a new era of prosperity and discovery for our society. And hence was my fall." I wasn't sure but I thought I heard him sob.

"How horrible! I'm so sorry."

"I remind you, take no pity on me, Argon. I deserve none. My place now is here in this derision of my former life. Here I am touted as having incredible powers and abilities yet I have none. It is a show that mocks me every day for I can no more help these lost souls than I could my own people."

"But what happened?"

"I struck a deal with the Xydoc Zyn."

"Sweet pickled beets! Space Pirates?!"

"Yes. You can see how foolish I was."

The Xydoc Zyn were space pirates that terrorized most of the galaxy. Every traveler in the blackness of space shuddered at the mention of them and slept a little less soundly in the darkness they knew would never hide them from the eyes of the pirates should their ship be boarded. A delivery pilot like myself had encountered them on a few occasions and the fact that I lived to tell the tales meant that I had much more than my share of luck and quick wits - despite what Winston may have evaluated.

Winston continued with his despondent tale: "The pirates were the first travelers that landed on my planet. I didn't know their reputation or what they sought. Like the fool I was I offered them the keys to the Capital City, Jirdonis. i fed them with elaborate feasts, gave them extravagant gifts, let them walk freely amongst the people who trusted me, who looked to me for protection!" The memory seemed to make Winston increasingly angry. I feared he may have an outburst that would alert Plood outside the tent but he paused for a moment and appeared to calm somewhat.

"More and more of them came from the skies. I still didn't suspect. I met with their leader and offered to buy ships from them. He agreed - much too rapidly I later realized. He asked me if I had the fortunes to complete the transaction. Ignorantly I assured him that I had. He pressed the issue explaining that while he was sure I was trustworthy he did not really know me. Ah! Such a fool I was. I was so worried about gaining his trust that I neglected the same feelings in myself."

"You were just naive. You hadn't had any exposure to the rest of the galaxy and the utter trash that make up a good part of it."

"If only I had had some of your guile, Mr....Argon. But I didn't despite all the warning signs that stood plainly in front of me. I took him to our massive vaults and showed him that I had the resources to purchase as large a fleet of ships as he could supply. It was then that the tables turned and he revealed himself for the true pirate he was."

It suddenly dawned on me who this arbiter of the Xydoc Zyn was. A cold, icy finger scratched across my spine. I shivered and whispered the name, "Rink SanDyer."

"You know of this devil?" Winston sounded startled.

"Stories. And none that I care to repeat."

"Truly. It was him."

"Shit," I breathed. Rink SanDyer, the leader of the Xydoc Zyn, is easily the most feared man in the galaxy. A shadow. A ghost. A specter that deals in death and gold.

"He took everything. He had strategically arranged his teeming followers across the planet. At his word they acted and before I could react it was over. They were everywhere. He knew just where to hit us to render my people helpless. He and his pirates ravaged the planet. He killed my entire family and...and..." he paused again to gather strength. "He reduced me to *this!*"

"A brain in a jar?"

"Yes, to put it so succinctly, Argon. You do have a way with words."

"Sorry."

"No need to apologize, my friend. I am just that - a lonely brain in a jar." Another sob? "It was in this state that I was forced to witness the destruction of everything I ever loved. Everything I ever held dear. My people were scattered to the stars as slaves. All resources of my planet sold off. They...HE!...left a used up husk in place of the shining beauty that was Mofisticar. All because of me."

"Damn," I whispered momentarily feeling the full weight of his guilt

"Yes, Argon. Damn. That is me. Damned for my pride."

I thought for a minute. There must be something I could do for this miserable creature. "Winston. Let me take you out of here."

"It's not possible," he argued.

"Yes it is. I can sneak you out of here. I have a ship..."

"A ship?" His tone shifted, buoyed by what I assumed was sudden hope.

"Yes. I can fly us far away from here. It won't bring your people or planet or family back but you don't need to service Plood and help him cheat more unsuspecting people."

"You're right! I am only making things worse. I am continuing to hurt even more innocents!"

"Right," I agreed.

"I will be forever in your debt. I have no way of paying you back."

"Not important."

"Oh, but it is! I simply *must* repay you in some way. I must make restitution for your generous nature or I have been as much a pirate as those that stole from me."

"I wouldn't go that far."

"I will have it no other way," Winston insisted.

"Okay, okay, we'll work something out. Now let's get out of here before that reprobate Plood manages to convince one of those people out there to pony up the credits to venture in here."

"Wait! I have a plan. It will help to pay you for your trouble, take revenge on Plood, and assure us he never seeks you or me out again."

"What would that be?"

"You could buy me!"

"What?"

"Purchase me. Then Plood wouldn't be able to come after me."

"Why would he sell you? You're his cash cow."

"Because he is greedy and if you got the price high enough..."

"How high?" I asked.

"How many credits do you have available?"

"Well," I did some rough calculating in my head, "I could probably go as high as...wait a second."

"Is there a problem? Do you need me to do the addition for you?"

"No," I said, slightly offended at yet another dig at my intelligence. "How does this compensate me for rescuing you?"

"I'm getting to that part. First I need to know what you can come up with to sweeten the bait enough for Plood to bite."

I thought again for a moment, having difficulty concentrating since Winston was putting extra pressure for me to be quick. I knew the more seconds that ticked by without my answer would generate the likelihood that he would make another snide remark. Finally, "About 1000."

"Not enough I fear. But you said you had a ship."

"Yes, the Space Spud."

"Catchy," he said with just a hint of sarcasm.

"She is worth quite a bit."

"What would you estimate?"

"At least 45."

"45 credits? What is it made of? Paper? Is it powered by dreams?"

"Idiot, 45 *thousand!*"

"Ah...that's better! We will throw that in," he suggested casually as if asking me to consider giving up my pocket lint.

"Wait, wait...that is my livelihood. I can't lose my ship!"

"Not asking you to. I know how we can secure your winning in a bet. Your um, *fortune* against me."

"How so?" I asked still unsure he knew what he was doing.

"There is a con that Plood uses to get a lot of money out of people. He asks a question only the victim knows the answer to and then puts up money to bet I will know the answer. The whole time Plood has a tiny, hidden microphone so I can hear the answer. He brings the mark in and asks me the question. I state the answer and he gets the winnings."

"What a weak scam." Such a transparent gimmick seemed destined to fail on even the most gullible person. "How do people ever fall for such an obvious ruse?"

"You would be surprised; people fall for it all the time. Plood can manage to get them so confused and wound up by his inane ponderings that they could be wearing their shoe as a hat and go to the Queen's Ball. Only this time, you'll have an in. Drum up his wager until he bets me out of desperation. Then when he asks, I'll give the wrong answer. You win, I'm free, and Plood is ruined! It is perfect!"

I thought about it for a moment, still nervous that Plood would be leading some poor fool into the tent at any moment. I was running out of time. Did I really want to get this involved for a complete stranger? I had been pretty much running solo for several years now and the thought of being overly concerned with the fate of a stranger, a kind of pathetic one at that, made me feel strange. My hard earned instincts pushed me to leave, not get further involved, but I knew that if I left now, knowing that I could have done something, made a difference in someone's life, it would haunt me for a long, long time.

"OK. I'm in."

Winston's voice became more joyful than at any time in all of the previous conversation. "Brilliant! Just hurry back out, making sure he doesn't see you leave, and engage him about how much of a fake he is. Drive up his indignation at being called out in front of the crowd so that he stops thinking and starts simply reacting. He'll go for it, you just watch."

"Done. See you in a few minutes."

I turned and cautiously eased out of the tent. When I peeked at the crowd there was no one watching me and Plood still had his back to me. I quickly ducked behind the tent and made my way further down the Midway so that I could come up from the direction of the main entrance. Within a minute I was back to nearing the front of Plood's exhibit. The crowd was still relatively small, about a dozen people with much less to do than most. Obviously they were starved for entertainment as this was a far cry from it. I even noticed a carnival official milling about as if Plood might do something underhanded - what irony as the whole blasted midway was a shanty town built of lies. Yet Plood still struggled onward to snag a willing victim.

"You will never witness anything as amazing as the Fabulous Winston! His incredible powers will astound and perplex you!"

I let him ramble on for awhile longer. It became clear that no one was going to bite. They seemed to be more interested in witnessing who might be fool enough to jump into this vat of crazy. Guess it would be me.

"Now hold on," I called out. "I don't believe all this flimflam one bit!" His head snapped around to pick me out of the thin pack.

"I say! You doubt my word on Winston's astonishing abilities, sir?"

"Yes I do. There is no way any disembodied brain can pick the thoughts from my head."

He laughed. "Just as easy as your dear mother picked the lice from it."

"Hey! You don't need to insult me."

"Nor do you. I make these statements not as boast but as my own experience I have witnessed these many years."

"Really? You claim a lot of things, Mr. Plood, but I believe only one thing."

"And what is that, my good fellow?"

"That everything you say is a lie." Judging from how his face was growing more crimson with my every incrimination I was having just the effect Winston had hoped for.

"This is only the opinion of a small minded man and one that appears to be just as small of financial stature as well!"

Ah, the subject of money. He got right to it. "What do you mean by that?"

"Well, for a few mere credits you can prove your accusation or my gospel." He smiled a wide grin that showed a dire need for extensive dental work. "Are you game, sir?"

I put forth the front that I was carefully considering his proposition. The throng around me finally took up more than a bored interest in the activities. They gave the impression they were excited their patience was finally paying off. After a few moments I drew in a deep breath and looked sternly at Plood. "I have an idea to determine which one of us is truly correct and proof that I am no man of 'small financial stature' either."

He raised an eyebrow wondering what I was going to propose. I could not tell if he was nervous or just playing coy. "Go on," he said.

"If I pay the couple of credits to go in there and see if that brain can do what you say and he fails I get ushered out the back and you go right on with your scheming ways. I want you to backup your claims with real money."

"Like a wager? Is that what you want? My money against yours to the truth of my declarations?"

"Yes. That is exactly what I want." He was falling right in line with Winston's plan. "If you really believe this rot about Winston's powers then you can back it up with a monetary guarantee."

"Well, this is highly irregular. I don't 'bet' on Winston. It would not be fair."

"AHA!" I exclaimed.

"My meaning, sir, is that you are sure to lose as Winston is never wrong. His very ability prevents him for losing. It would not be fair to you to take your money in such a way."

"I insist," I smiled.

He took a deep breath and seemed to stand a little taller while relaxing, almost as if he were casting off his charade and was being more himself. "Seriously. We have traded our barbs, you and I, but this is not a contest. I charge for the opportunity for people to see something they have never witnessed before. A ticket to another ideal; a place where the known meets the unknown. I do not want to take advantage of your own ignorance."

"So now you are calling me stupid?"

"No. You just have not had the experience I have had each day watching Winston perform."

"So he performs! Like a trick!" The crowd's heads swiveling to and fro as if watching a tennis match. I could tell they were also becoming invested in Plood's ultimate decision to 'put up or shut up'.

"That is not my meaning," he said, frustrated by my redirecting his own words.

"It is all just a game with you. Get your little puppet to perform his trick so you can steal money from these unsuspecting good people. What you are is a liar and a cheat!" I had to get him angrier if he was going to start to get irrational.

"That is uncalled for!" he shouted, offended by my blatant charge.

"I just call 'em as I see 'em. And what I see is a liar and a cheat."

"I am trying to be a fair man yet you try my patience and goodwill, Mr..."

"Bosch."

Yes, Mr. Bosch. I have no patience for your willful neglect of reason."

His face was redder than it had been during the whole argument. "You just keep hiding behind your false motivations, Plood. These people are finally seeing you for just what you and your little show are."

He was really mad now. "I have had enough of you, Mr. Bosch. I will take your bet!"

"Great! What can you bet? What price is this truth of yours?"

"Whatever your tiny pockets can produce."

"I have 1000 credits!" His eyes grew wide. I wondered if this seemed too high for an opening salvo.

He frowned. "I...I don't have that much. I can go as high as 800."

Perfect. I smiled, "Really, Mr. Plood? This is a sure thing to you. This is a chance to capitalize on your credibility. Surely you don't get this kind of chance very often."

"800. That is my offer. I think it will make my..."

"I will throw in my ship!"

The crowd, murmuring and buzzing with expectation and excitement just previously, suddenly grew quiet. They looked at me then to Plood.

"A ship you say?" He grew more serious.

"Yes! I have a small fast ship that is worth over 40,000 credits. I will put that on the line as well!"

"That is insane! You have lost your mind!" He took a step back in disbelief.

"Have I? Or have you lost your belief that Winston can come through for you?"

"I can't...I have no way to match that."

"But you do!" Both he and the now growing mass of spectators leaned their collective heads toward me. It felt like the whole Midway, the whole Carnival had dropped to silence. I thought even the steady breeze had died to heavy stillness. "Winston," I breathed and the crowd gasped.

"What! You have definitely lost your senses! I cannot sell Winston. He is not property."

"Correct, though I imagine he has little in the way of rights interned under your *care*. My wager is my 1000 credits and my ship for your 800 and Winston. Should I win I will allow Winston to go where ever he wants funded by your 800 credits."

"What would you get out of this then?"

"The satisfaction that a known huckster would be ruined and unable to further make a life preying on the gullible or naive."

Plood shook his large head and wiped a rag across his brow. "While this all seems noble in cause, I do not trust your motivations, Mr. Bosch. You are under the misunderstanding that Winston is a prisoner here."

"If he is not then you really have nothing to lose! He would elect to stay here and I would oblige him." I had turned the whole thing into a singular choice. Plood could not afford to say no as any resistance would show him as a fraud. And given what I know about the scam I was surprised that he was even debating the whole thing. He was a true showman; an accomplished thespian.

For the first time he acknowledged the official standing amidst the crowd. "Sir! I would ask you to officiate this barter, this wager."

The carnival officer walked over making himself more visible to the multitude that seemed to only have eyes for Plood and I. As he drew close to us he looked me up and down. "Are you sure about this, Mister?"

"Oh, I'm sure. This crook needs to be dealt with!"

He turned his attention to my current foil. "And you, Mr. Plood? Are you fine with this?"

"I have no choice, sir. I just hope you can make sure that this doesn't turn into something unsavory."

"Don't you worry about that! I will make sure that all funds and property are exchanged as per the details you both have laid out. Of that I am sure." His conviction and confidence were a little scary but at least I knew Plood couldn't welch when he lost.

"I have but one stipulation," I announced.

"I knew it!" shouted Plood. "What else are you asking for, Mr. Bosch? My body hung from a pike? Castration? My eternal soul?"

I chuckled. "Like you have a soul, Plood. Nothing so dramatic. I just require that this kind official and as many of these good people as you can cram into that tent of yours all get to witness Winston's answer. Surely there is no harm in that."

Plood was struck silent. For a long moment he simply stood and stared at me. I knew his mind was working to determine my angle on this. If he began to suspect that Winston and I were in collusion there was no doubt he would back out. But from all appearances he had not yet suspected a thing. Somewhat odd for a huckster that makes his living swindling people out of their money. Finally after some moments he spoke.

"I will abide by your demands, Mr. Bosch. But I warn you one last time that you do not understand the powers that you are dealing with. Do not condemn me when your means are lost."

"That won't happen."

"If nothing else, sir, I will always marvel at your conviction." He looked over the captivated crowd. Shaking his head slightly he said, "And so it shall be. Let us begin." He stepped away from the podium and came close to me. "If you will, tell me something that no one else in this eternal expanse knows about you. Something very personal. Something that would be impossible to guess. And, please, nothing as simple as favorite color or number. Remember, the stakes here are quite high."

I thought for a moment. My mind temporarily drifted across the highlights of my life and nothing much stood out. Leaving Earth, when I was only 10. My boring life on a new planet. Leaving my family for the promise of adventures across the galaxy. I needed something much more simple and precise. Something no one else knew. Something I never told anyone; something I probably had never even told myself.

I looked up, a melancholy smile on my lips but a tiny sadness in my eyes. "The name of the only girl I ever really loved. The girl I lost forever."

The crowd, which was buzzing with speculation and opinions, drew a collective breath. My revelation struck a chord within them and was almost too perfect - as if from some overly dramatic movie script. All we needed was for the crowd to part when I announced her name to watch her suddenly appear from amongst them, all forgiven, only to walk over to me and kiss me. Ride into the sunset and happily ever after to follow, of course.

Cripes...how maudlin.

"Then tell me, Mr. Bosch. Quietly now, what is the name of your long, lost love."

"Galaxia Newton-Jones," I whispered for only Plood to hear.

He pulled out a slip of paper and wrote it across the sheet and handed it to me. "Did I spell Galaxia Newton-Jones correctly?" I nodded. "Good, then hand that paper over to our official until we pose the same question to Winston and he announces his answer. At that point," he looked to the official, "reveal the written answer to the crowd and we shall all witness Winston's mysterious ability. Prepare to be *amazed*, Mr. Bosch"

"Oh, I am already *amazed*, Mr. Plood. Amazed that you've managed to pull these shenanigans off for so long."

He led me and several of the multitude into the tent. It was dark, damp, and smelled of unwashed laundry. I could see the cut out and Winston's glowing case beyond. I made my way to the front near Plood and the rest filled in every available space behind me. I heard a few gasps from the others as they first glimpsed Winston's quite unusual visage. It's not every day a person glimpses a brain floating in a jar.

"Hello," said Winston. More gasps and the random nervous chuckle.

Mr. Plood made the introductions. "Winston, these good people have come in to see your uncanny ability demonstrated. Our subject today is a Mr. Bosch. I fear he does not believe in my claims as to your astounding abilities. In fact he is quite sure that I am a charlatan."

"I'm sorry to hear that, Zantarif. I hope he won't be too upset when he finds he is wrong."

Plood sighed, "I fear he will be nothing but."

"Unfortunate," replied Winston.

Plood clapped his hands together. "Shall we get started then?" He gave me a quick glance, looked to see the carnival official was near by, and then turned to Winston. "Winston, Mr. Bosch has revealed the name of someone to me. Someone that is very special to him. In fact she was the one person he states ever truly loved him. Please sift through his memories and tell us all that name."

For the second time that day the crowd became deathly silent. Every ear was straining to hear what Winston would utter and would it be correct. Inside I was nervous with anticipation. What would Plood's reaction be? He was so confident in his ability to control Winston not even slightly suspecting that his tenuous grip was about to slip free forever. I felt a little sorry for him for a moment. He was about to be on the receiving end of his own deceptive ways.

"Galaxia Newton-Jones," said Winston with no hesitation.

"The paper, good captain," requested Plood with a self-satisfied bounce to his tone.

"Wait...what?" My head spun. Had I heard that right? What was the scheme again? What was Winston suppose to say? Stunned, I simply stood there as the carny officer handed the paper to Plood. He quickly unfolded it and held it up to the crowd then handed it to a random stranger.

"Dear lady, what does the paper read?"

"Galaxia Newton-Jones," she said with a twitter of excitement. A cheer went up from the throng. They seemed happy and relieved to have proof that their freaks and unexplained phenomena were still real. They could continue to believe in Santa Claus and the Tooth Fairy. Life made sense again.

Fuck 'em.

"But…" I started.

"But what, Mr. Bosch? Obviously you expected a different outcome. I warned you. I tried to dissuade you from being a fool."

It was all clear to me then. I was the mark all along. It was a set up from the moment I spied that open flap on the tent. Winston's story, my sympathy, all manipulations to get me to gamble away my entire world on a sure thing. Everything was starkly obvious. They played me.

Of course this also made me very angry. I was about to pull my gun from my holster and shoot Plood and Winston and a couple of the glad-handing crowd just for the fuck of it when the carny police guy shouldered up to me, a tight stare in his eyes. Was he in on it too?

"Will there be trouble, Mr. Bosch?" He pulled back his coat to reveal a sidearm that put mine to shame.

"Well, not now," I answered. "You know this is all a scam, right?"

"I'm not here to judge what is real and what isn't. I am just here to make sure there isn't any trouble."

"Right. I could call out the…"

"Who, Mr. Bosch? You are the one that wanted to gamble everything. Plood tried to talk you out of it. You have a couple dozen witnesses that heard it all. I think you just need to settle up and move on."

"How? He now has my ship and all of my money!"

"Guess you didn't think this out very well, then did you?"

"Apparently not."

Plood strolled up. "Sorry, Mr. Bosch. Maybe now you will believe," he smiled. I looked in his eyes and I finally saw it, that dark evil that motivated him. A cold calculating greed that consumed him completely. He lived for the conquest, the game. Nothing matter but the winning. Stranded alone in the desert he would con the heat out of the sand. This realization only made it feel worse. He held out his hand, not for a good natured shake but to receive the prize. I fished out my keys and all of my cash and dropped them in his hand. I held his gaze just long enough for him to realize that while he won I would never forget it. In that moment we both knew who he really was and I could sense that it made him just a little uneasy.

I spun on a heel and walked to the opening of the tent wanting desperately to put a lot of distance between me and The Grand Wheastoviac's Cavalcade of Freaks.

I guess I had wandered around a bit and found myself sitting in some low-class, dive of a bar. The waitress came by, she might have even been pretty but I had no eyes for anything but misery. I felt like a first class fool and the whole thing played over and over in my mind. I had been so wrapped up in the freakish nature of Winston and his moving story that I couldn't see I was being played. I was angry, pissed at Plood and Winston for playing me but, to be completely honest, I was mostly mad at myself. I had thought I was clever, wise in the ways of the Galaxy. A seasoned pilot that had seen a lot of the more remote corners of the open expanse of space. I had made good friends and even loved a great woman. I'd seen happiness and heartbreak. Had my mentor killed and my ship destroyed. Lost a fortune by leaving home but found a way to scratch out a living. Yeah, I was feeling pretty maudlin and self pity felt just about right at that point. I was swimming in it and paddling for the deep end.

"What can I get you, sweetie?" she asked.

"I don't care," I mumbled not even bothering to look up.

"Suit yourself," she replied and moved away. A few minutes later she returned with a black bottle of some brew I hadn't heard of before and a glass that hadn't seen a decent cleaning since it first left the store. "This should do the trick," she advised.

"Fine," I managed to toss out as I clutched at the bottle. I assumed she left but didn't look up to check. I just didn't give a damn...about anything.

I poured the bottle's contents into the glass and found myself being introduced to what would be a good, though harsh, friend. The heavy black liquid splashed into the glass and I caught my first whiff of the distinctive scent of Obsidian Ale. I took a hefty first gulp, emptying the glass in one chug. It hit my stomach like a rubber ball threatening to come tearing right back up the way it came. It was frightfully awful tasting and while it burned my throat it was more of a freezing sensation that was far from pleasant. Despite all of that I poured the rest of the bottle into the glass and threw it back like the first. I stared at the bottle and the label came in and out of focus and my head started to swim. "Blackhole - the Finest Obsidian Ale You'll Never Remember." Sounded just about right. Another bottle appeared on the table. After that I didn't remember much.

I came to not knowing where I was. Something crawled across my face and I sat up with a start. The sun was up and I blinked in the harsh light. Looking around I realized that I must have passed out either in the alley or in the bar and was thrown into the alley. I could hear my "alarm clock" skitter off into a trash heap and I was glad I didn't have to know what it was. My mouth tasted like it might have nested there and I had to piss something horrible. I stood and relieved myself against the alley wall and experienced my first Obsidian Ale urination. I looked down, jumped and almost peed on my own leg. I was pissing india ink! With no way to stop I just let it flow and then zipped up. I rubbed my eyes and looked around again. This was how my life had turned out? Waking up in a dirty alley peeing on myself. Oh yeah...I remembered. I needed a plan.

I spent the rest of the day and most of the night trying to formulate a brilliant plan of revenge that would get my life back and doom the soulless rat bastards that had put me here. Hung over, desperate, angry, and completely broke I headed for The Grand Wheastoviac's Cavalcade of Freaks.

I hid behind Plood's tent for a couple hours until the midway had cleared of traffic. I crept a bit closer and could hear Plood talking to

Winston. He seemed in a good mood, obviously happy with his recent windfall. Winston didn't say much seeming more content with listening to Plood run his mouth about how great he had done and how this scam was always the best one when they found someone stupid enough to fall for it. *Let's see how stupid he thinks I am now*, I thought as I rushed the tent's open flap.

Having entered the tent the same way the day before I knew what to expect but the trunks were situated near the entrance and packed full of clothing and items. I tripped on one that was spread open and lost my balance. "Shit!" I swore as I spun and fell into the trunk.

"What, what?" yipped Plood in surprise. He was startled by my sudden appearance but quickly recognized me. "Bosch! What's the meaning of this intrusion?"

I quickly tried to get to my feet to force my advantage of surprise but only managed to further entangle my feet in Plood's cursed clothing. I kicked and kicked and finally managed to stand. "Oh, you know why I am here you poor excuse for a hat!"

He looked at me quizzically. "What?"

"You heard me! You took my shit and ship" This was proving to not be my best oratory moment. That Obsidian Ale was still having an effect on me.

"I think you have taken leave of your senses, Bosch. You best leave before you get in even more trouble."

"Oh I'm in trouble like you are now. Wait. I mean you are the one in trouble now, not me."

"How's that?"

"If you don't fork my stuff over to me now I will be shooting to force you, I mean, forced to shooting you. No! Shoot you! And I will, you mad sock!"

Face it; I had lost my shit alright. I was talking gibberish and my plan consisted of my barging into his tent and forcing him to return my money and ship by threatening to shoot him with my gun. Oh yeah...my gun. I grabbed for it but found my holster was empty. Oh hell.

"I don't see a gun, Bosch. Maybe you lost that in a bet on whether the sun would rise or not." He began to laugh. "I have no time

41

for you. I have things to do." I finally noticed that the reason all of his clothes were by the tent flap was because he was packing his trunks with his possessions. He was leaving!

"You are not...being here soon?"

"Observant if not obtuse. Yes. With your ship and money we can get the hell out of this godforsaken freak show and move on. So if you don't leave now I will be obliged to call..."

"Who? Who are you going to call to your aid, Mr. Plood?" came a voice behind me. I spun around to see the carnival official standing in the tent opening with his large gun in hand.

Plood looked shocked and a little upset. "Jot? What's all this then? Do you have some ax to grind as well?"

The carny cop smiled, "An axe. I like that. Wish I had one." Something about what he said and the smile he presented made me feel uneasy. I took my first real hard look at him. He was very tall and thin, light complexion, not too out of the ordinary - especially when mixed in with the crowd and displays of a freakshow. He turned his head to look at me and I met his gaze. Something behind his pale eyes bespoke a harshness that would never let anything get between him and his goal. And I mean *anything*. I really hoped I wouldn't ever be that obstruction.

Plood wasn't quite as easily swayed by the official's steely determination. "Ha! Must you be so dramatic? I haven't the time for this."

The officer shot Plood in the leg. "Make time."

Plood barked out an agonized grunt and fell to the dirt floor. He looked up with a wet, perplexed glare. "You've really lost your mind! You shot me!"

"You think *I've* lost my mind? *I'm* not the one trying to escape this place without paying my *dues*. No one shorts me, Plood."

Plood, realizing his mistake, quickly began an attempt to repair the damage. "No, no, Garren. You have it all wrong. I was going to pay you up before I left."

"In the middle of the night?"

"In the morning. I was just getting ready. I have a lot of valuable property to pack up and ready for my trip. I just wanted to get that bit out of the way before I came to you to settle. Really! Why would I cross you? That would make no sense!"

"No, Plood, it wouldn't." He fired again and Plood's head splattered around the tent making a mess of his "valuable property."

I saw my opportunity. "Yeah. So I'll just be going now."

"Hold up, Mr. Bosch."

So, this was going to be how it ended. Me, shot by some local thug in the tent of the man who stole everything from me in the middle of a carnival freakshow on some backwater planet. Sounded just about right.

"Did you want to add anything?" he asked me.

"Uh...no. I think I'm fine. How about I just get out of here and forget all about The Grand Wheastoviac's Cavalcade of Freaks. Works for me."

"I don't think so," he replied and then Garren Jot did something that changed everything - he holstered his gun. "I think you need some encouragement to leave here." He went over to Plood's lifeless body and fished through his pockets. He pulled out a large wad of cash and some other objects. He peeled off a few bills and shoved them towards me. "Here. For the hassle."

I took the bills as if I was taking the apple from the serpent in Eden. This guy was hardcore and not one that I could trust no matter what he seemed to be doing. I gave a cursory glance at the bills and tallied the rough total, about a quarter of my monetary loss. I felt absolutely no inclination to argue. Considering everything that had transpired I was happy with that. Seriously. Then he tossed something else at me. I half suspected it was a grenade or something else that would suddenly end me. But when I instinctively caught it I knew what it was: the keys to my ship.

I wanted to say thanks but I wasn't sure it would be a sign of weakness or an indication that I wanted to be friends or something. This guy didn't have or want friends. I simply nodded and turned to leave.

"Bosch," he called out to me.

Oh, here it comes, I thought. Turn around and get shot in the face as well, evidence of my theft of Plood's ill-gotten gain in my possession. It would be an open and closed case once the officer made his report on what he "found." I winced and turned slightly, ready to drop or dodge or run. I only saw him leaning on Winston's case. "Forget something?"

"Uh, I'm certain I didn't. I have enough. Thanks. Good-bye."

"Take this damn brain thing with you. I don't want it left behind."

"Why?"

"Let's just say it could complicate things. Plus it kind of creeps me out. I certainly don't want it so you need to take it." Jot looked at me steadily. "That's not a problem, is it?"

I quickly just said, "Nope," and went over to Winston's case. I opened the door in the back and saw that the tubes and wires running from his jar all ended in a small metal box that hummed slightly with whatever apparatus was inside. I gathered them both up and went to leave...again.

"Bosch."

Holy hell! What now? This was turning into a game of Russian roulette and every turn the click of the trigger. The tension of feeling played with for some morbid fancy was fraying my nerves. I stopped and quickly turned around hoping that whatever he was going to finally do would be quick.

He gave me that same hard look. "I don't want to see you again." I just kept staring at him. "Ever. Do you understand me?"

I nodded a little too excessively and then said, "Thanks."

"Consider this all something you will soon forget."

"I think I already have, sir." This time I spun around and hastily walked out of the tent with no intent to stop or turn no matter what he said or I heard. A few moments later I was at my ship.

In record time I was inside with the engines warming. I placed Winston and his paraphernalia into the space behind my seat and kicked in the drive to lift me up over the city. Thrusters engaged and I set coordinates. I was bound for home at last. It was almost 3 hours before Winston said anything.

"That was fun."

It startled me, of course. I had forgotten he was aboard after feeling like I'd just pulled off the luckiest escape ever recorded.

"Shit! I forgot you were here."

"Typical."

"Hey, listen. You should basically just say 'Sorry' and 'Thanks' for the rest of the trip and for the remainder of the time I can see and/or hear you."

"Sorry and thanks."

"In fact, I should just toss you out into space for conning me like you did. You played me for a fool, Winston!"

"A part you were born to play."

"Are you shitting me now? That's it. I'm going to put you in the back cargo hold and open the outside hatch. You can deliver all of your sarcasm and snide remarks to the depths of space until the liquid in your little jar either boils or freezes. I've so had it with you."

"Sorry," he said in a tiny, humble voice. "And thanks."

"I don't get you, Winston. You played me like a cheap kazoo and when I could have just tossed you into a trash bin on my way to the dock but didn't and you *still* insult me."

"It was the way I was raised. A token souvenir of my youth."

"No, no, no. Don't you start to spin one of those stories again. I am in no mood for your bullshit."

"I am incapable of producing any kind of shit."

"Don't play dumb. You know what I mean and I am not going to fall for your stories, acting stupid or pitiful, or playing on my good nature."

"But you are the nicest man I have ever met since my father and he was killed while trying to fend off the savage K'lee Brain Boilers..."

"Stop! Just stop talking."

"Sorry. And thank-you."

Part of me still felt sorry for the pathetic thing. A damn brain floating forever in a jar. "Just don't talk for the rest of the trip. When I get home I will figure out what to do with you."

"Where is home?"

"Is that you still talking?"

"Sorry. And, of course, thank-you. Really."

We sat in silence for about ten minutes before I answered his question. "I live in Cyran." He did not respond with more questions, simply sitting behind me in silence. "I own a delivery company called the Jackleg Courier Service." Still nothing. "I've been running it solo for about a year and am not doing too bad." He remained mute for another 15 minutes.

"Sorry, may I ask a question? Thank-you."

"Go ahead."

"Thanks. Who takes orders and coordinates the deliveries when you aren't there? Sorry."

"I have to close the business down while I am gone. There is an answering service to handle inquiries. Plus there is a site for information."

He didn't respond for a few minutes. "Sorry. I am not questioning your keen intellect as it is quite obvious that you can take care of everything yourself with no help from anyone else but wouldn't it be even more successful if you were able to have someone there to handle business while you are away on important deliveries? Thanks."

I was about to snap at him knowing he was trying to manipulate me again but I knew he was making sense. I had often thought about hiring an office assistant to help with the business but didn't feel like it was an expenditure I could take on right now. But...

"Let me guess, Winston. You are making a play to be my employee. Am I right?"

"Sorry, yes. And thanks."

"Don't thank me yet. I am not hiring you." I said pointedly.

"Sorry. At least you are straight with me. Thank-you."

"If I did hire you, what guarantee would I have that you wouldn't betray me one day?"

"Thank-you. I didn't betray Zantarif when you offered to take me away from all of that. Sorry."

I grumbled under my breath. "That's because you were in on it! It's what you do - lure in saps and take their money. I don't think that counts as any sort of guarantee."

"Sorry. I'll tell you what, hire me on and don't pay me for six months. See how I work out. If it works out then we can negotiate a salary. It needn't be much as I don't require much, as you can likely tell. I know I can help you become more profitable. I can be very useful. Thanks."

I thought about it more and figured I didn't have much to lose if I stayed sharp and watched him like a hawk. "OK...six months. You pull any shit and you're out. And good luck with that."

Thank-you. I won't let you down. And I don't have any arms. Sorry."

"What are you talking about?"

"Sorry. I don't have any arms to pull anything, shit or otherwise. Thanks."

"Don't toy with me, Winston. You know what I mean."

"Sorry. Some of your Terran colloquialisms are beyond me. Thank-you."

I shook my head. I'd made a lot of mistakes in my life. What was one more? "You're hired, Winston. And you can stop with all that 'Sorry' and 'Thanks' crap."

"Sorry...er, thanks! Uh...I won't let you down, Mr. Bosch."

"Call me Argon. And I am sure you will, Winston."

"Thanks...sorry...oh shit."

I filled him on the Company for the rest of the flight back. Thirteen years later he's still there and I don't think he has ever said "Sorry" or "Thanks" since the day we landed.

"YOU CAN JUST RELAX. There is very little chance they will come looking for us," I assured Winston.

"And how can you be so sure?" he asked showing his usual lack of confidence in anything I do.

"Well, uh...because I think they all died when the space station exploded."

"What?! Oh please tell me that it had nothing to do with you."

"Pretty much."

"Pretty much you did or didn't have anything to do with destroying a space station and killing an enormous amount of people. And just to give me the slightest peace of mind that we won't be stormtrooped by a garrison of armed soldiers desperate for revenge, how big was this space station and how many people died?"

Sheepishly I mumbled, "It was the size of a small moon and contained thousands of people I imagine. No big deal."

Winston has the best hearing of anyone I have ever come across so why I try to mumble through a conversation I don't know. And, again, why I care what he says or thinks also escapes me. "A moon? Thousands? We are doomed! Doomed!"

"It wasn't me! They got attacked when I was there. I barely got out of there before it exploded. Yet you have no concern about me. Thanks a lot!"

"Argon, did you drop something into the machinery? Were you smoking?"

"Give it a rest, Winston. It wasn't me so drop it."

"Well, remember that time..."

"Drop. It. Now."

"OK but if you call me and need a lawyer..."

"Then you better get me one! Sheesh. Let it go!"

"Anyway, while you were gone..."

"Save it. I think you keep forgetting that I almost died. I am going to take some R and R. I've been going through way too much crap on these jobs lately and I need a break. We have enough of a cushion now to last a few days so I'm going to take a few days off." I was already thinking of my days visiting Harityko 8 and enjoying the relaxing resorts they had there.

"Sure, we have a cushion until I have to engage a lawyer." Winston was like a pin at a birthday party.

"I swear, Winston. If you don't let this go I will kick you off that table and you can flop on the floor like a fish until I get back."

"Enjoy your trip."

I walked out of the office with every intention to plan out my little vacation. It just never happened.

CHAPTER 3

I logged into my normal travel site to make reservations at a swanky resort hotel in Harityko 8's largest city, Brunstoak. Browsing through the suggestions I found one that was reasonably priced and had enough amenities to keep a tired old delivery pilot content for a few days. I sent out a request for a reservation and sat back to wait for a reply. I could practically smell the sweet air and feel the cool breeze. Exactly the opposite of my home city, Cyran.

Cyran was a huge city and one that had its fair share of odors and teaming masses which further helped make the city feel dirty, constrained and claustrophobic. It served as the main port for the planet of Mytopoli. Mytopoli was the main hub of the sector given its designation as a Gravity-Well Base (GWB) for interstellar travel. It had been on the navigational maps since the beginning of gravity-based flight and had taken its rightful place along the commerce lines that formed in those early days. In fact, if it weren't for the expansion of the trade routes and use of our Moon as a GWB for our sector we never would have been able to join the Galactic Community and been able to expand Humanity beyond our system. It catapulted us centuries into the future - ready or not. Without that discovery I'd still be on good old Earth probably working for the post office or stocking shelves at some big box retailer.

The reservation request bounced back a moment later all set for my payment info. A few seconds of input and I was greeted with a colorful welcome screen and a canned video greeting explaining how happy they all were that I was coming out to see them. How nice. Despite the obvious pandering I was excited to go. I couldn't remember the last vacation I had and this one was going to be a literal breath of fresh air.

Everything was in place. I got Winston on the intercom and let him know to inform clients that I would be "Out of the Office" for the next 5 days. I packed a small bag and tossed it in the Spud. I looked at my itinerary again and realized I had a few hours to kill before I needed to leave. I didn't want to hang around the Jackleg or engage Winston in some stupid conversation that would probably result in my blood pressure spiking. So I decided to head over to my neighborhood haunt, Galder's, for a couple drinks and some less annoying conversation.

"Winston," I said over the intercom. "I'm going to go over to Galder's for a bit before I leave."

"Right. Try not to catch anything before your trip."

"That's not why I'm going," I clarified.

"Oh, I'm sorry. I thought you said you were going to Galder's. All they serve are whores."

My intuition had paid off. Just telling Winston I was leaving had sparked enough from him in two sentences to piss me off. "They have a bar and music and some good people too."

"And...whores. Just because they will serve you alcohol, sing to you, and act nice doesn't mean you can discount that they are whores."

"You haven't even been there!"

"You never invite me."

"For reasons that are obviously apparent from our conversation," I pointed out.

"Whores?"

"I'm gone," I finished and swung out the door. I thought I heard something else from him but the door was already closing.

Chance Galder was an old school courier from the days of the

Shipping Wars, the rough and tumble years when the United Space Parcel Syndicate tried and succeeded to overtake the independent courier companies that previously had transported packages across the Galaxy. When the USPS finally took power after the war he, like many of the shipping companies, quit the business and sought his fortune elsewhere. He had hoped to open a luxury resort and enjoy the easy life. This was definitely not that.

As I walked into the familiar lounge the strong odor of smoke, sweat, and musk met me like an old friend. And not a well kept friend. "Argon!" came a shout from the bar. My eyes adjusted to the eternal dim that filled the place as if the ever present reek could somehow block light. I saw Galder waving at me.

"Chance," I said and walked over to shake his hand. "How is business today?"

He glanced around with a certain disgusted look. "Same as always...dreadful."

I laughed. "Oh, come on. It's not that bad."

"You have that sunny outlook because you get to come and go at your whim."

"You've got me..." A man stumbled from the bar, threw up on the floor, and half crawled out the door. I looked at Galder. "I see your point. Any closer and I'd have charged you for a shoe shine."

"And you wouldn't get it either." He turned his head and called to the backroom, "Fleep! Get a mop!"

He turned back toward me, "And what can I get for you? And don't say, 'What he was having'," motioning toward the door and the previous patron I could still hear retching outside.

"No thanks. I'll take an Obsidian. And is Dritzy here today?"

"Sure, but she's busy right now. Plus you have some old guy been waiting for you."

"What? Here? Plus if *you're* calling the guy 'old' he's likely to have died of old age while he was waiting."

He pointed to his face. "You won't find a smile here. Knock that shit off." He waved at a table near the back, "He was right over there but I don't see him now. Maybe he went to take a leak."

He placed a bottle of Blackhole in front of me, "Grab a chair at his table; he'll be back. He's been waiting for a couple days. I thought you had set something up."

"Now why would I ask someone to meet me here? My office is two blocks away."

"How the hell should I know? Lord knows what shady dealings you have running."

I tried to look offended, "Me? I don't think so. Strange, really." Galder didn't look to be offering any more information so I wandered to the table and took a seat. I sat there for close to half an hour and still the old man did not show up. Galder finally came by.

"He waits all that time and blows right before you get here? What's that about?"

"I've no idea, Chance. Did he say anything about his business?"

"Not really. I take great pains to *not* know people's business here, you get me?"

"Yeah. But what exactly did he say?"

He thought for a minute. "He came in a couple days ago and just sat down at this table. I came by and asked him what he wanted and he asked for a glass of water. I should have booted him then, I tell you."

"Right, cause you need the room. Sheesh, stick to reality, Chance."

He gave me an increased amount of scowl. "Shut it. After an hour I told him he either orders something *for money* or he can leave. So he orders a drink and I bring it over and then he asks about you."

"By name?"

"No, by description, you idiot. Man, I see what Winston means."

"Your turn to shut it, Galder. Is that all?"

"He wanted to know if you came in here and I told him you come in every so often but you could be off delivering something and it could be days before you get back. Didn't seem to deter him so I left him alone."

"Maybe he stopped by the Jackleg and Winston told him I would be back soon and...well, that doesn't make sense either. Why wouldn't he just wait there?"

"Maybe he was thirsty and I know how great of a host Winston can be."

54

"A stretch but I guess it could be. Anything else?"

"Well, after the first day I thought he'd shove off and I wouldn't see him again. Then the next morning, he's back. Pulls the same stupid shit with the water so I just cut to the chase and tell him this isn't a hotel and if he is going to be here all day he better pay rent by ordering. Spent the whole day nursing a bottle and eating a sandwich. Then he leaves when we close and I'll be damned if he isn't here the next morning again. Was like that until a few hours ago. He was sitting there when a couple of ugly types rolled in. I got the feeling they knew each other but they didn't sit at his table. He just kept looking at them."

"Are they still here?"

He looked at another table further back and scratched his head. "Looks like they left too."

I shook my head, "That doesn't sound good at all."

I got up from the table, took another draw from my Blackhole and told Galder to put it on my tab. I had a feeling I needed to get back to the Jackleg quickly.

The walk only takes about 10 minutes, shorter if I'm in a hurry, so I picked up the pace. The old guy leaving followed by some thugs seemed too coincidental especially if he was waiting for days specifically for me. I was getting close when a voice called out from a dark alley between two smaller buildings, "Argon Bosch!"

I turned and looked. An old man came out of the shade and approached me. I'm no detective but I made the hasty deduction that it was the man from the bar. He sported thick white hair and an equally snowy scruff of beard. I would have guessed he was human but we are part of a popular model when it comes to appearance throughout the galaxy.

"Who's asking?" I challenged.

"I am, you fool. Are you simple?"

"Listen, old timer, I am growing increasingly tired of people calling me stupid or a fool."

"Then don't be spouting nonsense, you idiot."

"The only thing I am spouting is your ability to make a snap judgment on a person you've never met before based on…"

"I have met you before," he revealed.

"What? When?"

"It was about 25 years ago. You were working for Galcursed on the Nir'don running cargo out of Dahlkirk."

I thought back to those days aboard the Nir'don. I had left my adopted planet, my friends, and what turned out to be a small fortune to feed my wandering spirit. Signing onto the crew of Captain Galcursed was a chance of a lifetime. He was a greatly respected pilot and captain and, more importantly, a person who was a mentor and eventually a close and trusted friend. Reflecting on those years I often realized they were the best years of my life. After he was murdered in a fare dispute my life became one of mostly solitude and poor choices.

"I don't recall meeting you."

He shook his head, "No, we never officially met but I was a good friend of Capt. Galcursed. We were close since the Shipping Wars."

"What's your name?"

"Abraxas Wun."

"Like the number?"

"I don't know of a number abraxas." He chuckled at his tiny joke like it was his practiced response to just such a question. I answered his little snicker with an eye roll.

"Uh, yeah. Still don't recall the name. I was familiar with most of his friends…" Suddenly it dawned on me - the nickname he mentioned frequently when talking about a great friend that had saved his life on a couple occasions. "You're A1!"

It was now his turn to roll his eyes. "Gad, I hate that name."

"But it is you."

"Yes. He gave me that name and it stuck. Everyone was calling me that by the time I left the Nir'don. I don't think I have had anyone call me that for a long time."

I grabbed his hand and gave it a sturdy shake. "I'm glad to meet you, A1. The Captain had a lot of nice things to say about you during my many years aboard the Nir'don."

"Sure, sure, "he mumbled impatiently. "The thing is I really need to talk to you about something important."

"Is that why you were waiting for me at Galder's?"

"Yes and no. I was waiting for you and hiding out from some hired muscle that was tailing me. I left them behind when I snuck out of that dive."

"They aren't there any longer," I pointed out.

"What? They left?" he exclaimed.

"Yeah. Galder tried to point them out when he was telling me about you but they were no longer at the table."

"Damn and tarnation! I wonder where they went?" He puzzled on this for less than a minute before his small eyes grew wide with alarm. "They might have heard me talking to that nosey barkeep about you."

"That can't be good."

"Certainly!" With that he began to move in the direction of my shop. "If they headed for your company then they might not be too happy when they find I'm not there." He picked up the pace.

This got me worried. He seemed to have some insight into what these thugs might do that unnerved him. And if it unnerved a man that didn't even know me, what kind of frantic state should I be in? Blind panic, is what and I immediately jumped to it. I sprinted past him.

When I got to the Jackleg a minute later he was surprisingly close behind. I hastily looked around and started for the door. Then I noticed, "The Spud is gone!"

"The what?"

"My ship! It's gone! Shit!"

"Calm down. It's not like anyone got hurt or killed."

My mind processed this unsubstantiated statement as I raced for the door. Even as I swung it open I knew what I would find - Winston's jar shattered on the floor, his brain stomped into a slimy mush. "Winston!" I yelled.

But, no. There was no smashed container or a large, wet stain that used to work for me. Instead Winston's desk was empty. He was gone. I half expected to suddenly hear the customer toilet flush and Winston asking, "Excuse me, can I trouble someone for a wipe?" as some kind of joke but there was only my heavy breathing and the sudden jingle from the entrance as A1 dashed in.

"Is everything OK? Does anyone work here besides you?"

"Yes," I panted, conflicting emotions crashing in my brain. "Winston."

We sat quietly in the office for some time, my mind a whirl of confusion. My ship. Winston. And above all...what the hell was going on? I knew that Winston did not possess the ability to pilot the Spud or even a way to physically get to it. Of course, he could have had help and hatched some plan to rob me of the ship but that didn't make sense. While Winston and I often had our disagreements and shared a mutual distrust, we were equally invested in the success of the business. Me, as a means of income and he as a shelter from the more nefarious elements that would easily see him harmed for any number of reasons and schemes. No, it had to be something else. But who and for what purpose? Those were the questions bouncing around in my head with no chance of coming to rest within the hole of revelation. But I had the feeling that there was someone that had some enlightenment.

"A1!" He jumped having almost fallen asleep during my stewing. "I know you have an idea what's going on. I need you to tell me. Now."

He gave me a quizzical look that either meant he wasn't sure what I meant or that he wasn't sure he could trust me. I had a strong sense that it was the latter. I pushed the issue. "You didn't seek me out because you had a friendship with Capt. Galcursed and thought it might be nice to get together with his ex-first mate and reminisce. You have an agenda and I have a feeling that whatever it is, it has gotten me embroiled into some shit that has caused my ship and employee to go missing. Am I warm?"

He continued his long stare and finally seemed resolved to talk though again I wasn't sure if it might be acceptance or desperation. "You're right. I did come looking for you for a reason."

"A good one I hope 'cause this isn't turning out to be a happy little introduction."

"Right, right. I need your help and I couldn't think of anyone else that might be able to fill the job."

"And what is this job?"

"Let's just say it has to do with delivering a package and that is something you are very familiar with."

In my line of work I try not to ask a lot of questions. As one might suspect with a huge juggernaut of a galactic wide corporation handling package deliveries that to compete the small time operators might have to haul some cargo that may blur the established legal, moral, ethical, and natural lines. So asking questions only complicates the situation and often creates undue weight on one's conscience. Better not to know how many laws you are breaking when toting some freight across the big, starry expanse. Never mind the fact that the customer most often does not want to answer such questions. He, she, or it doesn't necessarily want to think very hard on what boundaries they happen to be crossing or sins they might have to carry to their grave.

Me personally, I didn't really care what they had as long as it didn't affect me in some adverse way. I've been in trouble with the law many times for running something that pissed them off. But I've only been caught twice and both times I managed to slip the charges; though one time I did have a short stretch in jail before I got things right again. What worries me more is the stuff that isn't simply illegal and requires a certain stealthy tact to avoid the governmental patrols and checkpoints. No, it's the stuff that will kill me that scares me. Explosives, plague viruses, parasites, poisons, vicious animals, the occasional person, or the worst thing of all: avarice.

Transporting something that someone desperately wants means that they may make an extra special attempt to get it from you and that generally means they want to steal it and they usually don't give two turnips what happens to you in the course of their grab. That's the bad juju I have run into more times than all the others combined. And having to blindly accept a package not knowing what is in it or how it is going to blow up in your face makes for some nervous rides. Sure, I do ask one question about contents: Will it cause me harm. But the thing about people that ship stuff that the USPS won't touch, they don't have a problem with lying. Go figure.

So what A1 had for me made me worry even more. I really, really wanted to ask more questions.

"So, I just need to know, will it cause me harm?"

"There's a damn good chance," he said with a sincerity that knocked me back.

"Seriously?"

"Yup."

He was too candid about this. Nobody hires a courier being that honest. It costs too much. "You used to be a courier, right A1?"

"Yup. Near 50 years."

"Then you know that telling me that will either jack up my price by a large multiple or make me pass on the job altogether. And I am getting a strong feeling I'd be better off picking the second one."

"I am sure you are. I know I would be. But there are two things I am counting on."

"Which are?"

"Your inherent greed."

I nodded at his quick ability to judge my character. "Understood."

"And your desire to get your employee back."

I laughed. "I wouldn't put too much of a value on that."

"OK, your ship then."

"Better. But how is that connected with a delivery? What are you trying to get me in the middle of?"

"It is kind of a long story."

"The more you talk, A1, the more I worry," I informed him. "And I'll tell you, there will be a point where I just straight up kick your ass out of here rather than listen any longer."

"Hardly fair. You asked."

"For my own well being," I pointed out.

He considered it for a time and then said, "You're right. I'd have done the same thing." He looked out the front windows as if checking for someone snooping or maybe coming to kill us? All this mystery was starting to wear on me.

"You see, Argon, there are other people really interested in what I need you for and I think they grabbed your ship and employee to get to me."

"So you have something they want."

"In a manner of speaking, yes."

I shook my head, "I'm getting tired of these vague answers, A1. I think that point of kicking you out is approaching," I warned.

"Dammit! I don't have what they are after...yet. I need you to help me get it first. But there is no way in hell I am going to just hand it over to those thieving bastards!"

"But what about my ship?"

"And your employee?"

"Let's just focus on the important things first."

He gave me a look, "Uh, sure. Well, if that's how it is then once we find our cargo you'll be able to buy a fleet of new ships and hire enough employees to run this business from your local bar."

"That's a tall order. But let's go back to when you said 'find'. That's got me curious." I knew he was holding back.

He looked disgusted with himself for revealing too much too soon. "There is something valuable, *really* valuable, that we need to go get. Then we can make a delivery that will fill all our pockets." A huge grin crossed his lined face exposing his dark teeth. It wasn't something that made me smile. Or feel any more relaxed. It hinted slightly of insanity.

"Like I said, A1, the more you talk the more I don't want any part of this. I'm not a goddamned treasure hunter. I have enough trouble and adventure just trying to get a package from A to B. I don't need maps and rumors to complicate a simple strategy. I like simple. I *live* simple."

His grin softened slightly, losing that crazy look. "Oh, Argon. When I tell you what we are after you are going to beg me to help."

I laughed. It was clear to me now that Captain Galcursed's old best friend was crazier than a rabid schnoot and damn near as ugly. He had grown senile in his later years and now I was going to be the one to not only have to have him committed but to also take a financial loss due to his whacked out vision.

Then I thought for a second, if all that was true - who the hell had taken my ship. And, oh yeah, Winston. Obviously someone had the same belief as A1 and just as convinced in its value. Oh dear God...what did I step in?

"You laugh now but you will thank me when this is over," he panted full of optimism and self assurance.

"Oh, I doubt that." He simply smiled that self-satisfied smile at me. "What?"

"When I tell you what we are after you will be glad that I came to you."

"So tell me you old walnut," I demanded.

"Argon, we are going to go get the Lost Package of Dehrholm Flatt."

I looked him in the eyes as he waggled his eyebrows in satisfaction. "Holy batshit. Now I know you have lost your fucking mind."

CHAPTER 4

Life aboard the Nir'don was harsh at times and sometimes dangerous. Like the time we were running uncut sprik oil through Reen space and had the starboard engine fail. Ord, the engineer, got it running in record time but it was a very nervous three hours. I run small cargo and it is easy to avoid a lot of things in a small ship but the Nir'don was a Heriminious Class freighter and had a standard compliment of fifteen. Trouble could find us a lot easier.

"Bosch!"

"Captain?" I replied.

"I need us silent on this run. Your damn noise contraption is generating too much background static on any *wave pickers* in the area. Shut it down. Now."

"Understood, sir." Unfortunately I hadn't been paying attention to where we were on our course to Kritus 3. We were crossing the outskirts of Reenuvian space and sprik oil, especially uncut sprik oil, was a serious offense under interstellar boundary laws. Illegal in this quadrant due to its high toxicity to the Reen, it had once been used as a weapon during the Dark Skirmish and eventually became a serious war crime to use it on any Reen, even outside their sector of the Galaxy. But transporting it across their own space, in this quantity, well...my life would have been very different had we been caught - it would have ended much sooner.

So, not paying attention to our entry into Reen space caught me off guard. I was in the berthing compartment with a couple shipmates demonstrating the sheer awesomeness of Terran Classic Rock on my old jam box. It was one of the five things Earth contributed to the Galactic Community when we joined. In the many years since we were asked to join it had become very popular with almost the entire galaxy. Just something about it got you excited and that feeling seemed almost universal. So with only six months on board the Nir'don I was letting the guys listen to some choice cuts. I had just fired up one of the all-time greats, Head East's "There's Never Been Any Reason." And I was giving it to them as God intended: **LOUD!**

But, being an unauthorized ship sneaking across Reen space with a cargo hold full of poison, we wanted to remain undetected. *Wave pickers* were devices situated in deep space, usually along the borders, that detected subtle waves. All I needed was for my carelessness to get us all caught and sent to prison or killed. Or both.

I hastily switched off the device and turned to my bunkmates for some kind of support. I found none. While there can be a good amount of comradery on a ship, there is very little sympathy; it is considered a sign of weakness. So I gave them a stern look and said, "Next time you can just listen to your old Andojin tribal chants and I'll put my headphones on!" They gave me a manufactured scoff but I knew they were disappointed. Captain Galcursed seemed momentarily satisfied.

"Bosch," he said as he turned to leave, "Go down and double check the lower deck for high frequency sound roaches." I was new, I didn't know much as I had joined the crew at 17 and while it was what I most wanted to do in the whole universe, I didn't have any experience. Captain Galcursed took me on seeing something in me that nobody else ever noticed. So I did everything I could to impress him and ensure he felt he had made the right decision. So if that required checking for "high frequency sound roaches" that is exactly what I would do. Maybe a punishment, more likely a distraction.

"Aye aye, Captain," I chimed as I hurried out the door. I already felt foolish and I needed to get a bit of redemption flowing. I hastily made my way toward the bottom deck.

There were only four decks on the Nir'don and only three of them were suitable for the crew to inhabit. That left one nasty, dark, dank, stinky, cramped deck which, as guessed, was the lowest deck. It was where the various lines ran from forward to aft. Plumbing, electrical, communication - it all traversed through the lower deck. There were also storage areas, machinery for lowering the landing gear, and a lot of other junctions and devices crammed down there to make room for the crew above. It was rare when a person ventured down below yet here I went, smile on my face like a simpleton, to scare off some noisy bugs. Of course I didn't even know what these things supposedly looked like nor what I was supposed to do when I found one but that did not deter me in the least.

I opened the creaky hatch that led into the darkness and eased down the short ladder. The space was short enough that I had to stoop and try and navigate around the many pipes, cables, housings, and machinery. I clicked on my shoulder light and started looking for the targets. Usually the ship is filled with all kinds of racket as we scream through space but now, at the Captain's insistence, it was eerily quiet. The lack of noise and the dark claustrophobic spaces were unsettling. I found I was apprehensive and nervous as I crept through the jumble, banging against metal and bruising my head, arms, and legs not to mention a couple stubbed toes. Then there was the heat and the smell. The air was humid and close with no circulation while it reeked of oil, stagnant water, and waste. More than once I had to fight off a gag reflex. But I persevered and continued my hunt. Four times something scurried by me either in the insufficient shine of my shoulder light or, worse yet, outside of the glow leaving me to only imagine what it was. So, as time slithered on I managed to increasingly amp up my anxiety until I felt like I might explode.

Therefore it was no surprise when Ord stepped around a tall metal contraption and said, "Hey" that I nearly popped out of my skin. I will credit myself with not letting out a girlish scream that could be registered by a *picker* no matter the distance or obstructions

"You scared the shit out of me, Ord," I panted.

"I hope not, Bosch. It smells bad enough as it is."

"Funny, Ord."

Ord was Andojin like Captain Galcursed and most of the crew but as the chief engineer of the Nir'don, he was a little bit of a celebrity. He had been with Capt. Galcursed for 18 years and was the only member of the crew that could give the Captain a hard time and not get booted into space. But despite his standing with the crew, he didn't take it seriously. He was rather nonchalant about everything. We would grow into good friends after a few years and it was through him that I learned some valuable lessons. Like: the story of the Lost Package of Dehrholm Flatt.

"What are you doing down here, Ord?"

"I will ask you the same thing, Bosch. You come down here to get a taste?"

"What? A taste of what?" I asked somewhat disgusted at the thought of tasting anything down here in this fetid cesspool.

"My frag weed, you stump," he insinuated.

"Wait. You are down here smoking frag weed? Don't you know that the Captain will..."

"...do nothing, my youngish shipmate." He grinned and peered closely at me. "The Captain and me have an understanding. Here." He handed me a pipe.

"You might have an understanding, Ord, but I don't. I haven't been here long enough to push boundaries. The Captain gets wind that I've been crouched down in the hold smoking frag weed and I will be the one playing dodgeball with meteors and comets. No thanks!"

"Suit yourself, Bosch. You need to learn to not take everything so seriously." He took a long draw from the pipe and then looked at me. "So, if it's not the weed, then why would you be down here?"

"We are in Reen space and the Captain gave me the duty to make sure there weren't any high frequency sound roaches down here." I smiled like I had been appointed by the Queen.

He coughed out a bunch of smoke and started to laugh. After

enough time passed that I began to feel stupid and embarrassed he slowed his belly clutching and snorting only to look at me and start again. After a couple of those starts and stops I began to get pissed.

"Settle down, you bastard. What are you laughing at me for?"

He finally regained control of himself and smiled at me. "You *noxin*. There is no such thing as 'high frequency sound roaches.' It is an old trick played on unseasoned crew members."

"Son of a bitch," I fumed. Now I was angry at Ord and myself. Obviously the Captain didn't really think much of me to play such a trick. Being so young and inexperienced I found myself bordering on a pout. "Why would he do that to me?"

Ord took a draw from his pipe. "What were you doing when he gave you this honor?"

I looked at him for that subtle barb but I couldn't really muster up any real anger in my stare. I was just too disappointed. Maybe I had made a huge mistake running away from home. I was a fool. How could I feel any worse? "I was playing my music pretty loud for a couple guys. The Captain came in and made me shut it off before we got a hit on a picker."

He looked at me intently for a second then burst into laughter again! "Oh, Bosch! Sound doesn't travel in space! You could be banging on the hull with klegal wrenches and they wouldn't read a damn thing."

"Then why..."

"He hates that crazy Terran music! Can't stand it. In fact he uses the whole sound thing to finally get some peace and quiet on this crate. You just managed to piss him off."

Well, it seems I *could* feel worse. "Shit," I mumbled and sat on a low pipe. Ord must have sensed my feeling down.

"Hey, don't take it so hard, man. If the Cap really hated you he would have just kicked your ass into space. Or if he thought you weren't going to cut it you'd find yourself stranded on the first place we made planetfall." He put his hand on my shoulder, "Nah, you'll do ok, Bosch." I looked up at him and he gave me a big smile.

"Sorry, Ord. I just want this so bad," I wined.

"Yeah, I can tell." He took another hit from his pipe and we sat there in silence for a minute or two. "You know, Bosch, I can help you."

"How? With what?" I asked anxiously. I would have done anything to garner a secure position aboard the ship. I had a lot to prove and not just to my shipmates. I was on my own for the first time in my life and I needed to find my own sense of self worth in an enormous galaxy that couldn't give a rat's ass about me.

"Sadly, you're Terran and not Andojin so you aren't as use to this space life as we are. Our race is known for being spacefarers. The Cap is one hell of a pilot and I am a pretty sharp mechanic. I'll help you get used to this whole space thing. How would that be?"

"Seriously?" I was too naive to suspect he was working an angle and too desperate to question his motives if I had. As my luck would prove, he had only a sincere desire to see me succeed. That might have been the hardest thing for me to understand at that point.

"Yeah. Of course. You seem like a good kid. Just stick with me and I'll get you through it. Hell, maybe we can even make a decent pilot out of you." He suddenly laughed again. "Hell, no way! You Terrans suck at flying ships." He punched my shoulder. "But you are going to have to stop being such a *noxin*!"

Noxin was the Andojin word for 'baby' and on starships is used to refer to someone who is new and cannot care for themselves in their new surroundings. I hated that word.

"Call me that again and I will punch you right in the neck," I said with as much threat as I could muster. I was not going to be helpless.

"Whoa, randarc wrestler! I'll be your friend but if you start punching on me I'll grease fire you out of a waste disposal tube."

I laughed, which felt good and made me feel better about being on the ship. I had made assumptions about why the Captain had brought me aboard and now those seemed more or less fabricated by my subconscious desire to be accepted. Having Ord truly take interest in me and want to help me went a long way towards my hopes of being of value.

"But," he started, "you have to stop being so damn gullible. You will be exposed to a lot of talk that is pure shit and you better learn to smell the difference before you do something fatal. Hell, the next thing I know you'll be heading out to find the Lost Package of Dehrholm Flatt!"

"Who?"

"Dehrholm Flatt. He's the source of this wild, crazy folk tale and myth that has many a susceptible person squander all their money and life in hopes of finding him and the cargo he lost. Fools, every last one of them!" I detected bits of anger behind his words indicating that he had more than just a passing knowledge of this. Something personal had happened that made the subject a bitter one.

"I haven't heard about this," I confessed.

"Well, you would, given time and if I ever get wind that you are entertaining the idea of going out after it I will personally hunt you down and beat you with a dogging bar. And don't even think I am lying."

"Don't worry. My days of being a *noxin* are over. Especially regarding Derloam Flatt."

"Dehrholm."

"Yeah, right...Dehrholm Flatt."

"You'd be smart to give that craziness a wide berth," he continued to warn. His intensity continued to grow.

"Why do I get the sense that there is more to this than just the myth?" I asked.

He got more serious and shook his head sadly. "It got ahold of my father. He spent all of his years before I left home chasing after that goddamn package. It ruined his life and damn near ruined mine. Finally it ended up killing him but not before my mother and the rest of us left him behind. It's a Fool's Errand and one that I don't like to see anyone get wrapped up in."

"What's the actual story?" I asked wondering why I had never heard about this odd part of galactic lore.

"It is a simple thing like most of these things start out. A courier pilot named Dehrholm Flatt took a job to deliver a package to a destination across the galaxy. It was a long distance haul and ships were not quite as fast as some of the speedy little rigs we have these days so it was going to take him some time. He never made it to the delivery point and was never heard or seen again. Simple."

He was right, it was simple. Happens every day; some unlucky courier goes out on a run and mis-programs his NavCom and bounces too close to a sun or crosses paths with space pirates or decides the cargo is worth a lot more on the black market and "retires" early with the proceeds. Being an independent delivery pilot has a lot of risks and challenges. "So why the fuss?" I asked.

"Can't tell you for sure. But this thing got some traction and started to grow into a huge mystery. Part of it might be that the company that hired him, per the manifest - which is public record - was Singularity."

"Damn." Singularity was one of the largest interstellar companies in the galaxy. It was not only colossal but the amount of subsidiaries under its banner and the multitude of products and services it produced were staggering. Worst of all was the reputation that it had for being covert in a lot of its dealings. When people envisioned Singularity it was on par with a secret society with private agendas and secret handshakes. Only a select few had any true knowledge of its real inner workings. So the fact that it was involved would only add to the possibility of the missing cargo having some secretive background.

"Right," he agreed. "The cursed Singularity was also very uninformative when the insurance claim was processed. They didn't ask for anything. They told the insurance agents that the package was not valuable enough to warrant a claim and dismissed the investigation. This and the fact that there were two packages sent at the same time and neither made it to their destination produced the fertile rumor bed that simple people seem to thrive on. The other courier was hijacked by pirates lending the cargo a desirable validation. Roll it all together, smoke some frag weed and you have yourself a spooky mystery that screams fortune and powers beyond comprehension. There have been a wealth of books written about it and there was a movie that was loosely based on the whole stupid thing."

"And I've never heard of it?" I said with some curiosity.

"Never heard of 'Nebula Jones and the Orb of Power'?"

"What? Of course I have. Saw that movie 4 times."

"That was it," he revealed.

"Huh." This all made a lot of sense. "What do people think was in that package?"

"That's another part of the mystery and where imaginations reign. The manifest awkwardly doesn't have the dimensions, weight, or contents listed. So people can put whatever they want into that box. It is a bonafide McGuffin. Every theory is out there from the body of Xildaran the Obarnee Prophet to the Vengeance Stone to the Forgotten Books of Boge. You name it and someone has come up with evidence that it is in that cursed box."

"But it is all fabrication. No one knows anything for sure, right?"

"Yup," he agreed. "Not only do they not know what happened or what Flatt was carrying, they have no idea where it could be. There is a rough flight plan that would be the most logical path for Flatt to take from his origination to his destination but who can say for sure that he even went the direct route. He could have had another job or two that he knocked out while on the long trip and deviated from the straight course. This literally spans a good portion of the galaxy and looking for it is beyond insane." The disgust in his voice was heavy and fueled by childhood sadness and his own good sense as an established pilot and engineer.

Just then I could hear heavy footfalls on the deck above us and someone yelling. It sounded like the Captain.

"I think something is happening, Bosch," and he made his way toward the hatch in time to see the boots of Captain Galcursed appear on the steps. "Captain?" he called out.

The Captain crouched and his face came into view peering into the gloom of the lower deck space. "Ord? What in the seven suns are you doing down here? Is Bosch with you?"

"Yeah. I am helping him find those high frequency sound roaches you are so fired up about."

The Captain looked momentarily angry and then resolved to something more urgent. "We have a problem. The starboard engine has cut out and we are adrift. Maybe you can come take a look if it isn't too much trouble...Ord."

"Aye," replied Ord and he dodged his way through the space to reach the ladder and dart up above. Once I heard his footsteps bang across the overhead and off toward the engine room I was left with silence and a feeling of uselessness. It sounded like we were in trouble and I could offer nothing to help.

"Bosch!" came the Captain's voice booming from above. "You still down there?"

Apparently he did not leave with Ord. "Y...yes, sir!" I called back.

"Well, if you are done wasting time down there maybe you can come up and give us a hand at not getting caught by the Reen. That is, if I'm not disturbing your nap time."

Shit. I was disappointing him yet again. At this rate this day could be my last on the ship. I raced topside and stood at attention in front of Captain Galcursed. "Sir."

"Make use of yourself, Bosch! Go try and help Chief Ord. If we aren't moving soon we'll be found out for sure. And with this much illegal cargo the Reen will skip a trial and go straight to execution. Do you know how they execute criminals on Reen, Bosch?"

"No, sir."

"They crush their heads with a giant rock. Heard it makes one hell of a mess. You want that for us, Bosch?'

"NO, sir!"

"I don't want that, Bosch. Do you?"

"Then move your ass and try not to break anything else in the engine room or I will personally throw you out an airlock. Understood?"

"Yes, SIR!"

The Captain was a large Andojin and he towered over me; an imposing figure. He leaned down to bring his face within a breath of mine blocking the overhead lighting and casting me in the shadow of his frame. His pale eyes bored into mine. "Go."

I was off like an arrow from a tightly pulled string.

During the tense hour that followed I tried my best to help Ord repair the starboard engine I was as quick as I could be in following anything he said, be it, "Grab me a number three Klegal wrench!" to "Move! You're in my light." In time I even managed to anticipate his next order; like the next time I noticed I was casting a shadow into his work area - I moved before he even said anything. I felt we were becoming a team. I scrambled for tools and water, pushed buttons and flipped switches, and sat to the side and stayed silent. Despite his calm demeanor I could sense a burning tension under his skin that made me understand that no matter how he appeared, Ord was committed to the Nir'don and Captain Galcursed. And the fact that not once did the Captain come and check on Ord or ask for an update made me realize that the respect was mutual. Soon the engine roared to life and we made it the rest of the way to our destination without incident. It was the first of many such adventures and narrow escapes. It prepped me well for my future endeavors both as first mate of the Nir'don and as the owner of the Jackleg.

And those years also taught me that many a fool exists in the universe and that I best not be one of them.

A1 STARED AT ME WITH HARSH INTENSITY that not only let me know he was genuinely serious but that he also greatly resented my accusations as to his state of mind. While I granted him a certain respect due to his long standing and close relationship with a man I greatly admired, he was still basically a stranger and had yet to prove his character to me personally. Friend of the Captain or not, I would not be bullied.

"Sorry, A1" I started, "I am not going off to parts unknown to find something that is equal parts myth and fairy tale. I don't have the time or the lack of independent thought."

His strong gaze never wavered. "You know, I really thought Gal was right about you in all the things he told me but I can see you are just another small-minded loser with no sense of adventure or ambition."

"I resent that! I am not small-minded."

"Not funny, Bosch."

"Not meant to be. You won't ever hear me say I am ambitious and an adventurer. I have set up my life to *not* be those things. I don't want fame and fortune. I want peace and quiet. Adventure finds me way more often than I'd like. I am alive because I don't go looking for trouble."

"No," he said. "You are alive because when the Captain needed you, you weren't there. You are here because when the ship and crew needed you, you weren't there. Not looking for adventure, Bosch? Hell, you are running away from it and everything else that requires a commitment."

I won't lie, that stung. Badly.

"Get out, A1."

"Now just you wait a ..."

"Get out of my office. Now. Or so help me God I will shoot you right on that spot." I pulled my gun to accent my intent.

"What about your ship? Your employee?"

"I'll go without if it just means you get the hell outa here."

"There's something wrong with you, Bosch."

"Don't care." I never blinked nor looked away. I had every intention to shoot him if he didn't move toward the door. It is rare that I am that pissed off but when I am...

"Fine. I'll go. But know this: I sought you out because of a promise I made to *your* Captain and *your* friend. Your ship and employee are gone because of me and I want to set this right. So even if you don't want to go seek your fortune you could at least give two shits about your ship and maybe even your employee. Let me at least help you get them back and then, well, you can go crawl back under a little, safe rock and I won't bother you anymore."

"I can buy a new ship. And I can hire a new employee. And I can see you still standing in my office and in another minute you'll be dead and then I can forget this whole thing."

He gave me one last look, shook his head and left.

"Go fuck yourself, old man," I mumbled after he left. I went and locked the door, turned out the lights, and went to my room in the back of the building. I sat in the dark for a long while. Sure, I was really angry but something he said had drilled deep into me and opened up a long buried reservoir of crap I had hidden away another lifetime ago. Things I have trained myself not to think about. Or feel. Painful memories that had at one time tried to destroy me. Guilt is a horrible thing to live with and to survive we can make amends and seek forgiveness from those we have wronged and ourselves. Or we can jam that shit right into a little, black hole, cover it with every distraction and extravagance we can find, and tell ourselves everything is just plain okey doke. I've been doing that for 14 years. Maybe it was time to finally stop.

Kirk Nelson

CHAPTER 5

When I finally walked out of the Jackleg Courier Company office it was getting late and very dark. I could tell that at least a couple of Mytopoli's moons had to be up but the heavy cloud cover over Cyran blocked almost all of the light. All of the businesses around my company close in the early evening so their windows were all dark as well. It was primarily a business neighborhood so the lights on the street were spaced far apart offering little in the way of illumination. All the storefronts being closed for the night also meant there were no pedestrians milling about leaving me alone in gloomy night. It was quiet enough to hear the ships power up for departure at the docks several miles away. The roar of distant engines in the night was practically a lullaby for me. I loved the sound. I could instinctively tell if the engine was taxiing, ramping up for take-off or landing, what model it was, and based on that information - what kind of ship it was. Right then I knew that there were three ships landing and two prepping for take-off. Of those five craft, one was a Heriminious class freighter like the Nir'don, two were industrial Krayt style ships - the really big ones that the Syndicate uses, and the last two were small ones like mine that were for quick, small cargo. There was a part of me that wanted to run to the docks and sign onto any ship that would have me, the larger the better. Just leave Cyran behind as the huge starship would set course for somewhere far away, find the gravitational folds in space and literally skip across the galaxy like a flat stone on a smooth lake.

The night air was much cooler than the day had been and I sucked in a heavy breath, the dirty atmosphere of Cyran full of the scents I have grown to recognize as home. I stared up into the sky again and tried to imagine the sky without the clouds and pollution, to see the moons race around in their orbits, the stars twinkling in alien constellations, and the largest moon, Bor, showing me a gigantic red crescent on the ebony horizon. I remember that same feeling back on Earth when I was a child, staring into the dark sky, straining to see farther and farther into space. I knew even then that there was life, abundant life, all over the galaxy and that I so wanted to be a part of it. But those thoughts were all science fiction, fodder for imaginary trips into the void in my own little ship built under a table in the living room, shielded from the vacuum of space by sleeping blankets and beach towels. Within that tiny capacity I could find adventures that thrilled, providing me with tales of heroic feats and daring rescues won by luck and fate. I felt a kinship with space and I knew in those young years that my destiny did not lie on Earth but among the stars and planets that were home to races that would expand my understanding of what it meant to be "human."

For so long I considered myself fortunate to have lived the very life I had dreamed of every night as a child. The adventures of my make-believe spaceship manifested into reality at the simple age of 10 when we left Earth for a new "home" in the distant Neverland of the Galaxy. But as with any dream that becomes reality, the "reality" part is still a part of the mixture and always makes itself known - like onions in meatloaf, you know there are onions, you can sort of taste them but every so often, you bite into a big piece of one and you remember, "Oh yeah...onions. I hate onions" and you don't ask for seconds and remember why you don't seek out meatloaf for dinner anyway.

So after twenty years I had the job of my dreams, true friends that were from planets other than my own, and a woman that loved me. Then I bit into a giant, bitter onion and it was all gone. Hello Reality...it bites.

I walked around aimlessly for hours being melancholy about the past and maudlin about the present. I had made it a practice not to be sentimental and nostalgic and during this long stroll I was reminded why. In the end I accomplished nothing but get depressed and want to run away from everything. By some subconscious design I suddenly found myself circled back to Galder's and decided it was the best time for a drink and company.

Walking back in I felt the immediate familiarity I mentioned earlier but there was also a sensation that there were no answers for me here. It was a mirage that seemed to be what I needed but held no promise or solution. The place was about to close and so naturally there was a full push at the bar. Galder hadn't even looked up to see me yet so I turned to leave when a hand grabbed my shoulder. Having been in many a bar fight for reasons both good and bad I instinctively dropped my shoulder and spun to the outside ducking low and cocking my right arm back to deliver an uppercut if I was lucky, a block if I wasn't.

My quick movements surprised my assailant and I came a whisper from clocking him across the jaw stopped only by my own immediate recognition of that scraggly old face. "A1?"

"Still being an ass, I see."

I was still plenty angry at him - I *had* threatened to kill him just a few hours ago - but the heat of it had cooled somewhat. Maybe I would just beat the tar out of him. I was in a bar after all. "Hanging around for a beat down, then. I'll oblige." I drew my arm back again.

"Go ahead if that's what's going to bring you to your damned senses."

"My sense are fine, you old carburetor, because I sense an ass kicking." A drink or a fight, one or both of those was going to get me out of this funk.

He dropped his guard and gave me that same squared look. "Get at it then! But I'm going to tell you it won't help one bit."

"It won't help your looks, that's for sure." I swung hard and in the instant it was going to connect I realized he wasn't going to stop me. He was going to take it full on the chin with no pretense of self-defense. I've punched a lot of people before, even a couple of Farnok women, but I have never just *beat* on someone that refused to fight back. At the very last second I pulled the punch and altered the aim. It glanced off his forehead with a whack.

"Ow! Son of a bitch!" His hands went to his head. "You went ahead and did it! Do you feel better you sorry, hopeless ass?"

"My hand kind of hurts. You have a damn hard head, old man. But, yes, I do feel a little better. How about another one?" I squared off.

"If you do I'll be throwing punches back and I'll even toss in a couple a kicks. I can't believe you went ahead and struck an old man that wasn't fighting back. You *are* low."

"I thought you were just faking it, ready to counter with a swing or at least a dodge. Believe me, I pulled that punch," I confessed. But it had worked. All the steam was gone. I didn't want to fight. I didn't want to argue. I just wanted...hell, I wasn't sure *what* I wanted.

"Really? That was pulled? Guess I'm luckier than I thought. That was a pretty good hit if that was running on less than full steam. I'll give you that, Bosch, you can throw a punch."

"Fair enough." I dropped my hands and stood up straight sensing the quarrel was temporarily over.

"What are you doing here? If you came to apologize then you have a strange way of saying it."

"No. I was just wandering around thinking and ended up here," I admitted. "I didn't expect you to be here. I thought you'd be long gone."

"Where? I've only been to your place and here. Don't know where I should go."

"You don't have a ship?"

"No, lost it some time ago. I took the transport from Dahlkirk." He was still rubbing his head. A small lump and bruise was forming. Oddly, that made me feel even a little bit better.

"So how are we going to go find my ship?"

He looked up at me, "So, you're in?"

"I ain't saying that. Just seems your plan was a bit under-cooked."

"Didn't say I had a plan."

"Sounded like it. What with all this finding the lost package of

80

Dehrholm Flatt. Unless it is just down the street I don't see how we are supposed to go find it with no ship."

He gave me a pained expression. "You idiot, I figured *you* had a ship! You are a delivery pilot, aren't you? I didn't know somebody would steal it. That wasn't part of any plan."

"We are going to need a ship. Once we get one we'll go find *my* ship…"

"And your employee," A1 added.

I raised an eyebrow, "We'll see. But once we find my stuff, then I'll consider if I am going to go any further. I'm not making any promises, A1. You said you wanted to set things right with getting my ship pinched. I'm holding you to that."

"I will hope you reconsider on the package but I stand by what I said." He appeared genuine in his statement.

"So," I began, "We need a ship."

Ratsbak and Feldtac is a shipping brokerage. They act as an intermediary for people trying to ship something and those that want to deliver something. Most people that seek out independent couriers are shipping something special that doesn't quite fit within the stringent guidelines of the USPS. It is often quasi-illegal and almost always valuable. Independent couriers are not cheap and to warrant their fees the cargo must have a substantial worth. But as a lot of people don't make it a habit of sending off disreputable merchandise they don't know how to go about it. Finding a courier you can completely trust is difficult. Believe it or not, there are some that would easily sell you out to the authorities for a few credits or simply take the cargo and ignore your questions about what happened to it; the Galactic Legal Counsel doesn't represent victims of courier fraud. Therefore these inexperienced customers go to a shipping agent who, for a fee, brokers their cargo to the couriers they represent. The couriers bid on the job if it is a big payout, or the agents give out the jobs based on what it is and who they like that day.

I sometimes drop by the local Ratsbak and Feldtac office and grab a few jobs when things get thin. Vax Ratsbak runs the office in

Lynterus (the Capital City on Mytopoli) which is just an hour flight from Cyran. We go back to before I owned the Jackleg when I didn't have clients and was desperate for work. I thought he might be an avenue for renting a ship.

Vax, like his partner Voso Feldtac, is Klanx. I have no problem with the Klanx. They are good people, though a little too serious and work obsessed for me. They are one of the original three races in the Galactic Tribunal along with the Andojin and the Grantok. They have one characteristic that always bugs me: while they look a lot like really light skinned Terrans, they have no necks. It's not that they are just so fat or muscle bound that their necks are swallowed up by rolls of flesh or arcs of sinew; they simply don't have a neck. Their round heads sit directly atop their shoulders mildly resembling the upper half of a snowman. They can't turn, nod, or shake their heads. They have to bend at the waist to look up or down or twist at the hips to look right or left and they absolutely can't look behind themselves. It is an odd thing but I've been told, usually by Vax, that this is the key to their evolution as the galactic leader in industry and business: they are always looking forward. It is part of their culture and their lifestyle. But as the only race without necks, excepting, of course, the few that don't have a discernible head, I can attest to the fact that they are a little jealous. I have seen them wearing turtlenecks and scarves. Once I saw one with a crude attempt at a necktie. I know they feel a little left out on fashionable neckwear. Plus it is nearly impossible for them to dance, not that they are prone to dancing as they are insanely focused on work, but seeing one of them, stoned on blaganite, trying to dance to some classic Earth rock and roll...that is a sight!

"Vax!" I shouted as I entered the foyer of their posh office in the upscale, thriving business hub of Lynterus. "How is it going, my friend?"

Vax turned, bodily I might add, toward me from behind the counter. "Eye-level, Argon."

"Eye-level" is a great example of the no-neck culture of the Klanx bleeding into the phrases they use. It basically means "everything is as it should be."

"Glad to hear it, Vax. I need a ship." No sense in beating around the bush, the Klanx always prefer the efficiency of being straight to the point.

"Don't you have a ship, Argon? Don't tell me you lost it in some game of chance," he sighed.

"No, it was stolen and I need a ship to get it back."

He looked sad but I wasn't sure whether it was because I lost my ship or because the idea of borrowing a ship was distasteful. "You are aware, I am sure, that this is a brokerage, Argon, not a ship lending institution? We are not in the business of lending, selling, or otherwise procuring ships for our customers."

"I know that, Vax. But I thought you might have a lead on one or maybe someone that would be able to set me up."

"Nor are we an information service or some kind of matchmaking resource."

"Nothing but the business, right Vax?"

"Without question." He turned, bent, and signed some paper on the counter. He then lifted another up to his face and read through it.

While I like Vax, if I'm not setting up a delivery his conversations tend to always turn toward setting up a delivery.

I looked at A1 and he looked frustrated and a little impatient. He shrugged then I shrugged. Vax leveled his gaze at us and I wondered if he felt left out of our little mutual shrugging. I doubt it. "I am really desperate, Vax." I decided to throw in something close to a human element. "They even got Winston too."

"That is unfortunate. I will miss our conversations."

"I have to get him back, Vax!"

"Why was he taken?"

"I don't know."

"Who took him?"

"I don't know."

"How are you going to get him back?"

"I don't know."

"Argon, this seems like a losing proposition and you know how I feel about losing propositions."

"They are best left behind," I quoted what he had sometimes

said to me when I lowballed a job.

"Correct."

"But I do have a plan. My friend here knows what's going on and he can lead us right to Winston and get this whole mess straightened out." I slapped A1's shoulder giving him a wink to go along.

"Uh, right," he agreed. "I know just what is going on and I will get everything set right." He stepped over to Vax and offered his hand. "Abraxas Wun."

Vax shook his hand. "Like the number?" I cringed knowing what was coming next.

"I don't know of a number abraxas, Mr. Ratsbak." He grinned just like the old fool he was.

Then it happened. Vax laughed. Not a sympathy laugh but a hearty, full body laugh. I was stunned. Stunned that Vax laughed because in the 13 years I'd known him I never once heard him laugh. And I was stunned that he would think that stupid joke was amusing. Then he laughed some more. What crazy alternate universe had I mistakenly fallen into?

He finally recovered enough to speak, dabbing at his watering eyes at the same time. "Oh Mr. Wun..."

"Call me A1, please."

"A1 then. Oh, that was good. I haven't laughed that hard in days."

Days?!

"I am glad I could coax it out of you then," remarked A1. "But in all seriousness, I really hope you can help us out. It is my fault that Argon here lost his ship and loyal employee. I feel bad and I need to make it up to him. We can't...I can't manage to set this right unless we get us a ship. Can you please help us with that, Mr. Ratsbak?"

I was not sure Vax would fall for that play for sympathy but A1 was selling it like he was in his first school play. Vax was no fool.

"I may be a fool but I think I might be able to help you...A1. And please, call me Vax."

A1 bowed. "Thank you so very, very much, Vax. You have no idea what this means to me that you would help out a desperate stranger like this."

"I can see you are a man of honor, A1. And it is clear that you care what happens to Argon and his business - and I would hate to see his business fail."

"You understand me perfectly, Vax," said A1.

"I know a courier that is currently unable to fly due to a savage case of bowel-rush. Doctor says he won't be going anywhere for a few weeks. I am sure I could persuade him to lend you his ship for a small fee."

"That would be grand, Vax. You are a saint."

I feared A1 was layering his act with way too much honey. If he kept lathering it that thick Vax was going to see right through his pandering and it would be over. I had to move to the close...quick!

"Vax, you come through again, my friend," I interjected. "Man, I really appreciate this. I won't forget it, I promise." A1 looked at me and I knew he was pissed I had taken over his solo act but now was not the time to go for the encore. "If you could just give us the sickly gentleman's name and communication ID we will be on our way."

Vax smiled and said, "Sure. It is right over here." He walked over to his desk and waved through a shimmering display above it. It brought up a list of contacts and he quickly spun a finger here and passed a hand there and he seemed to have the information he was searching for. "I'll print it out for you."

"Thanks," said A1.

"Thanks," I added starting to sweat. It was all about just getting it and getting out. No more grand speeches, no more eloquent compliments. Just get out the door with the contact.

"Here you go," and Vax pulled the sheet from the printer. I strained to see the name but he waved the paper in the air like some high-school cheerleader at the big game. "I am so happy to help you." I would later swear that A1 had managed to slip Vax something to get him high after witnessing him being so damn near *giddy!* We had to go...*now!*

"I won't forget this, Vax. I will be coming back with a big repayment for your help," A1 started up again.

Oh no.

"No need to pay me back, A1," countered Vax.

"I insist! Why Argon here and I will have more than enough to share a hefty bonus just for you being so nice and all."

Oh sweet mother of donuts, no.

"How's that, A1? Why would you have this fortune?"

"Cause we're going to be rich!" exclaimed A1 with his usual mindless glee.

No, you damned fool! STOP! I just wanted to just clamp my hand over A1's mouth and rush him toward the door. In hindsight, I should have.

"I don't understand?" said Vax his face contorted in confusion.

"Me and Argon are going to go find the Lost Package of Dehrholm Flatt!"

Shit.

An inch. There was an inch between the paper and my hand. I saw it. A tiny inch. If only I had longer arms I would have had it. But in that last second Vax yanked it away. I'm not sure how he managed it but I swear he started tearing it up before he even brought it to his other hand. Like magic. It was there, then confetti. Son of a...

"You think me a fool, A1? That I would have anything to do with a get rich quick scheme that involved something as foolhardy as seeking the Lost Package of Dehrholm Flatt? And Argon!" I couldn't even look at him. I shrugged, which in hindsight, was not a good move to make again in front of an angry Klanx. "I am surprised and disgusted you would have anything to do with this. I thought you practical and a genuine businessman. But now I see you are a petty gambler, a reckless spender, an unworthy partner. Leave now and do not return." He turned away and put his back to us. It was one of the Klanx highest insults.

A1 began to speak but I stopped him. I shook my head and guided him to the exit. "But..."he started and I shoved him at the door.

"Shut up, A1. Just shut the hell up."

We were no closer to getting a ship and my options were running out. I didn't know if time was a factor but I suspected it was. A1 was proving to be no help and I hadn't even asked him where we were going to start looking. But until we had transportation there was no point in bringing it up. Without Vax's help I wasn't sure where else I could turn. Mortgage the Jackleg? That would take too long. Savings? Not enough to buy a ship. Hire a ship? I had no idea what A1's plan was going to entail time and effort wise so I couldn't manage to explain to the hired pilot our needs. Zero options. Dead in the water.

There was one person left I could ask and I simply did not want to do that. As it crossed my mind I pushed it away with thoughts of bussing tables at Galder's or cleaning restroom stalls down at the docks. And believe me, they both seemed a more pleasant alternative.

CHAPTER 6

My plan had blown up in my face due in no small part to my unfortunate partner, A1. Some may argue that it was A1 that offered an inroad to Vax's consideration and eventual cooperation but since he also was the cause of his staunch refusal I submit that I would have been no better off without him. And since he also managed to single handedly destroy my working relationship with a good source of revenue I figure I am worse off than if I were alone. Need I also bring up the source of this whole predicament that I now found myself embroiled in? I thought not.

I sat nursing a cup of coffee at a diner near the Transport Center in Lynterus with A1 across from me eating some kind of local...well, I'll just call it a sandwich.

"You should try this, Argon," he enunciated around a mouthful of food. "It has a very distinct flavor."

"I find 'distinct' another word for 'unusual' and that word, like 'exotic', when used in describing food, usually means I won't like it."

"How do you know unless you've tried it?" he unnecessarily argued.

"You have kids, don't you A1?"

He frowned for a moment as if the thought registered conflicting emotions. I was certain that he was going to come back with a negative but he surprised me. "I have a son named Abraham."

I couldn't resist. "What do they call him?"

"Abraham," he remarked with a raised eyebrow.

An opportunity lost. "Anyway," I sighed, "Your argument is a parent's argument and one that is as impractical as it is illogical. I've never eaten Prug Beast droppings but I know they will taste like shit."

"Because it *is* shit!"

"Regardless, it won't taste good, right?"

"Because. It. Is. Shit, you daft fool."

"My point is I know that some things will taste horrible before I ever try them. It is rare that I am surprised."

"I'm not getting that. We are talking about food here, not animal dung."

I tired to think of something disgusting that no one would ever eat. "What do Prug Beast testicles taste like?"

"Kind of like bitter tomatoes actually."

I tossed up my hands. "Alright. I imagine that, er, *sandwich* will taste terrible."

"Not to me it doesn't."

"Give me a bite, you shirtsleeve."

I took one bite, let it sit on my tongue for a second or two, stifled a gag, and spit it into a napkin I had at the ready.

"Shit."

"Really?" He actually seemed surprised and gave the "sandwich" a little sniff. "Strange."

"Not to me."

"Must be an acquired taste," he offered.

I rolled my eyes; the old fall back argument. Eat enough shit you will grow to like it. Well, I never wanted to invest that much time and effort into eating shit. "Moving on..."

"Good idea. What's your next plan?"

"You know, A1, I'm putting a lot of effort in having to come up with a way to secure a ship for us to go find *my* ship that *you* caused to disappear, so that we could go find something that *you* want. I would think perhaps you'd put forth a bit more effort into working this out."

He seemed a little put out by my statement. "I'm new here! I don't know anyone on this planet. Or even this sector. If you want to head over to my stomping ground I can get us a ship like that." He snapped his fingers but the grease from his meal produced only the gesture not the sound.

"Now wait," I said surprised at this revelation. "You can get a ship from somewhere?"

"Yes! I'm not completely useless. I've made a lot of contacts in my long career," he said with a swell of pride.

"Then what in the name of space monkeys are you doing here? You said you came to me because you knew I had a ship!" My voice revealed my growing annoyance with A1 and his harebrained scheme. I had barely met the man and I was already feeling equal desires to either punch him or slap his balding head.

"Not exactly. I said I knew you had a ship but that's not why I sought you out."

"You already admitted that you didn't really know me but you traveled across the galaxy to find me to go on this stone-cold crazy adventure. Did you draw my name out of hat?"

"No, no. You forgot what I said to you. I made a promise to our mutual friend, Captain Galcursed, about you," he jabbed a finger into my chest.

I suddenly did remember that tiny part of our conversation but had dismissed it when all the other crap bubbled to the surface. "What promise?"

"Back when Gal was still alive and you were the first mate on the Nir'don we ran into each other in a harbor-town. He had grown quite fond of you and seemed to be concerned with what would happen to you if suddenly he wasn't around."

"What was going to happen to him? Andojins live a hell of a lot longer than Terrans," I pointed out.

"Not that. I believe he suspected that something was already afoot with the Syndicate's play for galactic control over the delivery business. It was only a few months later that he was killed."

"By a Farnok over some payment dispute."

"Was it really though?" he questioned.

"Farnoks are pretty damn touchy about...well, everything. That's why no one likes to deal with them. I asked Captain Galcursed not to take the job but he did anyway."

"That's because he was in trouble. He had gathered a lot of debt trying to compete with the Syndicate. They were buying up independents all over the place and undercutting fees just to drive out the rest. It was a hard time for couriers back then."

"Hell, it's hard *now*," I reminded him.

"Nothing like then. You were first-mate, second in command, you should have had some idea."

He was getting close to touching a nerve with his thinly veiled accusations. "I wanted to but the Captain never let me. He insisted on handling cargo orders himself."

"Originally he did that because he didn't trust anyone else but later he did it to protect you from the difficulties he was having."

"Wait a second, A1. He told me that one day he would retire and I would take his place. Why would he hide anything from me? I would need to know about it."

He took a second to answer. "That's where the promise came in. He was really worried about the future of the Nir'don. Gal thought the Syndicate would squeeze everyone out, no matter how hard they struggled. He didn't think you would ever get the chance. Luckily the Joint Independent Courier Coalition came along and they managed to put up enough of a fight that the Syndicate had to back off. But that was after he was already gone."

"So what was the promise?"

"If I ever had an opportunity that would payout big enough to allow me to back out of the courier business that I would include you."

"What?" I suddenly felt like I was living a lie, that all the things that had gotten me to this point were built on false promises. The Captain had maneuvered me toward an icy tundra while describing a desert oasis. "Was it that bad? He was...my friend." The word had caught in my throat, another sign that there was a lot of heavy baggage I was carrying around with me.

"He thought of you as even more. He told me that you were like a son to him."

"Stop," I whispered.

"Really. He knew things were getting too out of control. He had to protect you."

"Stop."

"I think he even knew when he went to get payment from the Farnok that it was a Syndicate set up. That's why he made sure you stayed behind."

"Dammit...STOP!"

The people in the diner turned and looked at us. My head was down and I was having some trouble. Feelings came smashing into me and I struggled to hold it together but I could feel the control all slipping away. A1 reached out to grab my arm. I wasn't sure then if it was to comfort me or to restrain me, keep me from making a scene. I yanked my arm back. "This is bullshit, A1. He had no right to keep all this from me."

"He was only..."

I bolted up from the table, spilling what was left of my coffee. This did little to reduce the amount of attention our table was getting. I spun for the door and raced out, vaguely aware of eyes watching, heads turning to follow me. I thought I heard A1 call something after me or get up from the table but it was all outside of the storm cloud that had engulfed my head. I couldn't deal. So I did what I always do - I left.

A1 found me sometime later though I don't know how he did it. There were a lot of bars around the Transportation Center so he must have gone to every single one. It was late when he finally sat down next to me. I was on my fourth bottle of Blackhole and the familiar numb haze was settling down on me. The previous emotional dust up was starting to melt into a dreamy fantasy, far, far away from the reality of my Obsidian Ale, a band playing some kind of ethnic noise, and the very lovely female sitting across the bar from me. Much more along the lines of what I could and wanted to deal with. I was not happy to see him but my mouth wouldn't cooperate with my intent.

"A1, you sons of a Reen! Have me with a drink!"

"You need to come with me, Argon."

I tried to curse at him for what he put me through but it came out with different intent. "Only if lovely lady there can come too." I snickered at my odd statement and the sad double entendre I accidentally created.

To his credit, A1 never got upset or gave me any guff about it the next morning when I woke up. He had managed to get me out of the bar with no physical subduing. I believe he paid the female I had been eyeing to decoy me to the hotel where he had gotten us a room. She left immediately after I got to the bed and collapsed.

I was in the embarrassingly familiar state of the Obsidian Ale hangover when A1 walked in and brought me some breakfast. "I got you some simple, unexotic food. Hopefully your delicate palate won't be shocked or sickened by this sad display."

Taking a quick look at the plate I sort of recognized a couple things and shoved them into my mouth. I washed it quickly down with some kind of blue juice. "Thanks," I managed to mumble. "I don't feel too good."

"Not surprising."

I shrugged and jammed something else into my mouth. My taste buds hadn't kicked in yet so I didn't really care what I was eating.

He sat down on the edge of the bed. "I'm sorry about laying all of that on you at once. It was a lot to take in."

I could tell, even in my post-stupid stupor that he meant it. I couldn't totally fault him; I did ask. "Forget it."

He stood up, "Get yourself cleaned up, there is still the matter of a ship." I nodded and ate some more.

"What is this?"

"Do you like it?" he asked.

"Yeah, it's not too bad. Tastes a little like bitter tomatoes..." I quickly looked at him. "You didn't..."

He just smiled and left, closing the door behind him.

We met up in the lobby after A1 had checked us out. We had wasted a whole day and were no closer to a ship. I was feeling frustrated. I like things to be simple, easy, and familiar. I always want to know what is going on and what I need to do. I don't like ambiguity. I don't like confusion. And I certainly don't like uncertainty. But most of all I didn't like this helpless feeling I was having not knowing what to do.

"There must be some way to get us a ship," A1 tossed out. His slippery grasp on reality bothered me. It is easy to say something like that when it has no impact on anything. Just a general statement like, *"I could buy that if I had a million credits."*

"That's not much of a help, A1." We sat there for awhile not saying anything.

"Don't you have any friends that could help you out?" he asked.

"Not really."

" 'Not really' you don't have any friends or 'not really' you don't have ones that will help you?"

"Both, I suspect," I clarified.

"What do you mean by that?"

"I mean that I don't have any friends anymore and those few I did have are not likely to want to help me."

"Why?"

"You are asking a lot of questions, old man."

"Just seems to me you aren't trying very hard."

"Excuse me? *I'm* not trying very hard? Just what the hell are you doing? I don't see you contacting anyone to come to our rescue, A1."

"I'm..."

"...not from around here? Yeah, we covered that."

"OK, I'll call my old friend Tweed. He might be able to get here with a ship in a week. Do you want to wait that long?"

"Let me think about it...a week versus...*forever!* Not much of a contest."

"If you would quit moping around you could come up with something, someone," he assured.

"I only know of one guy that might, *might* be able to help us. *If* he will is a big unknown."

"Well, dammit, at least try. What have you got to lose?"

There it was, the question I had been dreading all along. What will I lose? I didn't know. After not talking to someone for almost 14 years what would he say? What would he do? I can live my life just fine on the presumption that a good friend hates me but to know for sure? That's a lot harder to carry around.

"I'll do it. I'll call him and see what he says. But I make no guarantees, A1. There is a pretty good chance he is going to tell me to go to hell if he talks to me at all."

"I can live with that," he said with no concern. Of course he could live with it but could I? It appeared I was finally going to find out.

"Is Mr. Spierlok in?" I asked the receptionist who materialized on the screen.

"Yes, sir. May I tell him who is calling?"

I was actually afraid to say my name. Would the line go dark immediately as I was well known at his business as the guy to never put through to the boss for any reason or you are fired? Or would I get the faux-polite "I'm sorry. He has left for the day. Please call back when the stars all go nova. Have a great day!"? Or maybe he would come on after a few minutes after he had time to jot down a few notes on all of the vitriol he needed to get out of his system. That is the one I dreaded. I would be happy to get the exploding sun line over actually seeing him staring at me on the view screen and unleashing years of hatred and disappointment.

"Please tell him it is Argon Bosch and that it is urgent. Thank you."

"Please hold," and she was off and I watched a slowly rotating logo for Orion Vacations. The irony of the situation was not wasted on me - me calling a travel agency for help instead of following up on my own vacation (the sudden thought of a wasted deposit fluttering down the drain making me quietly groan).

Minutes ticked by as I imagined him furiously pacing his office, dictating to his secretary all the points he didn't want to forget as he unleashed upon me. "Yes, Miss Nambipacker, take this down:

Dishonest, immoral, lazy, unscrupulous, deceitful, disloyal, malcontent, thieving, self-centered, cheap, dishonorable, did I say lazy? Never mind. See to it that I use all of those terms when I talk to Mr. Bosch. Give me a signal when I have cleared them all and then I can disconnect from him immediately. I prefer not to have to talk to that snake any longer than I have to. Egotistical bastard." I braced myself for the deluge.

Then his face came on and I heard the familiar, nasally voice, "Argon!"

"Doon," I replied, barely hiding a wince.

"You stupid son of a bitch." There it was, the beginning of the tirade I had coming and knew I deserved. *Let it go, Doon. Get it all out while I'm here.*

"Man, am I glad to hear from you after all these years!" His face split into that huge grin I was so fond of and that characteristically displayed his gregarious nature. "I really thought I wouldn't ever hear from you. I figure you must be desperate for something. Need some help?"

In those few short sentences he managed to wipe away my dread and toss me back to over a decade ago when such conversation would be commonplace. It was not until that moment that I realized just how much I had ached for this very thing: the comradery of a good friend.

"I...I thought you would be angry with me, Doon."

"Hell, buddy, I have only missed you. Just figured you needed to do your thing. Give you space and what not." His smile never wavered.

"Magnanimous as usual, Doon. I am beyond relieved that you aren't harboring some huge grudge against me. I did kind of give you the brush off."

"Kind of?" he laughed. "Brother, you just plain dropped off the edge of the galaxy!"

"Sorry," I mumbled sheepishly. He was right, there was no sense in trying to argue or explain. But as close as we were it became apparent that he understood much more than I ever gave him credit for.

"Damn, Argon. You were in a pretty bad place the last time I saw you. It was a lot for a guy to have to handle and I figure you would either snap out of it eventually or become an Obarnee Monk. Best I could do would be to welcome you back or sneak some Balasian Spine Fruit into your monastery. Am I close?"

"Yeah, kind of. Maybe a little of both," I admitted.

"Well, something pulled you out of hiding. My guess, something you need help with. Am I right?"

"Yes. On the nose." I wasn't sure how much to tell him, if I should go much beyond the immediate demand of finding who took my ship. And Winston. Caution said to stick to the immediate. Naturally I didn't do that.

"It is kind of a sticky situation, Doon. My ship got pinched."

"By the Tanaki? Failure to pay registration dues or not paying dock fees?"

"No, that's not..."

"Lost collateral?"

I shook my head. "No, it was more nefarious than that."

"Oh shit. You owed somebody big and they nabbed it!"

"Doon."

"Is a girl involved? Did you piss off her dad or something? Trying to get you to stay away from her, I bet! I've told you before..."

"Doon! Just let me tell you."

"Oh...sure. Fire away, AB."

Same old excitable Doonbridge Spierlok. "I got accidentally involved in some crazy scheme and some other interested party has decided to take my ship to slow me down, is my guess. I really don't know what the hell is going on."

"What's the scheme?" Of course he would attach significance to the least important part of my explanation.

"It is beyond stupid. I'm almost ashamed to say."

"Hey, it's me. Embarrassed? Ashamed? How about those four nights in South Kemnoshi City? Man, I don't think anything would out embarrass that set up. Hoo-boy! I'm getting a little warm-faced just thinking about it. Am I right?"

He did have me there. I had almost forgotten about that R and R we "enjoyed" with a few local "women." And here I had thought at the time that the Reen were a complicated gendered species. Uh...no.

"Er...yeah. Thanks for bringing that up, Doon. I had hoped to remove that from my mind forever."

"No secrets, my friend." He laughed with God knows what images going through his head. "*Definitely* no secrets."

With that anecdote out there, buck naked on a table, telling him about the Lost Package was going to be about as shameful as a trip to the market for bread. "Back to the subject at hand."

"Oh there were a lot of hands and *subjects* back..." he started with a strong nudge-nudge, wink-wink tone.

"Doon, for the love of peaches, man! Can we move on?"

He got a sudden blissful look on his face. "Peaches."

I rolled my eyes and struggled on. "They think I know where the Lost Package of Dehrholm Flatt is."

He was immediately silent and his eyes grew large as poached eggs. All thoughts of South Kemnoshi City flew from his mind like startled birds from a tree.

Finally he spoke, "Do you?"

"No."

"Then why do they think you do?"

"They don't, exactly, think *I* know."

"Then who?"

"An old friend of Captain Galcursed, A1."

"A1? Holy crap, Argon! I haven't heard that name in parsecs!"

"Parsecs are a measurement of distance, you dunce."

"Yeah, I know that. Just heard it somewhere I guess."

"You're a pilot, Doon. You know better."

"Right. Just thought it was a thing."

"Getting back to it..."

"Right! A1. Wow, what's he like?"

"Judging from this path he has put me on, crazier than a Navarian Flee Rabbit would be my bet."

"Seriously?" I could see the excitement on his face wilting at the thought of this mythical, iconic man being dashed into something less than desirable.

"Doon, he's after the damn Lost Package! Who does that but crazy people?"

"I'll go with him," he revealed, a sudden pride swelling up within him.

"Are you as insane as he is?"

"I guess."

"Why would you go after that blasted thing? It's a ghost, a story to tell kids and to laugh about when you hear tales of fortune seekers trying to track it down. It is the butt of a joke, Doon!"

"Argon, there have been rumors about its contents traveling through my family for decades. They believe it is a powerful Obarnee artifact. I'm Obarnee and if there is even a small chance then I need to take it. For my people." I now knew where the swell of pride came from.

"You are half Obarnee, Doon. Half. There is no more proof that it's this mystical artifact than there is that A1 knows where it is."

"I'm willing to take that chance, Argon. It is my duty as an Obarnee."

"Half. Tell you what, why don't you just tell the Obarnee people and let them go after it with A1. They can supply manpower and transportation and money to get the job done."

"You have had a lot of great adventures, Argon."

"Certainly not by choice," I muttered.

"But you have! I left the Nir'don much earlier than you. I didn't get to really see all the things you did. When I got my inheritance from Blag I went off and opened this travel agency. Now all I see are luxury resorts and exotic locales. Nothing exciting."

"Oh boo hoo. I don't care about adventure. I'm a delivery pilot. And thanks a lot for bringing up that whole Blag thing. Shit. Still gets me pissed." I didn't need more bad memories packed into the heavy emotional backpack I was carrying around these days. I needed to get this back on track so I could move on. Or away, as I usually do.

"Doon. Let's take one step at a time. Do you have access to a fast ship that we can use to find the rat bastards that stole my ship?"

He changed gears and I could see him thinking for a few

minutes. Then a tremendous grin spread across his skinny face. I didn't like the look of that but I was plainly desperate. "You know, AB, I don't really have a good ship like that, just my little light cruiser. But I am pretty damn sure I can get one." The grin, if possible, got bigger. "Where are you now?"

"We are at the Transport Center in Lynterus on the planet Mytopoli."

"I will meet you there in two days with a ship, ready for our adventure!"

"Doon. It's not an adventure. We are going to go look for my ship. That's it. No Lost Package. No Obarnee artifact. Just me getting my stinking ship back."

That grin still hung on strong no how much cold water I threw on it. "Ha ha, AB! You'll see. We are going on a goddamn adventure!" And he signed off.

My bad feeling meter pegged into the red and I was sure that his statement was going to be prophetic. Whatever we were going to do it was sure to be "damned."

"So this friend of yours is coming with a ship then?" questioned A1.

"Yes," I assured him...for the fourth time.

"I thought you didn't have any friends."

"So did I."

"Guess you were wrong."

"Yeah, I guess so. Do you have a point you want to make, A1?"

"Nope. Just can't wait to get going is all."

That brought up an important point in my mind that I kept letting slip away during all this mucking about. Who is involved and how will we find my ship. I didn't dare ask the "How" and "Where" about the Lost Package as there was no way I was prepared for that whole new world of crazy. The Captain loved A1 and would surely have indulged his wild fantasy but I was under no similar obligation.

"I have been thinking, who do you believe took my ship?"

"And your employee," he reminded.

"Whatever."

"I'm not entirely sure."

"And how is that going to help us?"

"Don't know."

"So this whole time I have been busting my ass to get us a ship and you don't even know where we need to go or who we need to find. That's just great!"

"I figure it'll come to us once we go get the Lost Package," he smiled.

Here came the Crazy. "Holy buckets, A1. So your plan is that we go try and find the Lost Package and the thieving bastards that stole my ship will find *us*? That's nuts!"

"Not really. I figure they were watching me when I came to you so they must be watching me now."

"And that doesn't bother you?"

"Not really; it's all part of my plan to get your ship back." It was obvious that he was very pleased with himself on his ability to figure out this elaborate, ingenious plan. Just what I would expect from him - unhinged as the old coot was.

"I told you my intention was to get my ship back and *then*, maybe, help with your rabid lust for foolishness."

"Right. It just so happens that they are both in the same direction."

"Maybe, but only one lies in the real world."

"I don't follow."

"If only," I said and stood up. "We have some time to kill. Is there anything to do around here? I'm usually too busy working when I blow through this place to notice any local color. It is the Capital, after all, they should have *something* to do or see."

"I haven't been here before so don't ask me," offered the generally useless A1.

"I figured as much." I turned in a circle giving the interior lobby of the Transport Center a more detailed look. It was a massive building holding all kinds of people making their way to the various transportation options available. Ticket and booking counters peppered the floor and all seemed engaged with travelers seeking fulfillment of their itineraries. Holographic displays hovered everywhere directing people and calling out schedules. It was a scrambling environment that made me miss my time alone in space.

I finally spotted a sign across the long expanse that advertised a Traveler's Bureau. I figured they might be able to come up with something. "A1, stay here a moment I want to go check something out."

"Right," he replied and continued to stare at nothing.

I took the lengthy stroll over to the booth and found a pleasant looking young woman sitting behind the counter. It appeared that with all of the hustle and bustle of the frantic travelers and their obvious tight schedules that this booth didn't get much business. She looked up from whatever was passing for mild entertainment on her small display device. "How may I help you, sir?" Her voice had an odd lilt to it that made me think she must be from the outer rim as most of those races don't grow up learning Common, so they often speak it with an accent if they bother to learn it at all.

"Hi. I am new to the city and was wondering if there were any interesting attractions I might take in while I am here." The line sounded so much like a pick-up line that I felt a sudden flush across my cheeks. Luckily it was quite obvious to me that she didn't take it as such.

"Oh, of course. What are you interested in?" She exuded a sincerity of purpose that seemed odd for such a mundane, and apparently underutilized, job.

"I don't know. A lot of things. Surprise me." That one sounded even worse. All I needed was to tag on a leer and she'd slap my face.

"Do you have a D-pad?"

"A what?"

She giggled. "A data pad! You know, for storing your data and stuff." Suddenly I felt like an old man asking his kid to turn down the music. I used to be cool and hip, a pilot was a daring, exciting profession. Lord, I was getting old. Had my interactions with females finally turned into come on lines, one night stands, and whorehouses? Why did my future just seem to get bleaker and bleaker?

I tried to salvage a little bit of suave. "I left it in my ship," I smiled.

She laughed, "Oh, don't worry. My dad does that all the time."

Really? Shoot me.

She spun her chair and pulled a few dusty brochures from a rack. "We keep these around for the old folks that don't have a D-pad or know how to use one. These should give you something to do." She smiled softly but I felt like there was a little hint of sympathy pulling at the corners of her eyes. An expression she would wear when she told her girlfriend, "Ah. Look at that poor, cute old man trying to get up those stairs." Then she suddenly leaned in close to me and cast a quick glance around. Maybe I was reading too much of my own existential crisis into the conversation. "And don't you worry, sir. I picked out ones that aren't too strenuous or long." She sat back and gave me a little wink. I turned around and looked for a place to die.

"Find out anything?" asked A1 when I sulked back to our original spot near the entrance.

"That I am a washed up has-been and that the best years of my life have long passed from sight."

"Holy crap, son. You were only gone a few minutes. Where the hell did you wander off to?"

"Reality."

"Say again?"

I looked down at him sitting content on his bench forever unaware of the chaos, madness, and plain old regret he had managed to drag into my life in the mere span of three days. "I have been spending too damn much time in your company, *old* man. You are sucking the life out of me."

"Where's all this coming from? I swear, Argon, you have some real issues."

"Which I had managed to mostly avoid until you came tumbling into my life like an avalanche of misery!"

"Hey now!"

"I have an idea, A1. Since we are obviously stuck with each other for however long this thing takes, why don't we split up until my friend gets here? We go our own ways and meet up here in two days. Doon will be here with the ship and we can get on with it. I think if I have to spend the next two days with you one of us won't make it aboard that ship."

"Fine by me. You kind of wear me out to be honest. All your fretting and complaining."

"OK. I'll see you here in two days. Don't be late. I want to get going as soon as he gets here."

"I'll be here, Argon. Just make sure you are. Don't go off and get stone drunk again."

"Don't worry about me you old cob. I'll be fine." I turned to leave and remembered the brochures in my hand. I handed them to A1. "Here, things to occupy your time."

He glanced at the leaflets. "Hey. A chair exhibit!" he remarked with more enthusiasm than any time since we met. I walked off, my decision already bearing fruit.

My first inclination was to find a bar. And a drink. And some company. Not a good direction as I figured that I should try and put some real thought into this whole stupid mess and how to resolve it. It was becoming quite clear that A1 was going to be no help. If I wanted to find my ship I was going to have to try and piece together what I surmised and what little information he had shared and formulate a plan. Doon promised to be here in two days and I needed something more than "Wait" as a strategy. He was helping me out in a big way, for reasons both unknown and unwarranted, and I couldn't force him to just sit around on the odd chance that something would happen. Knowing Doon, I am fairly certain that he would just wait patiently for weeks with that big, goofy grin on his face, happy as a dung mite in a crol turd. But that is not how I treat a friend - not that I had had much practice of late.

So that was my plan. Go back to the hotel we had checked out of that morning, grab a good meal and put some serious brain juice on this predicament. Perfect.

Two days later I woke up lying in bed with a hangover and some local Reen "female" draped across my stomach.

After quickly tossing on my clothes I left the hotel, grabbing some kind of pastry at the free breakfast available in the lobby. My stomach was not feeling well and I needed something to jump start my metabolism and get the rest of the alcohol out of my system so my head would clear. I wasn't sure what time Doon would arrive and I wanted to be ready and sharp when he got here. And, if time permitted, brainstorm my urgent need for a plan. Dashing out of the hotel I nearly collided with A1.

"Hey!" he shouted either in alarm or greeting, I couldn't tell which.

I blinked a few times in the sun and gathered my balance. "A1. Hello."

"Up late last night? I expected you at the Transport Center hours ago."

"Yeah, you might say that."

"You feeling alright, Bosch?" I wasn't sure of the motivation for his concern.

"Uh, yeah. I'm fine. Just feeling a little wonky. May be my dinner last night," I lied - I think.

"What did you have? I had some phenomenal boiled preebacks with some delicious steamed hrancis. It was one of the best meals I can recall lately." What was with this guy and food?

"Sounds...er, great? I haven't had either before," I managed to say as I was dodging speed-walking pedestrians on the moving sidewalk. Personal transports were speeding along the streets next to us and the occasional tram slowing to allow passengers to rush on or off. The city was in full swing and I just wanted to get to the Transport Center. A street vendor was selling something that smelled bad and looked even worse.

"You don't know what you're miss...Hey! Roast mulnd! I love those. Wait a second, Argon, I'll get us a couple. I'm kind of hungry, haven't had anything this morning 'cept coffee."

"No thanks."

"No. You have to try this. My treat."

I glanced at the roasted critters hanging from the canopy and they resembled some kind of skinned 6-legged animal with a large head, deep-fried on a stick. I didn't think that much time had been taken, if any, to remove anything other than its skin as the eyes were still present though popped and shriveled into the sockets. Suddenly the pastry was doing nothing to settle my stomach.

"Definitely no. And I would consider it a great personal favor if you skipped that thing and got something else at the Center."

"Aw," he whined. "But it…"

I didn't wait and picked up my pace hoping he would abandon his purchase in favor of keeping up with me. He did. Guess he wasn't that heart-set on getting that horrid thing.

We entered the Transport Center and it was as crazy as before if not worse. People everywhere.

I got my bearings and went to an "Arrivals" station that listed all ships that were scheduled to land for the day. Doon wouldn't have to schedule his landing time and could call in for a pad when he entered orbit but he was a pretty by-the-book guy so I figured he would schedule it if for no other reason than to give me a heads-up on when he would be here.

For once my timing paid off. I didn't know the type or name of his ship so he had requested the listing to just utilize his name. He was landing right then on Pad L5-P24. I went back and grabbed A1 who was just picking up something gross from a food vendor. I only glanced at it to assure my suspicion that it would be sickening and once confirmed, looked away.

"He's here. Level Five, let's go."

"Want a…"

"No," I said with conviction. I didn't even care what it might have been or how awesome it tasted. "Let's get up there and meet him before he changes his mind."

Between bites he said, "You think he might leave?"

"Not until he meets you."

"What?"

I deflected the question as we approached the elevators.

"Here's our lift," I pointed out and pressed the call button.

"I am excited to finally get going!"

"I am sure you are. It's all some kind of family outing for you, isn't it?"

He looked at me with a face that reflected a sadness and seriousness that I hadn't seen before. It took him a short span of moments before he could respond. "I know you don't think a lot of me but this *is* important to me. I'm not a young man. This might be the last chance I get to do something important. Really important. My son, that you asked about, he isn't too damn fond of me either. My wife? Ha, don't ask. I have been given the rare chance to redeem some of the crap I've done in my life, maybe escape dying alone, and also fulfill a promise to my last, great friend. So, I might not have any success in this but I am damn well going to give it my best shot. We'll find your ship and your employee and then do what you want but I *will* see this through to the end."

I had not seen that coming. He truly managed to surprise me. I can't say that he changed my mind about him in that moment but he sure did make me notice his tenacity. I wasn't suddenly going to clasp his hand and say, "I'm in it with you until the end, my friend!" but I think I felt a little more respect for him.

"Fair enough, A1. I appreciate the honesty." The doors pinged open on cue. "Now let's go meet our ride."

It was a short walk to Platform 24 and I could see the ship as we drew close and I had to stop for a moment and take it in. It was beauty. A Hanton Corsair. A model 88-G. Hanton is known for making fast ships and this one was a real screamer. Not as fast as mine but for its size it wasn't going to get passed by much. The sun caught it just right and the warm glow it gave the blue hull was a magnificent opalescence. Bright blue with jet black trim and bold red highlights. The Corsair wasn't a huge ship but much larger than the Spud. It could accommodate a crew of 8 but could easily be handled by as little as two. Doon had really come through. I couldn't imagine how he had secured this ship for us on such an unanticipated demand. The hatch was lowering as we finally approached.

We stood quietly and waited. Finally I saw Doon, all yellow and gangly, walk out of the opening. He saw me, raced down the gangway, and gathered me into his long arms. He was a continued welcome surprise.

"Argon! I am so damn happy to see you!" He practically shouted into my ear.

"Doon! You can't possibly be more happy than me."

Together we walked over to A1. I was happy to do the introductions except for…

"Doonbridge Spierlok meet…"

A1 stuck out his hand. "Abraxas Wun."

"Like the number?"

…that.

"I don't know of a number abraxas," chuckled A1. Doon got a giant grin on his face.

"You didn't just make that up, did you?"

"Make up what?" said A1 mirroring Doon's Cheshire cat face.

Then they both laughed and laughed. I won't ever understand that.

Once Doon had settled down to sniffs and coughs I asked him. "How in the Three Tribes did you get that ship, Doon? It is beautiful!"

His grin stayed large but I noticed a subtle change in his eyes: a hopeful nervousness maybe. A nervous look one might give a parent when you had done something with best intentions yet you felt it might have gone horribly wrong, like painting your dad's car with toothpaste and cream cheese. What had he done?

A voice suddenly called out from the open hatch of the ship, "Argon Bosch."

I didn't have to even turn around. I would have recognized that voice in a coma. Things had just gotten real.

CHAPTER 7

Life's a bitch. Maybe I should have led with that.

I had picked up that phrase before my eighth birthday back when I was still on Earth. Back when things were still a lot simpler. Back when people didn't know that there was a lot more life in this galaxy. When aliens from space were limited to science fiction themed movies, books, TV, and comics. Less than a year later the entire population of the world would get a wake up call from the Galactic Community shouting, "Hello!" Then, as one would suspect, everything changed. Everything.

But before that, in the Spring of my second grade year, my best friend was Franklin Samuels. We called him "Sammy." Frankie would have made more sense, I think, but he didn't answer to that. It could be because at that age kids had a tendency to call each other by their last name thinking it was cool. So I was "Bosch," Gary Deocampo was "Deo," and Franklin was "Sammy." The exception was our fourth musketeer, Maurice Mpayamaguru, who went by the clever moniker "Maurice" as we could never get our mouths around that jawbreaker last name anyhow. So when Sammy consistently started saying, "Life's a BITCH" (he always emphasized the "bitch") whenever anything went wrong or he encountered something he just didn't like, we just took it up as well. When Life revealed we failed the math quiz or we didn't sink an easy layup or we lost a hot dog to a poorly timed stumble we would all proclaim that it was a bitch.

Now a bunch of 2nd graders running around yelling "Life's a BITCH!" all the time may have seemed a tiny bit harsh but it was pretty tame compared to our classmate Tanner Church whose favorite word at that time was "shitface." He would use that constantly on the playground for any number of scenarios and found ingenious ways to work it into everyday conversations whenever he would talk to us. But despite his great fondness for the word he never said it around adults and not once got in trouble for it. I believe he became an escape artist, salesman, or one of those dread Space Pirates.

Later that year I dropped the "Life's a bitch" thing, as we all did eventually once the novelty vanished, and I was never very fond of it since. Oddly, while we had tossed it around constantly with such intensity, as if our very existence was in jeopardy, it was always for something much more mundane. Scraped elbows, bad grades, being grounded, or having to mow the lawn were all reasons to make an exasperated outcry, wailing against the injustice of the universe. The irony of it was that for most kids, Life wasn't a bitch. Not enough really bad things happened to us everyday to warrant such continued protests against Fate. It is not until we enter adulthood that we find suitable circumstances that prove that "Life *is* indeed a bitch." And even with that acknowledgement a lot of our lives are fairly even keeled. We settle into a groove, adapt to the barrage of misfortunes that land on us, and keep on going. But if I think back to those innocent days of my youth, yelling how Life was such a nasty, evil BITCH! when I dropped my school books, I know *that* "Bosch" was not ready for the "Life's a BITCH!" that was coming his way one day.

Don't get me wrong. My life off Earth and into my adult years was not always a sad sack of shit. In fact, when I think back and am honest there was way more good times than bad. There are schools of thought about why we always look back fondly on the great times when we get nostalgic or why absence makes the heart grow fonder. It is simple really: we need to remember the good things in our past to keep us from falling into a wretched, bleak depression. The memory of these happier times offers us the hope that they will soon return. It makes the current horrors we face tolerable. Recalling the sad times only makes us more resolute that "Life is absolutely...a bitch."

And a big sad memory had just walked off Doon's ship.

I quickly looked at him and that nervous grin was far more nervous and was growing smaller by the second. "What the hell did you do, Doon?" I whispered to him.

"Uh...tried to help?"

"Argon!" the voice came again, louder. I could hear footsteps down the gangway and then onto the tarmac. I had to decide if I should turn around or run. Running sounded infinitely better but I had a feeling I would be shot before I could clear the pad.

I gave one last blazing gaze at Doon and spun around. I threw my cheeriest smile on, said, "Fig!" and stretched out my arms in welcome.

Then she threw a punch that knocked me down.

I was dazed for a minute and I think Doon stepped over me to stop her from firing off a kick. I had the impression that A1 only laughed when I fell back on my ass.

"You son of a bitch," she spit.

"Another friend of yours, Argon?" asked A1.

I swiped the back of my hand across my mouth - blood. "I don't know yet but it would seem not." He held out a hand to help me up and I took it.

"Dammit, Fig!" I exclaimed.

She gave me what would normally pass for a stern, angry look but I knew her well enough to see conflict behind it. Tucked behind that scowl I saw some sadness. It was what prompted that sadness that really worried me.

IF SHE STARTED CRYING I knew I wouldn't be able to go through with it. But Fig wasn't a crier. After knowing her since I left Earth I had only ever seen her cry three times: before we had met when she, like most of the kids, stood by the huge portal and watched the Earth grow increasingly smaller and then when each of her parents died.

When we left Earth ("For bigger and better things!" - right) I was 10 and she was 4. I was acting tough (I wouldn't cry) but she was afraid of what was ahead and sad to see her world disappear forever. Most of the smaller kids were crying. All of the adults were celebrating; it was they who volunteered to take this first colonizing ship into space. So, sure, they were happy to be getting away from all the problems plaguing their homeworld. Kids are highly resilient and flexible, adults: not as much. The parents had to remain positive and think it was all a great and wonderful thing so as not to shit themselves in fear. Us kids, hell, we felt the loss and didn't have the overriding compulsion to remain positive in the face of change. A lot of our friends were still on Earth, never to be seen again. Would there be monsters (aliens!) on the new planet? And most of all, were there toy stores on the new planet? No, the youngsters saw it for what it was: a big, long, sad goodbye. Now they would have to make even more sacrifices because everyday in a kid's life is sacrifices. They have not the understanding or reasoning to know the importance of priorities and discipline. They run on impulses - candy before vegetables, play before study, toys before clothes and then they have to sacrifice that impulse to please or obey their parents. That is the world they know. Until they are saddled with responsibilities and consequences they live a life of innocent impulse and imminent sacrifice. So leaving something that they could *almost* understand for a complete unknown was the scariest thing they could imagine.

She was standing next to me, on tiptoes to see out the portal, crying. I looked down and saw her red face. She was trying to be brave but was losing rapidly. I was normally too self obsessed to care or get involved but something about her face, her tears, her fight to "be a big girl and not bawl," as she later described it, touched me and spurred me to do something, anything to lighten the load. So I looked down at her and told her the only wise thing I had ever learned.

"Hey," I said and she looked up at me with giant, brown eyes rimmed in red. "Life's a bitch."

She bit her lower lip and, if possible, her eyes got bigger. "You're not suppose to say that. It's a bad word," she managed between small sobs.

"Ha. Those are Earth rules," I said. "We aren't *on* Earth any more. We get to make up a whole new set of rules. And my first rule is that we can say 'bitch'."

She continued to look at me for a few moments, thinking about what I said. I noticed the jerking hitch of her sobs had stopped. She sniffed and said, "My name is Galaxia."

"My name is Argon," I replied. "Nice to meet you, Galaxia."

"Thanks," she said quietly and turned to look out the portal again as the Earth turned into a small, blue dot. I wasn't sure if she was simply acknowledging my greeting or was thankful of my unintentional council (she told me years later it was because I hadn't made fun of her name). I was 10, what did I care. We both looked out the ship's viewing window until the Earth was too small to see any longer. Then, in her quiet, tiny voice she said, "Life's a bitch." And I smiled.

But here I was now, at the other end of our relationship, telling her goodbye. For a moment I saw those same sad, big brown eyes looking at me, trying to be "a big girl," and not wanting to say goodbye. If one tear fell...

I was in a really bad mindset. I was depressed, tired, and drinking way more than I should have. I couldn't deal. I wanted to be alone. I wanted to run away.

My mentor and substitute father, Captain Galcursed, had been murdered a year previously. His idiot brother had taken over the Nir'don and was either going to ruin it or sell out to the Syndicate. He had demoted me from First Mate so he could put some rube of his into the post. I had learned that my substitute homeworld, Blag, had turned into a goldmine and all the inhabitants were now rich. Except me. I had left before I had become an "adult," according to some stupid law, and with both parents dead I had no claim to my portion of the fortune. Frozen out on a technicality. My best friend Doon had left the Nir'don to start his own business and now my girlfriend was going to do the same. The jealousy and anger were eating me alive like an acidic cancer. Sure, they both offered to help me get my own business going; they would *give* me the money. But my pride would have no part in it. I had to do it on my own. Charity? Bite me. I just couldn't have them succeed when I was just a second rate officer on a courier ship. They were the best friends I had ever had and I couldn't get past how I felt. I couldn't even be happy for them. It was all about me. Always was and I didn't see that changing. So, since I wouldn't change they would have to change. Into strangers. Memories.

I had already told Doon I was planning on leaving and that I didn't know where I was going to go. I told him maybe we would meet up again later. He took it hard but in the end he simply walked away. Now it was time to do the same with Galaxia.

Only, I didn't call her Galaxia anymore; hadn't for over 15 years at that time. She, Doon, and I had grown into a tight group of friends on Blag. When I left Blag to join the crew of the Nir'don both Doon and Galaxia stayed planetside. They were younger and their parents were still alive. So I was the first to leave. Years later Galaxia left to go to piloting school in Dahlkirk and we ran into each other. We hung out a lot when I was in port and as things seem to happen in such relationships, we became more than friends. She had always hated her name and often went by her initials, GNJ (pronounced Genj). I hated that nickname as it always sounded like "gunge" to me. So I would try different approaches and pet names to her consternation. Nothing worked. So, when we became a couple I introduced her to my crew mates as, "My gal, 'Axia." I only ever said that once as she hit me so hard I was knocked out, as the story goes. Actually, she swung at me and I tried to move out of the way and whacked my head on the bulkhead, got a concussion, and blacked out. When I came to in the medbay they didn't correct the tale that she had cold-cocked me so it stuck. Later I came up with calling her "Fig" because her last name was Newton-Jones and I was reminded of the cookie, which had become the most popular of the five Earth contributions to the Galactic Community. So one day I called her Fig in front of the crew and it stuck just like the insides of one of those cookies. She didn't care for it but it caught on too quickly for her to stamp out and it became cannon. Galaxia "Fig" Newton-Jones.

That first romance didn't work out. We were both too young. I was away too much and she finally graduated pilot school. We had a mutual break-up. We picked up a few years later when she was running transports out of Dahlkirk. It only lasted a couple months. Then there was the time she signed on to the Nir'don as a pilot. She left after just three weeks. Shipboard romances never last and the dynamic of the crews' attention on her and my jealousy tanked it. I also didn't like the way the Captain took a shine to her. I had to work hard to earn my stripes on the ship but she got on his good side as soon as she boarded. We mutually broke it off as soon as she left and that was the last time we were a couple until the Captain died. She came to see me and we fell right back into it like a recently slept in bed on a cold morning. But everything wasn't fine with me. I took the Captain's death too hard and I depended on her for everything. It wasn't fair to her but I had lost my way and I knew I was dragging her down in my self-loathing and misery. It is said that misery loves company. Of course it does. If you can stand on top of someone else at least they will drown in that lake of self-pity before you do.

So there we were. My best intention was to get away from everyone and maybe, just maybe, get my head straight before I doomed us all. After all, she and Doon had brand new careers to navigate with their newfound wealth. I would only be the poor one that got in the way.

"It's for the best," I argued halfheartedly.

"No. No it's not, Argon. I love you and I know you love me."

"It's not enough, Fig. I don't even feel it anymore; you or me. I can't do it."

I could see it in her eyes as she continued to fight the tears. I think she knew that if she broke down I would stay and there was no way she would allow our relationship to be built on the frailty of pity. But it was also clear by the look in her eyes that I was breaking her heart. There was no going back after this. My life was built on stupid choices, stupid luck, and stupid fate so I've dealt with a whole lot of stupid but this was going to be the single most stupid thing I would ever do. But of course I couldn't see it.

"Argon," she choked out and I saw it right then. I saw what was coming. She was going to lose it. She was overcome with sadness and she was that little girl watching her home float off into space. She was losing the battle and I couldn't watch it. I turned around and got on a city shuttle and left. I didn't look back and I didn't cry. I had closed the door on the best part of my life and also on the best part of myself.

Three days later the Nir'don exploded in the lower atmosphere as it was taking off for a routine delivery. I was in an Obsidian Ale coma sprawled across a whore's bed. I didn't even know I had missed departure until the following day. Now *everything* in my life was gone.

Life's a real fuckin' bitch.

A1 SEEMED AMUSED, Doon was worried, Fig looked upset, and I just wanted to, once again, run the hell away. I know I should have been more concerned and empathetic with these people (except for A1 who always had a back seat to any situation) since they were close friends of mine at one point but I had been alone far too long to suddenly, at the drop of a pilot's cap, be anything but annoyed. It was too immediate of a change from one pole to the opposite. I am a creature of habit, a lover of routine, and a despiser of change and yet here I was in some Cauldron of Chaos. But, to my credit and surprise, I stuck it out. I waited for the whole landing pad to instantaneously explode having suffered from such a volatile mixture of unstable personalities. Sadly, it didn't.

"What are you doing here, Fig?" I asked.

She turned and pointed at the ship behind her. "That's my ship! That's what I'm doing here."

I looked at Doon and he gave me a sheepish shrug. "Your doing, I assume?" I accused.

"Yes," he mumbled at me. I sensed he suddenly didn't want to be there any more than I did. I turned my attention back to Fig.

"Well...thanks?" I tossed out. I didn't know what had possessed her to fly all the way out here. From my sore jaw I knew it wasn't for some happy reunion. What the hell were her motives?

"That's it?" she said. "I volunteer my ship to bail you out of some jam that Doon can't even explain and all I get is an uncertain 'Thanks?' I guess I expected too much from you again, Argon. You are such a self-centered ass."

"Never said I was otherwise," I agreed. "And, for the record, I never asked Doon to wrangle you for a ship let alone invite you. You're the last person I wanted to see." Ah shit. As soon as that bypassed my brain and shot out my mouth I knew I had said exactly the wrong thing.

Fig actually looked surprised at my thoughtlessness. Maybe she still felt like I had some redeeming qualities left in me. So sorry to disappoint. Again. "I'm so out of here." She looked at Doon, who was growing more uncomfortable by the second. "Are you coming along or staying here with the asshole?"

It was plain to me that Doon did not want to make that decision so naturally he evaded the question. He looked at me with pleading eyes, desperately wanting me to fix it. "Argon?" he implored. Fig's eyes swiveled back in my direction.

"I'm sorry, Fig. I didn't mean it like that. I meant, given our history, I knew you, I mean...well, that I was pretty sure you didn't want to ever see me again. So I wasn't about to impose on you to help me or even put you in a position where you would have to consider it. It wouldn't be fair to you. It took me a long time to muster the courage to call on Doon and had I known that he was going to impede on you I wouldn't have ever called him up."

She turned back to face me. I thought I saw her face soften a little but I knew she was still angry. Any feelings she had regarding me, either good or bad, were bubbling just below her surface and even her punch or reaction to my callous admissions were but mild firecrackers compared to the warheads she was holding back.

"Truth?" she asked.

"Yes, of course," I clarified. "And I also need to point out that I wouldn't have contacted either of you if it wasn't for this old door stop dropping a huge load of shit on me and getting my ship stolen. I would have been happy never seeing either of you ever again." Again? Lord, I just need to shut up.

"Happy?" she replied, eyebrow raised.

"Shit. Again, not what I meant. Happy for you, maybe."

"And why is that, Argon?" she pushed.

"I told you both when I left that I wanted to be alone. And I did. I knew I wasn't fit company and pretty friggin' miserable to boot. But getting away from each of you was the best way to try and sort out my life and keep you out of the way of me and my own path of self destruction." I was on a streak. There was no way I had planned to reveal that much.

They both regarded me with equal parts sympathy and annoyance. Well, equal between them maybe.

Doon was easily looking more sympathetic. "I wish you hadn't done that, AB. I would have helped if I could. We both would have! We were...*are* your friends." I glanced at Fig and didn't see a lot of agreement on her face.

"I couldn't, Doon. Maybe it wasn't the right thing to do but it was what I had to do."

"Bullshit," remarked Fig. "You didn't have to do that and God knows it wasn't the right thing. You dumped us." For a second I thought she was going to say "me" instead of "us."

"You left us alone," she continued, "with no way to help when that's all we wanted to do. It wasn't right in the least and it was a damn shitty way to treat your friends."

"I can't argue any of that," I admitted. "It was all I could come up with."

"Of course it was. You only think about yourself. There was a time when..." She just left it at that. She shook her head and turned slightly away. When she looked back up she said, "So? Are you coming with me, Doon?"

He looked at me. I wasn't sure what to do. I didn't feel like begging. I hadn't asked for this convoluted mess. They were here...correction; *she* was here because she expected something else from me. Something I obviously didn't provide nor give the slightest hint that I ever would. She was resigned to the fact now that I was forever a dick and that she had no reason to stay. She started walking toward the ship.

A1, as concerned about everyone as he normally was, finally said something to me. "Stop her, Argon. We can't do anything without a ship!"

I cast him a glance. "You are such an ass." I surrendered to the inevitable: I harvested the seeds I had sown.

"Fig! Stop!" shouted Doon very uncharacteristically. He was a normally quiet guy and to have him shouting, well, it just seemed strange and unlike him. Fig, obviously thinking the same thing, turned back to look at him. He had at least succeeded in making her stop.

"We can't just leave," he complained.

"Watch me," she replied.

"No." And he said it with such a firmness and absolute that she didn't move or argue. She simply looked at him curious what he would say next. I wondered the same thing.

"We are supposed to be his friend," he said gesturing at me. "I asked you if you would help him and you said you would."

"Yeah but…"

"But nothing. You told me you would. All you manage to do was fly here and punch him in the mouth."

"You heard what he said," she pointed out.

"He hadn't said anything before you socked him. What should he say after that? Thanks?"

"Wouldn't hurt."

"Get real, Fig. We are his friends and if we can't come to his aid when he needs us then what good are we? And don't you bring up the past because we both know what happened. He was really hurting and that made him bitter and angry. He took it out on us and it hurt us too. But what did we do about it?"

"We did just what he asked us to do, Doon."

"Yeah, just what he asked. But friends don't always do that. Sometimes we have to do what we *should* do, not what we're told or want. A true friend takes care of a friend by doing what is really the best for him. And we both failed at that. He asked us to leave him alone and that was the last thing he needed. When Captain Galcursed died we knew he needed us. And when his ship blew up, where were we? We weren't there with him, helping him. We were off feeling bad for ourselves just like he was."

"Doon," she almost seemed to plead. "Don't."

"I'm sorry, Fig, I've got to say this. The fact that you dropped what you were doing and flew out here on a moments notice means you still feel something. Me? I'm glad he called. I've really missed him all these years and a chance to see him again and to actually help him? I'm thrilled! If you really don't care and want to run off again, fine. Go ahead. But I will stand with my friend."

I was actually moved by his speech. Not being a big talker it was odd to hear him defend me to such a degree. I knew right then that I was truly fortunate to have him as a friend.

"But he is a huge ass," said Fig.

Doon shrugged, "Sure, we all know that. But he is still our friend."

Hmmmm...

Fig contemplated his point and was moved to silence. Doon added, "I know you feel the same way. You came out here for him." She remained quiet but would not look at me. I didn't know how to read that. Was it because she still *did* feel something for me or was it the fact that the sight of me drove her to violence? Not a good choice to be unsure of.

After a pause that became long enough to make us all uneasy, she spoke. "I'll stay and help." Doon's face grew his signature grin once again and A1, whose only horse in this race was her ship, let out a whoop. "But I reserve the right to wallop Argon again if he pisses me off and God have mercy on him if he dares to try and get...close."

Doon looked uncomfortable. He slowly nodded agreement and his grin became unsteady. He looked sideways at me. I shrugged again. I wasn't sure yet what I thought of her amendments but if it got this whole business one step closer to being done, I was all for it even if one of the stipulations would deal me harm.

"I guess it's settled then," I proclaimed. "Should we board this beautiful ship, *Captain*?" I looked at Fig and she just kind of stared at me like I was some kind of simpleton asking if he can play with her gun knowing full well he'll break it or kill someone as soon as he touches it.

She finally looked at the rest of our motley crew, stopping briefly at A1, and then said, "Go ahead, get on board." There was a certain amount of surrender in her voice.

We collectively headed for the ramp. As we filed onto the ship she waited for A1 to step on and asked, "And who are you now?"

A1 got that damn stupid look on his face and said just what I feared, "My name is Abraxas Wun, Captain." He extended his hand.

I tried to will her to not say it. Didn't work.

"Like the number?" she clarified shaking his hand.

"I don't know of a number abraxas?" he shot out with his normal overzealous punchline.

Dammit.

Fig gave a small chuckle that sounded almost natural. I sincerely hoped it wasn't as it would certainly downgrade my opinion of her and retroactively void her entertained responses for any jokes of mine she had ever laughed at in the past.

"Cute," she said. "Welcome aboard the Sononi Heart, Mr. Wun."

"Thanks. Fig is it?"

"Sadly, yes."

I looked at Fig, still showing a little of my distaste for the "joke," and let her know she could call him by his nickname.

"Which is?"

"A1," I revealed.

It was just a second before I saw the recognition dawn on her. "*The* A1? Captain Galcursed great friend?"

A1 swelled with pride a bit at the recognition. "The very same."

"I am honored!" exclaimed Fig. "I was only on the Nir'don for a short time but he had spoken of you several times. You were quite special to him."

"As he was to me, miss."

She took his hand again. "I am so sorry he is gone. You must miss him terribly."

"Everyday." So help me, if he feigned a tear...

"Well, I am glad to have you aboard. Please, let me show you around."

"I would be delighted."

It was all so proper and civilized that I wanted to puke tea and crumpets all over them. I stepped into the ship and the ramp slid back into the hull and the hatch closed, hissing while the seals engaged.

Before things got too hoity toity I said to Fig, "We need to stop by my company and pick up a couple things. Plus I want to see if the thieves left any word on what they want."

She gave me yet another annoyed look. "What thieves? And what company? I still don't know why I am here or where we are going?"

I rolled my eyes and wanted to tell her that if she wasn't acting like such a child when she showed up much more explaining would have taken place. But, I decided (surprisingly) that saying that would not do me any good so I left it at: "I can explain some of it but A1 is the guy with the plan so he'll have to let all of us know the grand scheme. I own a courier company so let's get there and then we can figure this mess out. Can you hold out till then?"

I was feeling really uncomfortable around Fig and the looks she continued to give me weren't helping. I was like standing near to the slag geysers on Yhandoso. They were beautiful to see with the liquid metal shooting into the air, the light of the four moons reflecting off the silver as it crossed the clouds of steam. But get even a little of it on you and it would burn through to the bone. So only a fool would stand near one of them when the ground began to quake. And I could feel some rumblings where I was standing right then. I really needed to get some space between us.

"Point me to the navigation console and I'll input the coordinates," I suggested.

Her cold gaze never wavered from my face as she raised an arm and pointed down the corridor. I nodded and moved away. She turned back toward A1. "This way, A1," she encouraged with a voice suddenly replacing its bitter tone with honey.

I followed the main corridor down to the main cabin and sat down in the pilot's chair. It was like a dream.

I had flown small craft on Blag when I was growing up and had dreams of being a fighter pilot in the Dark Skirmish, the one war I had learned about in school. It was the last of the Great Wars, helping to finally unite most of the galaxy and providing a safe and secure base to encourage inclusion from all planets into the Galactic Community. So my young imagination fueled many an adventure fighting warring factions or encounters with Space Pirates. But I soon longed for more. And that's why I started hanging around on the docks to welcome new ships and maybe, just maybe, get a tour of the ship from one of the crew.

Since Blag was a giant armpit of a planet it had no tourist trade. It always rained and the weather was 475 days of heat and humidity - miserable. Did I mention that the solar year on Blag was 475 days? That's rain every single day. The dual suns provided more than enough heat on a planet with no axial tilt. Therefore the weather, day to day, was exactly the same the entire year. Temperatures ranged from 85 degrees at the poles to 170 degrees at the equator. Not a lot of people living there, just some really ornery critters with serious thick skin. The days were longer than Earth too, running just over 31 hours sunrise to sunrise.

The good and bad thing about Blag was that with that kind of weather, everything grew like weeds. Everything. Including a particular strain of mold that we managed to bring along with us when we left Earth for our new home. It was this mold that provided a sudden change to the economy of Blag after I was gone. But when I was there it thrived everywhere and was on everything. There was no escaping this fast growing reddish brown mold. So if the picture I am painting is of a horrid, miserable place then I have managed to capture the essence of Blag in stark photographic realism. It is of no surprise that I was desperate to leave there. The docks were the only way off the planet.

The Nir'don was a frequent presence on our local dock bringing us special goods and attention from the rest of the galaxy. Most of the standard supplies would come in on the regularly scheduled huge interstellar freighters. These were run by the Syndicate and made stops once every couple weeks. They didn't handle packages sent to us by friends and family or some items ordered by individuals. The extremely few passengers we got would show up either on a cargo freighter if they didn't have much coin or on the passenger liners that chauffeured individuals across the spaceways for a hefty cost.

The Nir'don impressed me as it was populated by mostly Andojins. Known as the Navigators of the Stars they were an impressive race when it came to space travel. If I wanted to learn about piloting ships these were the people I wanted to learn from. I did my best to visit the ship every time they put in. I gradually familiarized myself with the crew and did whatever I could to avail myself. After a few years I met the captain and while he was initially dismissive of my presence I eventually got the feeling that he wasn't completely annoyed by me. This was apparent by catching his interaction with other Terrans that, like me, made it a habit to hang around the docks. He wouldn't speak to them unless it was some harsh tone that warned them away from his ship and stop bothering his crew. He never took the same tone with me so I couldn't help but fantasize that it was due to some mutual respect between the two of us. A couple years after that, when my parents both died, I made a beeline to the docks directly after the funeral and found the Nir'don in port. I marched up, 17 years old and headstrong in my dreams to pilot space craft, and requested an audience with the captain. It took some persuading but I got called to his cabin. To his credit he didn't immediately boot me out when I requested, nearly demanded, he sign me onto his crew. He listened to my pleas/demands and gave me time to wind myself from constant, excited speech. Then he thought for a moment and to my surprise, offered me a position. I agreed before he even detailed out the job and the pay. I didn't care. I would have said yes to a job scrubbing frozen deep space sewage off the hull for free I wanted to be on the ship so bad. After 18 years he promoted me to First Mate, a title no Terran had ever achieved on an Andojin ship before. Five years later the Captain was killed and I was demoted by his brother, a fool who knew nothing about space travel and the courier business. A year after that the ship and crew were all gone anyway, blown to bits in a horrible explosion.

I had spent more of my life in deep space by that time than I had on a planet. It was in my blood and I would always feel more at home drifting through the nothingness of interstellar space than I ever would in the crushing gravity and claustrophobic closeness of a planet. It was the one thing I could count on in my feelings.

Sitting at the Nav console on Fig's ship I familiarized myself with the controls. It was a standard layout for a ship of that size. No real surprises. I punched in the coordinates for the Jackleg and sat back in the chair. It was a nice feeling sitting in the command chair of a large ship once again though I did feel a sudden sting missing my familiar Space Spud.

Fig roused me from my nostalgia. "Is the course laid in?" she asked.

I spun the chair around and smiled. "Yes." I motioned around me. "Fig, this is a beautiful ship. Really nice. I could get used to this."

"Don't."

"I'm sorry...what?"

"Don't get used to it. You won't be here long enough. Now, if you don't mind, you are sitting in my seat."

Her tone wasn't overly hostile but it was cold enough to inform me that I was not welcome here. I looked at her evenly. "Hey. I make no assumptions. This is your ship, of course. And I very much appreciate your help, as awkward as it may be." I leaned in slightly and dropped my voice. "I am sorry we got off on the wrong foot back there."

She kept her face as neutral as stone and replied, "There is no *right* foot, Argon. Just get us where we need to be and this will be over as quickly as possible. Then you can go back to your happy life and I'll go back to mine. Understood?"

She crossed her arms and stared at me. I could tell she wasn't waiting so much for me to answer as she was for me to move. I hastily got out of the chair. As she settled in she said, not even looking at me,

"Get settled in. We depart in 5."

I turned and left the Bridge and walked back down the corridor and followed voices to the crew's quarters where A1 and Doon were talking. I didn't catch what they were talking about but they stopped dead when I entered the room. "Talking about me?"

They looked at each other sheepishly and almost answered as one. "No."

I glanced at both of them and shook my head. "Fig says we are leaving in 5. Buckle up."

They grabbed seats and strapped in. Once a ship drops into gravity drive there is very seldom any turbulence but during initial departure or operating on thrusters a person can catch a few good bounces so it is a good rule to get a restraining belt on during takeoff and landing. I used the comm system to affirm we were ready to leave. Fig was a good pilot, I had no worries about her skills to provide a safe and smooth lift off.

"How long to our destination, Argon?" asked Doon.

"We should be there in about an hour."

"Good," said A1. "Maybe you can take the time to explain to me what in the 7 Moons of Gat you did to piss that poor woman off so much. Doon here tells me she hates you with a burning passion. How you manage to cock-up your life this bad is beyond this old man's comprehension."

I looked at Doon but he appeared extremely preoccupied with a loose bit of fabric on his armrest.

Life's a bitch.

CHAPTER 8

The Sononi Heart just managed to fit in the landing pad for the Jackleg. It hung a bit outside the property but the building next to mine was vacant so I didn't believe the property management company would be happening by to cite me for some violation. Just because the galaxy ran under a huge, advanced governmental system didn't mean anyone was safe from the annoying, speed-bump of bureaucratic oversight. Some things about governments, despite the size, never change.

We filed into the reception room and I once again had the odd feeling that Winston would be there, sarcasm at the ready, to greet us and belittle me. But his desk was empty and his presence a vacuum that I couldn't process. Did I miss him? Heaven forbid!

"Anything different?" asked A1. I guess he had hoped there would be some clue or note from the would-be brain-nappers and ship-stealers. I looked around but noticed nothing out of place or in addition to the normal clutter and bric-a-brac. It was early afternoon when we arrived and with the sunlight casting a warm glow to the office it seemed strange for it to be so empty and cold. I had put up a notice in the front window apologizing for the business's temporary closing due to personal issues and set the comm system to auto-answer any incoming calls with a similar message. So there were no clients waiting with packages, no comm lines buzzing for attention. Just an empty office.

"Is it always this empty?" questioned Doon.

I told them how I had addressed the closure. "And usually Winston is here taking care of any business."

"Who?" asked Fig.

"Winston. My employee."

"Is he here somewhere in the back or did you give him the time off?"

"No. He was kidnapped when they took my ship."

Both Fig and Doon turned to look at me, an alarmed look on their face. "You mean there is a person missing too? My God. No wonder you are so distraught," said Doon. "You should have said something when you called me."

"He probably forgot," suggested A1.

"What?" barked Fig.

"No," I argued. "I didn't forget. It just wasn't important."

Fig looked shocked. "It wasn't important? How have you become that callous? Does anything matter to...?"

"It's not like that. Dammit!" I was getting tired of her incessant badgering and poking. "You don't know Winston. There is a history here. He isn't even human."

"Oh is that how it is with you now? Degrading an employee to less than human. A possession. A piece of furniture. Oh Argon," she spat in disdain.

"C'mon Fig! You know that isn't me."

"I *thought* I knew you."

I clasped my head in frustration. "Oh the sanctimonious bullshit. Listen," I said as I turned on her, "Winston is a valuable part of this business. He is my partner. But he isn't a person in the strictest sense. He is a brain floating in a damn jar."

"Sacred Nebulas, Argon, a handicapped person? You didn't think someone suffering such an existence doesn't deserve consideration?" She shook her head in disgust.

"That's not it! I am just as concerned about him as I am my ship.

No, even more! He is pretty much helpless and can't really fend for himself. We built this company together from the beginning. But I didn't bring it up because it only would cause more explanations, which I didn't have time for. I needed action and I planned to tell you both when we got here. So just back off."

They grew quiet and I cast another stern look at A1, Mr. Troublemaker. I pointed a finger at him, "And you! Just wait your damn turn to speak. You'll have plenty of opportunity, once I lay the groundwork, to fill us all in on your elaborate plan. So for right now just shut the hell up." For once he didn't pop off with some stupid retort. "Follow me into my office and we'll talk this thing out."

I led them down the corridor to my office. Once again I found myself growing very weary of all of this drama. I just wanted my life to go back to a numb, bland existence.

"So that's when A1 and I got back here and discovered that my ship and Winston were gone. From there we tried to find a way to scavenge a vessel to go and look for the culprits. We didn't have any luck until I called Doon." I sat back, having finally divulged all of the information I had. Now it was up to A1.

Fig was watching and listening intently, elbows on the table, eyes never leaving me. She finally seemed to relax and took a deep breath. She spun her chair a bit and looked at A1. "So, what's the mystery here? What are you after that someone else would go these lengths to meddle in your affairs?"

A1 smiled. "I know how to find the Lost Package of Dehrholm Flatt!" He said it with such unbridled enthusiasm that I could tell the old fool actually believed she would be happy to hear such rot.

"Wait a second," started Fig. "You mean to tell me that all of this is for some insane ploy to find the Package? Really?"

Here we go. Finally someone with some damn sense. I was starting to feel like I was the lone scholar in the Lost Land of Misfits and Idiots.

"Yup," answered A1.

She looked at me with a quizzical squint. "You knew about

this?"

"Yes," I said. "And yet here I still sit. I wouldn't jump on this merry bandwagon of foolishness for any promise of wealth and fame but I am over the barrel here with Winston and my ship missing. I really wouldn't blame you for running out of here as fast as you can, jumping in your ship, and heading for the farthest reaches of the galaxy."

She thought about it for a long while. Then she surprised me by saying, "OK, I'm in."

"What?" I exclaimed. "You want to willing go along with this?"

"Yes." And she just left it at that. No explanation or justification for her acceptance of one of the most harebrained things I've ever been exposed to. She steps off her ship and punches me in the face because I didn't throw flower petals and strike up a band in appreciation of her arrival yet A1 casually says he wants to go look for a mythical box. My world no longer made sense. I had to just stare at her, my mouth slightly agape.

She noticed my slack-jaw. "What? Surprised that I am willing to help A1 out without being coerced or ransomed?"

"Surprised is too weak a word."

"Unlike you, not everything I do is motivated by my own self interests."

A1 piped in, "I am glad you will help me, Fig. I appreciate your understanding."

She turned to him and her face brightened significantly though I felt it was by design to further annoy me. "A1, out of respect for your deep friendship with Captain Galcursed I will gladly give use of my ship to further your quest. If we happen to find Argon's ship and employee so much the better."

I couldn't even speak at this point so I just sat and stared at her. "So tell me, A1, what is our plan of action?" This should be good. She was expecting a "plan" and the most A1 had was a vague notion, a slap-dash conviction fueled by mindless intention. He wanted this, wanted it bad, but what seed had sprouted this dream to then morph into something that spurred action had not yet been revealed. I had the distinct impression that when it was, I would be disappointed but not surprised.

A1 sat for a few minutes. I guessed that he was trying to come up with a way to say what he needed yet not scare any of us off. He was playing with words in his head that wouldn't make him sound as insane as he had impressed me. Finally he smiled and said, "I don't so much have a plan as I have a location."

"I don't follow, A1," said Fig, her full attention centered on him. "What do you mean?"

"Just that," he smiled. "I don't have a plan. I came to Argon because I know where the Package is I'm just not sure how to get it."

Fig sat back, her face unreadable. "Well, who was it that nabbed Argon's ship and Wilbur?"

"Winston," I corrected.

"OK...Winston then."

"I don't know but I suspect it was those same ugly fellows that were following me around."

Fig raised an eyebrow. "What guys?"

"There were a couple of ornery types that set on my tail when I left Dahlkirk," he explained. "I didn't notice them as following me at that point, just that they looked like trouble. I saw them again when I was waiting for Argon in a bar near here. They left after I managed to shake them by heading out the back when they thought I was in the toilet. I met up with Argon and when we got back here his ship and employee were gone."

She looked at me, "It could be a coincidence. Do you have any enemies that would do this to you?"

I smiled and spread out my arms, "Who doesn't love me?" I saw that I had suddenly come close to getting smacked again so I added, "Seriously though. Of course I do. What courier pilot doesn't? But they would come straight at me. They wouldn't bother with an old, busted-ass ship and a brain in a jar that's soaking in vinegar and pickled with bitterness and insults." I shrugged. "I think it's someone that is trying to get some leverage to get at what A1 knows."

"Who could that be?" she asked.

"Obviously someone as rolled in oats as A1 here." I felt I needed to point out the obvious. Fig did not look amused or in agreement.

She nodded toward A1, "So what do you think their play is *if* they are actually after the Package as you believe?"

"I think they'll continue to follow us to see where we go. At some point they will either grab us to get the information I have or wait until we find the package and jump us then."

"If they wait until we get it we'll all be dead of old age," I pointed out. Fig gave me another look hinting that she had a couple of knuckles looking for a face. I shrugged. "Just saying, is all."

She stood up. "Good enough. Argon, grab what you need and then we'll get underway."

A1 stood up next to her, "Do you want to know where we are going, first?"

She shook her head, "Wait until we get going. We can map the course on board." She headed for the door. "I'll get the preflight done and then we leave," and out the door she went.

I watched her leave then looked at Doon and A1. "You heard the lady." They started out leaving me behind. I went and grabbed a bag and started gathering up some gear. I was starting to feel like the one uncool kid at school or the one that didn't get the joke. I am no genius but I consider myself intelligent enough to see stupidity when it walks face first into a door. I was wondering if I was the one who didn't see the door.

After we broke orbit around Mytopoli I got out of my seat and walked to the Bridge. Fig was still checking readings and was heading slowly toward deep space. I watched her a few moments, noticing the little things that I had forgotten about her but that suddenly seemed as much a part of her memory as her face. "What is it, Argon?" she said without ever looking up at me.

"Oh, hey. I was just curious why you didn't press A1 for the location when we were in my office?"

"If the people that took your ship and Wilson…"

"Winston."

"Yes, Winston - and stop doing that - if those people are really watching A1 to find out what he knows, what is to stop them from bugging your office while they were there. Or even later when you both were trying to secure transportation?"

"Uh, good point," I conceded. Her ability to recognize that hidden threat caused me to wonder why she had so readily agreed to help A1 in his quest. "But seriously, Fig, are you really buying into this whole Lost Package nonsense?"

"I'm not saying I am or I'm not. But he seems pretty damn sure of it and he was the best friend of a man we both admired and respected. I think we owe it to the Captain to help his friend since we couldn't help him."

"Thanks, Fig," I said with genuine appreciation and turned to leave.

"Thanks for what?" she called after me.

"For saying 'we'."

I was in the crew's quarters with Doon and A1 looking through the cabinets for a snack when Fig came in. "Fig, do you have any Balasian spine fruit on this ship or do I have to starve?"

"Second cabinet to your right," she answered.

I swung open the door and pulled the short, blue tubes of sweetness off the shelf. I took a bite and then spit it on the floor.

"What's this crap?" I complained. "It tastes like ass."

"Boy," remarked A1, "you got a real food problem."

I gave him the look. "Shut it, garbage disposal." I looked back at Fig with my eyebrows raised. "What's the deal?"

"What? It's Balasian spine fruit like you asked," she shrugged.

I waved the stubby sticks in the air. "Like hell. Is it Sokasaki?"

She looked at the deck. "Well...no. It's SkeenCo brand."

"What?" I spit a couple more times to clear the sticky residue from my mouth. "Those hacks? I'm lucky to be alive!"

"Quit being so dramatic, Argon," she scolded. "It's all the same."

"My ass. If it's not Sokasaki Snack Company it's crap. You have me eating shit here."

"Here we got with the poop eatin' again," mumbled A1.

"Hey! Stay out of this," I warned him. I looked back at Fig. "Have you forgotten everything about me?"

She rolled her eyes. "If only." She shook her head and looked at A1. "Time to tell us where we are going, A1."

He got a big smile on his face and made a small bow. "Thanks for your patience. We need to set course for Farnok space, the planet G'toa."

"How about we just fly into a super nova," I remarked. "At least then we can go find the package as ghosts. It would be less painful way to die."

Fig looked at me perturbed. "Does every single thing you say have to be negative?"

"Often times...yes."

"A1, you know that Farnok space is very dangerous, right?" Like she was asking a little kid about playing in traffic.

"It is necessary."

"So the Package is on G'toa?"

"No. But we have to go there first."

"Why?"

"You'll just have to trust me on that one."

"That's a lot of trust, A1," Fig pointed out. "It is very dangerous there. We could end our journey before we even get to G'toa."

"True," he acknowledged. "But if we don't go, we end our journey right here, right now."

It sounded like an ultimatum to me but I could see Fig didn't take it that way. "OK, I'll go punch in a course to G'toa." She left for the Bridge.

I turned to A1. "What are you doing?"

"What do you mean?"

"She was nice enough to buy into your fantasy and you won't even level with her. Just tell her where we need to go and be done with it. Shit, A1!"

"I can't tell her where we are going more than G'toa. That's the first leg and that is all I know."

"Again - Shit, A1! You don't know where it is, do you? Just

another treasure map bouncing around the damn galaxy like a pinball hoping to find a bonus hole."

"That's not it, Bosch. You have to start to trust me." I gave him an angry sideways glance. "Like Fig does."

I turned on him, "Don't go there you delusional ass! She might be going along but that doesn't mean she's buying any of this drivel. Come clean for once and say it - you don't know where it is!"

"But I do and the first place we have to go is G'toa. You'll understand once we get there." He looked solemnly at me. "I promise."

"For your sake, A1, I hope we get blown to bits by space pirates before we get there. It'll go easier for all of us."

The trip to G'toa took the equivalent of 3 days time. After two days we had become familiar enough with the ship to settle into dull boredom. We had finally entered the Farnok sector giving us very long day of excitement crossing Pirate occupied space with every radar contact being just another chance to die in a horrible explosion. Sure, it sounded like fun but the practical side of me wasn't willing to play along. I just wanted to scream, "We are all going to die!" and be done with the subtleties.

The upside was that the tension needed an outlet and I knew just the solution to let off a little steam. I could finally impress them with my Vanderloon skills.

"I just happen to have a Vanderloon deck with me," I announced to anyone listening. "Anyone care for a game?"

Doon looked up curiously, "What game?"

I gave him a smile and said, "Just about the best card game ever invented! It is a lot of fun and can be played by up to four players, which we just happen to have with us!" I gestured around the room.

"Not me," said Fig. I had pretty much already written her off as a wet blanket.

"I'm in," agreed A1. He rubbed his hands furiously together, a gleeful smile on his face. I wondered if he was a ringer and that maybe I shouldn't recommend we add wagering to make it interesting.

Nah.

"To really make it fun, Doon, we should play for money," I casually suggested. "Not a lot of money, of course. Just a few credits between friends. It makes the game that much more exciting."

"Oh...okay. Sounds fun." I could see Doon was getting into the spirit of the game, he had an odd look and an almost electric energy of confined excitement. Kid needed to get out more, I thought. I eyed Fig one last time and wiggled my eyebrows in an attempt to entice her to play.

She'd have none of it. "No thanks, Doon. I've played Vanderloon and I've lost enough money on it. You boys have your fun; I'm going back up front."

"Just us then," I said as I dug the deck and chips out of my bag. We gathered around the table and I explained the game to Doon.

"It's all about matching colors and/or symbols on the cards. There are four colors and eight symbols. Four other cards are color wild, in other words, they match any symbol of the color represented on the card. And there are two Vanderloon cards that match anything. Those babies are great to have in your hand!" I flashed the deck to Doon, fanning out the round cards. "As you can see, there are different numbers of the symbols on each side of the card."

"They are round, they don't have sides," corrected Doon.

"What did you want me to say? Apex?"

"Would have made more sense. Or actually 'quadrants' would be more fitting as there are four sections represented on each..."

Just concentrate on the cards, Doon." He nodded sheepishly. "OK, so we have symbols, colors, and amounts of symbols on each...*in* each quadrant. You can use them to match the other cards. If you can match all of your cards you call out Vanderloon and you win! Simple, huh?"

He looked a little perplexed. This would be like taking candy from an infant. "Tell you what, let's play a trial hand and you'll see how easy it is. Fair enough?"

"Sure," he agreed.

We played through the first hand and Doon seemed lost at first but started to get more comfortable by the time A1 won the game.

"Vanderloon! I won!" he shouted.

"I Bosch," I replied.

He looked at me, curiosity crossing his face. "What? I don't get it."

"Seriously, Mr. 'I-don't-know-a-number-abraxas'?"

He shrugged, bewilderment overtaking him like an avalanche on a ski slope.

"Hopeless," I muttered and then started to gather and shuffle the cards. "Now...for money! Fun, right Doon?"

With a fairly confident tone he said, "Uh, sure."

"Great!" I dealt the cards and we started the round. The betting in Vanderloon is basically a whole different contest as it had been added after the game became popular. There are main bets, side bets, chance bets, and outcome bets. It gets very complicated very quickly and most newcomers, even those experienced at the game, lose sight of their bets and end up losing a lot of coin really fast. I had won a quite a few games over the years and financed several endeavors - though truth be told, the majority of it went towards less substantial enjoyments. The idea of fleecing some credits from Doon didn't really bother me as I figured he could afford it with his generous proceeds from Blag royalties. As for A1, I didn't mind jamming him for a hard loss by any means. He only won the first game because I threw the game his way to get him confident for the next game and the inclusion of betting. I was planning a clean sweep.

The game progressed much how I anticipated it would. Cards were played, bets made. I managed to subtly ease the betting along to get more money on the table. I even let Doon win a couple side bets though I could see that he wasn't comfortable in what he was actually wagering on. He even looked surprised when I shoved a pile of winnings toward him at one point. Fish in a barrel.

After enough time had passed I was ready to start to corral the game to a win for me and the various wagers were lining up for a grand sweep and a healthy score. I doubted Doon even knew how much he had on the table. I estimated two more rounds and I'd be just right to drop my charade and win the...

"Vanderloon!" shouted Doon.

"Wait. What?" I managed to say, stunned by the sudden announcement.

"Vanderloon, Argon," he grinned as he swept the winnings toward him. "A nice haul, really."

I peered across the table and saw that he had managed to turn a card and play a wildcard to join two separate legs of cards while emptying his hand to snatch an ingeniously planned Vanderloon right out from under me. It was not luck and wasn't a rookie move. There was something I was forgetting. Something...

"Wait a sec, Doon. That was some smart card play there. That's not just beginners luck."

He looked me straight in the eye and laughed. "Man, Argon, your memory is really getting bad! I think you have been living in your own head for too long."

I was perplexed what could he possibly be referring to?

Oh...yeah.

"Who do you think taught you to play Vanderloon, AB? Remember back on Blag?"

"Son of a..."

He laughed again. "I can't believe it! You have completely blanked it out! I taught you and Fig and we would play it all the time. That is until you rage quit one day because I was always beating you. You were ten years older than me but I could still beat you almost every hand."

I was flat-footed. It started coming back to me. All the games we played and I had hated it. This young kid, only 6 years old, would kick my ass all the time no matter how many times we played. It was embarrassing! And Fig would just laugh and laugh. I told them I'd never play that stupid game again. Ever! "But what about the Gambling par...oh, shit," I sputtered.

"Now you are getting it. I taught you how to wager in the game when I came back from shore leave on Stanolli Prime. You lost a month's wages the first weekend we played. Here I'd thought you'd have learned by now."

"You totally bagged me!" I exclaimed. I felt my cheeks redden as my overconfidence washed away to reveal my blind stupidity. I had spent decades fine tuning my Vanderloon game thinking I was a real player, pulling high stakes from heavy-pocketed marks that would stupidly fall into my traps to fleece them of their money and confidence. I had been playing the role so long that I had convinced myself that I was this great gambler. I'd bought into the con I'd created.

"Weren't you planning on doing the same thing to me?"

He had me. I eyed him, my humiliation getting ground under by anger, and saw him flash his usual toothy grin. Only this time I saw it for what it really was: not a goofy, innocent grin but the sly smile of a fox as it watches the hens file into the chicken coop for the night. I had been played and just when I thought I'd get pissed and punch the smart ass he said, "Sorry Argon...I win."

At that very moment the intercom crackled and Fig announced, "Incoming!"

And then the ship exploded.

CHAPTER 9

A lot of things happened at almost the same time, not the least of which was an explosion so unexpected and loud that it made me think my life was over.

Recalling the whole tumultuous event in hindsight offered me the chance to break it down into a brief timeline that started with Doon telling me he won. But his exclamation was drowned out by Fig's sudden shout over the comm system, "Incoming!" That confused me enough right there because I heard it as, "*Win* coming!" causing me to wonder how Fig knew Doon had won. So for about half a second I had grown even more baffled. Immediately the ship dropped out of gravity drive, accelerated, and pitched hard to starboard. My inner ear threw a tantrum for the next second stopping only for an enormous explosion that made the whole ship jump backward. This did nothing to calm my horrible vertigo and added the sudden discomfort of nausea. I would have let it fly except I still sensed I was about to die and didn't want my last word to be, "Blarf!"

I hit my head on a door frame and saw stars - ironic since I had just entertained the notion I might be floating amongst them soon. I shook my head to clear the fog and started toward the Bridge. The deck shuddered under my feet as we pulled another tight turn and the fuselage fought the ensuing inertia.

"What the hell is going on, Fig?" I yelled as I stepped onto the Bridge from the passageway. My bellow was semi swallowed by another immense explosion that dropped the ship from underneath me. There was an intense flash of light on the port side just behind the Bridge causing me to throw my arm up to block my eyes. When the flash subsided I grabbed for an overhead cable run to steady myself and looked over at Fig. She was fighting the controls to try and get the Sononi Heart to move in ways it was not designed. Fig turned her head for just a second to acknowledge my presence and give me a hard look. Her face was scrunched into a roadmap of concentration and I could almost taste the tension in the air. Something bad was going down.

"Just try and," she jerked the controls suddenly, "help somehow!" She looked at a readout, snapped a couple switches, and pulled back on the controls. I felt the pressure of my feet grow heavier against the deck as the ship rose harshly and the onboard gravity compensator fought to keep up. "We are under attack!"

"Who?"

"Farnok raiders, idiot!" Of course it was raiders. "Two ships."

"What about the weapons?"

She ignored my question for a scary couple of moments as more explosions bloomed around the Heart, at least one of which hit something and I saw a light come on her console. She snapped it off with a flick of her fingers and spun the ship a quick 180 degrees and banked sharply to port.

"Right! Topside...Gunner's Bubble. Can you handle a pair of Pysonite 250s?"

The last few days aboard the ship and none of us had thought to run drills on the weapon system. Seems idiotic given we were heading into hostile space. But I was flat footed in operating the guns or short range missiles. I knew trying to macho my way out of saying "No" would likely only get all of us killed. "My experience is in small arms."

She shook her head. "That's not good. I need someone to man

that station now!"

"I doubt A1 or Doon are familiar with them either. What about the missiles?"

"Can't get a..." Another explosion. "...lock. They're too quick. Have to use the guns."

"You know how to use them, right?"

"Of course! It's my ship. But who's going to fly..?"

"I'll take the stick. One thing I can do is fly."

I expected a cutting insult as to my ineptitude but instead she spun around and hopped out of the chair. "It's yours, Argon," and she rushed by me to get to the Bubble. That action, with nothing more being said, made me feel Fig had not completely written me off as useless. The only thing left was to make sure her confidence was not misplaced.

I jumped into the chair and did a very quick scan of the controls. They weren't the same as the Spud or the Nir'don but most ships designed for basic human specifications were laid out roughly the same. I grabbed the navigation stick and gave it a tug to the left. So, while most ships were *laid out the same* they seldom handled the same and I was going to need to know just what the Sononi Heart had to offer.

The ship swung smartly to port and with a couple more maneuvers I realized she handled like a dream. Responsive, quick, and smooth - all three characteristics the Spud didn't share. This would be...

There was a detonation directly in front of me and I felt the stick quiver in my hand as the force of it tried to knock the craft aside. I heard a tiny buzzing sound like a tiny angry insect trapped in a jar and realized there was a headset sitting atop the panel next to me. I donned the set and adjusted the mic. "Hello?"

"You need to fly *away* from the shots not towards them," instructed Fig. That momentary notion of her confidence in my abilities was ebbing away.

"Right! Just getting a feel for the ship, Fig," I said as calmly as I could trying desperately to sound nonchalant.

"Did you *feel* the explosion?"

"Of course. I've got it now. Just you worry about blasting those raiders."

"Then get me near them. You're flying away!"

"Just getting my bearings. I got this." I hoped that sounded authentic. I looked at the controls and checked the tracking screen. She was right, I was out distancing the two ships. If running away was the plan, I was executing it perfectly. But they would not give up on chasing us down, that much I knew. Farnok raiders are the most tenacious group one will ever come across. I had one follow me across an entire system before he crossed paths with a rogue comet. I didn't trust I'd get that lucky break twice in my lifetime.

I brought the Heart around and headed back at the two ships. I brought up their statistics and saw they were smaller than us and not as fast. But judging from their performance so far I figured they were also more maneuverable and carried more firepower. I was getting comfortable enough with the Heart's feel so I was sure I could handle her. The outcome was now up to Fig's marksmanship. The least I could do was get her something nice to shoot at.

"Get ready, girl! Fish entering the barrel!" I regretted that as soon as I said it.

"Seriously, Argon?"

"Just blast them, will ya?"

I kicked up the speed and aimed for a point directly toward the ships. They were already at full throttle having been trying to catch us so the distance between us was disappearing fast.

"Argon?" I heard Fig question, a nervous vibrato playing in my ear. I was on a direct collision course and I am sure it looked insane from her vantage point. Hell, it looked pretty damn crazy from the pilot seat. I could make out the ships clearly in front of us. They were dark with few running lights, excellent camouflage for deep space. They huddled together creating a tight ball that would be harder to hit and impossible to fly through. A small holographic call out on the front viewport alerted me to a weapon's lock. As soon as I registered the warning their guns blazed. Balls of plasma screamed across the inky black and impacted against the Sononi Heart's shields. I clearly saw the energy disperse across the deflecting field and it could almost be considered pretty if not for the teeth-jarring impact they carried. Shields were a godsend but they didn't lessen the feeling that you were getting smacked around by a giant hammer. I tried to dodge what I could to allow Fig a chance to aim.

I bet on them holding true to their kamikaze ways and keeping their course steady, waiting for me to chicken and veer off making an easy target for their weapons. And it worked perfectly. I steadily increased my speed and I brought the Heart dangerously close to colliding with their speeding vessels. They dare not shoot now as the debris field would shred their ships as they passed through. I wondered for a second if my luck would hold since they would soon come to the realization that should I continue they would die as well by the impact.

"Shoot UP, Fig," I told her and yanked back on the controls and then rolled 180 degrees. We flew directly over the two ships while inverted and I prayed that Fig followed my suggestion as there would only be time for a couple of bursts before we were well past them. I felt the hard nudge of the guns' recoil and was thankful their inertial dampeners were on to prevent the nudge from turning into a severe shove. There was an enormous shock wave and I saw one of the avatars on my tracking screen blink out. A shudder ran through the fuselage as I pulled a tight 270 degree oblong arc that brought us up right below the second pirate ship. The added Gs pushed on me like an immense fist. I felt Fig let loose with another long burst from her 250s. There was a forceful impact above us as the other target detonated. I could see the telltale streaks of flaming wreckage shoot past the forward view port as they quickly cooled and disappeared in the inky blackness.

"Anybody else out there you need to blow to kingdom come?" I asked Fig, a certain self confidence mixed in amongst the words.

"Not in the vicinity," she replied. There was a click and I knew she had disconnected the headset and left the Bubble. A minute later she was back on the Bridge with Doon and A1 following close behind. Doon had his usual oversized grin across his face and A1 wore a face that could only be identified as cautious optimism.

"That was some nice flying," remarked Fig. "Where'd you learn that trick?"

Again with the approval. I found it made me strangely uncomfortable. "A variation of a move the Captain showed me once while we were trying to evade some of these Farnok raiders."

"Farnok raiders? Isn't that the same as the Xydoc Zyn?" asked Doon.

"A lot of people make that assumption, Doon," I explained. "While the Xydoc Zyn are made up of a bunch of Farnok, there are a lot of other races comprising those cutthroat bastards. The Farnok Raiders are not nearly as nasty and deadly as the Xydoc Zyn. They are just a more extreme sect of the Farnok race. Of course there isn't a single Farnok known for being kind or civil. Never talked to one yet where I didn't have my pistol's safety off."

"Well, I gotta say you two make a pretty damn good team," blurted A1. I glanced at Fig and she did not meet my gaze. I could sense she was feeling as ill at ease as me.

Silence. Like someone had just let roar an enormous fart at a posh dinner party. It went on for what seemed like hours as we all just stood there staring at the floor, except for A1 who had some stupid smile going.

"People have to do what they have to do," I said trying to elevate the uncomfortable silence. "We just got lucky, I think," and got up from Fig's chair.

She looked at me and said quietly, "I don't think it was all luck." She started towards me then stopped. "Why don't you fly for awhile, Hotshot? I'm taking a break."

I hesitated sitting back down, "I can just switch it back to auto-pilot if you want to catch some shut-eye."

She shook her head at the suggestion. "Not here. Not in this space. We need a wary eye on that monitor. You'll do fine." She started to leave and turned briefly back and said, "Plus, I probably am saving you some money by keeping you away from Doon and his card games, Argon." There was just the hint of a smile on her lips and then she was gone. A1 and Doon just stood there and looked at me.

"Don't you guys have anything to do?"

As one they replied, "Nope."

"Well find something or I'll send you out to scrape space barnacles!" They quickly disappeared down the corridor like smoke.

The next several hours were tense. I killed the running lights and tried to keep the engines on a steady pace to avoid any disturbance that would be caused by acceleration or deceleration. I watched the instrument panel like a cat watching a mouse hole yet still every time something beeped I almost jumped from the chair. A couple of times a contact would pop onto the radar screen with a joyful little "ping" and send my heart into hectic thumping or a dead stall. It was not an easy station to hold. I was about to call Fig on the ship's comms when she just strolled onto the Bridge with a restful look in her eyes. She yawned and gave me another slight smile.

"It was nice to get some good sleep," she commented.

"Oh, sure. Glad you could catch up on your shut-eye. Hope the hammering of my heart didn't wake you."

"Not at all. Were there some problems?"

"Nothing I couldn't handle," I said with some bravado trying to sound fearless. My voice cracking caused it to fail. She smiled again, a little easier this time.

"I knew you could," she said with all sincerity.

"Look, Fig…" I started not sure what I was even going to say.

"I'll relieve you but I want to get something to eat first. Need me to bring anything back?"

"Nope, I'm good. I'll hit the kitchen when you get back."

"Sure," she said and left for the galley. I sat back and breathed a sigh of relief. I wanted to say something, something to make some kind of amends, just to settle the tension, but I didn't know what it was. Too much time had passed. We weren't the same people with the same shared experiences. Anything spoken in seriousness would come off dry and emotionless. I was sure she had moved on and I couldn't see anyway to recover even a slice of what we had before. It seemed she didn't want me to address it or even acknowledge it either. I decided I'd best just leave it alone but just like that loose scab, it itched for some attention.

About this time Doon walked on to the Bridge. "How's it going?"

"Fine," I replied. Just then a contact pinged on the radar and my blood chilled to ice. I eased the ship away from the contact and watched it steadily until it left our sensor field. After adjusting the course to compensate for the evasion I anxiously stared at the screen waiting for it to reappear. After a few moments it did not pursue us and I finally let my breath release. Doon had not moved nor said a word during this tense two minutes.

"Damn. Is it always like that?"

"Always. Unless, of course, it pops back on the screen after I turn, then I just shit myself."

He coughed a nervous laugh. "Does that happen often?"

"Let's just say I'm running out of underwear."

He gave a thin smile. "Sheesh. Sorry, Argon."

"No problem, Doon. Somebody's got to do it. I am happy to offer Fig a welcome break from it. She doesn't need to shoulder all of the stress of flying us through this living mine field."

"I can help too. I know how to fly."

"I know. Me and Fig can manage for now but thanks for offering." Doon was adequate at flying though I would never tell him that. He lacked the natural ability that makes for an exceptional pilot and I always knew it was more difficult for him than it was for Fig and I. I felt he took it on more because we both loved to fly and he didn't want to get left out rather than as an honest desire to soar through space.

"We made some great runs together when we were on the Nir'don," he said not pushing the issue. It only went towards confirming my suspicion. "Do you remember when the three of us ran that trade blockade on the Grantok border? Man, that was a close one!"

Of course I remembered that run, I almost died. Hell, we all almost bought it that time. And I could sense from Doon's excited recollection that he had a slightly different memory than I did.

"DOON! TURN TO PORT, 45 degrees...NOW!"

"I..."

"NOW!!" I shouted.

We were in the shit on this one and I really thought it was going to end badly for all three of us. The Nir'don had a load of contraband to deliver to a planet in the Grantok sector and needed a diversion to pull the blockade scout ships off their tail. The standard operating procedure for this play was to have the Nir'don's recon ships run the border and get the local scouts to follow leaving a hole for the Nir'don to sneak through. I'd done enough of these to consider it no big deal but this blockade was sanctioned by The Tribunal and so they had the Galactic Peace Keeping Force, the Tanaki, support to enforce it. Captain Galcursed decided I needed some support and had Doon and Fig join me. My guess was that he had thought since we were such great friends that we would make a great team flying this mission. He was only partially right. We made a great team...just not for this mission.

We had severely underestimated the amount of craft that would be securing this section of the border. As we sped through I caught sight of four Grantok scouts to port. If that was all there was I think we would have been fine but as soon as I alerted Doon and Fig that we had company Fig corrected my warning.

"No, Argon, it's six of them and they are at 2 o'clock."

"Dammit," I managed to say before I heard Doon's panicked voice crackle in my headset.

"I have ten ships surrounding us! Oh shit, oh shit, oh shit."

"Calm down, Doon," I said. "Kick up those thrusters and follow close on my tail. We stick with the plan and head for the nebula. We can outrun them and then lose them in the nebula cloud when we circle back to rendezvous with the Nir'don."

"Oh shit, oh shit, oh..."

"You said that already."

"Oh shit!" came a distinct voice that was not Doon's.

"Great. Now you too, Fig?" It was rare thing for me to hear any kind of fear in Fig's voice but it was there now.

"Argon?"

"What is it?"

"Dead ahead. In front of the nebula." She said it so controlled and quietly that I instantly got a chill down my spine. Something really had her spooked. I took my eyes off their positions and the ten scout ships and looked toward the nebula, really looked.

"Oh. Shit." Three Tanaki cruisers were floating there. Big ones. The scout ships were right behind us now and our escape plan was blocked by huge battleships. I knew enough about those Tanaki ships to know that each one had a massive weapons array and nested 45 Statacoi fighters. I have flown against a Statacoi fighter before and that was one bitch of a ship to evade. Forty-five of them and the cruisers and the scout ships. We didn't have a chance in hell of making it back out of Grantok space let alone to our escape nebula.

It was at that moment that the scout ships opened fire on us.

"Oh shit!" yelled Doon.

"Stop saying that!" I returned. There was no way we could outrun the ships and we didn't have nearly enough firepower to blast our way out. We would have to rely on something much less...confrontational. My mind was racing. Then Doon screamed out again.

"Doon! Turn to port, 45 degrees...NOW!"

"I..."

"NOW!!" I shouted.

"OH SHIT!"

"Doon! I told you..."

"I've been hit!" he revealed. Good enough reason then to start panicking. "Oh shit, Argon." I could see that Doon's vocabulary grew rather limited when he was overwrought. "We're doomed!"

I looked back to see how bad he was hit and saw a stream of smoke and flame trail off his starboard wing. His engines were fine but I knew the scout ships would target those next and if his ship didn't just explode immediately they would be drawing in for the easy kill. I had to come up with something or I was going to witness by best friends die right in front of me seconds before I was blown to space dust myself. It should have been just me out here. It wouldn't have increased my chances for survival but it would have spared my friends. I could have argued it with Captain Galcursed more, refused to fly the mission with them, but I wanted to show off. Show them I had a right to be the Captain's favorite.

There was a click over the headset. "Argon." Fig had switched over to private comms.

"Fig..."

"I'm going to come around and try and get them off of Doon. Try and make a break for open space, they should have their hands full with me buzzing all around them."

Damn her! That should have been my play. But there was no way I was going to try and escape and leave her and Doon behind. "Wait, Fig..."

"I can't. Doon needs me to turn around now. He's falling further behind. I swear once they peel off him I'll switch our ID beacons back on. Maybe they'll not shoot us..."

That was it! The ID beacons!

"No, Fig. Hold your course." I flicked us back into regular comms. "Doon! I have a plan. Everyone switch on your IDs and head for the Tanaki ships as fast as you can!"

"What..."

"Just do it! Quick!" I commanded and followed it with a silent prayer. This had better work or we were all, as Doon pointed out, doomed.

I switched on my ID and throttled up my ship toward the Tanaki warships. I could see they were deploying their fighters and my instruments indicated that they were locking weapons. In a few seconds we would know if this was going to work.

I clicked on my distress signal and made a call on the galactic emergency frequency.

"Emergency! Emergency!" I mistuned the frequency slightly during the call to make it appear my ship was having comm problems. I even flicked the ID beacon and distress signal on and off a few times as well to complete the illusion. "We are under attack from the Xydoc Zyn. We have been fired upon and one of our ships is damaged and in peril. Please assist!" I repeated it again.

"Attention ships in distress; this is Captain Jeenrow of the Tanaki ship Shohdinae. You are in breach of galactic law and have broken a blockade."

"Tanaki ship, we are in need of immediate assistance. Under fire from pirates. Please aid."

"Repeat. Ships in distress, this is Captain Jeenrow of the Tanaki ship Shohdinae. You have broken a blockade. Do you understand?"

"Communication garbled. Need help."

Silence. I hoped that was a good sign. I waited and I felt the air in my cockpit grow stale and hot. Sweat was starting to pop out on my forehead and under my arms. My throat was getting dry and I feared I might not be able to speak again if asked for more information. I kept a steady eye on Doon's ship. He was quite a way back now and I anticipated a huge fiery bloom would appear in his place in the next few seconds. *C'mon and buy it, you stupid Tanaki bastards*, I thought. Seconds crawled. I'd played out my best bluff and I was all in. If they didn't believe we were innocent and confused I would have nothing else to offer but a possible run for the stars.

Finally I saw the blockade scout ships pull away from Doon's ship and take up a more escort-type position on each side of us.

"This is Captain Jeenrow of the Shohdinae. Please allow the ships to escort you to us and dock in Bay 6. Any attempt to deviate from this course will result in your destruction. Do you copy?"

"I got enough of it. Bay 6. Copy." I switched back to our own encrypted comm system. "Ok, I think we are in the clear. Switch your comms to PROGRAM, type in the command 'BROKEN,' and switch back to INTERNAL. Once we land on the Tanaki ship I will do all of the talking. Understand...Doon?"

There was a moment of silence then, "Yes. Thanks, Argon."

"No communication until I say. Just follow my lead. Understood?"

They both came back with an "Affirmative" and we headed for the Tanaki ships.

"You came within seconds of getting vaporized, young man."

Captain Jeenrow was giving me a serious dressing down in Landing Bay 6. He wasn't a tall, imposing man but he had that stern, parental bearing that all captains seem to have that makes you feel both guilty and ashamed even when you've done nothing wrong.

"I understand, sir, but I can explain," I started.

He gave me a suspicious squint and said, "Oh, of that I am sure, Mr. Bosch, but I think I might get better answers from this young lady here." He nodded respectfully toward Fig. "I'd try this pale mop-handle over here but I fear he might faint if I look at him for more than a second." I glanced at Doon and saw a blush spread across his neck. Jeenrow was a good judge of people for such a quick and accurate appraisal. I was worried he was already onto my game.

"Unfortunately I am the leader of our little band and it was I who had the poor judgment to get us into this situation." I played my "poor leadership" card hoping it would get me more traction. It failed miserably.

"There is no doubt of that, Mr. Bosch. All the more reason to ask Miss..."

"Newton-Jones," offered Fig.

He gave a small nod, "Miss Newton-Jones...my pleasure. I feel Mr. Bosch, as your *leader*, will most definitely try and bend the facts to both rescue you all from this mess but also to endeavor to side step and deflect blame that would naturally fall upon his poor choices. Am I mistaken?"

This was not going well at all. I had the script all planned out. I had all of our comms programed to show they were defective. I had managed to partially disconnect my ID beacon and I had even jacked with my navigational console to show I wouldn't have known I was even near any blockade. But Fig didn't know any of this. I felt that hot, uncomfortable feeling wrap around me again like a heavy, itchy blanket. Here comes the sweat.

"You are probably right, Captain Jeenrow," admitted Fig. "He certainly isn't a leader. He barely qualifies as a friend." She looked over at me with disgust. It looked so genuine that I couldn't help but protest.

"Fig!"

"Hush now, Mr. Bosch," interjected Jeenrow. "You can be silent or you can be restrained. Your choice."

I didn't say anything else; I dared not. There was something very serious about this Tanaki Captain and I had greatly underestimated his savvy. I began to wonder if I could have hoodwinked him even if had gotten the chance.

He began to walk and lead Fig away from us and across the flight deck. She gave me one more contemptuous look and then smiled warmly at Jeenrow as she slowly walked alongside him. I was surprised she didn't take his arm. "I want to personally thank you for saving us from Argon...Mr. Bosch's near fatal mistake."

"It was close indeed, Miss Newton-Jones. Sadly, I have destroyed many a ship for far less. Those scout ships were even more inclined to do likewise."

Fig briefly rested her hand on Jeenrow's shoulder. "I sincerely hope we can sort this mess out though I don't know where I stand on Bosch's horrendous mistake." At which point they wandered far enough that I could no longer hear them clearly although I swore I heard her say, "...inbred, dim-witted sloff eater." That couldn't have been right.

My eyes never left them as I watched Fig and Jeenrow stroll around the deck like it was some summer evening at the Promenade. After 15 minutes they returned and I was relieved when Jeenrow motioned for the guards to lower their weapons.

"Mr. Bosch," he said looking at me with a mixture of annoyance and pity. "Miss Newton-Jones has filled me in on the circumstances of your misadventure here and while it is not my customary inclination I have decided to let all three of you return to your home ship and let her sort out your disciplinary action once you have been returned to your proper developmental school. It is obvious to me that your sponsor was much too trusting in your abilities and that your callous disregard for your friends' lives only reinforces the fact that you simply cannot yet be left without proper supervision in any social environment."

"I told you, Argon!" Fig scolded. "You aren't smart enough to be out here in space with us!"

Jeenrow turned toward Fig, "Are you sure he can be trusted to follow you both home? I could have him sent back later when we have a ship near your Homeworld. But I simply cannot keep him aboard as some slow minded janitorial lackey as you suggested. It is simply beyond a responsibility I would want to shoulder."

If Fig had painted me as a stupid mouth breather to Jeenrow I was certainly helping with the illusion as I stood there with my jaw slack and my eyes round with confusion during this whole discussion.

"I apologize for suggesting that solution, Captain Jeenrow. He tries my patience so. I find that this time he has practically driven me from my wits! It was a desperate plea from a desperate woman."

He took her hand and patted it. "I understand completely. I wish you luck and I hope that Mr. Bosch here will soon be taken under the State care as you have been seeking. Having to babysit a grown man of such small ability is trying for anyone." He released her hand and looked kindly at her. "If you find yourself in this sector again one day please inquire after me. I would so enjoy your company again."

Fig smiled warmly at him, "Yes, Captain, of course. And thank you once again."

He gave a small bow and turned to leave. The guards lingered to see we got aboard our craft. I looked at Fig, eyes pleading for details. "Hurry along, Argon. We must get you home. I fear your sponsor will be worried sick. Now get in your ship and follow us home." She turned and headed for her own ship. I decided it best to keep the charade and quickly trotted to mine. Doon, silent and dumbstruck the entire time, produced an ear-to-ear grin and then sprinted for his craft. Moments later we were in space and streaking away from the Tanaki fleet. There was no sign of the blockade scout ships.

After getting some distance between us and the Tanaki I clicked on my headset and barked, "What the hell was all that?"

Fig, her voice as cool as sorbet, responded, "That was me getting us out of hot water, that's what that was."

"I had it well in hand," I argued to try and restore my dignity.

"Did you now?"

"Well, I would have had Jeenrow let me speak. I had a plan."

"So you couldn't tell he was not going to go for that off-course-ship-trouble baloney you were about to spew?"

"I...I could have improvised. You didn't need to..."

"You're right, I didn't. But he chose me. I had to come up with something. Or did you expect me to play the poor, helpless damsel-in-distress character?"

"Well...no, but I..."

"But nothing. He was going to lock us all up and send us off to some penal planet. I'll admit you were clever enough to get us aboard his ship without any of us dying but once we got there it was pretty obvious he wasn't going to have anything to do with you."

"Yeah, a little bit, sure." I was between emotions here with the sudden elation of the compliment and the let down of her recognition that I wasn't going to save the day. It solidified even more what I had already known: that her opinion of me mattered much more to me than my own.

"Believe me, I would rather he hadn't picked me but he did. So I did the best I could. And considering the fact that we are flying back under our own power, all three of us, I think it was a win."

"You're right. You did great at getting us out of there on the fly. Pretty nice work, actually. You might make a pretty great smuggler after all."

"Not what I was going for, Argon. I skipped that course in flight school."

I laughed. I knew she was only on the crew of the Nir'don because of me and that she would leave at some point. But I did find the idea of her running blockades and contraband kind of sexy.

"Fair enough. I guess you shouldn't put this on your resume when you apply to the Syndicate for a piloting job then."

"Ha!" she tossed out a fake laugh. "The Syndicate? I wouldn't work for them. I plan on working for myself. Maybe open some kind of business. Maybe a courier company where I set my own rules and take the jobs I want to take."

"Right," I said, dipped in the proper amount of sarcasm.

"No, seriously Argon. Imagine not having a boss, calling the shots, running it the way you want to run it. Not having to take on these illegal jobs. Giving your customers the kind of service that the Syndicate could never provide. You'd have more jobs than you could ever deliver."

"It's a pipe dream, Fig."

"I don't think so," interjected Doon after his long silence.

"Oh, the boy wonder chimes in at last," I replied.

"She has a point, Argon. It would be perfect. I'd like to open a travel agency."

"A good idea given your piloting skills," I sniped.

"Argon! That's not called for," scolded Fig. "He does a good job. Don't knock him down just because we have a vision and want more for ourselves."

"I am just trying to be the voice of reason here. You guys can dream all you want but eventually you have to wake up and face the cold dawn of reality. It's not cheap starting up a new business. Plus going against the Syndicate is suicide these days. They are putting the squeeze on all independent couriers. They want it all and they are big enough to make that happen."

"I'm sorry, Argon, but I disagree. If you put the right amount of work into it people will use you instead of the Syndicate. And the Tribunal won't let them have a full monopoly on the courier business."

I shook my head even though they couldn't see me. "Hell, Fig. The Tribunal let the Syndicate rise to power. Those two are thick as thieves!"

"Really, Argon?" asked Doon. He was far too trusting to understand the sad state of governmental corruption. "They're the government for the whole Galaxy!"

"Yes, Doon. Even with their lofty, high-minded values they still roll toward the money. The Syndicate channels a lot of income to the various races and makes a lot of governmental big shots a lot of credits. They'll turn a blind eye if the Syndicate tries to squash you."

"Is that true, Fig?" asked Doon.

"To a degree, Doon. Argon always makes things sound much more dire than they are. His cynical side is less a side than a majority. Don't let him dissuade you. We need to stick to our dreams and let him struggle with reality."

"Thanks, Fig," Doon said with more cheer in his voice than I would have imagined. Maybe I did come off too gruff sometimes. I needed to work on that. "Hey! Maybe we could all work together and pool our money and open our own company!"

"Yeah, that'll happen." Dammit, there I went again. "Sorry, maybe someday, Doon. Maybe someday."

I had taken the time to radio an "All Clear" to the Nir'don as soon as the scout ships had taken pursuit of us when we crossed the blockade so they had delivered their cargo by now. I sent Fig and Doon the coordinates for the rendezvous. We talked more about our eventual company and soon found ourselves landing on the Nir'don and sharing our adventure with the crew. Doon seemed particularly happy about it and laughed and laughed at our near-death experience. I felt he had tied the experience in with the idea that we would all one day work together in our own business - the two things becoming melded together to allow him a great joy in the fact that we all nearly died. As I watched he and Fig recount the episode for the fourth time I smiled and took joy in watching my friends revel in the details of potential disaster. I loved those two. I didn't want to ever be away from them whether it be on the Nir'don or working for ourselves. As long as we were all together I didn't really care what we did.

Time and circumstance are the wind that can erode any dream.

"I RECALL THINGS A LITTLE MORE SEVERELY than you, I think," I pointed out to Doon though I know it would have no effect on dampening his enthusiasm and fondness for that horrid incident.

"I miss those days on the Nir'don," he said with that far away look that accompanies unrealistic nostalgia. "We had a lot of fun." He looked at me and his happy-go-lucky smile dimmed a bit. "I have really missed you Argon."

"I'm sorry, Doon."

"Why didn't you ever contact me? Did I let you down?"

There was no way I was ready for this conversation and it was the second most dreaded conversation I was fearing. Maybe in my whole life. I didn't have any answers and I certainly couldn't lie. While I knew I owed them both the truth I still would have lied if I thought for a moment that I could pull it off. There weren't any excuses and I couldn't come up with anything suitably sufficient as to why I had abandoned the best friends I had ever had. The truth, or what little I recognized as the truth, only would further reveal the man I never wanted to be in their eyes. And I knew I couldn't face that mirror right now, if ever.

"Doon...I don't know if I can explain."

He surprised me by asking, "Try." Doon isn't the kind of person that deals with confrontation. He doesn't like to push issues or make others feel uncomfortable. For him to attempt to nail me down to an answer was rare and out of character. It only displayed how important this was and the weight it placed on his mind over the years. It was obvious to me that while I had done my best to move beyond it, he was still wrestling with my abandoning him.

I gave him a look that was surprise with a little bit of a pleading tacked on. I didn't want him to push me into answering and I knew that he might just be the one person who could get me to cop to the truth.

"I...I don't really know what to say, Doon. It's something I don't know if I can really explain. Are you sure you want me to go into all of that?" I had turned my face away as I couldn't look him in the eye. I felt too raw, too naked. At that very moment I thought he could look right through me and into my soul. That as I sat there, shamed in what I had put him through and how I had simply walked away, he would see me as I really am and not the person he had looked up to for so many years. I would never be able to live with that. I would jump out an airlock and welcome the final embrace of empty space just to alleviate the shame.

"Yes, he wants to know."

My head popped up and I looked to see Fig standing in the hatchway behind Doon. She had a look of anticipation and something bordering on...sympathy? Both their gazes fell on me and it was way more than I could take. I felt emotion pooling up quickly like that overflowing toilet bowl that required immediate attention or there would be a godawful mess. I plunged it down as much as possible but the level kept rising.

There was a ping of a target and my attention immediately shifted to the screen. "What...?" started Doon.

"Quiet," I hissed as I tried to change course and also assess the threat. I eased the ship away from the direction of the object and waited for the identification data to trickle across one of the displays. A tense second and I finally got the blip to disappear out of range. I started to adjust the course when the sensor information filled in.

As data slowly clicked into place my eyes grew wide in panic. It was not a Farnok scout ship. It wasn't a Farnok cruiser or a random private ship out joy riding. At first I thought it was a massive Tanaki battleship that had somehow drifted way off course. The Tanaki rarely traveled into Farnok space since it wasn't under the jurisdiction of the 11 Chairs of Power. Without the Galactic Tribunal's okay the Tanaki could only enter the Farnok sector to respond to an emergency or at the request of the Farnok government. That last part never happened. The Farnok were far too set in their crazy, paranoid ways to allow any of the Tribunal's lackeys to go snooping around. And they damn well wouldn't ask for help even if their entire sector was about to get sucked out of existence by an immense, ravenous black hole.

No, this was something else altogether. It was huge yet the readings seemed contradictory as to the ship's configuration. The Farnok didn't have any ships that large. So who else freely flew around in Farnok space?

Then it hit me like a sledgehammer to the foot.

Sweet Christmas! We needed to leave here immediately.

While the reality of what we may be dealing with dawned on me Doon and Fig could only react to my features. And judging by their collective response I was expressing something grim.

"You are scaring me, Argon," whispered Doon, afraid to even talk in a normal register. "What is it?"

"Argon?" pleaded Fig. "Tell us what's going on. Your eyes are as big as plates. What did you see?"

I wasn't sure what to tell them. Should I tell them what I suspected or just brush it off now that we were in the clear? I looked at them and started to say it was nothing. "It was..."

And then the scanner pinged again with its little cute chirp belying the true weight of its tuneless indication. My eyes swung to the screen in time to see the same contact reappear. Only this time it was headed directly towards us and picking up speed. We had been spotted and it was moving with unwavering intent. I swallowed hard and returned my eyes to Doon and Fig. My fears became grounded as the readouts were able to better resolve the scans that were coming in from the Heart's sensors. The huge blip dissolved into several smaller objects. But I recognized the characteristics and knew it was not the Farnok. It was way worse.

"What goddammit?" demanded Fig.

"It's the Xydoc Zyn." While the heaviness of that statement was enough to cause at least one gasp the next one called up a chill like the sudden draft from opening the door at a slaughterhouse. "An entire fleet of Space Pirates."

CHAPTER 10

I wasn't sure what was worse, the horrified look on Doon and Fig's faces, the belief that I was most likely going to see them both die before my eyes, or the sudden clearly defined hatred I had for A1 for getting us here. As if on cue he appeared right then in the hatchway leading to the Bridge.

The fact that he was sporting his oblivious smile only further fueled my desire to punch his face off. "What's the meeting about? Trying to think of a good way to thank me?" It was all I could do not to jump from my chair but I had turned my attention back to the controls and readouts to make fruitless attempts at evading the numerous pursuing ships.

"Shut up, A1," whispered Fig (*God bless her*). "Things are tense right now so just don't say anything."

"Why," he asked and I was reminded of a small child asking why he couldn't have ice cream for dinner.

"Just be quiet," replied Fig and the tenseness of her voice managed to get A1 to remain silent.

I did my best to try and outfox the pursuing tight cluster of ships but they stuck to me like glue. I knew some tricks I had picked up over the years and they kept failing. I searched the area for possible places to hide or give them the slip but the only solid possibility was a lone pulsar that was still far out from our location. The odds of reaching it before the pirate fleet was upon us were bumping up against none. Yet still I set course for it on the slim chance we would make it.

"I'm going to head for that pulsar up ahead and hope we can make it," I informed them all. "It's the only chance we have." Fig gave me a nod of agreement.

"How will that help?" asked Doon, his piloting inexperience showing.

"Pulsars emit pulses of high intensity radiation that scramble most sensors," I explained. "If we can get close enough we might be able to lose ourselves within the static and hide until we make a jump or they give up."

"I know that star," said A1. "It's called 'The Blanket' due its ability to cover a signal."

I spun my chair to face Fig. "This is your craft. If anyone can squeeze some more speed out of her it is going to be you."

I could see she wanted to protest but then she said, "You're right. I'll do my best," and moved to take the piloting chair. I was happy to surrender it to her. Immediately I grabbed A1 by the elbow and ushered him out into the passageway.

"How do you know about that pulsar? Have you been here before?"

He indignantly pulled his arm out of my grasp and scowled at me. "This ain't my first rodeo, you ass."

"All right. So you *have* been here before," I confirmed.

"I've done a lot of traveling in my many years and in that time I have made a few trips into Farnok space. While they have never been a trusting lot, there was a time when they were more...friendly, I guess...to the casual traveler. Sure, those blasted pirates were always sneaking about so I knew the best places to hide if things went bad. Hang out in the right places and keep your ears open and you learn all the secrets for the parts you travel. I'd heard of The Blanket before. Great hiding place. You'll never know what's in there until you practically bump up against it. Had to use it once myself. Waited out a Farnok trader that came gunning after me when he thought I'd sold him some fake banderfot oil."

"Just once, A1, I'd like you to volunteer something you know before we have to discover it ourselves."

"I would if you kept me more in the loop," he argued.

"Seriously? This whole endeavor is in your 'loop!' We are here for no other reason than to fulfill your personal quixotic quest regardless of the reasoning behind it. This is your party, you oblivious sock puppet, maybe you should step up to the table."

"Would it have even made any difference?"

"Maybe you haven't been paying attention but every single thing makes a difference now. We are in hostile space with a shit-ton of pirate ships chasing after us. When they catch up to us they will snag our ship, board it, and then..." I had to stop. Suddenly my mind filled with horrible images of my friends at the hands of the Xydoc Zyn. Poor, innocent Doon getting tortured to death. And Fig! They wouldn't kill her right away. No, they keep her alive, pass her around and...

My hand shot out and grabbed A1 by his collar. "Pray, old man," I practically whispered into his face, now only and inch away from mine, my voice harsh with malice and desperation. "Pray we make it to that pulsar or the Xydoc Zyn won't be the only thing you'll have to fear." Then I pushed him away and spun toward the Bridge.

"Please tell me we are getting close," I said to Fig. She didn't turn her head but was intently scanning gauges, readouts, and various displays all while adjusting dials and sliders. I moved up next to her and watched over her shoulder. If there was any way to wring one more bit of thrust out of her ship she was using it. I looked toward the sensor display to check our situation and it looked dire. The fleet was making good time and would be close enough to snag our ship within minutes. The pulsar didn't seem closer but I could see we had shortened the distance substantially in the short time she had been at the controls. Would it be enough? I dared not consider falling short.

"Argon, are we going to make it?" asked Doon, the worry and fear crowding together in his voice. Anyone saying, "Honesty is the best policy" has never faced a situation like this. For what could easily lay ahead I needed to try and calm him down.

"It's going to be close but I think she'll get us there, Doon." I placed my hand on Fig's shoulder and softly said to her, "You're doing it, Fig. You're going to make it." She didn't acknowledge me but I thought I felt a small bit of tension leave her shoulder.

The Bridge became deathly quiet except for the beeping of the instruments, tension crowding around us like more warm bodies. I felt the first path of nervous sweat slide across my forehead and drop into my eye. I habitually swiped the back of my gloved hand across my face to stem what I was sure would evolve into an eventual flood and bent to look at the distance to the pulsar for the sixth time.

"Can you stop doing that?" hissed Fig. "We either make it or we don't. Staring at the display won't change anything."

"Sorry," I apologized. Then I leaned even closer and brought my voice low enough so only she could hear. "We're going to be short, Fig. We just need a little bit more and we can make it."

"Then why don't you just hop outside and push, dammit."

She turned her head to look at me and I could see the intense desperation on her face. But there was more blended into her features. Sadness. A deep sorrow in her eyes that stunned me in its absolute. She knew we wouldn't make it and that everything she was doing was for naught. It crushed my heart. So many things suddenly left unsaid to never be spoken, to never unburden. In an instant I was yanked back to that day we first met. The hopeless sadness of losing everything she had brought instantly back and for the tiniest of moments she was only 4 again and I was powerless to help her. Forty-seven years later I was no closer to helping than I was then and the feeling threatened to destroy me. Then, as if she had traveled right back to the beginning with me the corner of her mouth curled slightly into a faint smile.

"Life's a bitch," she whispered and the crushing weight of my own fear of disappointment and helplessness lifted.

I winked at her and said, "I think you hit on just what we need." I stood and turned heading for the passageway in one motion. I grabbed Doon as I passed him. "C'mon. Time to earn your way."

"Where..?"

"No time. Follow me."

I could hear A1 behind me questioning Fig, "Where are they going now?"

"I guess they're going to go push," she said with a voice that carried less tension than moments ago. And then we were out of earshot and racing toward the rear of the craft.

"Do *what* again?" asked Doon.

I was already scrambling back down the ladder and stuck my head back up into the gunner's bubble on top of the ship. "Aim toward the pirates and..."

"Where are they?"

"Right behind us. Now, when I tell you, give them everything we have. Don't let up until the guns run dry."

"I can't even see them! How will I hit them?"

"You won't. They are still out of range."

"Won't that just piss them off?"

"Doon! Just do it, OK? *Please.*" I didn't have time to argue or give more instructions. There simply was no time.

He sensed my desperation as his demeanor changed to compliance. "Sure, Argon. Shoot at them until the guns run dry. You got it! It'll probably scare them off, right?" But I was already down the ladder and on my way to the engine room.

When running hell bent through a ship with narrow corridors and some even narrower hatchways a person would need to be some kind of parkour champion to get through it unscathed. That wasn't me. I banged and bounced like a pinball through the ship. As I neared the engine room hatch there was a short staircase leading down a level which then culminated in a harsh left turn. My speed was impressive but my momentum was careless and I hit the downward slope with no chance to brake before the hatch and turn. I put out my left hand to grab the edge of the opening and used it to slingshot me around the tight corner. As I ended my descent my hand caught on some kind of cleat by the hatch. There was no stopping me and my body arced through the doorway like a pendulum. I heard a sickening snap as my wrist was unable to accommodate the impossible angle and broke. But it didn't release so my body swung full into the bulkhead. I don't think the pain of my wrist had even reached my brain when I felt my shoulder dislocate. My right hand shot to my shoulder and neglected to try and brace my impact with the wall. I had to rely on my nose for that. Another sickening crunch and I bounced off the bulkhead, lost my footing, and fell backward. By some miracle my hand freed itself from the cleat and I dropped onto the floor in a miserable heap. I may have lost consciousness but I could never be sure. I only remember lying on the deck, screaming and swearing, and hearing Doon's voice in my ear.

"Argon? Do I shoot now? Argon?"

I tried to right myself but when I put some pressure on my left hand to get up my whole arm just crumpled, my shoulder gave a little unnatural twist, and my brain exploded in pain again. My entire left arm was useless. I tried to just let it hang and not use it but it would have none of that. Hanging limp at my side only made it worse as the pull on my shoulder from dangling only further aggravated the area. The muscles cramped making it impossible for the joint to return home so it simply scraped, bone against bone, trying desperately to make me cry. And it was working. The pain was unbelievable. My eyes were watering and my nose was running with mucus and blood. I finally struggled to my feet and my head swam, my vision dimming and clouding at the same time. I was a mess.

"Argon! Please answer me," pleaded Doon. There was such desperation in his voice that it helped snap me back from my stupor. The pain intensified but I struggled on.

"I hear you, Doon. Just give me a minute," I replied trying to sound nonchalant but coming off loopier than calm. "I'm almost there."

I grimaced, took a deep breath, and then tucked my messed up left hand into my pants to try and give it just a modicum of stabilization. It might have worked but there were far too many active pain receptors in my brain that were otherwise occupied to notice. I gathered myself as best I could and headed into the engine room.

Luckily the couple of days of shipboard orientation had paid off. I knew where the control panels for the various parts and functions of the ship were and within seconds I had figured out the fire control panel. I swung open the cover and looked inside. I knew enough about ships to know that the inertial dampeners could not be disabled from the Bridge or through regular means. They would have to be released manually. I looked for the release but it wasn't there. SHIT!

"Argon?" There was distinct worry in Doon's voice. "Argon, the ships..."

I had to disengage the inertial dampeners now but they weren't here. Why weren't they in the fire control...?

Of course! They had nothing to do with controlling the weapons. Inertia was an environmental control. I spun around and searched for the correct control box. They were all labeled but the organizational order was lost on me. I didn't see it. Oh my God! Was it actually on the Bridge? I had to do it NOW!

I felt a sudden sense of defeat crush down on me. The pain took a momentary backseat to the anguish I suddenly felt. Failed to save my friends. Again.

I think I said something or swore or mumbled but Doon's voice was abruptly in my ear. "Argon? What did you say? The pirates are coming!"

I was about to say I was sorry and then I saw the panel on the other side of the room. I bolted for it and threw the cover open, my adrenalin causing my frantic grab to bend the hinge so badly it wouldn't ever close again. I scanned the interior and saw the controller box for the guns. I grabbed the top and pulled. It didn't budge. Oh for the love of mud nuts! I couldn't get a good grip and I needed two hands. This simply could not be happening.

I reached down and pulled my left hand free of my pants and raised it up to the box. My shoulder clicked and popped and sent a wave of pain so intense it almost made me throw up. Then I grabbed the box with my left hand and my wrist ground bone against nerve. I could feel my mind starting to float away from the situation to avoid the unbearable pain. When I let my left arm hang freely, gripping the box with as much strength as it was capable, I knew I only had one chance at this before I passed out. If I failed now there would be no second chance for the ship or for my friends. I dug the fingernails of my right hand into the small plastic box and threw myself backward. It popped with brief snap of intense light and the tang of ozone. I think it triggered an alarm but I couldn't be sure as there was only the drone of a loud thumping buzz filling my head.

"Now, Doon!" and I blacked out with a feeling that I had just been shot out of a canon.

I don't know how long I was out but I suspect it was only a minute or two as no one had come to find me yet. I awoke wedged into a corner of the engine room a couple yards from where the panel was. The Heart must have encountered turbulence or ran through some harsh maneuvers to cause my body to slide across the floor.

I tried to get up and was rather unpleasantly reminded that my body was a sad wreck. Sharp pain stabbed through me like jagged knives of fire. I fought it off as best I could and managed to stand, though not very steadily. Using my hand-in-pants trick to subdue my left arm a fraction I then stumbled and shuffled out of the engine room. The stairs proved a daunting task as I discovered my right knee was now banged up and didn't want to cooperate. I thought about just sitting down and resting for a few minutes and maybe think about pancakes. There was something comforting about thinking about pancakes. I don't know if it is the nice fluffy nature of them almost floating in a nice little stack or the pleasing image of them hot and steamy on a plate with butter melting across their surface and warm, sweet syrup slowly flowing down the sides. Yeah, I could have thought about pancakes for awhile.

"Argon!" screeched Doon's panicked voice in my ear. Seems pancakes would have to wait.

"Yes, Doon?"

"Oh thank God! I've been calling you and calling you and I thought...well, I thought maybe..."

"I'm fine. No, not exactly fine. But I'm here. What happened?"

"The guns! When I fired them they pushed us even faster or something and we made it into the pulsar's range. We made it! We lost 'em!"

I coughed and felt a twist of pain in my side. Turned out I had bruised a rib as well. Just my kind of day. "I'm heading for the Bridge."

"I'll see you there! Great job, Argon!" His voice was giddy with excitement and joy.

"I couldn't have done it without you, Doon. You did good. Thanks." he laughed heartedly and disconnected his comms. I drug myself up the stairs and down the passageway. It took me substantially longer getting back than it did when I lit out for the engine room. There was absolutely no surprise in that.

"Oh my God, Argon!" exclaimed Fig when I entered the Bridge. I was obviously not looking my best.

A1 took a look at me and then said, "What the hell are you doing with your hand down your pants? Keep that business to yourself. We're not monkeys here."

"Bite me, you dusty old fart," I said pushing past him.

"Watch your tone, willy wacker," he retorted and then punched me in the shoulder. Yeah, *that* shoulder. I dropped to my knees with a gasp. My left hand popped out of my pants and the wrist was over twice its normal size. I was in no shape to fight A1 but, man, I wanted to. Had I a hammer I know I would have at least taken at swing at smashing a toe or two from my prone position. Instead I think I just whimpered. Not exactly the same.

Fig rushed over and dropped down beside me. "What happened?"

"Misadventure, I fear. Took a bad spill in the engine room. Busted my wrist, dislocated my shoulder, banged up my knee. I think I might have bruised a rib or two," I said, ticking off the various injuries I had accomplished in the span of a few minutes.

"What about your face?"

"Oh yeah. Did a face-plant into a wall. Think my nose is broken."

"If we ever get into a fight, you and I, I think I am going to just sit back and watch," A1 tossed in his meaningful insight as usual. He ended it with a little chuckle.

"Yeah, that's a good one, A1. And by the way, you're welcome,"

I threw back at him.

"Right, right," he mumbled. "I guess I owe you one."

"One?!" I struggled to get up and cringed again. Fig tried to help but it was nearly impossible to grab me anywhere and it not hurt. A1 didn't feel the need to be as considerate.

"Here," he offered. "Let me help you up."

I knew what was going to happen. "No! Wait…" Too late, not that he would have listened to any warning. He grabbed me by the left elbow and hefted me up. There was a loud pop and I let out a scream that I am ashamed to say sounded far too feminine. But then I noticed an immediate lessening of pain in my shoulder. He had popped it back in and while still stiff it was a drastic improvement. "Wow. That's a lot better."

He winked at me. "Now, *you're* welcome."

I looked him in the eye. "I don't like you."

"The feeling is mutual, as they say," he returned.

"I bust myself up trying to save your ass and you still need to give me crap?" I questioned. "Really? Can't just be appreciative. Have to get your digs in. We're in deep shit and I didn't see you do anything but stand around and wait to get bailed out. That's all you do: wait. No ship; wait for someone to get you one. No plan; wait for someone to come up with one." I continued to rant at him and then I noticed he was no longer looking at me. He was looking past me. And I discovered no one else was saying anything. I turned my head and look at Fig. She wasn't looking at me either. "What the hell is it now?"

"You may want to hold off on counting all those accolades, son," said A1 with something halting in his speech, like he was distracted by something much more important. "In fact, I would be happy as piss if you managed to have another of your big plans handy right about now."

"What are you talk…?" I had turned around to see that everyone was looking wide eyed at the view screen. I felt my own eyes grow wide as I looked.

There, filling the entire screen, was the largest Xydoc Zyn ship I had ever seen in life or images. It was a monster. Its design was all hard-edged sweeping curves with wings that curved right along with them. It was all black except for the few running lights that gleamed amongst the darkness of the ship. Guns? There were so many guns it seemed the guns had guns. A number of sharp pointed antennas sprung out from it but then angled back to compliment the curved nature of the aesthetic. It could have been a beautiful ship but instead it radiated dread and menace. It was a ship that the Angel of Death would pilot. There was no good that would ever come from seeing this ship. And right in the middle of it immense black nose was a dark crimson emblem of the Xydoc Zyn.

In our frantic flight to evade the fleet we had unexpectedly run right into the hiding place of their leader. Out of the frying pan and into the fucking sun.

I said what I knew had to be the truth. "Rink SanDyer."

"Now I *do* have to apologize," said A1. "I think I just shit myself."

CHAPTER 11

There wasn't a lot I could do. I was busted up pretty badly and the pain was still intense enough to be a constant hindrance. Of course my body was pumping adrenalin like crazy but that only got me so far and it was nowhere near close enough to allow myself to birth some brilliant plan. To be honest, on my best day, in my best health, with every neuron in my brain firing at 100%, and a group of advisors at my back I would not have been able to devise a plan clever enough to get us out of this jam. Well...at least not in the time given.

There was a sudden shove against the ship as the enormous pirate ship reached out and grappled the Sononi Heart with its powerful tractor beam. I heard the outer hull squeal and protest as it buckled slightly under the force of the beam. It would be impossible for us to ever break free from its grasp. A quick lurching movement shook the Heart as the powerful beam started our journey into the lower bay.

As we drew closer the scale of the ship took on even more mammoth proportions as it became easier to recognize our dainty size in comparison. The entrance to the landing bay was so large I couldn't even fathom why it would be so immense. Were they planning on capturing a small moon to ransom later? Perhaps they salvaged rogue comets and asteroids to farm for minerals or jettison into disagreeable planets? My mind reeled as I tried to imagine the possibilities both realistic and foolish.

The whole of the experience was so absolutely shocking that not a single one of us spoke or moved. Even A1. And that was a feat indeed!

As the Heart finally rose up into the interior of the ship, I found my voice. "This sucks ass."

It wasn't exactly inspiring nor did it buoy my crewmates' hope but it did a good job of summing up our situation.

"Can we hide somewhere?" questioned A1.

"Like where?" I replied.

"I don't know. Under the deck plates, maybe?"

"So, they take the time to drag us in here and then when they come looking for us they simply give up because we aren't sitting here playing Vanderloon? 'Must be an empty, derelict ship just flying around through space,' they say. Who would do that?"

I looked him in the eye, "No, they are going to search and they *will* find us. They aren't idiots."

"It's worth a try," he argued. "Why just do nothing and let them just come in here and take us?"

"Because, it is their *job*. They would probably rather be drinking and screwing and counting their money than having to search every nook and cranny of this ship. So, if we make it even harder for them to find us then they will be even more angry. And since they don't really care about us anyway, why not just kill us on the spot and be done with it. Then they can get back to the important things."

"Like 'drinking and screwing'?" He raised an eyebrow mocking my statement.

"Exactly."

A1 thought for a couple more minutes and then said, "OK...well they are probably just going to kill us like you said so why not take a couple of those sons-a-bitches out with us before we go?"

"OK, again...this is their *job*. They don't *want* to do *anything*. Any inconvenience we offer them will only make things worse for us."

"Worse than dying?"

"Worse than dying *quickly* would be my point. These are the Xydoc Zyn. Goddamn Space Pirates! And this is very likely their leader's ship. So we have the worst-of-the-worst evil, reprobate, space faring mother-fuckers you will ever encounter in the entire galaxy. They have routine torture methods that you haven't ever imagined in your most horrid nightmares. They revel in pain and death. And that's when they are in a *good* mood! Imagine what they are like when you piss them off. There is no telling..."

"Stop, Argon!" pleaded Doon. "You are scaring the shit out of me. This isn't helping."

"He's right," agreed Fig. "Your little pep talk is not having the effect you think it is."

I looked at their collective worried faces and immediately felt guilty for letting A1 bait me once again into shooting off my mouth. I don't know what it was about that guy that just burrowed under my skin and caused such an unforgiving itch. "I'm sorry. The point I wanted to make is that if there is any chance at getting through this alive the best first step is to not make them mad." They nodded in agreement, A1 included.

Even during my bleak discourse I was still fighting off images of my friends' possible fate at the hands of the Zyn. I could not face that. Despite the odds I simply had to find a way out of this. There had to be a way, the alternative was far too ghastly to contemplate.

A heavy bump indicated we had come to rest on the deck of the immense landing bay. "Open it up and deploy the ramp, Fig," I instructed, struggling to keep my voice steady. "Let's see what's waiting for us out there." She complied and I led the way to the hatch, trying my best to not display the jolts of pain that accompanied each movement.

"Let me go first, Argon," volunteered Doon. A grand gesture not wasted on me.

"Thanks, Doon, but I need to go first. You wouldn't be here if it wasn't for me." He tried to argue but I'd have none of it. If nothing else I could at least do this for them. My right hand slid down to my holster and I unclasped my pistol. I silently vowed that if it looked like it was going to go bad from the start that I would take care of my friends before I would allow them to fall into the sadistic hands of the Zyn. That was the other thing that I could do for them. But with each grimace I prayed that it wouldn't come to that being my last act of my life.

There was a hiss of equalizing pressure and the hatch seals popped and it began to rise. My heart began to pound drowning out the grind of gears and pistons working to raise the heavy door. Sweat beads popped out on my forehead and a tiny rivulet crept down into my eye. My hand twitched as a constant stream of adrenalin pumped through my body, every nerve alert, every muscle primed for action. Fight or flight; one of those was not an option. After seconds that felt like a lifetime the hatch was open and I was staring right into...

The face of an incredibly beautiful woman.

A bald incredibly beautiful woman.

With an eye patch.

And a long jagged scar that ran from the forehead just above her patch, down across her cheek, touching upon the corner of her mouth, and ending abruptly just under her chin. It seemed obvious that what had caused the scar had also taken her eye. And yet, despite her imperfection and commitment to having no hair, she was still one of the most stunning women, of any race, I had ever met.

It was such a shock that it took me a few moments to get past that startling revelation. Stunned into silence I merely stood flat footed and stared at her while she looked me over and cocked her head to one side, favoring her good eye. I could hear the rest of the crew mumbling behind me but their voices simply droned into a background static like the sputtering hum of the ventilation system. My world collapsed into a single focus, the rest of it ceasing to exist. Had I died right then I doubt my first glances of Heaven would impact me as much. There was only me and this exquisite vision before me. And a space monkey.

A space monkey? A space monkey wearing a little hat that reminded me of a sombrero. It gave the already awful looking thing an unsettling comic look like a gorilla wearing a bow tie or a great white shark with sunglasses.

The disgusting creature leaped upon my shoulder and attempted to stick its mangy finger in my ear. I was immediately pulled from my revelry and plopped unceremoniously into a very harsh reality. Annoyed and frustrated with its presence I swatted at the vermin but it evaded my attempts skittering around my body like I was a tree. I would have feared its bite or claws but I was far too upset to worry and only wanted to free myself from its disgusting grip.

"Squirty!" she suddenly shouted and the foul creature leapt from me onto the ground and then scuttled behind her legs and peered at me with its large, bulbous eyes. It gave a little hiss and were I not sure it would have doomed us all I would have shot it right then and there.

"I apologize for my pet's behavior Mr..."

"Bosch," I finished. "Argon Bosch. And you are?"

"Trixie," she answered.

At least I *heard* "Trixie." Of course that was not her name. But I was just so enthralled by her beauty that she could have said anything and I would have just heard "Trixie."

I WAS TRANSPORTED, VIA NOSTALGIA, to my late teens growing up on Blag. I didn't have a knack for school and preferred to spend my time hanging out at the docks and listening to the various crews' wild tales of the spaceways. My parents had at first complained and disciplined me in an attempt at forcing me to put forth more effort into my studies but, after many a failed change of direction, they finally relented to let me squeak by on my school work and entertain myself with my daily trips to the docks. It was on one of these trips that I met Trixie.

I had run down to the docks to greet the ships arriving and one in particular that I had grown familiar with, The Rontarr. I was more tolerated by that crew than any other and I was anxious to be there as the crew disembarked. In my zealous haste I ran headlong into one of the crew who was just leaving the open hatch. I managed to not knock her back but grabbed her to steady us both. I shook off my startled sensation and discovered I was looking right into the eyes of the most beautiful girl I had ever seen.

She smiled and I felt my knees grow weak. "Sorry. Usually people show that sort of enthusiasm in leaving the ship not entering it," she laughed. My face flushed and I managed to blurt out that I was sorry for my clumsiness and lack of awareness and begged for her forgiveness. She would tell me much later that what I really stammered out was, "S...sorry. Me." and "Dammit."

"Are you part of our crew? I don't think I've met you." She offered a hand.

"Um, uh...my name is Argon."

"Nice to meet you Argon. My name is Trixie."

She was six years my senior and was part of a crew that had signed on a month ago after they left Blag. I didn't have much of an eye for the girls in my class but she presented such an exotic beauty that I couldn't help but be awestruck and swept away at first glance. From that first encounter she became the subject of my infatuated heart.

Her father was a long time space pilot and some of his desire to travel the spaceways was imparted to her. She had taken his lead and ventured out into space to find adventure. I didn't recognize it until much later but her experience was the idea that later germinated in my desire to leave Blag and join a crew on a freighter.

She was a striking figure of a young woman with a head of brilliant crimson hair and a dark complexion to further contrast. She wore a kind of black bandana-thing to reign in her wild hair with a pair of goggles perched atop. I would find that she wore this headgear often and when she took it off her hair would blossom into a cascade of red which, in certain lights, seemed ablaze with dark flame. Her eyes were a bright emerald green and carried their own inner light. She was tough but had a kindness that would tolerate my foolish puppy-like following. When she started to recognize me on later visits it only cemented my youthful passion. And when she began actually talking to me she couldn't help but become my first love.

Even though I continued to hang around like a buzzing pest she grew fond of me for a reason I never could comprehend. It was apparent to anyone of even marginal sight that she was far beyond my league. Yet each time she came back to our port I would be anxiously waiting and clamoring to hear of her latest adventures. Of course, she would only occasionally have anything remotely close to being an adventure but I still sat and listened intently glued to every word like a lamprey - feeding on each casual glance or innocent attention. And then one day, after over a year of this seemingly futile exercise, something so strange happened that I still cannot completely understand it.

I had been waiting for The Rontarr to dock like I always did; straining to catch that first glance of my "sweetheart." She was late coming off the ship and for a few tense and dreadful moments I feared she would not appear at all. But finally she did and I ran towards her with my characteristically foolish exuberance, giving her an immense hug and rambling on about how much I had missed her. But then she looked at me and gave me such a wide smile that it seemed to actually echo the feelings I was already showering on her. There was a welcome in her eyes that had never been there before and an assurance in her smile that made me feel like she had, for the first time, really wanted to see me.

Then she kissed me.

And the galaxy dissolved around me and rebuilt itself into something that was entirely different. It became a place where I mattered.

After our lips parted and she looked deep into my eyes I felt like I was floating, *we* were floating, to somewhere only we existed. The whole thing became surreal and I started to doubt whether I was even awake at that point. Surely it was a dream and not reality. She took in my goofy look and laughed but not at me but because of me. It was a joyous, happy laugh that seemed to fill me with its essence because I realized that I was the cause of that joy. I've lived a lot of years since then but I don't know if there was ever a time since where I had felt such complete and innocent happiness.

"I missed you, Argon Bosch," she whispered in my ear. "Come

with me." She took my hand and pulled me after her as she ran from the dock. I raced along close behind unsure what lay ahead but anxious for it all the same. Normally we would have ended up at some dock pub surrounded by her crewmates anxious to one-up each other in outrageous stories but instead she led me far from the docks. Before I could even ask our destination we ended up out near a lake that bordered the city. I collapsed under a tree and panted so vigorous was our pace. She turned and stood over me, that same smile beaming from her beautiful face aglow with exertion from the run, and pulled her bandana from her hair. The suns were setting and the amber twilight backlit her causing a rosy halo. As her chest heaved from each breath and her face looked down at me with such welcome I felt a tear slip across my cheek. A momentary concern touched her, "Are you okay, Argon?"

"I...I'm just so happy I don't know what to do. I may burst," I tried to explain.

"Why?"

I was not accustomed to talking to her about anything of any substance, let alone the true feelings I had, but this sudden intensity of feelings and reciprocation had my mind muddled and confused - otherwise I would never had said it. "I love you."

A strange series of feelings played across her face and I couldn't read her. In the end something like understanding fixed there and she gave me an accepting smile. She kneeled down next to me on the soft, mossy ground. "I don't know if I ever consciously knew that but when you said it some part of me seems to have always known it." She took my hand in hers and then touched my hair with her other hand. "You have always been nice to me, Argon. And you made this place almost seem like home."

I wanted to suddenly say so much to her. Share the secret daydreams that would while away my days when she was gone. The captive memories I clung to awaiting her return. The countless futures I created out of tiny threads of hope and prayer. But it was all too sudden and I couldn't find the words. "You *are* home, Trix."

A deep sadness seemed to overtake her but she fought it off

with a valiant smile though not before a tear of her own sprung free from those beautiful green eyes. I reached up and touched it. "I love you, Trix," I repeated.

She grasped my hand firmly in hers and leaned in close to me. "Show me."

We made love next to that lake as the suns finally set and a million stars filled the sky.

When we were finished I noticed she had tears in her eyes and somehow I understood that they weren't from sadness. Something had happened to her and I didn't know what or why but when she composed herself, giving me a quiet laugh and a smile that melted any concern, I knew everything was going to be fine. She held me then, pulling me tightly to her and nuzzled her lips to my neck. I closed my eyes and smiled. Then so unexpectedly that I almost missed it she whispered, "I love you, Argon."

We had three days and nights before The Rontarr was scheduled to leave and we spent every moment of them together. There will never be words to explain the content and joy I felt in those three days or the pain I felt when I kissed her goodbye as she boarded her ship. She would be back in four months and, while I had waited twice that before just to see her ship return with less promise than I had now, I could no longer tolerate the thought of even one day without her.

I returned home, my eyes rimmed in red from tears, inconsolable. My parents, deep in some discussion when I came in, scolded me for being gone for three days and not contacting them. My father seemed more agitated than I would have expected and even threatened me. My mother voiced her own worry over my welfare. I couldn't do anything but sit and rock myself trying not to break down in front of them. After a few moments my mother realized how upset I was and asked what had happened. My father stopped his tirade and repeated her question. How could I explain? How could I tell them? I finally just got up and walked to my room and locked the door. I stood by the window and watched the suns set and when they had finally both dipped below the horizon I dropped on my bed and cried until I fell asleep.

Had I known what my world would be like six months later I would never have woken up.

"**I'M SORRY.** You said your name is 'Trixie?'" I tried to clarify.

She gave me an annoyed look and shook her head. "Tricks E?" she repeated pronouncing the name as two separate words, like a first and last name. "I clearly said my name is Zyryn. Maybe you have some kind of hearing difficulty."

"That's the least of my difficulties right now." I shook my head. "This is a huge mistake."

She gave me a wry smile. "Mistake? On whose part, Mr. Bosch? Ours?"

"No. I mean, well...I, um," I continued to fumble for something for a few moments. I finally decided it might be best if I didn't look directly at her since her appearance was causing a distraction. I took a deep breath and tried to start again. "What I am trying to say is..."

"That you are fucked," she completed my thought with more clarity than I was going to.

"That could be a distinct possibility depending on your intention, Zyryn."

"You have managed to discover the ship of Rink SanDyer. What do you suppose my intention is?"

I scratched my chin and looked thoughtfully at the ground. "I would assume you are going to kill us all by one means or another but that could have been easily handled by blasting us to atoms when we came upon your ship but you brought us aboard for some reason."

"I could say it is because we would rather salvage your ship. No sense in destroying a perfectly good vessel." Her smile was captivating and beautiful. I could see no hint of malice. It was a chilling feeling as I knew I was dealing with a stone cold killer. I wouldn't want to sit across the table from her in a game of Vanderloon.

"Uh...yeah. We wouldn't want that."

"An attempt at humor, Mr. Bosch?"

"More an attempt to not think about your actual meaning really."

Her smile grew broader. "I like that. But we have put the proverbial cart before the horse as you Terrans say. I am here to determine why you are here and what it is you are trying to do."

I looked her in the eye, caught myself, and then gave her a sideways glance. "That is a long story that seems to grow longer every time I have to tell it. Which happens to be more often than I'd like." I cast a weary eye toward A1.

"I think you may need to tell it, though not quite yet. Follow me." She turned to lead us off somewhere and I was momentarily surprised that she hadn't made any assertions concerning us being prisoners. Hell, she hadn't even asked who all was on the ship or for us to surrender our weapons. Maybe A1's goofy ploy to hide in the ship might have worked after all. Perhaps my paranoia was getting the best of me.

She turned her head and looked back at me as she walked. "You *are* going to have the rest of the crew accompany us, aren't you Mr. Bosch?"

"Uh, right. Wasn't sure you'd want their company while we, uh...spoke," I offered with a smile.

She sniffed and replied, "You have the wrong impression." She waved a hand in the air. "Gleef, have your men search the craft for any further passengers and kill any you find immediately." One of the men standing along the gangway, Gleef I assume, motioned to a few others and the small company of men surged toward the entrance to the Sononi Heart but not before Fig, Doon, and A1 came bolting out and raced down the ramp.

"Wait up, Argon," called A1. I gave him a knowing look which he failed to acknowledge.

Zyryn stopped and looked at me with a slight intensity that I found unsettling. "We are pirates after all, Mr. Bosch."

"Oh, I haven't forgotten that for a second," I admitted.

She gave me an appraising look and then remarked, "They don't care for you, do they?"

"What? Who?"

"Your crew. It looks like they have taken turns beating you with pipes." I had forgotten about my sad appearance from my Engineering mishap. And her shocking presence and our situation had temporarily taken my mind of the pain. That ended immediately. I grimaced.

"First off, they are not my crew. Secondly, I managed to do this all on my own."

She broke a slight smile on the corner of her mouth crossed by the scar. "You are a strange one, Mr. Bosch. I am not sure what to think of you."

"I get that a lot," I muttered and we headed down the corridor.

Rink SanDyer's ship was not as impressive as some I had been aboard. It was massive and the spaciousness of the passageways and compartments made me recognize the more confined nature of the ships I was used to. But there was not the lavishness of detail and blatant extravagance I would have suspected of the Captain of the Space Pirates, the Most Feared Man in the Galaxy. I was looking for gleaming platinum and gold. Jeweled adornments and the intense glow of krenon plasma fixtures. The kind of stuff I had seen in adventure movies of my youth. Even Zyryn was a little bit of a let down, dramatically speaking of course. I expected to be greeted by some 9 foot hulking cyber-troll that eats kittens like popcorn. Why we weren't shackled in irons and being poked by laser lances was beyond my comprehension. Zyryn was dressed in body-hugging black leather and body armor with a couple of weapons hanging from her hips and a long, barbed pole thing across her back. If it weren't for her amazing beauty she would strike an intimidating figure. Even then, knowing her vocation, I continued to find her both arousing and threatening - a mix I found conflicting.

Walking behind her as we continued down a long dim corridor offered me a few stolen glances of her from behind and it was enough a distraction to keep me from fretting myself into a lather. But between Fig's close proximity and the three men that followed alongside her I dared not let those quick looks rest too long lest I get an elbow from Fig or a knife in my eye from her personal guard. But were they worth the chance? Oh yes. Just as I chanced another glance her repugnant pet peeked over her shoulder and gave me an angry scowl followed by its little teeth-baring hiss. That mean-spirited monkey was going to come to a bad end.

I began to wonder just who this woman was. It was obvious she was Farnok given her name. The Common Xydoc Zyn translation from Farnok was "The Horrid Death" and I strongly suspected that Zyryn was a derivative of Zyn but I couldn't remember enough about Farnok syntax to know if Zyn meant "Horrid" or "Death" - though neither was a suitable name for woman.

She had three personal guards if I read the situation clearly. The three men were next to her when I opened the hatch and they were never more than two steps away from her. They kept watching her and then watching us as if we might pose a threat to her while we strolled along a corridor on Rink SanDyer's ship. A ship chock full of bloodthirsty space pirates. Either they were overly vigilant or incredibly poor judges of character. Did they even look at A1? These guys were not just standard off-the-street thugs. Two were likely Farnok and one was probably Terran given his garb. The Farnok males wore dark body armor and heavy coats festooned with large caliber handguns and a various sized blades. The Terran wore a garish crimson tunic with just a pistol of some sort on his hip. He was diligent in his duties but stood out like a coal lump in a snowbank.

"We are here," she finally announced as the two Farnok pirates raced ahead to open the large double doors ahead of us.

As the doors swung wide I heard my group take a simultaneous breath. This is what I had been expecting.

The room was bright and open. There were large portals in the overhead that presented grand vistas of the surrounding space. I could clearly see the pulsar throbbing in the distance with a brilliant orange nebula arcing across behind.

Immense columns rose to the ceiling with soft glowing bands of light at regular intervals. The floor was Darneesh Marble polished to a gentle shine that helped keep the room warm and not garish. A contingent of surly looking Xydoc Zyn stood in full battle gear seemingly waiting for a sudden call to action. They made Zyryn's body guards look complacent by comparison. In the center was an elevated chair that simply cried out to be called a throne. In it sat Rink SanDyer.

He was quietly conversing with a fetching young female that was of a race I had not encountered. She was tall, thin, and covered in a light fur. Her tail swished seductively as he whispered something causing them both to laugh. He continued in his flirtations for several minutes before she slid away on graceful feet. He gave his D-pad a cursory glance before finally looking up at us and then Zyryn.

"Who have you brought me, Zyryn, and why are they not dead?"

"I thought they might..." she started and I sensed that even she felt intimidated in front of him.

"What? Further waste my time with their babblings on top of your own?"

"No, fa..." she began once more only to be cut off again.

"No indeed." He looked us over slowly, taking his time in the silence to meet each one of our gazes in turn. Most of us could not hold his scrutiny and were forced to look down. I didn't but not because I wasn't afraid (I was terrified) or because I felt I had a chance to disturb his dominance but simply because I was curious. Here was a legend, a historical figure from my early memories on Blag, that was every nightmare's germinating seed. I cannot count the number of times I woke up crying as a young boy having dreamed I was stolen from my home by Rink SanDyer and his band of evil pirates. I didn't have enough understanding of the depths of human depravity to fill in the parts that came after simply knowing that it was not anything I would ever want to go through. The tales that were told in whispers behind school walls and in late night conversations at camp sites leading to the inevitable sleepless nights were legendary and saturated with menace. As adults we still had the icy grasp of this villain clutched tightly around our subconscious, just ready to give a squeeze to our adrenal glands to rack up our pulses and quicken our step when we would hear the click of a heel behind us on a desolate street. He was always with us to some degree and those that staunchly professed that they had no fear of Rink SanDyer still found themselves lowering their voices when proclaiming this lie. The very personification of evil and suddenly I was standing before him.

His unwavering eyes finally returned to mine and he recognized that it wasn't defiance that made me not look away but a strange sense of wonder. Something passed between us then and he stood from his elaborate chair and calmly stepped down to the floor level. His eyes never left mine as he walked toward me. As each step brought him closer I was sure that I would loose my bowels or at least my bladder recognizing that he would not be able to simply let this charade of courage go unpunished. I could clearly imagine when once within striking distance he would pull a blade from concealment and, with an elaborate flourish, bury it to the hilt in my neck. And even with my certainty of approaching death I could not drop my gaze.

Then, just as I thought my heart was about to explode as well as my straining sphincter, he stopped and said, "And who are you?"

So sure had I been that I was about to be skewered that it took a moment or two to actually realize he was talking and then to recreate what he had said. I tried to recover and respond but being Argon Bosch such simple things are sometimes beyond me. My mind, fueled by the hormone release of my fight-or-flight instincts, started to formulate a retort. Should I attempt to be funny? Challenging? Disrespectful? Helpful? I didn't have anything that would remotely be considered experience for this so I couldn't rely on my usual smooth, oratory prowess. Right. So, in the end, after he watched me stand there motionless and mute for what had to seem like a day and a half, I spoke.

"No one of any consequence." I knew I had heard that in a movie somewhere.

"For some reason I doubt that. What is your name?"

"Argon Bosch. I'm just a delivery pilot actually. Nobody special."

"You keep saying that like you are trying to convince me," he suggested.

"Uh, no. I just know who you are and so I figured I'd just be upfront about it."

"You know who I am? Have we met before?"

I raised my eyebrows. Was he really trying to be coy with me? "Seriously? You're Rink SanDyer, man. Who wouldn't know who you are? A newborn maybe. But even then I imagine there is some kind of racial memory imbedded in their primal brain."

He smiled and let out a chuckle. "You flatter me, Mr. Bosch."

"Well...you're welcome but that wasn't my intent. I was only trying to establish that you are a galactic presence that is extremely well known."

"I know who I am. I am just not sure I know who you are. Perhaps you could start by telling me why you are here."

"We are here because you captured us. I can assure you that we definitely would not be here otherwise." Never hurts to state the obvious when at a loss of what to say. This assumption proved to be wrong.

He slapped me hard across the face.

"You toy with me? Maybe you *don't* know who I am."

I could taste blood in my mouth and felt the tingle of numbness changing to pain on the side of my face. He was making me angry and I had an even better chance of acting foolish when I was angry.

"I answered your question. Maybe next time ask a better one." Yeah, that was the wrong thing to say but when I got mad, common sense, what little I possessed, flew right out the window. And that innate terror I had been feeling went right along with it. Before I could utter another stupid thing he had a knife pressed against my throat.

"Now you are insulting me. On my ship. In front of my crew." He brought his face in close to mine. "Do you really wish to die that strongly?"

I could hear protests arising from behind me but the sound of blood pounding in my ears drowned out the exact words. I suddenly thought of my friends' fate if I continued to act so irrationally. I calmed slightly and regained my senses.

"I don't mean disrespect. I just don't appreciate getting slapped in front of *mine*."

He thought for a second then pulled the blade away and stood back.

"I understand. I will give you one more chance to tell me what I want to know before I kill *your* crew." He pulled a sidearm and aimed it at my friends. Apparently fun and social niceties were over.

"OK, OK." I held up my hands in surrender. "We found you by accident."

"Just careening around the galaxy with no plan or goal. I don't find that remotely believable." He leveled the gun.

"No, wait. We weren't looking for you! My God, who would do such an insane thing?"

"You would be surprised. I have a substantial bounty on my head by the Galactic Council. Alive or dead, they don't seem to care which. So you're right, Mr. Bosch, who would be crazy enough to try and find me? Bounty hunters, that's who!" He took aim though more for dramatic effect and stalling as he could vaporize anyone at such a short distance with even the most casual of pointing.

"Do we look like bounty hunters?"

"Of course not. My scullery crew looks more like bounty hunters. But that is just the ruse I would suspect a bounty hunter to use to put me off my guard." I began to get the feeling this guy was rather paranoid. But I guess in his line of work it would be warranted.

"It seems to me the more I argue we aren't bounty hunters the more it will convince you that we are," I reasoned. "So I cannot possibly change your mind."

"Why don't you tell me what reason you would have to be in Farnok space and I'll judge what your profession really is."

"We are seeking the Lost Package of Dehrholm Flatt," I announced with disgust. Behind me I heard A1 bleat a complaint.

He let the gun fall to his side and looked at me. There was a tense minute and then he started laughing. When he stopped he looked back at me, eyes wet from his outburst, and then started again. After several minutes he finally managed to compose himself and wiped at his damp cheeks. "Oh, Argon. I have not laughed that hard in years."

My disgust only deepened. "I am glad I could amuse you."

"Indeed you have. The Lost Package. What a rube. I should just release you and let the Raiders take you. It would be a better end than the sad state you will be when you and your happily confused cohorts finally destroy yourselves in that miserable falsehood."

"How magnanimous of you," I said dryly.

He raised his eyebrows. "Oh, it wouldn't be out of any misplaced charity. More pity - even from my black heart. What an utter dolt you must be."

"Now wait a minute. It isn't my idea." I pointed my thumb over my shoulder in A1's direction. "It's that old coot's insane idea. I just got pulled along for reasons I still don't understand."

He smirked and said, "That's even better. You can't even extricate yourself from a mad old man and a fool's quest. I don't think any bounty hunter I would need to fear would be capable of such a pitiful cover."

I smiled. Who cares what this reprobate pirate thinks as long we aren't a danger.

"So we can just leave then?"

"Oh no, Argon, my friend. We're still going to kill all of you. Did you forget?" He gave me a sinister grin that was blood chilling. "We're fucking pirates."

CHAPTER 12

"**W**hat is that smell?" I asked rhetorically. We were all standing around in a dark, dank pirate dungeon cell. And it smelled horrible.

"I suppose it is whatever is left of the last person that was in here," suggested A1.

"Alright. I guess it's not that bad then." I glared at him but he wasn't looking at me to notice. Doon wandered over and looked me over.

"You're quite a mess, Argon."

He was right. I didn't have the benefit of a mirror but I had a visual in my mind that I was pretty sure was a good approximation of how I appeared. I could feel the crusted blood still itching on my upper lip and chin and my ribs were a constant ache with each breath. I looked down at my left wrist and it had swollen into something belonging on another, much larger body. My knee still throbbed and my shoulder felt stiff and angry. At least I wasn't having to cradle it any longer. And to top it off I had fallen into a pool of something wet and rancid smelling when they pushed me into the room. Sure, I didn't look too good but now I smelled even worse.

"What are we going to do?" asked Doon. I felt bad for him. He had always been a great friend and I had come to the realization quite some time ago that in the universal friend equation he came up short on the reciprocation part. He'd stuck with me through everything since we met and all I did was leave him behind when I could have used him the most.

I WASN'T SURE WHERE DOON was but I couldn't even be bothered to try and find him. I'd had it and I just wanted to be left alone and sure as hell didn't want his sympathy and reassurance that everything was going to be fine. It wasn't. Ever. And if anyone tried to convince me otherwise I would have no part of it and likely punch them in the jaw for the effort. Misery loves company. Bullshit. When you are really down and feeling like the whole Universe is out to just beat you with sticks you don't want help, you don't want pity, and you sure as hell don't want somebody trying to blow happy tidings up your ass. You simply want to be alone and find someway, anyway, to forget about everything. At that low point in your life the most desirable thing is a coma. At least that was how I felt.

I had all my gear packed and I had sold everything else I couldn't carry. Along with the coin I managed to weasel out of the insurance company after the Nir'don had exploded I had a tidy little sum that would last me quite awhile. I needed to use it to make a stake in what would be my next endeavor but with my black mood enveloping me wholly I couldn't focus on anything other than the Now. And that Now consisted of getting drunk and renting some female company. It solved nothing but made me forget for awhile. And that is all I ever wanted.

I had already pushed Fig away from me and set her adrift in some kind of broken hearted world. She'd never forgive me and deep down I never wanted her to. Doon had walked away well before then and was now off somewhere trying to turn his Blag fortune into a business. Fig had done it already - used her income from Blag to set up a transport service and knowing her it was going to be a success. That was what had driven the final nail for me. They had both come into a cargo ship load of credits and I couldn't feel good for them. I didn't get my share and I resented them for it. Of course it wasn't their fault but I couldn't use the reality of the facts to get past the feeling of disappointment and betrayal. We grew up together and were inseparable friends but at that point in my life I wanted nothing to do with them.

DOONBRIDGE SPIERLOK? It didn't sound like a name anyone would ever have. Turned out he was half Obarnee - mother's side. His father had met his mother when she visited Earth in the early days of The Introduction, when our entire race suddenly discovered that we were very far from being alone in the Universe. It was a chaotic and, as my parents had explained it to me, a hugely exciting time. Over the course of a few days we discovered an alien base on the moon, made first contact with aliens of several races (the envoy that came to Earth when they knew their secrecy was gone), were exposed to technology eons beyond what we had, and found out that when it came to the Galactic Community, we were looked upon like some isolated South Pacific Island tribe. I was seven at the time. To me it was a crazy sci-fi movie come to life. I just hoped there would be action figures (there were)!

Doon's dad, Deter, like many human males (or Terran, as we grew to call ourselves - using the term "human" to include all races that had our general appearance), became obsessed with the exotic qualities of alien females. He was a prominent scientist and was drafted to the international council that was assigned the responsibility of working with the alien scientists that helped teach us about our new Galaxy Community and the technical wonders it offered. It was there he met his future wife, Dimcha. She was Obarnee and their female anatomy was not only compatible with Terran but had the extra benefit of four breasts and a very distinct yellow coloring that offset their ebony hair and eyes in a certain sensual way. It was not long after they met that

Doonbridge was born. Rumors had been circulating that a Terran could not impregnate an Obarnee so both Deter and Dimcha were quite surprised. Later they married and as Earth's first inter-planetary marriage it sparked some controversy. The uproar in the more conservative media, desperate to show our galactic benefactors in a bad light, snapped on this like a rabid piranha. Before he knew it Deter and his wife were unable to lead their normal lives and he soon lost his position on the council. When the opportunity arose for volunteers to leave earth and start a new colony on Blag they jumped on it. Doon, named after Dimcha's grandfather, was only one when the ship left Earth. But I didn't meet Doon until he was six.

I was aware of him because he hung around with Fig who happened to hang around with me. She was nine and had this habit of always being wherever I happened to be. Like her I didn't have any siblings of my own so after our encounter on the trip to Blag she kind of became my unofficial sister. She didn't show a lot of interest in me until right around the time she turned nine and then I couldn't get rid of her. Not that I wanted to. She was funny and we had shared enough common history to be comfortable around each other. And then, one day, there was Doon strolling along the walkway next to Fig. He had lighter hair than an Obarnee and his coloring resembled more of a jaundice than their distinct yellow coloring. He was thin and tall for his age so overall he just looked sickly. But he had this wide grin that was infectious and often times, in the years to come, would help drag me out of some foul mood.

Fig waved at me. "Argon!"

"Hi, Galaxia." It was still a long time and a lot of crazy history before she picked up the nickname "Fig."

"This is my friend Doonbridge Spierlok," she announced motioning toward the boy standing next to her.

"*Dune Bridge Spear Lock?*" I repeated. "What kind of name is that? It sounds like a bad anagram of a real name."

"He's Obarnee," she revealed.

I was about to call bullshit given his appearance but he suddenly said, "*Half* Obarnee. My Dad is Terran."

"Guess that makes sense then."

Fig looked at Doon and explained excitedly, "Argon is super cool. He can fly a duster!" A *duster* was a small flying craft that we used on Blag to spread anti-fungal dust across fields of the ever encroaching moss-like mold to try and kill it off. If only we knew then what we would find out later we would have been doing the opposite.

He looked up at me with an expression of awe. I found it uncomfortable. "Not that big a deal, Doonbridge."

"Call me Doon. All of my friends do."

"Uh, sure." I looked at both of them. "So what're you both up to?"

"Just wanted to see what you were doing and thought we could all hang out together," said Fig. I was just about to go check in with my boss on any work he had for me. I had picked up a part time job with Halley's Dusting Service a few months previously and even though I was young my ability to fly a duster got me some sporadic work. Despite my age I was one of their better pilots and could often have better luck navigating some of the rougher areas. The pay was pretty good for a teenager and it gave me something to do on our new Homeworld. Our city, Freeport, was as boring a place for a kid as I could imagine at the time so piloting a speedy little flyer was a welcome diversion. And it seemed to impress both Fig and Doon quite a bit. Years later, after Fig and I were involved in our first romance, she confessed to me that she had a huge crush on me and the fact that I was a pilot had a large part in that. She even told me her desire to be a pilot was born from that feeling and her desire to impress me. Go figure.

"I have to check in at work and see if I have to make any runs."

"Can we come along?" asked Fig.

"I, uh…"

"Yeah!" shouted Doon. "It would be so cool!"

"I guess so."

"And maybe you could give us a ride?" hinted Fig eagerly.

"Wait a sec," I looked at Fig. "You weren't supposed to tell people about that. I could get in big trouble!" Dusters were a single occupant craft and flying with a passenger (sitting on your lap) was against all the rules and I could lose my license if found out.

She looked up at me sheepishly. "I'm sorry. I just had to tell Doon. It is just so great to be flying with you."

I gave her a momentary glare and then switched too Doon. "You'd better not tell anyone," I warned.

"I won't," he said. "But I would just love to fly with you just once. Please?"

"No. Don't even think about it." I said as threatening as I could. "And don't ever ask again!"

They both bowed their heads and looked at the ground.

I quickly felt bad for them and added, "You can come with me and if I have a run you can watch me. But no rides! Understand?" They nodded reluctantly finding some joy in the simple possibility of nearness to my ship.

Sure enough. I checked in and I had a run waiting for me. A tricky one just outside of Freeport near the mountains. I looked over the specs of the job and then headed for the landing pads to ready my duster. Fig and Doon loitered outside while I was checking in and then raced along beside me as I headed for the ships. They were like kids at the circus.

After finishing the preflight checks I opened the cockpit and started to climb aboard. I looked down at them and gave a little salute. They both still wore giant smiles but I could tell disappointment was hanging heavily at the corners of their mouths. Looking at them my steely resolve began to erode in the flow of their pure childhood exuberance. I glanced around and saw the area was empty of any other pilots. "OK, c'mon Fig. Saddle up."

She practically beamed with happiness and then she looked over at Doon. I could see her mind working and conflict cross her face. "I think Doon should go," she offered.

"What?" he choked.

"Fig?"

"I've been up with you a buncha times. Doon's never flown before. I think he should get a chance."

I was surprised at her unselfishness. It was a trait I would later find I loved in her. But at that point it just seemed out of character for a nine year old. "Are you sure?"

"Yes," she said firmly.

I looked around again and then motioned to Doon. "Climb on up, buddy." He hesitated for just a second, as if he wasn't sure it was actually okay with Fig and I then he scurried up the ladder like a squirrel on an oak tree.

I climbed in and had him plop down on my lap. I buckled us in and then closed the cockpit bubble. "Here we go," I exclaimed and he let out an excited giggle.

Flying a duster was almost automatic to me, requiring very little actual concentration as the ship just felt like a natural extension of myself. It was a great feeling soaring through the sky. Like nothing else in the world.

Soon we were over the target area and I needed to start my approach. I've been told that it is similar to an old operation on Earth called crop dusting. I am sure that had something to do with the term "duster" being attached to these small craft. Just come in low and spray out a load of chemicals that would try to inhibit the growth of the mold. I didn't think it ever did much good but it made me money and gave people hope that they had some control over their difficult environment.

I did the first few runs without even thinking. Standard stuff. Drop in close, unload the dust, close the dump vents, climb, turn, do it again. Simple. But then I drew close to the mountain and the wind started to create an updraft I was not expecting. On the next pass a sudden gust caught my starboard wing and the ship started to corkscrew. I could have fought it and compensated for the lift but it would have required me to end my pass prematurely and I'd have to try and make up for the area I missed. So I let the wind push me into a roll-over and then I remembered that Doon was on my lap and definitely not prepared for such a maneuver. Too late. We rolled.

And he laughed and laughed.

I was shocked that this little kid wouldn't freak out or get sick or both. Instead he was laughing through the whole thing and then said,

"Again!" when we leveled off. It made me smile.

"Seriously?"

"Yeah!" he shouted between gasps of laughter.

On the next pass I could feel a few more updrafts pushing at my port wing. I let them and used the force to corkscrew through most of the pass. Even I felt a little nauseous after that one but then suddenly grew concerned for Doon thinking I had probably scared him with my careless showboating. He was quiet and I could feel him trembling. I raised my goggles and looked around at his face. I then realized that he was laughing so hard he couldn't even make a sound and his whole body was shaking from the effort. Finally he let out a huge, exhausted gasp and chortled with glee. I started laughing myself. This kid was fearless! I worked in some other moves during the runs that had me rolling, diving, and slipping sideways through the sky. I even roared high into the atmosphere and did an inverted stall, letting the ship fall out from under us simulating zero Gs. He would only laugh harder each time.

A half hour later we landed on the field and I popped the hatch. Doon shot out of the cockpit and raced to Fig. "It was the best! The. Best!" he yelled. He started to dance around and laugh. Fig just looked from me to him and smiled.

I got down and started for the office to sign off on the job when he came running up to me. I turned around and he latched onto my leg. "Easy, Doon. I have to turn in my keys. Stay here, okay?"

He clung tightly for a moment then finally let go. He looked up at me, cheeks flushed, wet tears still balanced in his eyes, and said, "Thanks Argon! That was the best time I've ever had ever!" Then he ran off towards Fig.

I turned and headed into the office feeling pretty special. I never had a little brother until that day.

BEING IN THE PIRATE PRISON was making everyone edgy. My wrist was numb from pain as long as the swelling didn't deflate. So I sat myself in the corner and laid it gingerly across my lap. I tried not to think about it or the fate of our disenchanted little group. We had been standing around in here for half a day and while we had discussed ideas for escape they all seemed to fall between sitcom slapstick goofiness and overblown spy movie impossibility. Nothing feasible came from it so eventually we grew into silence and went to separate corners. I suggested sleep but there was no way that was going to happen. I looked across at Fig and saw she was staring at me with a strange look on her face. When I caught her eye she looked away and wouldn't glance back my way no matter how long I watched. Finally Doon walked over and sat down next to me.

"What's eating her?" I asked.

"You really don't know, do you?"

I looked at him and furrowed my brow having no idea what he was referring to. "No," I admitted. "I have not one single clue."

He gave me a sad little smile. "That actually explains a lot."

"Spill it, Mr. Detective. What am I in the dark about?"

"The same things you are always in the dark about."

"You are making my head hurt, Doon. You're reminding me of A1." I glanced over at the old coot and saw him leaned back against the wall, sleeping. Figured.

"Yet another thing you don't have a clue about."

"Stop talking if you want to talk in riddles and insinuations of my ignorance. I don't need any more of that shit. In case you haven't noticed I am beat to hell, stuck in some godforsaken pirate dungeon waiting to die, and there is next to nothing I can do about it." He just looked at me with some kind of placating sad smile. "And did I mention I am soaked with something horrible?"

He wrinkled his nose. "I noticed."

"So I don't need any mysterious double talk to make it even worse. If you know something helpful now would not be the time to be coy."

"It's your inability to read people."

"I think I read people fine. It is part of my job."

"No. Your job is to deliver packages. Your job is to get things done."

"I still have to read people," I continued to argue.

"Well, I know that if that was your only job you would be broke."

"That's a fine thing to say."

"I'm trying to not be coy, like you said."

"Smart ass."

"If you have to be an ass it's best to be a smart one. Or a rich one." He gave me a nudge. "Isn't that what you always used to tell me?"

I smiled. "Yeah." Then I looked at him, "But maybe *you* don't need to be an ass." He understood. "Now, level with me. What am I not seeing? Who can't I read? Fig?"

With no warning the door burst open and Rink SanDyer walked in followed by a half dozen grizzled, mean looking pirates.

A1 was sitting right near the door and with no hesitation SanDyer gave him a sharp kick to his leg and said, "Get up, old man." A1 let out a grunt and started to get to his feet. I got up as quickly as I could. I guessed this was how it was going to start: grab each one of us one at a time and then lead us off never to be seen again. Torture. Rape. Death. I wasn't going to go out without a fight. I balled up my fist and started forward. The SanDyer looked straight at me. "I want to know about Dehrholm's package."

I was stunned. I thought for sure he was coming in to personally select each of us, taking great joy in our fear and dread. "Why?" I asked.

"I have some interest in this missing package. It is the thing of myth and folklore. A value as priceless as any I have ever acquired. Should you, by some strange happenstance, actually know the whereabouts of this prize I would be a fool to let that secret die with you."

"Guess that makes sense," I muttered.

He drew close to me. "I take it you are the leader of this," he glanced back at the others, "...crew?" His mocking and derogatory tone impossible to miss.

"I wouldn't go so far as to say leader but I am the reason they are here together."

"Fair enough. Will you tell me where this package is?"

"I would, honest, but I don't know."

"So. You are a liar as well as a reluctant leader," he insinuated.

"No. We are on a quest to get the damn thing but I don't know where it is."

"A fool's errand then. Guards, kill them all. I have no use for them."

"Wait!" I shouted. He turned back toward me, eyeing me curiously. "I don't have all of the details but that is because it wasn't my idea to go get it."

"Then who?" I pointed at A1 who then gave me a mean stare. "The old man?" he said with some surprise.

"I ain't that old," called out A1.

Rink SanDyer slowly walked towards A1, never letting his eyes waver from his destination. Like watching an animal stalk its prey. "So, what do you know about this? Will you tell me where the package is?"

I will give A1 credit. He never once failed to meet SanDyer's intense gaze and stood straight revealing no sign of fear. "I don't know if I *would* tell you but I know I can't."

"You show a lot of backbone, old man. But backbones can be broken...in many painful ways. I am curious if I can pick out just the right one for you."

"You can torture me all you want but in the end I won't tell you because I can't."

"Some ancient oath perhaps? Maybe a promise to a long lost loved one? It matters not. Once I have completed my work all of your secrets will be laid bare, along with most of your internal organs." He gave a little chuckle at his play on words. A1 just continued to keep his head held high but I was feeling a little sick.

"SanDyer!" I yelled and he spun towards me. "Look. He actually can't tell you because the location hasn't been revealed to him yet."

"Some kind of vision quest? A holy journey led by some spiritual being?" he laughed. "Pathetic. Guards, I tire of this. Kill them quickly." He raised a finger. "But...keep the old man's head. I want to mount it on the wall to remind me of the foolishness of not instantly killing anyone that boards my ship."

"Would you just listen to him?" I offered. "You've nothing to lose."

"Except my patience." He swung back to A1 and slowly placed his hand on the top of his head. When his face was inches from A1's he said, "Talk to me, old man."

"No one knows the whole thing," explained A1. "There are just people that know parts and when you know enough parts, you can find the package."

"And you know all these parts, I suspect?"

"No, of course not. But I do know how to find the parts."

SanDyer thought for a moment then said, "This is all far too convenient. I don't think you know anything. It is a simple ruse to avoid me killing your entire hapless band of halfwits."

"Why would we chance crossing through Farnok space if we didn't need to?" I asserted. "It wouldn't make sense."

The dread pirate looked back at me. "I'm not expecting sense out of any of you. There are plenty of lost fools who stumble across my path. They all have a story and I find the ending always the same."

"Which is?"

"I grow bored and they grow dead," he said with a hint of dry humor flavoring his more matter-of-fact tone. "And I am getting oh so bored right now. Guards..."

"I think you need to believe them," came a voice from beyond the door. Then Zyryn crowded into the room with her three constant companions. The one in the scarlet shirt seemed wary and nervous like he was expecting danger at any second. "Twitchy" would have been a good name for him.

SanDyer looked shocked and a bit annoyed. "Why are you here?"

"I just have a feeling these people actually might be onto something. I think they may really have some clues as to where the package is."

"Based on what?" he asked. "Some vague intuition, I suppose."

"Yes," she confessed. "But you know I have been right before.

Remember when I knew we shouldn't board that Reen freighter yet you took a crew there anyway and were almost captured? There were a lot of times that happened."

SanDyer seemed angry at her defense. "Even a blind prok finds a bleed nut once in awhile. You just get lucky. I will put no stock in your damned intuition beliefs." She began to argue but SanDyer raised his hand in finality. "Quiet," he commanded. "I will have no more of this talk." Silence fell across everyone and he looked deeply at A1 before turning and walking toward me. He stopped, took one more look around the room, then faced me.

"I am not going to kill you...yet." he announced. "I will give you a chance to find this package. If you succeed, which I highly doubt, you will bring it back here to me and I will let you live. If you fail to deliver the package within one week I will see to it that you are all killed immediately."

"You are going with us then?" I guessed.

He laughed his amused laugh. "Of course not. Do you really think I have the time and necessary patience to travel around the galaxy with the likes of you? I'd likely kill you all before we even left the system out of simple annoyance. No, I will not be going along on your moronic journey. But I will send someone along to make sure you do what you say you are going to do. And if you fail, those I send will ensure my threat is carried out."

"What if your goons get a little too rambunctious and end up killing us just for sport?" I questioned. "I don't like the idea of traveling across space with a bunch of simple minded, loose cannons on our ship. It is a recipe for disaster."

"That is why I am sending someone I trust to make sure things go as I want them to."

"And how do I know I can trust you? You could just kill us as soon as we find the package."

"You can't trust me. I'm a pirate, remember? But I could just as well kill you now and not have to give you a second thought. I don't think you have two clues to string together into a plan so I have nothing to lose. But *you* might have something to gain. Your choice."

"I wouldn't consider it a choice, more like a lack of choice. But we'll take it. Which scary henchman are you saddling us with?"

"No henchman. I am sending Zyryn, my daughter."

My eyes flew to Zyryn and I could tell she did not seem overjoyed with SanDyer's decision. He turned to look back at Zyryn. "No arguments I assume? It is basically your idea."

She looked at him for a minute in silence then I could see surrender overtake her. "Of course. I will take my men and we will make sure they deliver the package."

"To me," he added. "They deliver the package *to me*."

"Yes. To you."

"Splendid."

I looked at Zyryn and then her three stooges. "That's eight people. It is going to be a little crowded."

"If you'd like I can hold one of your crew behind. Perhaps this lovely lady," he threatened, looking salaciously at Fig.

"No!" I instantly shouted. He spun surprised. "I mean...it is her ship. She's the only one that can really fly it, especially if we are going anywhere dangerous. Which I'm sure we are."

His look only darkened. "It would be good insurance to hold her here then, I think."

"I thought you trusted your daughter to enforce your will. If she isn't up to the task then maybe you need to pick someone else," I suggested rather more boldly than I should have.

That seemed to anger him but I sensed that the anger wasn't directed at me.

"Fine! Take your whole damned crew. But don't you dare disappoint me." He spun and glared at me.

"Uh...sure. Won't be doing that," I assured him while not having the least bit of faith that we would find the cursed item.

"Zyryn," he called out. "Gather up these fools and get underway at once. I am annoyed and feel the need to kill someone."

"Yes, sir," she muttered.

Rink SanDyer started for the door and then stopped again in front of A1. He looked him up and down. "I hope for your friends' sakes that you up to the task, old man."

"Close enough, I think," replied A1.

"You have some character, I must admit. I don't trust you but I think you know more than you are letting on and in that I think you might get further than most."

"Well, I think so."

"What is your name, curmudgeon?"

At that moment I felt like I needed to just run despite the fact that I would get shot down before reaching the door. I just didn't want to see the slow motion train wreck I knew was coming. Even death seemed a more favorable choice. I silently mouthed the word "No" at A1 as emphatically as I dared.

"Abraxas Wun, pirate."

"Like the number?" asked SanDyer.

Shit.

"I don't know of a number abraxas?" came the hackneyed reply.

I hoped I had been wrong; that his practiced joke was far funnier than I had ever imagined. I prayed that my sense of humor was undeveloped and lacked any recognition of wit. That somehow I was the stupid one that couldn't find the humor in the phrasing. Oh PLEASE! I squeezed my eyes together fearful of the inevitable outcome.

There was silence.

And then...laughter.

I snapped my eyes open and looked at SanDyer ever hopeful that the peals of laughter were issuing from his mouth. But no. He wasn't laughing. He wasn't even smiling. He turned and looked toward Zyryn. One of her lackeys was howling. Doubled over. Chortling, if ever there was a person who chortled. It was "Twitchy," the guy in the red shirt.

SanDyer pulled his blaster out, said, "That isn't fucking funny," and shot Twitchy without any hesitation. There was a loud ZAP! noise, a flash of brilliance, and a puff of smoke where he had stood a second before. Zyryn looked next to her in silent shock.

"Not the least bit funny," remarked SanDyer. "Anyone else think that was funny?"

"Hell no!" I said, shaking my head vigorously. "No matter how many times I hear it."

"Fine." He spun on A1. "I hear you say that again and I will burn your head off with a construction torch."

Sounded about right.

"Uh, sure," agreed A1.

"Bob?" I heard Zyryn say quietly looking at the small dust pile next to her.

SanDyer holstered his weapon and remarked to no one in particular, "I do feel a little better now." He turned back to A1 and said, "We clear, old man?"

A1 got a sudden mean squint in his eyes and replied. "One day I am going to kill you."

SanDyer seemed nonplused by the statement as if he heard it everyday. "If you really feel that way you best find that Package. Otherwise, I don't think we'll ever be seeing each other again." He then looked at his daughter. "And you best get on your way." He gave a passing glance at the smoldering pile that was Bob. "Always hated the color red," and was gone out the door.

After a moment I headed for the door as well. "Guess it won't be *quite* as crowded." Fig punched me in the shoulder and gave me a scowl.

As we started for the landing bays and the Sononi Heart I heard Zyryn say behind me, "Bob."

CHAPTER 13

We cleared Rink SanDyer's ship and The Blanket without incident. From what I was assuming was a desire to keep me in good enough shape to accomplish the task, SanDyer had allowed me use of the ship's medical facility before we left. I was sure it wasn't due to any sense of sympathy or humanitarian aid on his part. The MedBay was far from what I had expected. I had pictured some disgusting, dimly lit room with blood stained floors and the occasional finger or toe lying about. But it was clean and in good working condition with a couple of people on staff that had more than a passing knowledge of anatomy for several races. They were patching up a Brott when I entered and those people are not easy to look at, let alone sew up. What would one use to bandage up an incision with all that nasty slime? Before long they had me close to good as new with just a small wrap on my wrist and a small bandage across my nose.

We got an escort of pirate ships to accompany us across Farnok space lest any of the Raiders decided to give us another go. The last I heard from SanDyer was a brief transmission as we headed into space.

"I have assigned two ships to insure you leave the region unscathed. You have 10 days, Bosch. Then Zyryn is ordered to kill all of you in anyway she fancies. So I will next see you with the package or dead. Should I not hear from Zyryn after that time I will assume you have killed her and run off to hide. At that point I *will* hunt you down myself and *when* I find you, believe me, it will not be merciful or quick. In fact, a part of me hopes you try and escape. It could possibly be even more rewarding than some dusty, old box." And then he was gone. A shiver raced up my spine and I hoped nothing happened to Zyryn despite her orders to kill us when we failed.

Yes, I fully expected us to fail in finding the Lost Package. This was due to my firm belief, imparted to me by my old friend, Ord, that the stupid thing didn't exist. It was a fairytale. It was an urban myth of galactic proportions. It would be the equivalent of finding the body of the prophet Kreey d'nas Uilghnsi or the mystical planet Qwee. Such things have circulated for far longer periods than the Lost Package of Dehrholm Flatt. And they were quite a bit more interesting. So A1's fixation on this sham of a quest had now officially doomed us all. The only bright spot in all of this was the tiny satisfaction I would get in the last few moments of my miserable life when I could give him one hell of an "I told you so!" Not quite enough to make me happy. But close.

After several hours flying uneventfully through Farnok space I went to look for Fig. I knew she was on the Bridge piloting her ship and I thought I could finally get some time to talk to her. I was in the engine room checking on the Gravity Drive. Being the most technically knowledgeable person on board, doing a little preventive maintenance couldn't hurt. It also kept my mind off the horrors that would surely befall my friends within a week's time.

As I started up the ladder I was stopped by another person coming down. It turned out to be Zyryn without her usual entourage - minus Bob, of course. I backed up and bounced off a bulkhead. The woman just made me that uncomfortable.

"Hey," I said. "Where are your bodyguards?"

"They are not bodyguards. My father has them follow me around though I am sure it is not for my safety." Just standing there talking to her for a couple seconds was causing my hands to sweat. My inclination was not to look directly at her to prevent me from staring but I couldn't. She was hypnotizing in her beauty and while I didn't know anything about her, I got the strong impression that she was not comfortable in her own skin. That only succeeded in making her more attractive.

"Why do you say that?" I asked thinking it was a strange admission concerning her father.

"Because I don't think he would ever think to keep me safe. Most likely the reason he insisted I escort your crew..."

"They're not my crew."

"Friends, then."

"Better, though A1..."

She shifted uncomfortably and gave me a sigh. "Regardless, I think he sent me with you so that whatever happens to you on this foolish journey will also do me in."

"First off," I started, "I am happy to hear that you think this is foolish. I enjoy the dose of sanity. And, secondly, why would your own father not care about your welfare? I know he is...well, um..."

"Evil?" she offered.

"Uh...yes."

"Sadistic?"

"Fair enough."

"A stone cold killer and the most feared man in the Galaxy?"

"If you want to label him - sure."

"Well, here is a little known fact: he is also the worst father in the entire galaxy. Maybe in the Universe."

"Now that's a real claim to fame." I tried smiling but she didn't reciprocate. Her statement was made as sad fact and not unpleasant exaggeration.

"I'm not kidding. He is a real bastard." There was a profound sadness that hung behind her eyes; one I sensed had been there most of her life. She was Rink SanDyer's daughter, a card carrying member of the Xydoc Zyn, most assuredly a murderer, and right now the woman most likely to shoot me dead in a few days time. Yet I found myself feeling pity for her.

"OK, we can agree on most of the words we have used to describe your father but how mean can he really be to his own flesh and blood? Maybe your view is colored by the environment you were raised in?"

She scowled at me," You know *nothing!*" Then she turned and raced up the steps of the ladder.

I stayed behind for a few minutes. Something told me not to pursue her. I half feared she would be at the top of the stairs, crying, and then either fall into my arms for comfort or shoot me out of embarrassment. Either way, it would not turn out well for me.

After enough time had passed I cautiously climbed the ladder to the passageway and peered about. She was gone. I decided not to head for the Bridge. Between Zyryn's running off suddenly upset and Fig's odd behavior I didn't feel any desire to be around any females. So I figured maybe I'd go try and finish that conversation with Doon. Actually, at that point I might have considered a light-hearted talk with A1. Well...maybe not.

I hadn't gotten through the Galley when I encountered one of Zyryn's thug friends (*not* a bodyguard). The other one drifted up behind him from the adjoining passageway.

"Where's Zyryn, asshole?" he barked. Along with his rancid breath, his general demeanor was also quite unpleasant. His head, along with his buddy's, was shaved. I would have thought it might be some sign of solidarity given Zyryn's bald head but poor, unfortunate Bob had sported a healthy mane. The man also displayed a few deep scars across his face and neck and had a long, curved moustache which end's hung below his chin. I had already taken note of his look on SanDyer's ship and, while I still didn't know his name, I had started to recognize him as "Stash." I also had noticed his mostly silent friend had a large skull tattooed on the back of his shaved head so I had come to think of him as "Skully."

"Aren't you supposed to be watching her, fellow asshole?"

He growled at me like some B-movie henchman and looked back at his partner then to me. "Shut your face. Now where is she?"

I didn't respond.

"I said where is she? You better answer me or I will gut you right here."

"You told me to shut my face. I can't respond if you say that."

He growled again and pulled a very nasty blade from a sheath on his hip and leaned in. "Just tell me."

I raised my hands in surrender and said, "OK, OK...easy. I don't know where she is. I talked to her a moment ago and she ran off. I don't know why or where she went. Now put that thing away before there is an accident."

He studied me for a few seconds and my pulse quickened at his hesitation. Then he finally jammed the knife back into its sheath while continuing to scowl. The moment was made even worse since he was a dedicated mouth-breather. I thought he looked Terran but I didn't know of any Earth dish that would produce such a fetid stench.

"What'd you say to her?" asked his colleague. From where I stood I got a clue they had shared some recent meal.

"She was talking about her dad. I didn't say anything."

They looked at each other and nodded as if some insight was clarified then they left without another word. I stood there for a few minutes hoping the drama quotient for the day had been satisfied and then made my way toward the crew quarters. Maybe A1 *would* be good for a chat.

I encountered Doon inside the lounge area. He was alone, sitting quietly reading something on a D-pad. As I entered he raised his head and then smiled a greeting. "Is it safe in here?" I asked.

He raised an eyebrow, "Why? What happened now?"

I explained about Zyryn and my encounter with her minions. He nodded, "Sounds like she has some issues."

"You think?"

"Well, she is a space pirate after all. That might make a person less stable."

"I think it is more than that. Some kind of father issues. But I don't have time for extra drama, seeing as we all are going to..." Uncharacteristically I stopped talking before I blurted out something that would not be sensitive to Doon's feelings. I wasn't used to being so mannered so I didn't know what to say to finish the thought.

"We are all going to what?" he asked after a moment.

"Uh...have a hard enough time finding that blasted package. We need to focus on the task at hand and not get a lot of distractions with some pirate's personal issues. Don't you think so?"

"Sure. We have to get that package! We will, won't we, Argon?"

"Of course. We have the old team together again, right?" He nodded to me emphatically. "And we have tackled worse than this, right?" Doon nodded again. "So how could we fail?" He shrugged. I put my hand on his shoulder and said, "I will make sure we will, Doon. You know that about me."

He looked down sheepishly. "Uh, sure."

"What?"

When he looked up that grin was gone. "You just left me, Argon. I really could have used your help a few times but you left. I didn't know how to get ahold of you. But I always thought that any time now you were going to just pop up and save the day. But you never did. Fig said you'd come back soon but after 5 years she stopped saying that. Then after another 5 years neither of us even looked for you to show up. That was hard. Really hard. I missed you a lot. I am glad you are here now and we are off on another adventure but I keep thinking that once we find the package you'll be gone again and I may never see you again."

"Doon..." I started.

"You hurt us both really badly, Argon. I don't think Fig ever got over it but I know that she is thinking the same thing I am: How long until he is gone again?"

And what was it I had just said about not needing any more drama? Man, I sure didn't need to hear all of that. Doon was essentially my little brother and I had flat out abandoned him. While I was extremely surprised that he took me back and welcomed me with open arms, I knew then that his pain was much deeper than what he portrayed. I had hurt him bad and I felt I would not get the opportunity to make it up to him. But I swore right then that I would do everything within my power to safeguard him through this and I would also do whatever I could to get him away from this disaster alive and healthy.

"I'm not going anywhere, buddy. We are in this together and after we recover that thing I promise I will not disappear."

Magically his grin returned and he suddenly gave me a huge hug. It caught me off guard while at the same time made me feel guilty. My only satisfaction was that I wouldn't have to worry about that last bit. I didn't expect to walk away from this thing.

"You really need to tell that to Fig," he added after he released me.

"I suppose so."

"And maybe throw in an 'I'm sorry' as well."

"Will it help?"

"It can't hurt!"

"Then...I'm sorry," I said to him.

"No. To her, not me."

"No. To *you*. I am sorry, Doon, that I did what I did and that it took until now for me to say that."

"I always knew you were an ass, Argon," he grinned. "But I love you anyway, brother." He shook my hand.

"I love you too, brother." And to my sudden realization I knew I really meant it.

"Now go find Fig and tell her. She *really* needs to hear it."

"I'll do just that."

It was just a couple moments later that I once again encountered Zyryn's lackeys. They were blocking the passageway to the Bridge. The duo gave me a stern look when I approached.

"What's up, boys?"

Stash walked towards me. "We found Zyryn. She wants to see you."

"Uh...fine. I just need to talk to the pilot and then I'll come find her."

"If Zyryn wants to see you, you go now, not later," he explained. "She is in her quarters. We'll take you there."

When the pirate clan moved on board to eventually kill us all, Zyryn SanDyer commandeered Fig's room putting her out amongst the rest of us. The Sononi Heart only had bunk space for six crew besides the Captain so we weren't as roomy as before. Fig had not been happy about the accommodations but she went along with it since the alternative was likely death or being left behind with Rink SanDyer.

"I know where that is and I will come see her as soon as I finish," I said.

"No. Now," he demanded.

"Listen, pal. I am not a prisoner here and I don't answer to you or Mister Personality over there."

"Argue and I will hurt you."

"Hurt me and I will hurt you right back," I challenged. I had had just about enough of these two-bit thugs. Sure, they looked like they would just as soon toss me out an airlock as have to talk to me but I was starting to get pissed off and that never made me very considerate of circumstances or outcomes.

He glanced at Skully and said, "Sounds like arguing." Then he punched me in the side of the head and for a few seconds I was floating in space, not able to feel my body and seeing blackness with sparkles of light. When my brain finally re-entered my body I shook my head, decided that was a mistake, then shook it again using the pain to snap me out of the fog. When my eyes refocused on the pirate he was smiling at me.

"Anything else to say, brim?" Brim was a slang term for useless cargo.

"Just that I think I have a little more argument left in me."

That made him angry and he tried to throw the same punch just as I had hoped. I ducked inside close to him and brought my head up hard underneath his chin. I heard his jaw snap together with a distinct CLACK! and then he staggered back. I had my pistol out before either of them could react. "This is my attorney, Mr. Gun" I nodded to my sidearm. "He can do any further arguing on my behalf."

Stash held up his hands and calmly said, "Easy. No need to pull a weapon. You need to think this through."

"The time for thinking is over."

"No. If you kill us Zyryn will kill *all* of you. She has nothing to lose but a little quicker trip home. If you somehow manage to kill her then you will have the entire Xydoc Zyn after you until you are caught. I

218

think you know what happens then. Right?"

He had me there. My threat was empty and they knew it. Damn how I hated being outsmarted by a pinhead.

"Alright," I said as I lowered my gun. "I'll go with you." I holstered my pistol and followed them to the Captain's quarters.

"Just don't think I will forget you pulled your gun on me cause I won't."

"Whatever," I mumbled.

When we approached the door to the cabin Stash gave it a sharp rap and waited for a response. "Barry?" came Zyryn's voice from inside.

Barry?! What the hell?

"Yes, Madame Zyn. I have Bosch with me."

"Come in," she replied.

"Your name is Barry?" I asked him as he opened the door.

"Problem?" he retorted.

I smiled. "No. None at all. What's his name?" I asked thumbing toward Skully.

"Bruce. Why?"

My smile grew into a grin. "No reason." We entered the room.

Zyryn was sitting in a chair. Her jacket was off and I could see her arms were heavily tattooed from shoulder to wrist with one design continuing down across her chest. The top she wore counted as clothing in only the most forgiving of definitions. The room was not very big and while nicer than the crew quarters it didn't seem very luxurious. Tasteful but not fancy.

"Leave us," ordered Zyryn.

"Are you sure?" asked Barry. Sheesh...*Barry*. A fearsome pirate named Barry. Then it hit me: Barry, Bruce, and *Bob*. I couldn't even make up something that weird.

Zyryn simply glared at him and he and Bruce spun and left, closing the door behind them.

"What do you want with me that's so damn important that you had to have Barry and Bruce run me down here with the threat of killing me if I don't?"

"They threatened you?"

"My head is still a little tender right here," I motioned around the reddish left side of my face, "from a punch he nailed me with."

"Barry!" she yelled.

The door opened and Barry stuck his head in. "Yes?"

"Did you strike Mr. Bosch?"

He looked a little embarrassed. "Yes. He wouldn't..."

"Did I tell you to hit him?"

"No, but..."

"But what, Barry?"

"He wouldn't come with us immediately."

She shook her head. "Did I ask for him to be brought here *immediately*? I said to tell him to come see me as soon as he could. Right?" Even with my immediate dislike of Barry I cringed with the heavy condescension of her remarks.

"I misunderstood, Madame Zyn. I just wanted to make sure..."

"I have told you that my orders are to be followed precisely, Barry. There is no interpretation or improvisation. Right?"

"Yes, Madame Zyn." He hung his head.

"Then leave here and take Bruce with you. When I want you I will come find you."

"Madame..."

"GO!"

The door closed and I heard some muttering in the passageway from Barry and Bruce and then they were gone.

"I still, uh, don't know why you wanted to see me. We shouldn't be at the coordinates for a while yet."

"Sit down, Mr. Bosch." I looked around and there wasn't anywhere else to sit but on the bed as she was occupying the single chair. I sat down and looked at her, then made an effort to look like I was surveying the room so as to *not* to look at her. Something about her made me uncomfortable.

"I needed to apologize for my anger before and to clear the air between us."

"What? Why?" The surprise of her statement forced me to look back at her again.

"Because I was upset and you were only trying to understand me," she explained. "I have some issues with my father and it often makes me upset even when I don't want to be."

"Hey. You don't have to explain anything to me." I raised my hands and looked at her again. "At this point you don't even have to talk to me. Chances are you'll be killing me within a week's time so no need to get chummy."

"Why do you say such things?" She actually sounded sincere. I feared she really thought we were going to find that Package.

"Listen. I'm realistic to the point of pessimism. I don't have any hope of finding this thing. In fact I am pretty damn certain we won't. A1 is an old man with old man dreams. If anything, he is likely senile and doesn't even understand half of what he says. I was along for a sense of obligation and because something important was taken from me and I wanted to get it back."

"What was taken?"

"My ship was stolen right when A1 showed up. We suspect there were some other interested parties that were tailing him in the hopes he would lead them to the Package. My hope was to lure them along and then trick them into thinking we had found it and get my ship back. And my employee."

"Your employee? Where is your employee?"

"It would appear he was taken at the same time as my ship."

"Couldn't he have just taken your ship?" she suggested.

"Uh, no. He's just a brain in a jar. He doesn't have the physical ability to move let alone get to my ship and pilot it."

"A brain in a jar, you say?"

"It is not important."

She concentrated for a moment. "It might be. That seems familiar. What is his name?"

"Winston," I answered.

"Hmmm…" A couple of minutes passed while she contemplated what I had told her.

Finally I broke the uncomfortable silence. "Well, that is all moot as I still imagine being dead before this all gets sorted out."

She looked at me and smiled. I hadn't seen her smile before. I stated I was ill at ease before but that was nothing compared to how I now felt. I just needed to leave as my mind was starting to go in a direction I didn't think it should.

"You are just all doom and gloom, aren't you Mr. Bosch? Or can I call you Argon?"

"Just call me Doomy Gloom, if you want. Right now I don't care."

She continued to smile and then moved to the bed to sit beside me. "You are a strange one."

"I think I should just leave," I croaked and started to get up.

"I don't want you to leave. I called you here for a reason."

I grew more unsettled as she spoke. Her proximity was only adding to the tension. I really needed to get out of that room yet I still furthered the conversation. "And what is that reason?"

She looked down for a moment while she organized her thoughts. At least that was how it seemed. When she finished she looked back up at me and there was that damned sadness again and a tear waiting at the corner of her one visible eye. "You think of me as my father's daughter; a woman...a pirate, born in violence and raised in evil but that is not me. I am not that which you would think I am. And..." he voice caught. "And I don't want you to see me that way." The tear finally fell as she trembled in a sob.

"I'm sorry," I said. "But I don't understand." Then she fell against me and grabbed me as if I was a life raft in a turbulent sea.

I could feel her clinging and fighting to not break down. After a moment she sat back up but would not meet my gaze. "When I was born my father had wanted a son but he got me instead. I was then and would always be a disappointment to him. He hated my mother for giving him a "useless female" as he would say and he hated me as the unwanted daughter."

"That kind of shit still exists? Some dude that can't accept equality in the sexes?"

She sniffed and gave a sad little chuckle. "Oh, you are an odd one alright, Argon." I caught the edge of a smile in her profile. "You are well traveled I assume but naive in your understanding of the galaxy we live in."

"I know there are a lot of different cultures that still draw a harsh line between the sexes but most of the more advanced worlds seem to have mostly put that behind them seeing that only limits possibilities and opportunities."

She reached over and took my hand. "Pirates aren't one of those."

"Really? Seems those blood thirsty murderers would want every person onboard to be wielding either a knife or a gun or some kind of knife-gun."

"Oh, they try and do that but my father will have none of it concerning me. He will have women fight and kill but for his family, it must be a son to carry on the line, be his heir."

"Old school," I mumbled.

"I have spent my whole life trying to change his mind. I dress like one of the men and even shaved off my hair to not remind him I am a woman. Not his son." She paused to gather herself. "I have grown to hate him and despise the things he does."

I sensed that there might be a flaw in SanDyer's plan. "So you aren't going to kill us?"

"That is not what I want. I hope I can convince you that I am not evil and violent. But for now I must put on a facade for Barry and Bruce."

"About that..." I started but she went on.

"They are loyal only to me because of my father's orders. I don't believe he completely trusts me and wants to see what I do in this mission. If I let on that I am against him they will tell him and most likely I will be killed alongside you." She clutched my hand tightly and looked directly into my eyes. "You must help me come up with a plan to stop them and save us all."

Great, another person I have to save. Why not.

"I don't know if I can but I will try."

She smiled with relief and let out a loud sigh. "Thank you. It means the world to me that you will give me a chance. That you will trust me."

Hmmm...trust? I don't think I would go that far yet. But I did sense that she needed me to help her.

She didn't say anything more but continued to look into my eyes. After the silence went on a for a moment or two longer I began to get very uncomfortable and figured I'd best just get up and leave. And then she was kissing me.

It wasn't just a tender little, thank you kiss. No, she was going for it and had her lips tight against mine and her tongue in my mouth. It was not wholly unpleasant. Then she took the hand she had been holding and placed against her breast. Muscle memory took over and I felt myself getting swept up in the moment. Then two things happened at almost the same time. I heard a quiet "click" come from the door. And, at that very moment, she pulled away from me and quickly pulled my hand off of her breast saying, "I can't do this." She turned away from me and started to get up.

I was very confused at her sudden passion and then the equally sudden lack of it. What was going on, I thought. Then I turned my head slightly to see what that noise had been and saw Fig standing in the doorway. "Argon?"

Oh fuck me.

CHAPTER 14

I was off the bed in a shot but still Fig was gone from the doorway already.

"What's wrong?" asked Zyryn noticing the distressed look on my face. "I'm sorry I pulled away. I just...I just got carried away in the moment. I was feeling..."

I didn't wait around for her to finish that idea as I raced for the Bridge to find Fig. Even at my most breakneck pace I couldn't catch sight of her making me think she didn't head back to the Bridge. But she would have to be on the Bridge unless...

The gravity engine was off. I hadn't noticed before but I could hear and feel the difference between the main engine and the pulse drive. She was away from the Bridge because we were in orbit.

Finally I got to the Bridge and she was back at her seat talking on the radio.

"Well, fuck-you very much," she said very sweetly to whoever was on the other end and then disconnected.

"Uh...friends of yours?" I asked timidly.

She spun around and the first thing I noticed was the harsh coldness in her eyes. It was only too obvious that she was genuinely upset but like the tough woman she is it was the only telltale sign that she was bothered at all.

"Our escorts letting me know they were leaving." Her voice was calm and surprisingly not hostile. "I'm sorry I barged in on you earlier. I just wanted to let you know we had reached the coordinates that A1 had given us." She offered a thin-lipped smile that displayed no real emotion.

"Right. Um...about that..."

"You don't need to explain." The same tight, joyless smile.

"No, I should. Zyryn was upset..."

"I am sure she was." immediately, as the last sound exited her mouth the forced smile replaced it.

"No really, Fig. She was upset about her father and I think I may be coming up with a way out of this."

"Terrific." Smile.

"Seriously. I think there is some kind of tension..."

"Sexual tension? I understand." Smile.

"Wait. What?"

"I've seen the way you look at her. You are attracted to her." And...smile.

"Yes, I mean...no. Sure, she is good looking..."

"In a one-eyed, bald pirate kind of way." Her smile was there but it looked like the effort to keep it there was intensifying.

"Now Fig. She might be able to help..."

"I'm sure she would love to help you though, from what I saw, it looked like you were the one trying to help." The smile was definitely losing ground.

"No. I wasn't. I didn't. I mean..."

She stood up and the smile finally fell away leaving only hurt and anger. "Were you trying to take advantage of her?"

"What?"

"You were practically forcing yourself on her!"

"What? No! That's not right. She came onto me!"

"Oh, right. *She* put *your* hand on *her* breast."

"Huh? Oh." I scratched my head. "Come to think of it, yes she did."

She folded her arms and cocked an eyebrow. "Sure she did. She just overpowered you and made you squeeze her tit. Do you really expect me to believe that, Argon? Just be a man and stop lying. Take responsibility. Why try and hide it?"

This was going badly. I knew that if she could just get past her feelings she knew me well enough to know I wouldn't do such a thing. "I'm not, Fig. You have me all wrong. I was on my way up here to talk to you."

"And then you decided to stop by *my* cabin and get a little fresh with the local pirate queen. That is so like you."

"No it's..." My previous several years of existence flashed before me. "OK, maybe a little. But I was on my way to see you. I wanted to talk to you."

"Next time try harder." She paused and then her anger became more apparent. "Actually, scratch that. Don't try at all because I don't want to hear your bullshit. Tell your stories to her if she doesn't mind your brash advances." She stood up and crossed her arms across her chest.

"I am trying to find a way to save us all," I tried to explain.

She smirked. "You overestimate your charm."

"Not like that."

"Well, while you were off making out with a pirate I have been trying to get us to the coordinates that A1 gave us. Plus the whole time I have had to contend with *that*," she said pointing toward a corner of the Bridge.

And there it was. Squirty, Zyryn's pet. It met my gaze with its signature hiss.

"I had forgotten about that thing," I explained.

"I haven't! He has been in here since we left. He won't leave. He just stares at me and makes odd little noises and..." she hesitated.

"And what? And how do you know it is a male?"

She looked at me and I could see color warm on her cheeks. She was embarrassed. I couldn't recall that last time, if there even was one, when I had witnessed Fig embarrassed.

"I, he ..." She couldn't go on.

"I don't get it. What happened? What did it, er...he do?"

She struggled for another moment then she looked down and quietly said, "I think he was...masturbating. While he was looking at me." She glanced back up with an uncomfortable look on her face.

"That horny little fucker." I pulled my pistol.

"Don't shoot him!" she exclaimed. "Do you want Zyryn to kill us all?"

I holstered my gun and said, "I'm not sure I want that thing running around loose. God knows what he is capable of. If anything I want him locked up in Zyryn's, I mean, your cabin." It hissed at me again.

I have always hated these so called "Space Monkeys" since the first time I saw one. I remember encountering one when I was 13 on Blag. A kid at school had purchased one and it followed him around constantly. It was butt-ugly. Disgusting. While they are referred to as monkeys they are neither simian nor even mammalian. They are more closely related to birds having short feathers covering their bodies. Their beak is blunt, short, and rounded giving it a similar look to a chimp's muzzle-like mouth. They have tufts that resemble ears, a long, ropey prehensile tail, claws that have more in common with feet, and arms instead of wings. So, kind of like a monkey with feathers. Their eyes are extra large and bulbous giving them their revolting little faces. The kid on Blag eventually got bit on the back by the thing and it disappeared after that. I didn't see much of their kind until I signed onto the Nir'don. They are a popular pet but I don't trust them and their repugnant ways. Yet after seeing hundreds of the creatures through the years I have never known one to jerk off.

"It won't leave. I've had Doon up here a couple times and A1 once. They tried to coax it off the Bridge with treats but it wouldn't budge. A1 even tried to give it a kick and it looked like it was going to bite him."

"Sounds about right," I mumbled.

"Argon! I'm serious. I think it is attracted to me."

"You think? Was it his long enamored looks or his grabbing his dick?"

"That's not funny."

I couldn't help but smile. "Oh, I think it is." Then the absurdity of it struck her and she started to laugh. I joined in.

"Why is it that every male that falls for me is just some over-hormoned ape?"

I laughed and but abruptly stopped understanding her meaning. "Wait a second..." She just laughed harder.

Then Zyryn walked onto the Bridge. "What's so funny?" She spied Squirty sitting in the corner. "My little boy!" she called. "Where have you been all this time?" He quickly skittered across the deck and leaped into her arms. I hadn't paid much attention before in their interaction but given the previous revelation I couldn't help but notice that Squirty seemed very happy to nuzzle in between Zyryn's breasts while cradled in her arms.

I also noticed that Fig had stopped laughing and her smile was gone.

Zyryn looked at me, "I was worried how you ran after one of your crew. Did she do something wrong?" She glanced dismissively at Fig.

"She is not one of my crew. She owns this ship," I explained.

"So you hired her then."

"Not exactly. She came to help me."

"For a share of the profits." She looked again at Fig. "Shame you got caught up in this unfortunate outcome, isn't it sweetheart?"

The condescension in Zyryn's voice was sandpaper to Fig's ears. I thought I could see it producing smoke.

"No, Zyryn. Fig is a dear friend of mine who dropped everything to come and help me." I had to make some points back with Fig and try and prove there was nothing between me and SanDyer's daughter.

She took no real notice of my comment but just scratched Squirty on the head and turned to leave. "When you sort out whatever this woman's done wrong return to my cabin and we can continue our...talk." And out she went.

I feared looking back at Fig but knew I had to. Surprisingly she was just standing there, looking at the deck with a slightly bemused look.

"I'm sorry about her. I'm sure I got her to rethink your position here."

"Oh, I doubt that. But she is expecting you. Better not keep her waiting. Or Squirty." She walked by me. "I'm going to go let A1 know we have arrived at the first designation." And out she went also.

Well, that had gone just about perfect.

I wasn't sure what I should do but I knew that going to see Zyryn was not one of the options so I finally hurried after Fig to see what A1 had to say. God help us.

"His name is Olovane and he is there," A1 was saying as I walked into the lounge.

"Here?" questioned Fig. I hadn't even taken the time to see where "here" was.

"At the coordinates I gave you, yes."

"There isn't anything here, A1," informed Fig. "I don't see G'toa. Dead Space. Nothing." Then she added, "Unless he is floating around in a space suit."

"Hmmm..." said A1 as if he actually considering it. Crazy bastard. "I wouldn't think so. Let's go check what *is* out there."

We went back to the Bridge and A1 looked out the view screen for a few moments then went and checked the scanners for...a guy in a space suit? Who knows what he could be looking for given his penchant for the absurd.

A1 stood up and marched to the screen again. He quickly scanned an area and then increased the magnification. With a pointing finger he exclaimed, "There!" We all crowded toward the screen to see what he was pointing at.

"An asteroid?" questioned Fig. "He lives on an asteroid?"

"It would appear so," reasoned A1. "That asteroid or planetoid must be G'toa."

"Makes perfect sense," I added.

Fig turned to me, "How so?"

"Because every single bit of this whole thing has been crazy. I can't wait to meet Olovane who I imagine is the mummified remains of a Dirnarian spit weasel."

"Why would he be mummified?" asked A1, scratching at his head to further muss his thin, wispy hair.

"Are you kidding me?" I replied.

He turned toward Fig. "Can you scan that rock and let me know if you find any life signs?"

She shrugged. "I guess so," then turned and went to the scanners. Minutes later she sighed and spun her chair towards us. "There is something there, beneath the surface. An environment and a life sign."

"Let's go then," said A1.

"Wait. How do we get to this sanctuary underground? Burrow?" I looked at Fig and shrugged.

A1 replied, "Well, first we land then we go looking for a way in."

"Fig, how big of a diameter is this thing?"

"Roughly 850 miles."

"Better yet," I suggested. "Let's try and hail him and see if he can invite us in."

"Or, we can do that," agreed A1.

Fig grabbed up the communications headset and started making calls to the surface on the more general frequencies. Finally, there was a response.

"What do you want?" came a deep voice with a strange accent.

"This is the ship Sononi Heart. We are looking for Olovane."

"Then your search will continue," was the reply.

A1 took the headset from Fig and said, "This is A1, a friend of Flashburn Brill, the prospector from Nandecious Prime."

There was just the hiss of static silence for two full minutes and then, "Sending landing coordinates. But if this is a trick, you *will* regret it." Even with the odd accent his tone registered real menace.

"Well, that settles that," smiled A1 slapping his hands together like he had just finished digging a ditch.

"I guess we'd better let our guests know," I mentioned and I would have had to be blind to miss the look Fig gave me.

Within the hour we had landed at the position Olovane had passed along. It was an inhospitable landscape with huge stretches of rough plateaus crisscrossed with deep fissures. Within a canyon-like crack the landing bay was housed, camouflaged from casual view. There was just enough room for the Heart to squeeze in and land. The bay was carved from raw stone and was fitted with lights and the standard pass-through field that kept the atmosphere inside the bay when ships came and went. There were hatches against the rock walls and what looked to be a control room high up projecting slightly from the facing stone wall.

"Do you think he will be coming to meet us or do we just go look for him?" asked Doon.

"I figure he'll come looking," said A1.

It wasn't long. We stood around the Bridge like lost children until I saw a figure dressed in a long, hooded cloak make his way toward our ship. "That must be Olovane!" remarked A1 with his usual exuberance.

"Ya think?" I mumbled with my own exuberant sarcasm. I simply got another in a series of elbows from Fig. "Why don't we open the hatch and go meet him. No sense in the old git having to walk all the way over here just to have us all walk all that way back."

Fig led the way toward the hatch saying to no one in particular but just loud enough for me to hear, "Let me open the hatch this time so I can fall in love with the first person I see." Ouch.

I tried to give her my best are-you-kidding-me-with-this-shit look but she got ahead of me and didn't look back. I wasn't the best one to read a woman's thoughts but even a musty vegetable could have picked up that frosty attitude.

We walked down the ramp to the landing pad floor and started toward Olovane. I was a little wary of the whole setup. It seemed too trite and easy. Nothing had been this smooth this entire venture so why would that change all of a sudden? I did my best to stay vigilant for some hidden danger. Perhaps some secreted army waiting in ambush or laser weapons tracking our every move, drawing a bead on us for the inevitable head shot. Or maybe I was just getting too cynical and had watched far too many pulpy adventure movies over the years. So as we neared Olovane I only felt myself continuing to tense.

A1 spoke up treating him like they were old friends even though I was fully aware that A1 had never seen Olovane before and I was sure that the same was true of our mysterious host.

"My name is A1, Olovane," he said with his normal child-like enthusiasm. "It is a pleasure to meet you." He extended his hand. As Olovane drew near he raised his arm up to return the clasp when suddenly a metallic hand shot out from the long, heavy sleeve and clutched A1's with mechanical precision. A1 let out a small grunt and I could see that the pressure on his own hand was causing him severe pain. Reflexively I pulled my pistol and leveled it at Olovane.

"Let him go, Olovane or I will shoot that hand off at the wrist." I am a pretty good shot and at that short range I had no doubt I could hit his wrist but as to the outcome from the blast, I couldn't 100% guarantee that A1 would not lose his own hand as well.

Before I could flinch, shoot, or blink an eye Olovane produced a gun from somewhere inside his robe and leveled it at me face. He wasn't even looking at me as far as I could tell, seeing as his head beneath the hood never swayed.

The voice we had heard before spoke softly and unhurried from the shadow of the hood. "I would think again," it cautioned with the same strange accent. I realized then that the accent was actually part of the speech synthesis that Olovane was using. "I can break A1's hand and shoot you directly in the face before you can cause your gun to fire. Consider your actions."

I raised my left hand slowly and holstered my sidearm at the same time with my right. "OK, ok...I hear you. Just stop hurting A1 and we'll all get along just fine." His response was to turn toward me and raise his head. The darkness of the hood was complete but I could just make out the gleam of metal in the dark and a glow from two eyes fixed on me. He slowly released A1's hand and took a small step back. After a moment he replaced the gun in its hiding spot and looked back at A1.

"I apologize for the injury. This shell has much more strength than my previous one. My intention was only one of greeting. Welcome to my home."

"Olovane," started A1, "we are here looking for something and I was told by Flashburn that you were the first step in finding it."

"If it was Flashburn that sent you then you must be looking for the Lost Package of Dehrholm Flatt," surmised Olovane. I have to admit I was pretty shocked that this thing was resolving so easily. For such a mysterious and almost mystical object the Package was rather simple to find.

"Great!" I exclaimed. "Just go get it and we'll be out of your hair. Then you can work on your handshaking skills all you'd like."

He turned to look at me once again. "You actually think it is here? And no one ever just came here and took it before you? Are you that ignorant?"

"Hey, one question at a time, tinman. You seem to know quite easily what we are after so this can't be news to you. I figure this Flashpan guy figured out you were sitting on this Lost Package and he gave A1 here the heads up. So, just give it to us and then we can leave and, believe me, we really do need to leave."

He regarded me with a slight tilt to his head and said, "I guess that answers my question about being ignorant."

I frowned at him. "I'm not. I just know what's what and I think you are holding back on something and I am guessing it's that damn Package."

"I don't have it."

"Then at least you know where it is."

"No," he answered.

I started to get annoyed which would soon blossom into frustration which, in turn, would morph into equal measures of anger and stupidity. "You know, I just wish I had one person on this damned tour of insanity that would just speak straight. None of this beating around the bush and tossing out meaningless rhetoric. Can't anyone just say something straight up?"

"I am," replied Olovane. "I don't have it nor do I know where it is."

"Then why..."

"Because Flashburn Brill was convinced that I was some part of a larger map that one could assemble to locate the eventual resting place of the Package. Brill stumbled upon my retreat while prospecting asteroids for rare minerals. He was starving and ill so I took him in and nursed him back to health. We talked very little really so I have no understanding as to why he thought I was a clue related to this prize you seek. I fear you, like Brill, have misplaced your trust and faith. I am no more a stepping stone to fortune than any of you."

"Then I guess we get to kill them now, right Mistress Zyn?" piped up Barry. I had almost forgotten he was standing behind us along with Zyryn. Bruce had stayed on the ship for security reasons. Guess Zyryn didn't want any of us sneaking back onboard during the talk with Olovane and blasting back into space.

"No," she said. "This isn't over yet, I think." She gave me a long look that was easily noticed by Fig. I looked away from both of them and back to A1.

"Well, A1, what now?" I asked him.

He rubbed at his bristled chin. "I...I'm not sure. Flashburn was very convincing. He swore to me that this was the clue that would lead me to the Package."

"He could have lied, A1," offered Fig.

"I don't think so," he replied.

"Why's that? Maybe he was trying to trick you," suggested Doon. "What was he doing when he told you?"

"Dying," said A1 a bit too casually. "He was dying from a blaster wound and wanted to let me know before he died. I managed to kill his adversary but not before I swore to him I'd try and find it."

"Good enough for me," said Doon shaking his head.

"I suppose," I mumbled. I turned back to our mysterious host, Olovane. "Maybe that Brill character was confused or delusional but we did have to go through a lot to get here. Maybe you can indulge us a little in this crazy quest and tell us what your story is."

"I don't have a story," he said with slight hesitation. Something about him didn't sit well with me and my instincts told me to push for more.

"Let me see..." I started. "You are living alone - on an asteroid -

in the ass-end of Farnok space. I am not sure what the deal is with your body but if I had to guess I'd say you are part cyborg or something. If I put all that together my feeling is that you went through some horrid trauma and are now hiding out here from somebody. And it wouldn't be the Xydoc Zyn because you are camping out in their backyard. Am I close to your non-story?"

He didn't say anything for awhile and we all just stood there looking at him. I half suspected he would just suddenly vanish and we'd find ourselves in some kind of holographic simulation. Like that would ever happen.

Finally he spoke. "You are an observant man, sir." He lowered his hood and I saw that his head was entirely robotic; a shiny copper-colored metal head with two yellow eyes, no nose, and a mouth that was more a slit to break up his face than a function of speech. "I am all mechanical with just my brain to link me to my former humanity. This...shell is something I have been dealing with for a long time. I have had to replace it from time to time, each incarnation a hopeful improvement from the last. But this newest one has some adjusting to do given the damage I almost caused your friend here."

"But what happened to you that you are like this and living all the way out here by yourself?" asked Fig.

"It is a long unfortunate tale to be sure. But suffice it to say that I saw some hardship and am now actually in the service of Rink SanDyer."

Zyryn stepped forward. "I am his daughter."

"Then I feel pity for you as I am a creature of a very long life span and I have never encountered such a devious and evil person as the Grand Xydoc, SanDyer. He is a man whose very presence taints this region of space."

"What is it you do here? My father has never spoken of you or this place."

"I don't know that it is a secret. I merely man this lonesome listening post for which SanDyer leaves me alone. I relay information I pick up through a network of spy-receivers littered throughout this asteroid field. What he does with it all I care not to know. I cherish my solitude. My life has had enough upheaval and tragedy to allow me the appreciation of my time alone."

"For a man with no story, that sounds like a fairly full one. And I suspect that is the Made-for-TV version." I was lucky to get him as forthcoming as he was. I felt any further pressure for more would not gain me any better insight. But I still wondered what Brill had found in his short exposure that made him believe that Olovane's life was a clue to the whereabouts of the Package.

I turned to look at A1. "Any ideas where to head next, scout master? For being the first clue it looks more like a dead end."

He scowled at me. "If it were easy then anybody could find it and it'd damn well be gone by now. So maybe you need to put your big genius know-it-all brain to work on clue finding instead of fault finding. Then maybe we will have some luck for a change."

"Now you listen, you old handbag. I'm here at your insistence not because I wanted to. It's your damn party, A1. Now be a good host and either figure it out or close it down." I looked over at Zyryn and her minion. "Which, by the way, just means we all die."

"Argon!" scolded Fig. "We are all in this together!"

"Not by choice."

"We are all here by choice except you," she pointed out. "You are the *only* one who didn't volunteer to come along and since some of us are here because of you maybe you could try and help a little more so we don't all die."

I opened my mouth to retort but the words caught in my throat before I could argue them. She was right and, try as I might, I couldn't find anything to debate that sounded remotely true. Fig and Doon came along to help me and hadn't bitched about this mess despite the fact that we were probably going to be dead before it was over. So I did the only thing I could. I pointed at A1.

"He was the one that started it!" This only garnered an eye-roll from everyone with the exception of Olovane mostly due the mechanical limits of his robot eyes. "Okay, okay. You're right. I'll try and stop being an anchor to this thing and work on solving the riddle." I again looked at A1. "But he needs to help as well. You all may have volunteered but this all started because of him." Fig started to say something again but I cut her off. "But, we are all here now and for better or likely worse, I'm in and I'll do my best to get along with Humphrey Bogart over here," thumbing toward A1. From the look in their eyes I could tell that my reference was lost yet they all nodded silently. I turned to Olovane.

"So, before we try to head out into deep, dark space again, maybe we can hang out here for a bit and leave in the morning. Would that be OK?"

"You are on an asteroid in the middle of space," reminded Olovane. "There is no 'morning'."

"You know what I mean, Olovane. You did once live on a planet with a day/night cycle, right? We will stay here for the...*night* and then be off on our way. Problem with that?"

"No. I will appreciate the company. I have plenty of rooms that go unused. You needn't stay aboard your cramped ship for the...evening."

"Great. And I could use a nice hot shower as well." Then I remembered his metallic body. "You have those?"

He nodded. "Yes, of course. This station was manned by several of the Zyn before I took over here. There needs were met. Follow me and I will show you to your quarters."

"I could eat something," injected A1; ever the popular guest. "I'm growing tired of our shipboard chow."

"There is food as well. Everything you will need to make your stay comfortable," our mechanical host assured. "This way."

Zyryn drew up close to me. "Why are we staying here?" she asked quietly. "You are under a fairly severe deadline."

I smiled at her. "*Dead*line. Clever."

"I'm not trying to be funny. You don't have a lot of time to waste."

"I know that. But we don't have any clue as to where we should be heading. I am really hoping that I might be able to stumble upon something that Brill managed to discover that made him believe there was some connection between Olovane and Derholm's Package. I just need to find it like he did. I am guessing that since he was laid up here and unable to get around that whatever he saw would be in the same area that we will be hanging out in."

She looked at me shocked. "You are trying to help."

"I ain't giving up yet. You are just going to have to wait a little longer to kill me." Then I quickened my pace to catch up with Olovane. "Is there a chance I could visit your medical facilities while I'm here? This wrist of mine is still giving me a lot of pain."

"Sure," he said. "Just let me get your friends settled and I'll take you there."

Now all I had to do was be some kind of super observant detective and we'd be home free.

Cake.

CHAPTER 15

The trickiest part of getting used to space travel was the whole problem with time. Now a lot of people get hung up on the whole relativity thing that Einstein was all gung-ho about. Yeah, sad to say, he just didn't quite get that right. In fact he was looking left when he should have been looking right. One of the first things we learned when we made contact with aliens during The Introduction was how wrong we had gotten a lot of science. Sure, it made sense while we were just sitting on our own little sand particle in space but when you got out there on the *beach*, well...it just didn't hold true.

So we were told by the Galactic Society that basically one could travel faster than the speed of light and that Time was basically a constant. It took a long time for the brain trust of Earth's scientific community to accept it. The rest of us just went along for the ride. The fact that there actually were aliens visiting us from worlds light years away proved that much of our scientific beliefs were wrong. Even Einstein knew there was a more unifying force to the Universe so he referred to his discoveries on Relativity as *theories*. Face it; the dude knew more than he was letting on.

But while Time was, for the most part, a constant, it didn't help when you traveled to a planet way across the galaxy that had days that were twice as long as yours. And that a year there was 597 Earth days long but only 298 of their days. It would seriously mess up your head. Calendars were useless once you left planetside. No two planets were ever exactly the same. 32 hours in a day? Check. 18 days in a week? Yup. 7 months in a year? You bet. Almost anything you can think of was out there somewhere. So there had to be some way of knowing what the time was on the planet you were on. So every ship had a syncing chronometer (a syncrometer) that could show current time on the planet you just landed on or one you wanted to know about but what if you were running around a city and had to be somewhere by 3PM? Who could keep setting their watch that way? It was bad enough with the different time zones on Earth let alone resetting your watch to a planet that had more hours in a day than your watch had numbers. Crazy.

So most people that engaged in a lot of space travel wore a syncrometer on their wrist, referred to as a *skono*. They looked like a watch but would sync with the time of the planet you were on by utilizing a standardized signal that each planet transmitted. The one thing the Galactic Tribunal was ahead of the curve on when they united the galaxy was to standardize everything they could. Want to join? Then get your shit set up right. No more different protocols. All measurement was the same system galaxy wide. You could have your own systems but there was an official form of almost everything. And it had to be used and understood. It made moving between worlds so much easier. I had my own Greenman Skono Avenger. Greenman made some of the best skonos and I liked the techy style of the Avenger. Plus, like many of them, it had a dual time function that could be set for your particular biorhythm so you could stay on a more standardized sleep cycle rather than having to stay awake for 50 hours straight.

So, when I had told Olovane we would stay for the night it was due to my skono telling me it was almost 10PM. This was my own custom setting and it kept me more alert and rested. No one complained so I felt they must be feeling tired. Hopefully it would give me some time to look around.

The medbay was more deluxe that I would have thought. Given

the obvious little need that Olovane presented, there had been pirates manning the station previously and I imagined those guys didn't have any medical needs other than a bone saw, fish-gut, and leather for biting down on. But there was some hi-tech stuff in there and I made use of the Regenerator to help finish the mend on my wrist. Pretty much good as new. I poked around a little after Olovane moved on and didn't see anything that gave me a clue as to a loose corner Flashburn might have noticed during his time in the infirmary. A dead end.

While he had taken the time to show each of us our quarters prior to leaving me in the medbay it wasn't going to be my next stop. I decided to take a little tour around the place just to see what I could see; making special attention of anywhere I figured Brill had visited during his short stay.

In the cafeteria - which again was much fancier than I would have expected - I decided to make myself a sandwich. This would provide a suitable excuse should Olovane find me going through cupboards and drawers. After finally crafting my snack and not finding one damn thing in my hasty search I decided to wander around further. It was during this random strolling that I encountered Olovane in what I could only guess to be a library. These damn pirates are not living up to my expectations one bit!

"Is there something I can help you with, Mr. Bosch?" he asked not looking up from his display.

"Restless. Thought a quick bite might get the blood out of my head so I can sleep." Olovane hadn't shown any aggression or appeared less than forthcoming but I still thought he was holding back something and I didn't want to let on about my search.

"I would imagine that would help. Any luck?"

"Not a damn bit, I'm afraid. Doing some reading?"

"Yes. I find it keeps my mind distracted from the tedium."

"I ain't sleeping so I guess I have some time to kill. What's the rest of your story, Olovane?"

He finally looked up. "What do you mean?"

"Why do you stay here?"

"I do not have a ship," he said matter-of-factly.

"I'm not buying it. Flashburn Brill was here and you coaxed him back to health and off he went to discover the whereabouts of the Lost Package and claim his prize. You could have left with him."

"I...I had to safeguard his departure," he stuttered.

"Even robots lie."

"I am not a robot."

"Not the point, Olovane. Come clean - why haven't you left?"

"I cannot."

"We already covered that," I pushed. "You could leave if you wanted to. And yet you stay here. Listen, that's fine. I guess it could be ok given your current state of being a robot and all…"

"I am not a robot!" he yelled.

"Sorry. You just look like one and so I have a tendency to think of you as one."

"I am human like you. Or…I was." A certain sad lilt came through his voice despite the synthesis used to create it. His head drooped.

"What happened, man? Why are you a robot…?" His head snapped back up. "Sorry. Why are you trapped in the cybernetic body?"

"It is a long, melancholy tale that explains little. Suffice it to say, I once was a person of esteem and had all that I could ever want but a conflict arose between me and my two brothers. In this none of us could ever bend or compromise. It led to our inevitable downfalls. I stay here because I should. I am not fit for a place amongst people."

I wandered around the room looking at some of the items there: long forgotten tomes with labels I could not read, some odd, unidentifiable objects that could have been crafted or grown, it was impossible to tell just by looking, and a few pictures hung on one wall. "That sounds like a sad story all right. What was this conflict over?"

He stood and slowly walked around the room, his hands clasped behind his back. I wasn't sure if he was just composing his thoughts or intercepting me as I drew near the pictures. Finally, after some moments, he answered my question. "As with far too many unnecessary disputes it was over a woman."

He was drawing close and I got the impression he was trying to pull my attention away from the pictures. "A woman? Really?" I asked attempting to sound nonchalant while running my gaze more intently across the pictures. There were three. One was a recent candid shot of Olovane with what I assumed were Xydoc Zyn. He was engaged in an arm wrestling competition with a sizable, well muscled Zyn who had a worried grimace etched on his heavily tattooed and scarred face. The large pirate was losing. The other was of a man I did not recognize looking forlorn and lost in thought. The final picture sandwiched between them was of three men, handsome and well dressed, standing close together toasting glasses. They were in front of a very large building with huge letters above it. Just as I read the letters Olovane sidled up next to me.

"Yes," he said and I turned to face him trying to keep the surprise of what I saw off of my face. "My brothers and I had all fallen for the affections of the same woman and in the end, none of us won her and we traded our fraternal closeness for hate and jealousy. Our bonds were burned in the intensity of our rivalry. Of this I am ashamed. I gave up my brothers, whom I had loved dearly, for nothing more than the attention of a woman. I am the oldest and I should have been the one to safeguard the others from themselves but I failed them and myself. I succumbed to the same lure as they. I have since looked for no comfort but only the solitude where I can pay penance for my sins and reflect on all that I have done."

"Shit," I muttered putting my attention back into the conversation as I slowly moved away from the pictures and passed a hand over what might have been a real human skull.

"Your summation, while brief, is accurate."

"Sorry. Didn't mean to discount your story. But, it is an old one. Can't count the number of times I've come across something similar. Great wars have sprung from just such a thing. And in the end, nobody wins."

"A true lesson, Mr. Bosch. Yet one that seems never learned."

"Ought to teach that one in High School," I suggested and took a seat next to where Olovane had been sitting when I entered.

"Excuse me?"

"Never mind, Olovane." I thought about his story for a minute. "During your time with Brill did you tell him about your past?"

"He was here for a few days and his relentless curiosity rivaled even yours so, yes, I did tell him some of it."

Something told me this was a connection. Something here. "What became of your brothers?"

Olovane sat back in his chair facing me. "One, the youngest, was a compulsive liar and conniver. A cheat. While I loved him dearly he was the initial cause for the rivalry as he proclaimed his love of my other brother's wife before I had."

"Wait. His wife? You were in love with his wife? Here I thought it was some space wench in a local pub with a full bosom and a pretty smile."

"You simplify things too much, Mr. Bosch. My brother, Linus, was married to the most wonderful and intoxicating woman I had ever met. Yet I stood my ground despite her advances toward me."

"Again...what? She came on to you and you are living on a rock in space?"

"Casual flirtations but ones that only fueled my growing love for her. But my youngest brother, also smitten, tried to wrestle her heart away from Linus and by doing so sparked my affection for her into a roaring fire. I could not let him have her nor could I let Linus keep her."

"So one brother was a complete bastard and the other one now an angry, jealous husband. Bet Thanksgiving was fun."

"I don't understand."

"Skip it. So where are they now?"

He stood across the room from me and in the low light he suddenly seemed more human that before. His shoulders were slightly curved from the weight these memories were putting on him. "We all went our separate ways not to see each other again. And many, many years passed but then 20 years ago, before I took my place on this asteroid..."

"You've been here for 20 years?!"

"Almost, yes. I ran across Linus and we spoke for a short time. Even given the long stretch of time since we had fought the wounds still bled fresh. It was after talking to him that I realized that I needed to extricate myself from society and seek shelter alone with my thoughts and grief. Soon after this position presented itself and I have been here ever since."

"Shit."

"I think you have already said that."

"So your youngest brother?"

"I do not know where he is or if he even still lives. I would think, given his penchant for dishonesty, that he would have befallen some karmic fate. But he could be a politician I suppose."

"And where is Linus?"

"He lived in the small city of Adarenah on D'Moc. I have not heard or seen him since. While I do miss him I know that he also lives a life of sad regret. He has no need to seek me out and I am sure he will never forgive me."

"Time can change a lot of things, Olovane. I think I read somewhere that Time wears down the largest mountain."

"The analogy is not lost on me, Mr. Bosch. But I fear I will not have that much time."

I turned to leave and head for my quarters for some sleep then spun back toward Olovane as I entered the doorway. "Did you tell Brill where your brother was?"

"I believe I did mention it. Do you believe it significant?"

"Perhaps," I said and left the Library.

Bingo.

I got back to my room and opened the door. As soon as the lights snapped on I felt stomach tighten. Zyryn was sitting on my bed. Barry wasn't with her so I knew this wasn't anything "official." I decided to leave the door open.

"Hey," I said cautiously entering the room.

"Close the door," she ordered, judging by her tone.

"Uh...not a good idea considering what happened last time we were in a room together. Alone."

She actually got a sad look on her face. "Please?"

I shook my head. "Why are you here?"

"I wish you would close the door. I need to talk to you and it could go badly if certain people overhear what I have to say."

"You got that right!" I agreed. "But I prefer the door open."

"Then you at least need to come over here so we can keep our voices low."

I started for the bed then stopped a pace away. I stood there. "I can hear plenty fine from here. What do you need?"

Again the sad face. I was wondering what this woman was playing at. For a pirate, let alone the daughter of the most feared pirate of all, she was not acting like one. I would place her reactions more on the pouty, spoiled princess side. Had she pulled a knife or pistol I might have been more worried but I think I would also have been more at ease.

"I don't want to have to kill you," she stated rather bluntly.

"Then don't. I won't be disappointed. Really."

"I am not joking."

"Nor am I."

"What I mean is that we need to find this thing but if we don't, well...I still don't want to kill you. But I cannot make sure that my father doesn't find out with Barry and Bruce around. I told you before that they are loyal only to my father. I will have to find a way to convince them you are dead."

"They aren't loyal to you at all? I thought they were your personal guard."

"The three of them were assigned by my father but the only one that I trusted, that would be absolutely loyal, was Bob. He and I were...close."

"O...k. So you were lovers then?"

It seemed she was about to blush but recovered. "Yes. But I have not had that closeness with Barry and Bruce even though I tried."

"Lord! At the same time?"

She seemed to ponder the idea which made me very uncomfortable. She smiled slightly. "Hmmm...I hadn't thought of that. It may have worked. I think they are gay."

"Oh shit," I mumbled.

"But I think that is why my father never liked Bob. He had lost his control over him and therefore another spy into my world. I miss him."

"I bet. So you don't want to kill us - let's get back to that part," I nudged, growing more ill at ease by the second.

"Yes, of course. You know that I hate my father so I despise the fact that he ordered me to kill you...either way this goes."

"Hold on. You're telling me that you are supposed to kill us even if we found the Package? What kind of bullshit is that?" Then I remembered I was taking the word of a space pirate. I am so dumb.

"He doesn't care about the Package at all. This is a test for me. He is testing my loyalty and I am supposed to be his executioner. I won't do it. I was afraid to tell you earlier but I decided it is best I let you know you were deceived. You and your friends are dead no matter what happens. But I want to change that. I want you to live whether we find it or not."

I scratched my head. Wow. "Well, I guess you could say that is what I want too."

She smiled that incredible smile and said, "Great. We want the same thing then. Now we just need to make sure it happens." She then stood up and approached me. "We will talk more soon. I will come up with a plan to rid us of Barry and Bruce but for now we need to make every effort to find the Package. Have you had any luck locating the next clue?"

I wasn't sure how honest to be with her but her intent seemed sincere. Besides, she was traveling with us, she'd know anyway where I planned to go. "I think I know where we are heading next."

She smiled again. "Brilliant! I knew you'd figure it out. We'll leave in six hours."

"Works for me."

She grabbed me, pulled me tight to her and kissed me hard on the lips again. But then before I could struggle she released me and headed out the door without a word. I fell onto the bed and stared up at the ceiling. "Oh this is not going to end well for me at all."

Approximately six hours later we were all meeting in the kitchen for some quick breakfast and heading back out into space our next destination.

As the last of our strange group stumbled in - A1, of course - I explained our next step.

"I have searched as best I could and I believe we need to go to the planet D'Moc, to a little city named Adarenah. I think our next clue lies there."

"How do you know this?" asked A1 around some kind of bread and sausage.

"You'll just need to trust me."

"I'd like a little more actually," he replied.

"You don't get to ask questions, A1. You got us this far but you haven't come up with anything else so I figure it is my turn. I said I'd try my best to help and this is me trying. So we are going to D'Moc. Now let's get back on the ship and go. We don't have a lot of time. D'Moc is almost five days from here."

Zyryn looked at Barry and Bruce. "You heard him. He has nothing to lose but his life for guessing wrong so this is likely his best effort. Get on board."

We all headed for the Heart and to take our leave of Olovane's asteroid.

"Go ahead and get on board, I need to talk to Olovane one last time," I shouted to them as I turned and ran back toward the dock exit. As I suspected Olovane was in the monitoring room watching for unwanted traffic along the Farnok border. He looked up as I entered.

"Something amiss? I thought you were leaving."

"Nothing wrong and we are leaving but I wanted to ask you something else really quickly before we left."

"Yes?"

"We are going to go see your brother Linus, or at least we are going to try and find him on D'Moc. If we do, is there anything you would like me to tell him?"

He took a minute to think then slowly shook his head. "No. There is nothing left to say. I have deeply wronged him and asked for his forgiveness. Anything else is up to Linus; I have done all I can."

"You don't happen to have a picture of him, do you?"

"I do." He walked over to a D-pad sitting on a desk near the door. He tapped the screen and I heard a distinct crack. "I have broken it," he muttered. "It is these clumsy hands I am cursed with." He looked back up at me. "I'm sorry. I fear I cannot help you to easily identify him."

"That was your only picture?" I questioned.

"My images were stored on the device. I can work toward retrieving them from the mainframe storage aboard SanDyer's ship if you'd care to wait. It would take me a few hours to locate them amongst all of the data. I know you are in a hurry..."

"Thanks Olovane. I don't have the time to wait. I'll take my chances. Good luck to you."

"More so to you, Mr. Bosch. I fear you will need it more than I."

With that helpful wish of good fortune I raced back to the Sononi Heart and we left the asteroid landing bay behind as Fig's ship streaked across the stars. I'd need to try and piece together my hunch quickly as our time was rapidly running out.

CHAPTER 16

I was on the Bridge with Fig plotting the course to D'Moc trying my best to be charming and tear down the tension that was hanging like a curtain of sandpaper between us. She was still being frosty no matter how nice I tried to be.

"We can't go that way," I protested.

"It will cut over three days off the trip!" she argued back. "With only seven days to find that package five days is a big chunk. Plus we have already used up almost two days."

"I don't care if it was ten days to D'Moc and we'd be there tomorrow if we took your shortcut, we are not going that way." I crossed my arms. "That's my final say."

She stood back and looked at me. "Really? You're the captain now?"

"No. This is your ship. I'm just saying if you go that route I will have to leave."

She smirked, "Where? And...how?"

"I don't care. Hell, I'll just put on a suit and try and jet pack back to Olovane's." I looked at her with my best serious, all-business face. "I know your course is a bad idea. Farnok space was better."

She paused. "You are serious. What is so bad about the Flatlands?"

"I've been there."

"You have?" She actually sounded both surprised and impressed. "I've heard stories about it but I figured we are just cutting through the corner of it. Now how bad could that be?"

"I won't take the chance. I flew through there for weeks and almost lost my mind. You just don't understand. It's just one giant void in space. Nothing. No planets, no stars, nothing. It's like parking your ship in a hanger and turning out the lights. I had someone helping from outside to keep me on course. We don't have that. If we were to drift even slightly we might never leave there. I will not take that chance. That's final."

"Aw...scared of the dark, little boy," she teased.

"Stop it! I ain't clowning here. We go in there we don't come out. You want that responsibility then fine, take it." I was getting angry and her jibe didn't help one bit.

"Okay, okay. Sorry. We'll take the longer way." She turned back to the charting display. I wanted to tell her that it might not make any difference as we were dead either way but I didn't want to frighten her. She was tough and could take it but I didn't want her to walk around with that hanging over her. I had a small chance with Zyryn to maybe work that part out and it would be better if no one knew.

"I'm sorry, Fig." I walked over to the display and looked at the course. She didn't look up at me but plotted it in.

"We'll have to navigate the Keszler Bridge to get there from here in four days. The Nesher Gravity Well won't align in time."

"I've never had to go through the Keszler Bridge. I heard it can be tricky."

She finally looked up at me. "I have. It's no picnic but I can manage. Just keep that damned monkey off my bridge and we'll be fine."

"The monkey?" I had forgotten about it again but it appears Fig had not. As if on cue I saw the thing dart in and scurry into a darkened corner, its little hat bouncing atop its head... "Shit. It just ran in here."

"Kill it," she said. I knew she wasn't kidding.

"I can't, you know that. But I will get it out of here."

"Good luck," she mumbled as she sat down at the controls.

How hard could it be to scare off one stupid space monkey? I walked over to where it had run and peered into the darkness. I couldn't see it as there was a small cabinet blocking my view of the corner. As I placed my hands on top of it and leaned over to see if it was behind it suddenly felt it bump against my leg as it ran off to another part of the bridge. "Dammit!"

"See?"

"Hush. I'll get him." I looked around for the thing but while the Bridge was not large, there were a lot of dark corners and consoles everywhere. I pulled out my flashlight and snapped it on. The small cone of light played across the floor and quickly bettered my chances at success. I got down on my hands and knees and started aiming it under things and into corners. After a moment or two I still hadn't spotted the vermin.

"I think maybe he ran out..." It landed on my back with a thump and a hiss. The sudden pounce startled me and I quickly stood but banged my head on an overhanging corner. "Shit! Ouch!"

"Guess he's not gone then?"

"Stow it." I wasn't going to let this damn thing beat me. Beat me? That's was it! "I'll be right back, Fig. Don't worry." I headed out the hatchway.

"No! Don't leave me alone with this thing, Argon!" she called out as I left.

But I didn't leave. I went halfway down the passageway and turned around quietly sneaking back to the opening to the Bridge. I hoped I wouldn't have to wait long. And I didn't.

I stood stone still just outside the Bridge and then I heard it, a soft little "fapping" noise. A sure sign the monkey was otherwise engaged.

"Oh shit," I heard Fig say disgustedly. "Not again."

I tried to locate the sound within the room and narrowed it down to the forward left corner. Horny little creature.

I raced in and shot straight for the area where the noise was coming from. Fig gave a jump as I sped past her and right to the monkey. There he was, tiny penis in hand, just slapping away like he had a train to catch. His eyes had been fixed on Fig but snapped to me as soon as I approached. I'll give the critter credit as even with a startled look on his face he never missed a beat. With a single motion I grabbed him by the neck and spun around. I then drop-kicked the repugnant thing out the door and into the passageway where he landed on the deck and slid a couple feet. His stupid tiny hat sprung free of his head and rolled a narrowing arc around his prone form. He lay there twitching slightly though I could not tell if it was due to an injury, loss of consciousness, or the results of his endeavors. Honestly, I didn't want to know.

I tried to catch my breath and huffed out, "Told you...I'd...get him."

Fig was trying not to laugh. "Yeah, thanks for that." Her eyes remained on the view screen.

"I don't think he will be...bothering you again, Fig." I looked up and saw Squirty sway to his feet and slowly make his way down the hall. He didn't look back. I couldn't imagine how the whole voyage could get any stranger.

With that bizarre annoyance out of the way I returned my attention to the matter at hand. "How long will it be until we enter Keszler Bridge?"

"About a day," she said.

"Is it going to be bad?"

She thought for a minute. "Not much worse than this trip has been so far."

I picked up on the inference and decided to not let it go unnoticed. "About that, Fig. I think you got the wrong idea."

"And what idea is that, Argon?" a definite chill in her tone.

"That there is something going on between me and Zyryn."

"Ah yes, the pirate hooker. I often forget she is on board."

"Come on, Fig. She isn't a hooker - though I do question if she is even a pirate," I mumbled. "Don't be this way."

"What way is that?"

"Playing to the lowest common denominator. You are better

than that. I know it."

She didn't say anything and I thought I might have cracked the armor she was currently wearing but then she simply said, "I need to get these coordinates input and map this route out. You can come relieve me in eight hours...if you're not too busy."

I knew then that she was still very upset about everything and that my continued presence would only antagonize her further. Sometimes experience helps you understand what your choices are. My choice was simple - leave.

"I'll see you in eight hours," and I left the Bridge.

I was hanging out in the crew quarters thinking about sleeping when A1 came walking in. Joy.

"Why is it that most of the time I see you it is just you doing nothing?" asked A1, his odd idea of a greeting. Man, I couldn't stand that old fart.

"And why is it that whenever I see you I just want to punch you in the face? Oh yeah, it's cause you are an asshole."

"You have some real anger issues, boy."

"Did you just call me 'boy'?"

"You are just a kid from my view. Just a snot-nosed kid that doesn't know anything about anything but acts like he has full command of everything."

"Go find me something to write on. And make it big to accommodate your failing eyesight."

"What do you need that for?"

"So I can draw up a big old scorecard and we can see just who knows something and who is just along for the ride."

He shook his head and gave me the *brush off* gesture with his hand. "I don't want to get into your whole 'I saved everybody' speech again. I am tired of you thinking you are the only one doing anything around here."

I stood up and pointed my finger at him. "No. I'm not the only one doing something but I am not the only one doing nothing. What are you contributing to this again, A1?"

"I don't need to justify myself to you. You wouldn't be here if it wasn't for me."

"Finally! The truest thing you've said the whole time since I met you. Yet for some reason you have that down as a *good* thing."

"It is a good thing if you weren't so damn blind."

"You are certifiably insane, you couch cushion. I am on a one way trip to dead with my best friends along to share the ride and there is likely not a damn thing I can do to stop it. Yeah...thanks!"

"You can thank me later," he said and glared at me. Then he walked out before I could fulfill my punching desire. *Thank him later?* He was crazy from the start but now I was thinking he might have finally lost all touch with reality. I was going to have to keep an eye on him now as he could just as likely cause someone harm in his carelessness and warped perspective. Great, one more thing to worry about. I sat back down on my cot and then, with little effort at all, fell fast asleep.

"Fig is asking for you on the Bridge."

I awoke with a start and flipped over to see who was talking to me. I squinted in the light and finally focused my eyes on Doon. "Wha..?"

"Fig is waiting for you on the Bridge. You were supposed to relieve her an hour ago.

"Right, right. Shit. I was out!" I rubbed some more at my eyes and sat up. My stomach growled slightly. "Go tell her I'll be there in a minute. Just gotta grab something from the galley."

Doon walked off and I stood up, stretched, and looked in the mirror. I looked a mess but needed to get going so I threw on my gear and headed for food. As I walked into the mess deck I saw the dynamic duo of Barry and Bruce sitting at a table drinking something and talking low. They became silent when I walked in and both watched me head into the kitchen.

"What?" I said. "Is there a problem?"

"Did you do something to Squirty?"

"Who? That monkey thing?"

"Yeah. Zyryn's pet. He is hiding in her room and doesn't want to leave. She thinks somebody did something mean to him."

"And why would anyone do anything to that cute little guy?" I asked feigning ignorance - my most common ploy.

"Because he is an annoying, disgusting vermin in a constant state of arousal," admitted Barry. I was surprised at his very accurate appraisal. I had suspected he and his buddy routinely overlooked Squirty's more unpleasant habits in lieu of their dedication to Zyryn. But given the revelation that they served Rink rather than Zyryn made the statement more in tune with their eventual loyalty.

"Yeah!" piped up Bruce. "In fact one time Madame Zyn had us…"

"Bruce!" yelled Barry. Bruce stopped, leaving the rest of his admission to my imagination and what I came up with was equal parts appalling and embarrassing. I hoped I was far from the truth - for their sakes.

"So what did you do, Bosch?" returned Barry. "I know you are protective of that pilot woman and Squirty was giving her a bunch of the old 'tug and stare' while she was on the Bridge before. Something tells me she was looking to you for some kind of intervention."

"In case you haven't been paying attention, boys, Fig doesn't want anything to do with me."

Barry gave a chuckle. "Of course. That's because you are having a go at Madame Zyn."

"That's bullshit!" I asserted. "We don't have anything going on between us."

"Not according to her. She told us herself. I saw her coming out of your room last night on the asteroid. She told me she had dropped in for a little late night bump and tickle."

Shit. How could I counter her excuse for plotting against Barry and Bruce and not throw some suspicion on her. I didn't want to perpetuate the rumor but I had to safeguard Zyryn for the chance she will be able to get us out of this alive. She had a plan and I needed to make sure I did what I could to give that plan a chance to succeed. So, if admitting to some crazy story about her and I being lovers, well, I would just have to go along with for the time being. As long as it didn't get back to Fig to further anger her I was okay with it. And how would she ever know different since she didn't have any contact with Barry or Bruce.

"She can say what she wants but I'm not going to confirm or deny it. You'll have to draw your own conclusions."

"Fuckin' her," said Barry.

"Definitely," agreed Bruce.

"Grow up, you idiots," I replied and left with the meager snack I had rounded up.

"I bet Squirty likes to watch," said Bruce as I walked toward the Bridge.

"I just hope he doesn't join in!" added Barry and they both laughed.

Did I say this couldn't get any stranger? I was wrong.

"Sorry I'm late," I started as I walked onto the Bridge.

"How do you make a living as a courier, Argon?" she asked. "You are *always* late."

"I try. I really try. I don't know what it is - shit just happens. Always."

"Anyway...we are still pretty far out from Keszler Bridge. I'm going to go eat and get some sleep. I'm bushed."

"Fig..."

"And thanks for earlier. With Squirty. I appreciated that." She said all of this without looking at me directly but it was still nice to hear. One of the few nice things she had said to me since we started.

"I was glad to do it. But I wanted to tell you..."

She still wouldn't meet my gaze. She was avoiding me. "Later, Argon. I'm too tired to chat."

So I stopped trying to engage her. "Sleep well, Fig. I'll see you later." And off she went.

I'd known Fig for most of my life and I was familiar with how she acted and reacted. But ever since she joined us at the Transport Center in Lynterus she seemed like someone different; not her usual self. I thought at first it was due to our history and the abrupt circumstances of my departure years before. I had expected that, after awhile, she would become more like her old self but that had not happened. She was distant and cold. I never expected she would see me the same way but I had hoped she would at least treat me more like a friend after we had been around each other more often. Fig was not a vindictive person. She could carry her share of emotional baggage but a grudge wasn't ever one of those bags. She had always been quick to forgive and one to let things slide. I had always admired her for that as I was quite the opposite. You hand me a good, solid grudge and I will clutch it like my life depended on it. And if it gets a little slippery I will wrap it in a coat of righteous indignation just to keep my firm grip. No, I don't let that shit go.

Having some time to be alone on the Bridge gave me time to think. I didn't like that. Over the years I had developed obsessions and distractions to always keep my mind occupied so I didn't have to just sit and think about things. I found that when I pondered Fate, Life, and Destiny it became too full of ugly Regret and Hurt. I didn't like my life and I certainly didn't like where I was in it but sitting around thinking about it only served to magnify the things I didn't like about it and the little control I had. It just bummed me out so it was always best to avoid that self reflection by drinking, whoring, gambling, and getting myself into bad situations. I had become quite good at it.

So sitting there, while everyone slept away the "night," staring out at the endless expanse of space as we zipped along, gradually drew me into a state of deep melancholy. I tried to distract myself but it wouldn't work. Too much was going on and I just felt an enormous dread about our collective future and the sudden end I feared we all faced. So after several hours I was a raw patch of emotion and frustration and ripe for anything that would get my mind off my sad, pathetic life.

"Permission to enter the Bridge, Captain Bosch."

I recognized Zyryn's voice as soon as she spoke and I would have normally been ready to deal with her but found myself too into my own issues to try and dismiss her presence. I spun my chair to face her. She was wearing her black leather outfit but not the various belts, weapons, and armor that normally broke up her figure. The front of it was undone to a level lower that I would think could afford secure movement.

"Madame Zyn," I greeted.

She smiled playfully. "I see we can both be rather formal."

"To correct you, I am not the Captain. That's Fig's title. Currently I'm just the pilot."

"You will always be the Captain to me, Argon. You know you command the most respect of any on board."

"Uh...thanks, I guess. But this *is* Fig's ship."

"I believe that is only due to yours being stolen from you."

I laughed. "Oh, Zyryn. There's barely room for two on my ship let alone seven. If we were on my ship you'd be practically sitting on my lap." I knew that was a mistake as soon as I said it. She immediately came over and sat on my lap.

"I thought you'd never ask," she grinned.

I was uncomfortable but at the same time I did nothing to remove her. Her attentions were just the distraction I needed to get my mind off myself. "Uh...I'm not so sure..."

She put her arms around my neck and kissed me hard on the lips. I suddenly had a replay of the unexpected interruption Fig created when she walked in on us in almost the same position - except my hand wasn't on her breast. Yet.

I pulled away and said, "I don't think we should be doing this, Zyryn."

She looked at me surprised and replied, "I am sure you can put the ship on autopilot if you think you need your hands for something besides manning the controls."

"No, that's not it. I mean you and me. Making out. I...well, I..." I paused losing my train of thought. The woman was intoxicating and she definitely scrambled my brain when she was around. "I don't know what I mean."

To my surprise she got up from my lap and sat in the copilot seat next to me. She looked down and quietly said, "I'm sorry. I just thought you liked me."

"No, that's not it. It's me, not you." I couldn't believe I just said that. It was the epitome of cliché.

"You don't need to make excuses or try and not hurt my feelings. I understand. It is the way I look."

"What?"

"The way I look. My bald head and my...eye."

She had never ever mentioned her eye before. Since I had only known her for a few days and she had that patch and scar from day one it was something I didn't repeatedly find shocking. But when she mentioned it and my attention was drawn solely to it I couldn't help but feel that it was a crime that she had been disfigured so...personally. It was the kind of wound that was both heavily physical and emotional. It changed a person and how they viewed themselves. Every person that ever saw you would notice it and every time you looked in the mirror you would remember what you looked like before. There was just no getting around it - your eye was gone and a horrid looking scar raked across its old resting place. It reminded me of a brand. A mark placed on something to claim ownership or to display a hidden shame - like the Scarlet Letter. I only hoped that the person that did it had been made to pay severely. They had tried to ruin an object of beauty. I desperately hoped that it was not done purposely to hinder her looks...

Oh. My. God. The thought crashed into my mind like a wrecking ball.

"Did your father do that to you? That motherfucker!" I almost shouted, my anger already boiling up in the back of my throat. That incredible, evil, hateful man. No matter what happened on this trip I was going to find a way to kill him.

She looked at me and I saw that my blossoming rage surprised her and for some strange reason, touched her deeply. Her eye instantly filled with tears yet it didn't appear to be triggered by sadness.

"Oh Argon, you surprise me with your outburst. I am flattered that you feel so outraged by the cause of my scar. That such a thought of my father trying to remove my feminine features from my face could spur you to such exasperation moves me. I did not think anyone would ever feel like that toward me. To defend me against an injustice as grave as this," she motioned across her face.

The tears fell across her face and I was touched by the sudden softness she displayed. I didn't see her as Rink SanDyer's daughter or as a leader of the blood thirsty Xydoc Zyn but instead of a woman that had been forced to live a life she never wanted by circumstances well beyond her control. A young girl traumatized by a father with a heart as black as deepest Space. It tore at my heart. "I'm so sorry he did that to you. I know why you hate him so much." I gently wiped my thumb across her cheek and she took my hand in hers and pressed her wet cheek hard against it as if drawing strength and comfort from it.

She closed her eye and was silent for a short time, a soft smile on her lips. Finally she spoke. "I am truly touched by your kindness, Argon. You are a good man." She looked up at me, a pained look washing away her momentary solace. "But I need to tell you that my father did not do this to me."

I was shocked. How could I have misread the situation so completely? I was sure he was the cause of the outward scar she carried for the torment she carried inside.

She closed her eye again and the discomfort on her features intensified for a second as she struggled to reveal something I knew she didn't want to say. I gripped her hand tightly and placed my other hand atop it. "What happened then? Who did this to you?"

Zyryn finally opened her eye and looked at me. "It was me."

What?

She could read my expression and knew I didn't understand. "You'll think I am some kind of crazed lunatic but I did this to myself." She tried to laugh it off but failed as the laugh stuck in her throat, caught on an unyielding fragment of sorrow.

I continued to just stare at her in bewilderment. Why on Earth would she do something so horrible to herself? I was familiar with children who would cut themselves or bang their head against things all out of conflicted emotions and frustration but to savagely slice out your own eye? She was right, it did sound like the actions of an insane person.

She finally looked away and released a heavy sob. "I have scared you. Made you even more repelled by me. I should not have told you. I am such a fool!" She started to cry and tried to stand but I reached out, took her hand again and pulled her back down to the copilot seat.

"Tell me why. I want to understand." She looked at me. "Really."

She composed herself and then looked at me and gave a pained smile. "I never told anyone this before. I don't know why I am telling you." I just shook my head because I couldn't figure it out either. "As I've told you, my father hated the fact that I was not born a son. He wanted someone to carry on his legacy and a girl was just not going to do it for him. He considered women weaker and less of threat. He wanted a son and I was just a nagging disappointment. He grew to hate me for what I was and the reminder I caused. Knowing this as a small child made me even more desperate for his attention and approval but no matter what I did I always came up short. And the harder I tried by dressing like a boy, keeping my hair short and eventually shaving my head, it all never was enough and I grew more and more depressed."

"But it wasn't your fault," I offered.

"That wasn't a thought that would survive in my mind. I could tell myself that a million times but in the end I just wouldn't believe it and the shame I had blaming myself continued to grow. After my mother left him I was alone with his hatred and it only got worse. He became abusive and as I continued to develop into a young woman it became harder to downplay my femininity. And with this came the attention of men. I did my best to discourage their affections but they grew more insistent. Then I met Kreen. He wasn't like the others whose hormones were the only contributing factor to their attention. He was first a friend who treated me the same as everyone else, like he didn't notice whether I was a boy or a girl. We grew close over a couple years and then we grew closer, if you know what I mean."

I nodded having a pretty good idea and then my mind flashed back to Trixie and those few days that early summer. I knew what she was talking about.

She continued her story. "I am not ashamed to say that I believe I truly loved him despite the horrid life I was living. But knowing how my father felt about me, his learning that I was in love with a boy would drive the final nail into his hatred for me and I actually feared he would kill me. But in my ignorance I never thought about what he would do to Kreen."

"Oh shit," I said having a feeling where this story was going.

"Yes, he found out and flew into a rage when he caught Kreen one night in my quarters. He wasted no time and knocked Kreen from my bed and ran a knife through his neck. I stood there watching his blood flow across the floor and I could do nothing. My father slapped me so hard I fell to the floor, the room swirling in my vision. He looked down on me and sneered telling me that I was a curse upon him and that my own good looks would be my undoing as well as his. No one would ever feel threatened by me. I would serve only as a thing to be fucked and then tossed aside. I screamed at him that I never wanted to be beautiful and that it was a curse to me as well. I just kept yelling at him, waving at my face, 'I never asked for this! I never wanted this!'" Then several guards came running into the room hearing the noise and saw Kreen stabbed on the floor and me lying naked in his blood. My father was distracted by them and I reached over and pulled his knife from Kreen's neck. I yelled at him, 'I don't want this!' and yanked the knife across my face, cutting deep and slicing across my own eye. 'No one will ever love me now!' I spat at him before I passed out."

"Oh my God," I whispered. "That's horrible."

"My *wonderful* father looked down at me, passed out, naked, bloody, and missing an eye and I would have hoped he would have felt some sort of sorrow or at least pity, but no. He decided to take advantage of the situation. I found out later when I finally woke up that he covered the whole thing up. He found my blaster in its holster lying by the bed with my clothes. He yanked it free and shot all of the guards in the room. He then put the gun in my hand and ran from the room. He left me to be found by another guard an hour later when I was almost dead from blood loss. When the guard summoned him he convinced everyone that Kreen and the guards had entered my quarters and that Kreen had raped me while the guards waited their turn. And that I had fought back, gunned down the guards and when Kreen had slashed my

266

eye, forced the knife from his hand and drove into his neck. He turned me into a thing to be feared, not loved or lusted over. And in my sick and twisted need to please my father I went along with it. I lived the role. I turned down procedures to fix my face or replace my eye. I became the thing my father had designed me to be - a stone cold killer. Men feared me. I would take lovers by force and no one would ever question me. I became my father's son in spirit and perception if not in sex."

"Holy shit, Zyryn, that is one messed up story."

"The worst part is that I think the story he made up was supposed to be posthumous. I truly believe he expected me to die in my room and that the guard that found me was not suppose to be there for another few hours. The fact that I still lived after that was yet another in a long string of disappointments I have provided."

I just shook my head not wanting to believe that Zyryn could be the focus of such cruelty. It only strengthened my vow to kill that son of a bitch.

"I went along with it, Argon. I cannot forgive myself for that. I let that story become the truth. The one man I loved in my life is remembered as a rapist and attempted murderer of the daughter of Rink SanDyer. He was a wonderful man and I have forever sullied his name by allowing my father's lies to erase the truth. I am a partner to this and I am no better than he."

She was threatening to fall back into tears and sobs so I moved to her and held her. "You are only trying to survive in a nightmare. What made this change? Why are you trying to free yourself now?"

"My mother contacted me after all of these years." Hope sprang up in her eyes. "I thought she was dead but she is alive! She was in hiding fearing my father's wrath but she finally realized that after almost 30 years that he wasn't looking. She started trying to find out if I was alive or where I might be. Trying to learn about the daughter of the head of the pirates is not an easy task. It's not like she could just ask people. But finally she was able to learn I was alive and still with the Xydoc Zyn. After a lot of effort she managed to sneak a message to me through outside channels. I couldn't believe it! We haven't been able to communicate much but I know that she is sorry for what happened and leaving me behind. She still loves me and she has made me want to leave and run away from my father. I finally have the courage to escape. That is why when you brought this information about one of the most mysterious and sought after objects in the Galaxy I knew it was my ticket out. With the money from the Lost Package I can finance my escape."

"Is it that hard?" I asked. "You have to be rich; you're a pirate!"

"Harder than you think. Pirating is not as profitable as it once was. The Tanaki chase us everywhere. My father rarely leaves The Blanket as it is one of the best hiding places in open space. He would never admit it but he fears the Tanaki and is sure they would someday catch him. Our operations have far less reach than twenty years ago. I am not given a lot of our spoils as he takes most of it and doles out what he thinks I should have. I admit I don't go for wanting but to run away and start a new life for me and my mother I need much, much more."

"So you get the Package and what happens to me?"

Her face lit up and the last traces of sadness dropped away. "You can come with me!"

"I can't leave my friends to just die."

"That's why we need to stage your destruction along with the Package so that my father will not come looking for you or the package. But Bruce and Barry will have to be dealt with. They are not loyal to me, only to my father. They are here as much to watch me as you."

I rubbed my chin trying to take it all in. I sat back in my chair and looked at her. It was a hell of a lot to digest and I didn't really know what to think.

She got up and knelt in front of me. "Argon," she almost pleaded. "I want you to come with me. We would be good together."

"I don't doubt that but..."

Then she rose up to take my face in her hands and kiss me. Caught up in it all I did not protest. And when she slid back down and began to undo my belt and holster, I made no move to stop her.

"What was that noise?" she said suddenly.

The moment was broken like a dry twig. I stood quickly and spun to the entrance of the Bridge sure that I would see Fig standing there, a shock, hurt look on her face. But as I quickly swiveled toward the hatchway I found it empty.

"No. There is a noise on the hull. From outside. And the ship's not moving any longer."

I heard it then and turned back around and, glancing at the controls to affirm we had indeed stopped, looked out the viewscreen. What I saw chilled my blood and deflated any interest I had in what Zyryn had been doing.

"This is not going to be good," I said.

CHAPTER 17

The scene outside the ship was unlike anything I had seen in my almost 40 years of space travel. It was both spectacularly odd while still being downright terrifying. Had I not been witnessing it I would have scoffed at anyone telling me about it. In fact I was already feeling sad that I would most likely never be able to relate the experience to another soul due to the pure unbelievability of it. That and the fact that I was most likely going to die.

Outside the ship I could see the muted colors of a huge gas cloud backlit by a twin star system. Rays from the stars streaked through the darkness of space like the Sun back home on Earth poking through massive rain clouds right after a summer storm had just passed. It was one of the sights I always enjoyed while ripping along through the cosmos.

But the beauty of the nebula was offset by the horror between it and our ship. Most people on Earth believed that space was exhaustively empty expanses of nothing broken up by occasional specks of dust; namely planets, stars, and other inconsequential debris. While that is generally true, it is biased by the fact that the Earth hangs out near the edge of the galaxy and therefore is amongst the regions of the outer rim where things have spread pretty thin. We were much, much closer to the dense center and here it was almost crowded.

Nearer the hub of the galaxy there was a lot of dust, gas, and dark matter. And amongst all of that grew a strange and impossible ecosystem. There was life in space despite the incredible improbability of it. And the majority of it was things called crip. Crip were relatively small creatures that subsided on the minerals that made up the cosmic flotsam. Subsiding on space dust and cosmic radiation these tiny things drifted around the galaxy in what could only be called schools, like some kind of interstellar krill.

Before the development of repulser and deflector technology these things had wreaked havoc on early space travel. With any real speed necessary to travel between planets, let alone star systems, the nuisance creatures would pierce the hull of a fast ship like bullets. The ingenuity of several of those early races helped usher in the later major improvements in space travel: helium ion engines, pulse-fire technology, and the big daddy of all space travel - gravity drives. So maybe these inconsequential animals helped unite our galaxy. Or maybe they just slowed us down.

But with a plentiful food source just drifting carefree through the galaxy, more creatures would evolve to hunt them down. So, while rare (I had only ever seen a *picture* of one in my entire life), the hahkarnish was the most massive animal to develop in this food chain - basically a galactic whale of sorts. Immense beasts that sailed along on solar winds and feasted on the crip. I would have thought it was the presence of this gigantic creature that had caused us to drop out of gravity drive but it wasn't. Even the fact that there were three of them pushing through a thick patch of crip would likely not have caused us to stop. And it would have simply been an amazing sight to witness for the first time in my life with no regard for the safety of ship and crew. But that was not all that was out there. I was witness to history seeing something that had only been whispered in rumor and shared as legend. The Sot n'Gayth.

A galactic kraken.

"Is that what I think it is?" whispered Zyryn, her eyes not wavering from the screen.

"I don't know what you might be thinking it is but I am fairly sure I know what it is," I answered. "Our doom."

"The Sot n'Gayth - the devourer of worlds." There was both fear and awe in her voice and I couldn't help but feel the same way. Despite my reverie I heard a sudden commotion behind me.

"Why did we stop?" I heard Fig's annoyed shout coming up the passageway. I didn't need to answer as I knew her attitude would change as soon as she set foot on the Bridge and took a gander at what was outside.

And sure enough. "Argon! You better not have broke..." Silence. I heard others behind her but I couldn't take my eyes from the scene before me to see who else had followed. For what seemed like minutes we all stood in rapt silence fixated on the scene unfolding just outside the ship.

While the crip slowly buoyed their way along the cosmic winds, some bouncing along the hull of the ship causing the noise Zyryn and I had heard, most were swallowed by the floating hahkarnish. The Sot n'Gayth was narrowing the gap as it closed on a prey that would better satisfy its enormous hunger. And somewhere amongst all of this demonstration of Nature's complete evolutionary madness was the Sononi Heart sure to be crushed by the behemoths crowding towards us.

As huge as the hahkarnish were - roughly two times the size of the ship - the Sot n'Gayth was over twice their size. It was staggering how immense the thing was. With four arms and two legs, what seemed to be smallish wings upon its back, and a mouth ringed with groping tentacles it reminded me of the legends of the Elder Ones, the most famous being Cthulhu. Perhaps Lovecraft managed to spy one of these things in a telescope or talked to someone who had. The resemblance possibly being just another example of the coincidental nature of the Universe. I would have loved to ponder the subject with my crewmates but I was too busy witnessing the slow approach of the folkloric creatures that would undoubtedly end up killing us all.

"I'll be damned!" came A1's voice behind me. "That is a Voraith! I'd always thought they were some bullshit made up by seasoned pilots to frighten new crew members and to populate their exaggerated space stories."

"Well, if we live through this you'll be one of those old codgers running his mouth in a rundown bar at the ass-end of the Galaxy," I noted. He mumbled a response that I neither heard nor cared about. The gigantic monster that was the Sot n'Gayth (or Voraith as it was called amongst old space pilots) was drawing closer to the three hahkarnish who themselves were heading headlong for our ship. In mere moments we would be smack dab in the middle of an epic battle for survival between these giants who showed us no more care than a bug.

"Do something!" yelled Fig stirring me from my awe.

"Like what? Take a picture?"

"Ass," she replied shoving me aside and sat in the pilot's chair to take command of the ship's controls. I wanted to tell her that we wouldn't be able to outrun them nor maneuver out of the way in time but my annoyance at her inability to credit me with common sense overcame my desire to share the obvious. In a flash she came to my same conclusion. "The engines are off. The disturbance to the gravity drive knocked them dead. How did this happen?" She spun her chair to confront me and then looked up at me in disgust. "Your fly's open." Her eyes flew to Zyryn who was still watching our fate unfold.

"Uh..." I didn't know what to say so just closed my mouth.

Fig stood and shoved a finger into my chest. "You are such a worthless prick. All you had to do was watch the controls for a few hours and you led us to this," her finger swept to the screen. "Can you not do anything?"

While she had a point, my temper was on the rise not willing to take her chastisement without a fight. "How would I know we would come across this impossible situation? Who would suspect running into a herd of hahkarnish and a fucking Voraith?"

She squinted a mean look at me. "See that blinking light? That warns you of unrecognized disruptions within the fold of the gravity drive. You have flown a ship before, right? Isn't that your job?"

"Uh, yeah. I know that but..." I couldn't come up with anything remotely resembling an excuse. "That's not the only thing I have to keep my eye on you know." Weak.

She looked even more disgusted and shook her head. "I bet you had plenty else to look at," she looked again towards Zyryn who still wouldn't look back at us now clearly pretending to be transfixed by the sight outside the ship. "What a piece of work. So we just sit here and wait to be crushed?"

"Can't we shoot it?" asked Doon.

"Sorry, Doon," I said. "Those things are too huge. Wouldn't hurt them."

He looked exasperated. "Can't we at least try? It's better than just sitting here doing nothing!"

"Kid's got a point," said A1.

It looked to be my opportunity to get off the Bridge and maybe die in peace far from Fig's accusations and damning tone. "Fine! Fine, I'll do it." I raced down the passageway to the entrance to the gun blister on the top of the Heart. I slapped the headset on and spun the weapon toward the creatures. Sitting in the bubble and looking out at the things drove the scale of them home. Not viewing from the confines of the ship's interior I felt like I was alone in space with the gargantuan monsters. They now took up most of my view and all four were far too close. A couple crip bumped against the side of the bubble and nearly made me crap my pants.

"What was that scream?" asked Fig.

"I didn't hear anything," I lied. I trained the gun on the titans and prepared to fire. Maybe I would get lucky and the shots would scare them in another direction but at the short distance I had the feeling that their turn radius was far too wide to miss us even if that worked. But it was the only chance we had.

I think I might have uttered a short prayer and then I pulled the trigger.

There was a harsh noise and a jolt and I held the trigger back down and just let them fly. My eyes were closed.

When I stopped firing - I think due to Fig's shouting in my ear to stop - I opened my eyes and fully expected them to be right on top of us, angered from my fire, and seconds from smashing us to dust. But there was nothing there. It was like they had just disappeared. A few crip drifted by but the behemoths were nowhere to be seen. Had my shots scared them off and they had some means of spontaneous acceleration? It seemed impossible but as I craned my neck to search the vicinity the fact was there were no huge monsters of rare imagination. Just space. Space and stupid, impossible crip.

"What..?" was all I could say.

There was the momentary static and snuffling in my ear as the Bridge headset rustled with activity. Doon's voice boomed in my ear. "You did it! You destroyed them!"

"What? How?"

"You shot them and they just exploded!"

"Come again?"

"They exploded, Argon! They're gone!"

I pulled the headset off and clamored down to the passageway. As I started for the Bridge Doon met me at the door. He quickly grabbed me in his long arms and hugged me. "You did it!"

I squirmed free. "It was your idea, buddy. I just did what you said." He simply grinned at me. I walked onto the Bridge and looked at Fig. "What happened?"

"It is just what Doon said," she reiterated. "They exploded when you hit them."

"Why? They were huge! The rounds should have just bounced off or just made them angry."

Many years later I would learn that these giants of the spaceways were incredibly delicate things. Given the environmental challenges of living in zero gravity with no air made them mostly just enormous, fragile husks. Their bulk was filled with stored nutrients and whatever gas and dust they could gather in their lonely sojourn across the Galaxy. With little to draw from in their journeys they simply took advantage of everything they came across and stored anything not immediately digested, like camels storing water. Movement was indeed another obstacle of survival so they remained as light as possible to require the least amount of energy to propel themselves when faced with gravitational forces. A testament to the adaptability of Nature and the bizarre picture this sense of purpose presents.

"It was like they were just made of gossamer and tissue paper. Once the round pierced one of them it popped like a balloon and the others quickly followed suit. They just turned to dust." She was smiling and obviously relieved. I secretly hoped the events that led up to this salvation were forgotten but I knew I would never be that lucky. My mistakes would surface again. But for now everything was perfect and I was fine with that. I turned back towards Doon.

"You're a hero, my friend. You saved us all."

"But you…" he started.

"No. It was you and just you." I moved closer to him so only he could hear. "You take this, Doon. You take all of it and always know that when all the rest of us could do was stare and shit ourselves you knew what to do. You saved us. You." I hugged him and then left the Bridge. I needed a drink.

I walked down the passageway with the sounds of the glad handing around Doon. I was honestly happy for him but the contrast of their collective view of him and of me only managed to make me feel worse about things. I wasn't a hero and I wasn't even a good guy. I had almost gotten us killed with my single minded womanizing. As soon as I got back to the crew quarters I managed to scrounge a bottle of some foul smelling liquor. After splashing some in a glass and throwing it back I decided it wasn't as bad as it smelled and poured a good portion into the glass and sat on the edge of my bunk. I let my mind drift through my sack of assorted self-pitying memories searching for one that might make this dreadful time seem like a party. It wasn't long before I found one. A good one.

I HAD BEEN A RESTLESS YOUTH OF COURSE but when my mother passed away I was like a balloon that had escaped its tether to the earth. She had become sick and had been diagnosed the day Trixie had left. Five months later she finally succumbed to the disease and my father had been hit hard by the loss. I had taken it less so as I was now a young man with plans and dreams and love. I wouldn't let sadness cloud my "sunny day" so I did more of what I wanted to do and less of what I didn't. I constantly fought my father on everything and he was too overcome with sadness to fight back. I can look back in hindsight and see that the loss of my mother destroyed him. He was never the same. Sure, I missed her but as with most teenagers I was too self absorbed to understand the impact it would have. I spent more and more time away from home with Fig and Doon and hanging out at the docks waiting for Trixie to come back.

I skipped school constantly and it was soon apparent that I would not graduate, yet I never really cared. My father finally gave up nagging me about it sensing his words and threats had no effect. The only thing that kept me going was the thought of Trixie coming back to Blag. The memories of those three perfect days were a constant hum in the back of my mind and it was the fuel that powered my days and nights. I ached for her in a way that only the first love of adolescence can.

I hadn't really paid much attention to my father and his steady decline. My life was too full of hope and impossible dreams to bother with anything else around me. The day the Rontarr was supposed to dock was the day I had been straining for. I couldn't sleep and I was up at dawn to get ready and head for the docks a full seven hours before Trixie's ship was scheduled to dock. After over six long months this day was going to be the longest part of the wait. I burst into the kitchen a wreck of nervous energy and anxious stomach in search of something to quiet the rumblings.

"Where are you off to?" asked a voice in the early morning gloom of the kitchen nook. My father was sitting in his usual spot drinking. He had been there every morning I left and every night I returned but that strange fact never connected to anything in my infatuated, crowded brain.

"I'm off to the docks, Dad." I fished a pastry from a sack in the pantry noticing only mildly that it was the last one and quite stale.

"Isn't it a school day?" he asked, a slight slur to his words.

"Isn't it a work day?" I snapped back at him having noticed that he never left the house.

"Don't be smart with me, Argon."

I finally looked at him and saw his sad state. He was unshaven, dirty and impossibly thin. My dad has always been a tall, lean man but the figure staring at me from the shadow was a gaunt caricature of the man I had known as my father. He held his drink in both hands as if it was the only thing anchoring him to this world. His eyes were sunken and rimmed in red and looked at me with a sadness that pleaded for something I couldn't understand but could have given without effort. Yet despite this sudden moment of clarity, seeing my father as he really was right then, it offered no more resistance to my trajectory than the clouds in the sky. I dismissed him without a thought.

"You do what you want and I'll do what I want."

He paused long enough for me to take a bite of my pastry and I turned away from him one last time.

"Son," he rasped between sips of his drink. "Life is hard but whatever happens..."

"...happens," I finished for him. "I gotta roll out, Pops. I might be gone for a few days. See you when I see you," and I was out the door never looking back.

The seven hours at the dock turned into thirteen when the Rontarr finally docked. I was a mess by then and had not eaten nor drank a single thing. The constant mugginess of the damp Blag weather was having its toll. I was wet, tired, and sick with anxious feelings but my hope kept me steadfast. My mom had told me once that Hope is the charity of Dreams and I never understood what that meant. But I would soon find out.

As the Rontarr finally finished mooring and the cargo began to be removed from the storage bays I saw crew members start to leave the ship. I started for the gangway and only then did I notice the scoring across the hull. As it drew more of my attention I took notice of the severity of the damage along the side of the ship; parts of the hull patched or replaced entirely. It was apparent that the ship had been damaged by something. I don't know why but with that realization my

Kirk Nelson

anxiousness to see Trixie changed to something closer to panic. I hastily ran for the entrance to the ship.

Just as I reached the hatch a few more crew members came walking out almost colliding with me. One of them recognized me from my many visits. He was an older, stout man with a bald head and numerous tattoos. I was fairly sure his name was Tug.

"Argon?" he said.

I shook his hand. "Tug, right?"

"Yeah. What's the rush, son?"

"I saw the ship had some damage and I was concerned about..."

"Yeah. Ran afoul of those blasted Xydoc Zyn. Gave us a bad run. We was lucky enough to get clear and make it to port."

My sick feeling only grew more at the mention of the dreaded Xydoc Zyn. "Is Trix coming out soon? I really need to see her. She doesn't have the first duty shift does she?"

His expression changed in an instant and my whole world stopped cold. I knew what he was going to say, I knew it when I saw the damage on the side of the ship, I knew it from the look of pity that had crowded its way onto his face but I couldn't do anything to change it. I couldn't move. I couldn't speak. I was forced by shock to stand and listen to him say it.

"I'm sorry, Argon. She didn't make it. She was lost during a boarding party raid. She was a tough one and a hell of a crewmate but those damn pirates are evil relentless bastards. She fought to the end and that helped fend them off. I'm just glad it wasn't a bigger ship that hit us." He looked at me with empathy. I don't know what Trixie had ever said to the rest of her crew so our relationship could be unknown to Tug and his mates but I sensed he knew something. "I'm sorry." He placed a hand on my shoulder. I spun around and started walking down the gangway. I heard him still talking but the world around me held no reality. There was no hope, there was no charity. There were no dreams.

I don't remember how long I sat on a stubby bollard on the pier but it was dark and growing cold. I was soaking wet and trembling but I just didn't care. My eyes had run dry of tears and the numbness of the damp cold was paltry compared to my emotions.

Tug came walking up then and handed me a coat. I didn't move so he just draped it over my shoulders. "You should just go home, Argon."

"What's the point?"

"The point is that she's gone but you're not. You need to keep going. You're a young man with a long life ahead of you. You need to focus on that."

"I can't."

"You will. As hard as this is now, you will manage to get past it. Everybody does. Son, life is tough and whatever happens, happens."

The phrase shot through my brain like a bullet and I suddenly thought about my dad. "Not everybody gets past it," I realized. How could I have not seen what was happening to him? I quickly stood to leave.

"Here," and Tug reached into his pocket and pulled out something dark to hand to me. I reached out and took it. In the faint light I held it out and recognized it immediately - the bandana-thing Trixie always wore and her goggles. "She would have wanted you to have this. I found them after we managed to fend off the Zyn."

I looked at Tug, said a hasty "Thank you" and raced off towards home. All the way there I replayed the tearing feeling of my heart breaking and the boundless empty feeling left behind. And I would see this reflected in my father who had lost the love of his life. But I had loved Trixie for such a short time compared to his thirty years of marriage. It didn't lessen my pain instead lifting my selfish blinders from my eyes to reveal how insensitive I had been the last five months. I throttled my flyer until the engine screamed near its breaking point. It was clear to me then that I needed him and he needed me. That together we could weather the loneliness and sorrow that wanted to destroy us.

When I approached the house I felt the same nervous dread that had overtaken me at the docks. The house was dark and silent. Bursting through the door I raced to the kitchen praying I would see my father sitting, unmoved, in his normal spot in the nook. He wasn't there. "Dad!" I called out but no reply ever came. I screamed his name over and over as I raced through our small house. Finally I entered his bedroom and discovered him there. I froze. As I looked up at him I saw the horrible reality of what my mother's death had done to him. "Dad," I sobbed and grabbed a chair to get him down. I wondered if this is what love really produces - an ache so deep and complete that life itself loses all meaning. Why would anyone ever want such a thing. Why would I? I gently loosed the rope from his neck and placed him on the floor. All I desperately wanted was for him to hold me and tell me he still loved me but nothing was left within him. I felt my eyes sting with the promise of tears but none would come having spent them all at the docks. I just crumbled there in the dark beside the body of my father and choked on a gasping sob. Never in my short life had I felt so utterly alone.

Ten days later I was signed on to the Nir'don under Captain Galcursed and saying my goodbyes to Galaxia and Doonbridge. I swore to never lay eyes on the cursed planet Blag again and I couldn't even keep that promise.

"ARE YOU CRYING?" she said so suddenly that I jumped. I spun around and looked up to see Fig looking down at me. She put a hand on my shoulder. "Are you okay?" There was genuine concern in her voice and for a second I was straddling the death of Trixie and my father and the utter fuck-up my life was currently. Sure I was crying, who wouldn't?

I wiped at my face. "No. Don't be silly. Why would I be crying?" I forced out a small laugh that fell flat and only proved that I had been. I stood and tried a covering gesture by stretching. I yawned and said, "Are we at the wormhole yet?" I didn't make eye contact.

"Argon?"

I was really trying to force a high degree of nonchalance into my voice. "Yes?" I finally looked at her.

"Doon told me what you said to him."

"Sorry? What did I say?" At this point I was actually looking at my fingernails like some hackneyed cartoon.

She punched my shoulder. "Stop it."

"What?" I said with all the confused innocence I could fake.

She just stood there, hands on hips, and gave me a stern look. "I came to find you to tell you how sweet, surprisingly, that it was for you to tell that to Doon and I find you sitting on a bunk whimpering. What the hell is wrong with you?"

"I wasn't 'whimpering'."

"Your eyes are still red."

"Allergies."

"We're on a spaceship, you idiot."

"I'm allergic to A1."

"Stop it. Just stop it."

I looked at her and I saw something in her face that showed she was concerned, really concerned. My shoulders fell and I raised my hands in surrender. "I give up."

"What?" she questioned.

"I am a full fledged asshole and I don't deserve to be around people. You'd do best to just stay away from me. Once this stupid shit is over I expect you to race the fuck away from me just as fast as this ship can go until the only Argon you know is sitting on a periodic table."

"Why do you say that?" she said with a hint of sadness in her voice. It caught me completely by surprise.

I raised an eyebrow staring at her confused. "Uh...because I am a disease that attacks and kills happiness. Look at me. My life is shit and not only do I have to sit and splash around in it but I have the rare gift of dragging those I love..." I stopped.

"Go on," she prompted.

"I mean. No...uh..."

"Yes?"

"Don't you have a ship to fly or something?"

"Don't change the subject. You were saying something?"

"Fig."

"Yes?"

"I...I'm..." The room seemed to spin a little throwing me off balance. I thought maybe I was passing out until Fig fell into my arms stumbling as the ship pitched hard to port.

"What's happening, Argon?" she said with alarm. It wasn't me, the ship was starting rolling and I could hear the engines laboring to keep the ship stable. I held her tight so she wouldn't fall.

"Hey you lovebirds!" shouted A1 from the entrance. "If you can quit making out for a minute there seems to be something wrong with the ship."

Son of a bitch.

CHAPTER 18

I was freezing. The wind was blasting at me and I hadn't much wardrobe to pull from to insulate me from the frigid weather. My meager gloves were fingerless which, while looking cool, held no protection in what one might consider the important part of gloves in general: keeping your hands warm. And as luck would have it, my luck that is, I was on an ice ball in space trying to pull flesh out of the engine vents with my semi-bare hands.

The Sononi Heart had lost thrust in the port engine after our encounter with the rather bizarre deep space creatures that I ended up blowing apart. While it had appeared to all of those watching that they simply vaporized, in actuality the enormous beasts had blown apart and their skin and flesh flew everywhere. It was discovered later that a large amount of it flew onto the hull of the Heart and had managed to clog several important orifices of the vessel. When Doon had applied the thrusters to try and maneuver us back on course the port engine failed and we spun and bucked like a crazed dervish. Fortunately we were able to land the ship on a nearby moon to make repairs. Little gravity or atmosphere and freezing cold all contributed to the misery of all as we fervently tried to pull the disgusting muck from the vents.

"This stuff is freezing solid," remarked Doon over the comm channel. "I am going to have to bust it out with a pick!"

"Careful," warned Fig. "A wild swing and we might not be able to take off from here."

"Noted," acknowledged Doon.

"Did the rest of you hear that?" I added, my gaze directed at A1 who was swinging his pick like he was mining for Feronium ore.

Zyryn, Brad, and Bruce all chimed in and I waited for A1 to at least grunt. "A1?"

"What? I'm working here!"

"Take it easy on those vents. Bust a fuel line or cut a wire and we might be stuck here."

"I know what I'm doing!" he shouted back, no change in his tempo.

"Go easy on it, you jackhammer! I want to leave as much as anybody but..."

There was an intense flash of light and the mildest feeling of an explosion and suddenly A1 was cartwheeling across the frozen comet. A steady stream of cursing filled the comm channel as A1 grabbed furtively at the smooth ice, the occasional outcropping, and finally empty space as he began to float off the comet.

The suddenness of the whole thing seemed to dull the reactions of the rest of the crew as they simply stared at him all the while imagining he would just stop. I'd witnessed this before and knew, there would be no stopping until he was snagged by a star's gravity and pulled into its insatiably furnace. Or he gets hit by a passing ship. Not a pleasant sight having been witness to it once before.

I had luckily grabbed a tether line when we exited the Heart just to ensure I didn't do what A1 was doing right then. Some others had as well but they had mostly just left them coiled on the ice. So I started running.

Running in low gravity is a sure fire recipe for disaster. If your feet hit hard enough you just bounce up and don't come down. The crew of my old ship, the Nir'don, used to have races on low G moons, asteroids, and comets. A kind of space parkour. It was a lot of fun and we carried tether lines and thrust packs to make sure we could get down to the surface if we got careless. Only lost one of the crew that way and I have always remembered that day. The Sononi Heart didn't carry thruster packs so tethers were the only thing we had. I would have to make do with just a bunch of rope.

I started my best running/skating style across the ice quickly grabbing up what loops of cord I passed. A1 was not traveling fast but the less distance I had to travel the better.

"Hey you old turnip, throw me your pick!" I shouted to him on the comm channel.

"Who are you calling...?"

"Just throw it!"

"Why?" he argued.

"Bruce needs a tool and you aren't going to be using yours."

"Well Bruce can just..."

"I'm kidding, you clod! Throw me the pick!"

He was rotating slowly but managed to give a decent toss of the pick. I grabbed it, quickly tied an end of the cord to it and drove it into the ice with all my might. It took hold and I quickly ran a few more feet and launched myself at A1. I had been tying the separate loops of cord together as I was running along and now had a substantial length to utilize in my rescue attempt. Doon had chased after me when he saw me race after A1's drifting form so I called back to him.

"Make sure that pick stays anchored, Doon, or I will be spending the rest of my short life with that cagey old fart."

"You got it, Argon," he answered.

I had gotten a little more speed in my jump than A1's velocity so I was gradually closing the distance. I feared I might run out of tether before I reached him but I would give it my best try.

"A1!" I yelled on the comm. "I'm coming out after you. Watch for me 'cause we are only getting one shot at this and it will be close."

He just mumbled something and tried to right himself to face me. Sadly, in space, you don't have anything to push against so only very minor changes can be impacted by body movements. The rope was uncoiling faster than I'd like to see and it would be only seconds before I snapped at the end. I fashioned a quick loop on the end and placed my foot through it so my hands would be free. Then I dropped the remainder as I couldn't stand the tension of seeing it run to its end in my hands. I focused on A1 and got ready to make one final grab.

As we closed he swung around slowly and I could see his face and for the first time since our unfortunate meeting I saw real dread and concern on his face. He knew what was at stake and realized that this had a good chance of not ending well for him. Or he simply loathed the fact that I might be his only chance for salvation.

The span between us grew shorter and I could not bring myself to look back and see what little rope was left. It was all or nothing.

It was nothing.

I felt the rope tug on my foot just as I reached him and my arms shot out with every bit of extra length I could get, willing my joints to extend as far as they could. I was just shy as my fingers almost brushed against his ass. I actually felt sick knowing I wouldn't reach him. I shouldn't have cared at all but after all the time we had spent together I can at least say he was a person I knew and I didn't want to see him die in such a horrible fashion.

And then his body rotated around and I was able to just snag his boot with my fingers!

There was a small loop near the heel and one of my fingers managed to hook into it. It was a one in a million chance of logistics and trigonometry. I wasted no time in dragging him closer and grasping his boot with both hands.

"Doon! Reel us in!"

"Uh..." he uttered and the sound of it was not reassuring. I looked back down and was first shocked to see how far from the surface I was and then at the fact that Doon was not standing on the surface either.

"What the hell?" I exclaimed.

"I saw you weren't going to make it so I grabbed the pick out of the ice and started running to give you more rope. When you got too high I had to stop and..."

"My momentum pulled you off the ground," I finished, another sick feeling in my stomach.

"Yeah. Sorry."

From my high vantage point I saw figures scrambling across the icy waste heading for Doon. One was far in the lead and I knew it was Fig. She still had her tether and she had it attached to her pick and was whirling it over her head like some old fashioned cowboy on a steer round-up.

"Doon! Catch!" she blasted into the comms. She let it fly and it rocketed straight at him with a velocity that made me worry for his safety. It ended up sailing just over his head and he reached out with one hand and grabbed the rope. I suddenly had visions of Fig being pulled free of the comet as well and eventually we would be just like a length of toy monkeys and floating along in a strangely connected string. But at the last second I saw the other figures cluster onto Fig and anchor her to the ground. We all stopped moving and a second later I felt the first pull towards the surface.

It took awhile but we all finally got back down to the surface. I was never so relieved to have the ground under my feet.

"That completely sucked ass," I remarked in a puff of exasperation. I glared at A1 who went out of his way to not return it. I walked over and gave his shoulder a shove. "Well?"

"I got carried away. It was cold. I wanted…"

"You wanted to get yourself killed is what you were trying to do!" I felt my rage clouding my brain and working my jaw. "If you want to be stupid just stay in the ship. Fig warned us about the vents."

"I didn't hear her," he sputtered but I could tell he was lying. He still wouldn't look me in the eye.

"Is that the best you got 'cause I ain't buying that. You were just being as careless as you usually are. Just causing more shit and then we have to drop everything because good old A1 needs help. I'm sick of it."

He just stood there looking at the ice beneath his feet. If I were more sensitive I would have recognized he was defeated; that he couldn't even fight back. But I was far too pissed to let up and allow reason to intercept my anger.

"I should have let you drift away into space! But with my luck and your tenacity to be a pain in my ass we would have had your dusty old body float into an intake vent and blow the ship up. That would have been about right considering the huge fucking mess you have made of everything since I bumped into you outside of Galder's. I wonder if those thugs you were running from were just some poor blokes that had had the unfortunate experience of knowing you."

I could feel Fig at my elbow. "Argon! Leave him alone."

I shook her off and turned toward her. "Why? He is useless! If it weren't for him you'd be happily sitting in your office counting your Blag money and living your grand, carefree life. But nope, you are stuck here on this dirty chunk of ice with a busted-ass ship and some ancient bastard wailing away on it like he was building a bridge." I waved my arm at everyone now standing around looking at me going quickly insane. "That goes for all of us! We would all be somewhere else, doing anything else, and not have the horrid misfortune of knowing this worthless piece of shit!" I spun around and pointed straight at A1 to accentuate my point.

He finally looked up at me and I could see through his helmet that he was upset. His face was pale and his eyes looked red. He just looked at me for a moment then turned and walked back to the ship.

"What a first-class ass clown!" I said watching him slowly trudge across the ice. "How does he get through life? I am constantly having to pick up his slack. Who'd he have to save his life before me? A squad of highly trained military storm troopers, a room of genius tacticians, and a sweet old nursemaid?" I turned back toward the rest of the crew, pleased with myself for finally putting him in his place, only to find the only person still standing there was Doon. Fig was almost back to the ship along with Zyryn, Bruce, and Barry. Doon was staring at me with a particularly repulsed look on his face. I thought momentarily that it was due to me not thanking him for saving my life.

"Hey," I smiled. "Sorry buddy. I got carried away and forgot to thank you for saving me."

"I can't yell at you like you do to other people but if I could you'd feel worse than A1."

"What?"

"You heard me. And next time you want to point out an asshole, look in the mirror." He headed back to the ship with the others leaving me alone. Arguing or pressing the issue wouldn't help, I knew that much. It takes a lot to upset Doon and I was having a hard time figuring out why. I had not hesitated to put myself at risk to rescue a man I basically hated. To me that is what a hero does. So why the cold shoulder by everyone, I wondered. With nothing left to do I started toward the ship.

"So what the hell did I do?" I asked Fig.

We were now back on course, trying to make up for lost time. Fig was at the controls and I was trying to figure out why she was being so cold. I thought we were finally starting to gain some ground on our relationship as friends but suddenly we were back where we started this trip and I feared she would haul off and punch me in the face again.

No response.

"Fig! What is it?" Nothing still. "C'mon! Just tell me what it is? You can't possibly be this upset about me calling out A1 for being a royal pain in the ass. You know I was right!'

She still just sat there and pretended that navigating through space took all of her concentration. It didn't.

"I'm not leaving. I've know you too long to put up with this pouting. Just tell me."

She turned to look at me and I could see the hurt in her expression. And it was something deep and painful. I was at a complete and utter loss. "My God, Fig. What is it?"

"Argon," she started and I could pick up the slightest tremor in her voice as she fought to keep it steady. "You are insufferable. I don't remember what I ever saw in you. I've known you all of my life since we left Earth and yet after these many decades you still manage to surprise me with just how insensitive and hurtful you can be. I had hoped I was over your effect on me but you can still manage to crush me with a simple off-handed remark that cuts like razors and leaves me a crumpled mess. And the thing is, you are so insensitive to not even know what you have done." The last word caught for just a brief moment but long enough to know she was failing in her fight to stay strong. She was as angry as she could get but the pain was winning the battle.

"I don't know how this is all going to end - maybe I'll just be dead - but I will tell you this: I want nothing, NOTHING, to do with you once it's finished. I am done with you. Done."

"That's hardly fair," I protested having no clue as to what else to do. Her anger and hurt were a complete mystery. Unless she had found out about Zyryn. But I hurriedly ran it through my mind and couldn't place a way for her to suddenly find out while we were out on the ice. It had to have been something else. Something I did? Something I said?

"Fair?! Are you just trying to stoop even lower because it isn't possible you complete ignorant fuck!" Her anger was now winning. "Get out of here!"

I wandered off down the main corridor scratching my head in puzzlement. Something about being fair had sparked her rage. Fair? What had I said that would hurt her about being fair? And then the door opened in my memory and it all made sense.

Blag.

"IT'S NOT FUCKING FAIR, FIG!" I shouted. "This fucking planet just keeps fucking with me! I fucking hate it! Fuck!"

"Nice rounded vocabulary, Argon," she jibed. "May I suggest a thesaurus?"

"Don't do that. Don't make light of this, Fig. It's not...freakin' funny."

"Yeah, doesn't have the same punch."

I just stared at her. I wasn't letting go of my anger no matter what she said. People in the bar were looking at us but I didn't care. I was about to stand up and start yelling at them just to let some of my steam out before my head exploded. Doon put his hand on my shoulder.

"Don't stand up and start bellowing like a mad thing. That won't help."

I folded my arms across my chest and glared at the table. I needed to kick something in the worst possible way. Never a trash can around when you need one.

Fig and Doon looked at each other and then back at me. "What exactly did they say?" asked Fig.

Time for a little history refresher course:

The first colony to leave Earth was the ship my family was on. Among the other thousand families were Fig and Doon's families. As part of the compensation for establishing a Galactic Well Base on our moon without the Earth's permission the Galactic Tribunal provided a colony ship to a planet set aside just for us. That planet was Blag. And it sucked ass.

It rained about 95% of the time so it was hot and humid and contained a huge amount of plant life. After being there for a short while a new strain of tenacious mold began to proliferate on the planet. Scientists theorized that it was the genetic accident of a cross pollination of an Earth mold that arrived with us and a hearty native moss. In no time at all the stuff was everywhere. It grew at an amazing rate and seemed impervious to anything we could throw at it. Hell, stand still long enough and you'd find it growing across your shoes. It was only dangerous in its rampant growth but posed no danger to us. But it sure made life unbearable. The big brain-trust on the planet finally managed to come up with a retardant that could slow the growth but it was just a way to manage it not extinguish it. My first job was a duster pilot trying to spray the life out of the disgusting mold which we had nicknamed the "creep." A bunch of well meaning people tried to utilize it for anything useful they could imagine. Growing up I had had my fill of creep soup, salad, tea, bread, chips, snacks, and jerky. Then there was the cloth for clothing, bricks for building, and fuel for fires. It was almost comical the things desperate people would try and use it for. But it tasted horrible; animals would eat it only out of desperation. Any products made from it were short lived - the cloth caused you to itch, the bricks dried out and crumbled, and as fuel it stunk like a dirty diaper burning in a hair fire. It was, in a word, utterly useless. And we were surrounded by it. Everywhere.

Then, one fateful day, some Klanx got lost, got their ship all busted, and ended up landing on our planet. It was while they were waiting that things started to get strange. Klanx are all business and don't have any room in their harried schedules for "waiting around." So the idea of wasting a couple days on some backwater planet like Blag made them extremely uncomfortable and pretty damn cranky. And that was exactly how it was. For one day.

By the second day they were going crazy. They were drinking, partying, and having sex with anyone that might offer them an opportunity. Since Klanx do nothing but work and hoard their money they are all fairly well heeled. And they were spending money like they couldn't get rid of the stuff fast enough. No one had ever seen them cut loose like that before and they had no intention of stopping. It took only two days to repair their ship but they wouldn't leave. After a couple weeks more Klanx came looking for them. Then they wouldn't leave either. Before you knew it Klanx were coming to Blag by the hundreds. And it was all due to that damn mold.

It turned out that the mold was some kind of drug to them. After being on the planet for a day they had managed to breathe enough spores from the stuff to develop a contact high. If they ingested it in any way it was even quicker and stronger. It was christened "blaganite." Overnight a huge demand had sprung up for all the useless crap we had tried to make out of it. The people of Blag started shipping out huge quantities of blaganite tea to all of the Klanx worlds. Suddenly Blag was a holiday destination for a huge section of the Galaxy. The Terrans that settled there were rich!

But not me.

I had left Blag to join the crew of the Nir'don years before the Klanx ever landed. When I finally heard about all the money all the people of Blag were getting from the blaganite I took a leave and headed for home for my piece of the pie. But as I soon found out, there wasn't any pie for Argon Bosch.

"They said I don't have a claim," I snapped. "I had left and unlike you two, my parents are both dead. I don't get a stake in this cash cow.

Nothing."

"That can't be right," said Doon. "You grew up here just like us. You are listed as a founding colonist just like me and Fig."

"That's right," agreed Fig. "There has to be a mistake. There has to be." Her head dropped into her hands.

"You don't think I pointed that out to them? They saw the records. But in their eyes I had left with no one here to establish a claim. If one of my parents had still been alive..." I stopped myself there not wanting to finish the thought. As greedy as I might be I couldn't blame my parents. Thinking about it caused far too much contact with feelings I had buried long ago.

"We need to go to the government with this," announced Fig. "We'll make a big case out of this. We'll get the media involved too."

"Right," agreed Doon. "They won't get away with this. You're entitled to your share, Argon. And Fig and I are going to make sure you get it!"

Fig smiled and stood, "That's right! They won't have a chance against the three of us!"

"Shut the hell up!" yelled a stoned Klanx from the next table, a bevy of empty tea glasses ringing the table.

Fig walked over and slapped the glass from his hand. "You shut up or we'll kick you off OUR planet."

He quickly turned back to his table searching the other glasses for some sign of liquid.

"Let's go set them straight," announced Doon. I stood up with them and we marched out the door together with a confidence and righteousness that was sure to move a bureaucratic mountain. I finally had some hope.

A week later that too was all gone.

"I'm really sorry, Argon. I'll be happy to keep fighting if you want," offered Fig.

I hugged her and smiled. "Thanks but it won't do any good. You are wasting your money and time. They aren't going to bend."

"Well, I already talked to Doon about this and he agreed, we'll give you some of our money. Split it equally amongst the three of us."

I gave her a long look, not because I doubted the honesty of their generous offer but because I couldn't believe the pity in her eyes. All our lives she and Doon had looked up to me. Doon even idolized me. And now suddenly I was some sad charity case that couldn't make it and needed their help to get by. It hurt my pride and I couldn't take the sudden decline in stature.

"Seriously?"

"Of course!" she assured. "You deserve it as much as we do and we'd feel horrible if you didn't share in the fortune. It just wouldn't be right."

And the last words carried along the same sentiment: pity. The more she talked and pushed the offer the more it banged against my pride. I could start to feel my hurt and indignation give way to anger and resentment. When it finally erased all perception of good intent I quickly stood.

"I don't want your charity. I don't want your money," I said a bit too loud.

She looked at me surprised. "It isn't charity, Argon. It is the thing one friend would do for another."

"Yeah. A friend that felt sorry for the other is what you mean. I don't need your pity. I'll be fine by myself just like I always have."

She looked a little hurt and a bit angry. That only increased my self righteousness. "So you and Doon can sail through life on your cloud of free money, not worrying about a thing and your old friend Argon will just have to earn his own way."

"Damn you, Argon, you stubborn ass! You know that's not what I mean. We are your friends and it is what friends do!" She gave me her best glare and I decided I'd had enough of it. I turned to leave.

"Where are you going? Let's talk this out, Argon. Argon?" But I was already heading out the door. She ran after me and stopped at the doorway. "Argon, please. Just stop. I'm sorry." And I knew even right then that she meant it. Despite my own juvenile outburst she felt sorry and apologized. But as time would show again and again, once I got angry I ceased to care or have rational thoughts. I didn't look back and just kept walking. Fig knew me well enough to know that no amount of pleading was going to change my attitude so she just watched me go.

I made a straight path to the other side of the city and was soon in the seedier section that had sprung up to accommodate the Klanx and their blaganite fueled debauchery. I walked into a random bar and brothel and stayed there. Three days later I walked out, headed for my ship, and left Blag far behind and haven't been back since. I never said goodbye to Fig or Doon and it would be several years before I would see them again.

IN MY STUPID RANTING I had mentioned her Blag fortune. God, I was a horrid thing. I swung around and headed back to the Bridge.

"I am sorry, Fig. I lost my head. I shouldn't have…"

"No, you shouldn't have. But you can't help yourself, can you? You get mad or upset and you can just say whatever you want. Just punch people who care about you with your careless words. And then come walking back all humble and apologetic and expect that everything will be OK. Well I'm here to tell you that's not the way it works. Not then, not now, not ever! You have managed to hurt me more than any other person I have ever met. Or poor innocent Doon. The suns rose and set by you. He idolized you. When I was hurt by some mean thing you casually did or said he was always the one that argued on your behalf. He never failed to come to your defense. But you never saw that in him. But you were so quick to dismiss him just like me. Turn your back on him; leave him alone without even a 'goodbye.' All because of your wonderful captain dying."

"Now wait a second. There was a lot more to that. I loved that man like a father. And then he was…"

"Gone. Right. So you lost people in your life. We all have but that doesn't give us the right to turn our back on those that love us and need us. So sure, you lost a man that was a surrogate father to you when you left home. But he was taken from you. How do you think it feels to have someone you loved with all your heart just walk away from you like you were just some piece of useless furniture? That is real hurt." She paused and there was pleading in her eyes. "I loved you." She started to cry. The words triggered my auto-defenses and I had plenty of sharp comebacks at the ready but I couldn't say them. They couldn't get past the sudden extreme sense of loss I felt. She spoke of her feelings in the past tense and after all I had done to her and all I had said it finally became clear to me that I had lost her. She was really gone. I had finally spewed enough hurtful things to kill the root of her affection for me. It wouldn't grow back. The seed I had planted as we watched the Earth grow smaller, leaving our home for a new one far across the emptiness of space, was dead. And I was the one that murdered it. By my own hand. The most precious gift I had ever received. Gone. And by now I think everyone knows how I react to loss.

Fig was crying and the sobs seemed to take all the words she ached to shout away from her. So I left the Bridge and walked to the Galley. I pulled two bottles of liquor out of a cabinet and walked to Fig's stateroom. I swung open the door and found Zyryn standing near the closet changing out of her space gear. She looked surprised to see me but not in an unwelcome way. I glanced down and saw Squirty by the door. After giving him one stern look he fled the room. I closed the door and locked it.

"Keszler Bridge," I announced looking out the viewport on the Bridge. I had seen a wormhole before so it wasn't a strange an aspiration as others would think. Something akin to an inverted bubble in space. The Keszler Bridge was one of the few more stable wormholes in the galaxy and was anchored at this end by a nebula. It gave the look of the wormhole entrance a much more noticeable appearance whereas one that was located out in open space could easily be missed amongst the black.

The semi-stable wormholes were all called bridges as they linked to locations and provided a short cut. But no wormhole is stable forever and there have been a few that have collapsed while supporting traffic causing a terrible catastrophe of loss. The Quinion, T'Thell, and

Birky Bridges are a few that have cautioned many from utilizing bridges in their travels. No one has ever been found that was the victim of a bridge collapse. There are a lot of theories as to what happens to them but there is no proof of any of the theories. The one that scares the shit out of me is that you are simply crushed for infinity, never dying. That nightmare will wake you up in a sweat. So, this will be my first trip through one.

Zyryn was standing next to me as I piloted the ship up to the opening. We were the only two on the Bridge but my announcement over the ship's address system would have the others coming up soon. There was no way I was going to try and navigate the bridge. That duty fell squarely on Fig's shoulders as this was her ship and she had actually gone through Keszler Bridge once before.

I hadn't seen or talked to Fig since her breakdown and I knew she was as much avoiding me as I was her. I had taken over the piloting duties from Doon and he didn't want to have anything to do with me either. I guess my defender had finally relinquished his cause. I told myself they were better off without me and any allegiance would simply expose both of them to even more shit.

"My father mentioned this wormhole before," offered Zyryn. "I believe he has used it to outrun those trying to capture him. He made mention of a certain effect."

"What effect?" I asked.

"He didn't say except to mention that it was very unpleasant."

"I really don't like the sound of that."

"Move," came Fig's voice as she entered the Bridge. "Now."

I hastily gave up the chair and let her take her spot. She never gave me a glance, simply grabbing the controls, scanning the readouts, and bringing the ship directly in front of the wormhole. I sensed that this was the new way of things.

"Zyryn said there might be some side effect of flying through this. Is that true?" I asked trying to seem unfazed by Fig's icy manner.

"You'll see," she clipped and went back to prepping her ship. I suddenly noticed that no one else was present on the Bridge and that made me suspect that they may have been forewarned about any impending effects. I hoped that Fig's feelings towards me had not degraded to the point of wishing me extreme harm but given the whole "woman scorned" thing I determined it may be best if we find a suitable place to weather the ride.

"Hold on," was all she said and the Heart shot forward. I grabbed Zyryn's hand and pulled her with me as I attempted to get us free of the Bridge and into someplace that might offer protection - though I had no idea from what.

We made it to the forward passageway just beyond the Bridge when we flew into the entrance. We both turned to look out the viewport and then the effect hit us.

It wasn't wholly unpleasant but it was uncomfortable and very unique.

The first thing I noticed was the odd light that filled the screen. Then there was an intense pull of inertia that lifted our feet from the ground until we were parallel to the deck. I grabbed a hold of Zyryn's boots as she reached for a support beam that ran floor to ceiling near the door. The sensation was like my feet were being pulled backward. Then it hit me, the nausea. I felt like I was going to throw up as the ship suddenly sped up faster and faster and started to spin. With all this motion I still mostly just felt the odd pulling on my feet. And then I threw up. Yet I didn't. My mouth opened and I waited for the wretch but it didn't come. Instead I felt the bile moving back down my throat and the unique sensation I mentioned began. I could actually feel the contents of my stomach moving down through my body and not up and out of my mouth. And it just continued down. I was a tube of toothpaste getting the squeeze. Too late I realized what was going to happen as the entire contents of my digestive system was going to be looking for a way out. I tried to clench but I would have had better luck stopping a firehose with the palm of my hand. I had a bit of luck delaying the inevitable. Unfortunately Zyryn did not and everything came blasting out the bottom of her tight pants and onto her shoes and beyond. I let go thinking the pull on my feet would allow me to create some distance between me and Zyryn's reverse enema but surprisingly I didn't move. It only managed to duplicate the same pull on my hands as my feet and they snapped to my sides. Zyryn gave me everything she had right in the face.

At just that moment we cleared the wormhole and I dropped straight to the floor and promptly shit myself.

I vowed to never, ever fly through a wormhole again.

CHAPTER 19

Over the next couple days I tried to keep a low profile. I was frankly embarrassed about the events journeying through the Keszler Bridge and had received my share of comments, jokes, and jabs. If anyone accused me of having a "shit eating grin" one more time I would likely pull my pistol and shoot them on the spot. Zyryn alone seemed my only ally and so naturally I was drawn to her company versus the constant harassment I endured around everyone else. And while Doon didn't want anything to do with me, I purposely kept my distance from Fig. If I encountered her in a passageway I would avoid eye contact at all costs and keep my head down. The events of Keszler Bridge, my humiliation, and the way I had acted previously all spelled certain doom to the two friendships I treasured more than anything else. The circumstances and my resulting feelings only managed to render in stark reality just how far I had fallen from the man I once was. But, as I am prone to do, rather than accept the responsibility for my actions and try and come back from the chasm of self loathing, I just stayed my path and further felt even sorrier for myself. Not a good or healthy decision but one that I was all too familiar with. At least it gave me ample time to think about the puzzle that had formed in my head. I would need to get a clearer idea of where the package was or our little joy ride was going to end soon.

If I could try and paint any kind of happy face on this it would be that after all this had happened, A1 was as silent as a shamed puppy. He avoided me and never made a wise crack about my shitty afternoon. If anything, after all of his cajoling during this adventure he seemed, for the first time, repentant for the predicament we were now a part of.

It was a pleasant experience and damn bit strange. I decided finally to tempt Fate and confront him since I had nothing to lose except peace and quiet.

I found him in the aft control room staring wistfully at some scrap of paper in his hand. It appeared to be a deeply personal moment of reflection so I cleared my throat as I approached so as to alert him to my presence. He looked up with a start and quickly shoved the paper into his pocket.

"A1," I said in greeting.

"Bosch," he acknowledged. "What are you doing here?" His voice was even and didn't carry the usual defensive or accusatory tone I had come to expect.

"Making the rounds; trying to keep a low profile. You?"

"Just trying to be alone and stay out of everyone's way."

"Why?"

He looked at me in surprise. "Really?"

"Yeah," I said. "You always seem to be in the thick of it."

"And where does that get me?"

"What do you mean?" I asked.

Again the surprised look. "I am a giant pain in the ass."

"Why do you say that?"

"Bosch, don't play at me. You above all people here know the answer to that."

"Meaning?"

"Holy crap. After that tongue lashing you hit me with on that comet you are going to stand there and not know why I might be trying to stay clear of the crew? Hell, boy! They all heard what you said. I'm surprised Zyryn's goons haven't tried to shove me into an airlock."

"Nothing I ever said in all the days we have been forced

together has had any impact on your behavior but suddenly you have a change of heart over one speech? No, that ain't right."

He stood up from the equipment he had perched on. "It wasn't just that. After all you had done and said to me you still were the only one that dropped everything and raced to save my life - with a good chance of losing your own - and yet you never hesitated. You never once thought to just let this old fool just drift away into space."

The flattery, intentional or not, struck me hard. I wasn't sure what to say. "I...I would have done it for anyone. Well, maybe not Bruce or Barry; I hate those guys."

"It was me and until that moment I figured you hated me with everything you had. And if you actually cared enough to put your life on the line for me when nobody else did, then I figured you were a straight shooter and all that shit you gave me must've been deserved." He looked a bit sheepish and looked down at the deck no longer wanting to make eye contact. He was quiet for a moment and finally looked back up at me, his eyes having that same redness I noticed on the comet after we were back on the ground.

"But before I could even spit out a thanks you were tearing into me like some kind of starving riprat. In front of everyone and feeling the way I already did I guessed I deserved every damn bit of it! That's not a position I am accustomed to, Bosch. And I was feeling mighty low and ashamed. So I will say right now, thanks for saving me. And for what it's worth, I will stay clear of you for as long as this damn thing takes and then I am gone. You won't have to see me again. I owe you that much."

The entire change of attitude almost knocked me down. I was speechless. I ended up just shrugging not knowing what I could or should say or do. He walked closer and for just a second I thought it might have been a ploy to get me to drop my guard so he could sucker-punch me. But to my eternal surprise he walked up and threw his arms around me in a huge hug. I was ill prepared for the gesture and my level of discomfort rose to an all time high. If he would have started to cry I think I might have had to punch him. But he didn't and a moment later he had released me.

"What the hell was that?" I coughed out still stunned by the whole display.

"I want you to know I am sincere. This isn't some gag or a performance. Despite everything we've been through you saved my life. I was wrong about you. You do have some character and I was too stubborn to see it."

The awkwardness of the situation finally pulverized my defenses and I suddenly felt myself moved by A1's act of humility. Maybe he wasn't the only one that was unable to see people for who they really are.

"Thanks, A1. That actually means a lot to me."

His mood lightened a bit and he almost smiled. "Sorry it wasn't sooner. Maybe we could have avoided some of this crap."

"If only..."

He sat back down and looked at nothing, his quiet solitude returning.

"Can I ask something?"

He looked back up at me as if not realizing I hadn't left. "Uh, sure. What?"

"What were you doing when I walked in? What were you looking at?"

He reached into his pocket and drew out a crumpled piece of paper. "I was reading over yet another of my great mistakes. Something else that stabs at my regrets."

He didn't offer it over as an explanation so I was forced to ask what it was. "It is a final letter from my daughter," he revealed.

I didn't know which of the multitude of questions that avalanched into my head I should ask so I settled for the obvious one. "You have a daughter?"

He nodded. "Actually 'had' would be a more appropriate word. My daughter, Abigail, was my oldest. My son is 4 years her junior."

"Oh yeah, Abraham," I recalled aloud still thinking of the obvious thematic oversight. "You never mentioned her...uh, Abigail."

"It is a sore subject. It is not a memory I like to return to very often. Plus, we weren't known for being the kind of shipmates to share a lot of personal history, right?"

"You've got me there," I surrendered. "So what happened?"

He looked down at the note again. "She had left home at an early age. She was a bit too much like her old man; always restless and feeling the draw of the spaceways. I was signed onto the Nir'don as you know and she wanted to do the same but I wouldn't allow it. I told Galcursed that if she joined the crew I would leave so he didn't sign her on. But that wouldn't have stopped me so it sure as shit didn't stop her. She argued and we fought and I argued and we fought and in the end we both said a lot of things we didn't mean. Finally I came home from a long trip and she was gone. All that was left was this note telling me how much she hated me and to never come looking." He shook the note hard in the air as if his aggressive action could change the wording on it. "Well, you know how goddamn stubborn I am so I left it at that. Figured I was better off, knowing full well I was wrong. And then, years later, just out of the black of space she contacts me. She says she is sorry and how she wants to come home. All that kind of stuff. But you know what kind of asshole I was, Argon?"

"Not the kind I imagine, seeing where this might be going."

"Yeah, just that kind! I wouldn't forgive her. I told her she wasn't welcome, her ship was her home now." His voice caught for a moment and he gathered himself to finish. "I told her to leave me alone and closed the connection. That was the last I ever heard from her."

"Why have you not gone after her now? Obviously you have had some change of heart. What are you waiting for, man?"

He turned his head and looked at me, his eyes wet and pained. "Because she is dead. She died not long after that."

I was stunned. I thought that kind of horrible shit only happened to me. "My God."

"I got word that she had been killed by those fucking Xydoc Zyn fuckers."

"I'm sorry, A1. What did your wife say? Did she know...?"

"My wife died before Abby ever left. It was one of those things where we both felt her loss differently and it only helped drive her further away. I never told my son about her call until after I heard she was gone. He left me shortly after that and I haven't seen him since. I can't blame him. Had I let her come home she would still be alive today. I know you have some regrets, Argon, but they just don't measure up."

His story hit home resonating with several chords of my own sad song. I felt bad for him; old and alone, carrying around such a heavy burden of guilt. It was crushing.

He managed to look back at me again. "What ties us together, oddly enough, is that you ended up taking my place on the Nir'don. After I left they promoted old what's-his-name..."

"Sirons Iknatus."

"Yeah, him. Promoted that useless turd to First Officer. A couple other shuffles and there was a hole left for some young know-nothing. That'd be you."

"So I heard. I didn't pay much attention at first but when the Captain took a shine to me I kept hearing about how great you were over and over."

"I didn't quite measure up did I? Don't answer that!"

"I know you and the Captain kept in touch and he saw you on occasion but you never returned to the ship."

"I couldn't. I never went back out, gave up the whole space thing for a job as a package broker. It's been a long, long time."

"I'm sorry, A1. I just never knew. Guess it explains a few things."

"I think you and I are a lot alike, Bosch. But while my life is pretty much a short, straight line, you still have some opportunity to set some things right. Starting with that captain up on the Bridge."

"That's done," I admitted.

"Ain't done till it's done, I always say."

"You don't understand..."

"Don't I? You just heard my sorry story. I think I understand plenty. You can still make this right, you ass. It didn't take me long to tell you two had a history and judging from that right cross she threw at you when she first saw you, I'd say she's still feeling it plenty."

"But that was before..."

"Stop your yapping and go talk to her! There's nothing you got to say that I need to hear. Now git!"

With that I figured I'd better go see Fig.

As I journeyed to the Bridge I found myself thinking again about this whole mess and how it was a nightmare from the very beginning. So many random elements jammed together in one galactic stew pot of angst and moronic situations. But the more I pondered it the more it cleared in my mind that something was amiss. While I could contribute much of the haphazard journey this adventure had taken to my own inability to deal with almost any difficulty, we had continued to make inroads toward a solution. This fact bothered me. How in the hell were we still on the trail of a lost package that had been a sought after prize by millions? We should be lost amongst the stars and no closer to solving this mystery than when we started. We had encountered Farnok Raiders, Space Pirates, giant floating creatures in the void of space, and were traveling with actual members of said Space Pirates aboard the ship. Rink SanDyer's own daughter was traveling with us to ensure the prize would return to him yet the very first clue was on a listening station that was part of his realm. And why had he given us just a week to find it? People had searched their entire lives and never found a single clue yet he half expected us to find it in a week based on the inane ramblings of an old codger? There was more going on here than what I had witnessed. It was almost like…

"Argon!"

I spun around to see Doon walking quickly toward me. "What?"

"Grab a seat. We are landing on D'Moc."

"Already?"

He passed me continuing toward the Bridge. "Wake up and get back in the game," he tossed back at me. I couldn't help but pick up on the disgust in his voice. I turned to call after him but he was already around the corner. I headed for the crew quarters to grab a chair.

"Libertine, the capital city of D'Moc," Zyryn said as we stepped off the ship and onto the landing deck. It was a busy port and the hustle and bustle of people and freight crisscrossed it like ants on the march. We gathered up our group with Bruce and A1 staying behind to watch the ship. The weather had a chilly bite in it and there was the distinct tang of chlorine in the air.

"Is there a pool near by because...damn!" I coughed a little, the chlorine stinging my eyes and throat. I pulled up my bandana and placed my goggles over my eyes. It helped a little but I could still feel the caustic chemical assaulting my senses. "Or are they just a bunch of clean-freaks and afraid of germs?" I was transported to a dreadful summer back on Earth when I was five and had to take weeks of swimming lessons in an over-chlorinated pool that bleached my hair and reddened my eyes. I still can't swim.

Zyryn waved at her face and coughed. "That is so strong!"

Fig gave an exasperated sigh. "If you had done any research you'd know that D'Moc is known for its chloride mines. The natives actually are able to metabolize it. While it can become an irritant after prolonged exposure it has no long lasting effects provided we don't spend more than 8 hours in their environment. I suggest we split up since we have no idea who we are looking for."

"We know his name is Linus and he has a brother named Olovane," I pointed out, the fruitlessness of the task dropping on me even as I uttered the almost pointless clues we had. Doon just rolled her eyes.

"Uh...right. We split up and meet back here in 7 hours. If the air is getting to you there are stores that sell breathers for off-worlders. Pick one up if you can't handle a little gas." She looked at me with some disgust then added, "I'm going to the city records building to see what I can find. Doon's going to the revenue building. Maybe you two can find some way to be useful besides finding a room to rent." Then she and Doon walked away.

Zyryn snuggled up close to me. "That sounds like a good idea."

I slipped from her grasp and looked at Barry. "Maybe you should look for the local law enforcement. They might have some record."

"Give you two a chance for some foolin' around, ay?"

Zyryn gave him a cold scowl. "Just do it, Barry!" He shot off without another word.

"Looks like it is just the two of us, Argon," she purred.

Oddly I didn't feel interested at all in her advances. She was a stunningly beautiful woman that I had been mysteriously drawn to since we met but impossibly I just wanted to find Linus and get off this planet. Maybe it was the chlorine.

"I'm sorry, Zyryn. We just need to find Linus quick. We're running out of time and your father will be coming after us soon."

"He won't. It was just a threat. I told you that." She grabbed my hands and drew close again. "I'm supposed to kill you as soon as we find it, remember?"

"How could I forget?"

"But I'm not, stupid. After we find this stupid package then we are going to ditch these idiots and go find my mother."

"Right, okay. I know that. But we still need to find Linus and I don't know if we will be able to. I think he is hiding and this is a big planet. It's worse than a needle in a haystack. It's a needle in a planet full of nothing but haystacks."

"What's a haystack?"

"Forget it. Let's just split up and see what we can find."

I thought for a second she was going to give me some kind of pouty-face but she didn't. She looked angry but stood back from me. "Where should I go?"

"Surely you have some kind of contacts here. Part of some secret space pirate hangout or clubhouse or something? Maybe a local chapter of the Xydoc Zyn?"

"Haha...you are so funny," she said without any mirth. "How about I go see what I can find in the seedier parts of this city. At least there I might get a friendly grope."

"Oh come on, Zyryn."

"You had your chance, fly boy." And she headed off for some place I felt she might get just that. I could say I worried about her but I had the strong impression that she could easily take care of herself. That left me to my own devices and I knew just where to go.

It took me two hours but I finally found the largest local package broker in the city. Everybody needed to send or receive something at some point and if Linus was trying to keep a low profile like I thought it would stand to reason that he wouldn't use the Syndicate for his shipping.

Ferrin Pack and Ship had a nice building just beyond the city proper and seemed to be the only brokerage in town. I walked in and looked around taking in the place. It was fairly standard with a good bit of traffic running through. The employees were efficient and pleasant enough so I finally singled out who I thought might get me what I need, information.

Just as I approached a voice called out my name. I turned to see a man walking toward me, a large grin on his face. Jimmy Dutch.

When I had first acquired the Jackleg Courier Service I hired Jimmy as a delivery pilot and assistant since I didn't really have any experience in running an independent courier company. Jimmy was a big help in the early days and he helped me get the company turned around. A few years later he left to find steadier income through a more established company. I couldn't blame him as the Jackleg has always been a bit up and down on the business sense. I wished him luck and while we kept in touch for a couple years, it eventually trickled to a holiday card here and there and finally nothing. I was very surprised to see him.

"Jimmy, you old space dog!" I shouted and grabbed him up in a big hug. "It has been far too long, my friend. How are you?"

"Right now I am just surprised to see you. You may well be the last person I expected to walk through my doors." He gave me another quick hug and then asked me why I was here. "Last I knew you were still haunting the lonely offices of the Jackleg. Close shop or expanding operations to D'Moc? If it is the latter you may want to rethink that as Ferrin pretty much has this region sewn up for independent courier work."

"I have heard of Ferrin and they have a good reputation. I wouldn't dream of taking them on."

His face grew more solemn, "Need a job then?"

"Oh, no no no. I am still running the Jackleg and am out this way on business."

His smile returned. "Oh good! You love the Jackleg and I know how proud of her you are. I would be very sad to hear she folded. You aren't still flying that damned Spud are you? I wouldn't think so as it was on its last legs back when I worked there and that was over ten years ago!"

I laughed. "Well, I am still flying her and she is just as good now as she was then."

"So pretty bad then, huh?" He feigned deep concern.

"You never liked that ship."

"If you weren't so blind you'd recognize her for the piece of junk she is," he grinned.

"Hey! That's my ship you're talking about. If I didn't still like you I'd have punched your mouth before you could've finished that sentence."

"Old man, you would have *tried* to punch me."

"Keep talking like that and we might just test that theory before we're done here."

He gave a quick laugh and slapped my shoulder. "But I do need to ask, since you like to hold onto things for a long time, did you ever get back together with Fig?"

My mood immediately changed and Jimmy took notice. "Er...sorry, Argon. I know you were pining for her while I was there and I just hoped..."

"Best to let that one go, Jimmy."

"I'm not the one that needs to let it go, my friend. I can tell that chapter ain't finished even yet."

I quickly changed the subject. "What I do need, more than love advice and critiques of my ship is some information. Think you can help with that?"

He studied me for a minute and then decided not to probe any further into my affairs. "Sure. If I can help, I will. What do you need?"

"I am looking for someone. I am hoping you might have a line on him. I don't have much to go on so it won't be easy as I don't have much to go on."

"Shoot."

"All I know is his name is Linus and he lived in Adarenah for a short time. We went there but that town is…"

"Gone. Yeah I know. The whole town was destroyed by some weird disaster, an explosion of some sort. A bomb maybe. Horrible, horrible thing. Happened about 15 years ago before I ever got here. I don't know much about it other than everyone there was killed. No survivors. If he lived there he ain't living anymore."

"I am hoping maybe he wasn't there when that happened. I really need to find him. Libertine is the closest city and I am going to have to hope he was here when that happened."

"What else can you tell me about him?" asked Jimmy.

"He has two brothers. One is named Olovane. I don't know the other brother's name." I mentally kicked my own ass for not asking Olovane even that simple question. I am not a detective by trade so while I may have enough deductive reasoning to connect and "A" and a "B" there is a good chance I won't recognize a "C".

"You're right, that is not much to go on. I'll see what I can find. How much time do I have?"

"None really," I replied, a hint of stress coming through. "I am on a pretty strict timeline here. But I will wait and see what you can come up with."

"Alright. I'll see what I can do. How can I reach you?"

"You can find me at the landing bays in the city."

"The Spud?" he smiled.

I pretended to cock my arm then shook my head. "No, a larger ship. The Sononi Heart. I'll be there the rest of the day."

He looked at me with a raised eyebrow. "Argon, you old softy. I wouldn't have guessed that'd be your ship."

"It's not. But why do you say that?"

"Obviously there is a sad tale wrapped up in there somewhere," and he walked away. "I'll find you and let you know what I find. Great to see you, Argon!"

I scratched my head and walked out into the thick chlorinated air. "What the hell was he talking about?" I mumbled. A passing burtradite looked up at me with some shock. Rather pious are those diminutive burtradite zealots and they don't take kindly to even the most casual of curse words. Had I uttered something worse the small religious compulsive might have just shot me dead on the spot. Despite their strict beliefs they didn't hold life in as high esteem as a stranger uttering the word "fuck" in public. I was no fan of their crazed religion nor the look of disgust this one was glaring at me with.

"Have you no sensitivity or control to use such language within earshot of others?" he barked at me. "I find your lack of manners disgusting and sacrilegious. I will not allow such behavior on the streets of this fine city."

I bent over to stare in his face and was ready to yell, "Blow me!" when suddenly a tight grouping of laser shots impacted the wall directly behind where my head had been. I quickly spun and punted the diminutive burtradite priest into a bush and raced behind a column supporting the overhang to the Ferrin Building entrance. Another laser blast struck a man crossing in front of me and I heard a woman scream. Immediately there was chaos in the courtyard in front of the building and I was sure that someone was gunning for me. I didn't know why somebody was trying to kill me but it wasn't a new sensation. I drew my pistol and slowly spied around the edge of the column. I didn't see anything but running bodies everywhere and I knew it would only be seconds before the local law enforcement came screaming out of nowhere and secured the area. I didn't have anything to hide but I didn't want to get involved in a lot of questions and paperwork. I decided it best if I just tried to leave without getting shot.

I ducked down behind the stanchion and then rolled into the shrubbery. From there I crawled around the corner of the building and when I finally figured I was far enough from my starting place I popped up and looked around. With no further shots fired at me I stood and ran for the nearest building to try and put something substantial between me and my assailant. Just as I skidded to a stop next to the large building across the street I chanced a quick glance and saw a figure darting through the crowds in my direction. His face was covered and I just made out the glint of what could be a pistol in his hand. Then he was lost in a mass of scrambling pedestrians. I didn't want to wait for him to get any closer and spot me so I continued to make my way through crowds and traffic, buildings and alleys until I was fairly confident that I had lost him. Of course I had no way of telling it was a male given the loose kaftan-like outfit he was wearing but I let my imagination suppose the gunner was a dude.

I chanced a short break to catch my breath and communicate with my fellow crew members. "Anyone see a suspicious person tailing them be warned; I have had some fool taking pot shots at me."

There was a scratchy "What?' in response but otherwise silence.

"Someone is trying to kill me. Be careful in case there are more of them," I cautioned.

"Received," answered Fig with little in the way of concern or sympathy.

I was not too far from the landing field where the Heart rested so I moved in the direction, wary of my surroundings and any sketchy figures in my vicinity. After a few blocks I got the sensation of being watched and I stopped to more carefully scan the area around me. I wasn't being very surreptitious about my search so if I was being followed my personal assassin was likely to know. Nothing. I picked up my pace, soon resorting to a run, and tried to make for a more difficult target. I was doing fine until I ran into a small throng of those damn burtradites rounding a tight corner. They scattered like bowling pins with me taking a header into the ground. I managed to roll on my shoulder and stood up ready to continue. "Watch where you are going!" one of them shouted.

"Bite me, you little asshole," I retorted in a manner I was accustomed to. Too late I recognized my mistake.

"Eess lana farnoo," one of them chanted in their religious sing-songy dialect and took a stance that I could only guess to be combat based. These guys were like those old Chinese monks I had seen in the old movies of my youth that were all about peace and tolerance but could suddenly remove your gallbladder before you could say "Excuse me." The one difference was that the burtradites really weren't that committed to the peace and solitude thing. They were much less tolerant and unforgiving preferring to settle issues through violence and ass kicking.

In the bustle of the collision I had dropped my pistol and I now scrambled to snatch it back up off the ground to try and ward off the small, crazed fanatics. "You best just keep on going before you start something I am going to finish," I said trying to stall their inevitable attack.

More of them started to chant and pose and I knew that soon I would have them bouncing around and kicking like some strange dance troupe. I just laid my hand on my gun when the first of them launched into some kind of spinning attack. His foot collided with my shoulder and it felt similar to what I would suspect a large baby might inflict if it hit me as hard as it could. The burtradite landed softly and displayed a flourish of hand movements before hissing out some kind of satisfied grunt. I was not impressed and the next one that leaped at me received my own skilled defense by way of a quick slap. It flew off into a bush. The others, surprised that I had managed to strike the creature, stood stunned for a moment. "You will not live long enough to regret your action," one of them warned. He found himself promptly launched into the air at the end of my boot. While they were not much of a threat alone, the sheer weight of numbers started to worry me. I started punting them as quick as I could to keep them off guard hoping to wear down their resolve and garner myself enough of a break to retreat. I suffered a few blows that stung when they landed on my face but not enough to faze me or weaken my attack. So while they seemed easy enough to thwart they were tenacious in their attack. I was growing tired as they just continued their merry jumping and striking.

Just then a blast caught one of them and he fairly exploded from the force/size ratio. This broke their frantic attack and they looked around stunned at the fate of their comrade. I took the pause to grab my fallen pistol and restart my rapid retreat to the Heart. My personal assassin had returned.

I didn't see any other evidence of shots as I raced for cover. A quick glance back showed the burtradites scattering in different directions. I surmised they had lost their fearless posturing and realized a blaster more than leveled their playing field. I had hoped they might offer some temporary distraction to my follower but no respite was forthcoming.

If my attacker had been following me since we landed I figured he also knew where I was heading. His continued shots also meant he intended to finish me before I got back to the ship either to avoid the added threat of my shipmates or to prevent me from leaving. Either way, he was bound to follow my path to bar my escape. I decided to take advantage of that and go on the offense.

I found a small niche in a large building I was passing and squeezed myself into the spot, gun drawn, ready for him to pass. It was tight but I figured the element of surprise would allow me one good shot.

I heard him before I could see him; the quick footsteps and the rustle of cloth. I readied myself and prepared to fire. Just as he crossed the narrow gap I started forward but my shoulders wedged tightly between the walls and my arm didn't raise all of the way up. The pistol fired but the shot went low and gouged a chunk of the walkway out just ahead of his step. He was quick and managed to stop and spin towards me at the same time. His gun was already rising towards me. Luckily I had just cleared my shoulders by turning slightly and my pistol fired a second time hitting him in the waist. It was a glancing shot but enough to knock him back and down. I freed myself from the gap and leveled my gun at him as he hit the ground. His own pistol came up even as he hit. But the impact caused his shot to miss me by the narrowest of margins and my shot destroyed his gun and part of his hand.

And then he was gone, up and racing across the courtyard next to the building with uncanny speed and agility. On my best day I could not have hit him even with a steady arm and non heaving chest. I decided against a victory dance in case he was quick to return. With the threat passed I headed for the ship in all haste hoping my friends hadn't encountered a like situation.

"I didn't have anyone try and shoot me," announced Doon. After seeing everyone back at the ship and no one leaking blood I laid out my encounter with the would-be killer. "Looks like he was just after you, Argon."

"I'm lucky that way," I said. "I'm glad no one else had to deal with that. He was rather single minded."

Zyryn slid up next to me, "I'm so glad you are okay. I was worried when I got your alert."

I tried to create a bit of space between us but she latched onto my arm. "Not my first rodeo, Zyryn."

"What's a rodeo?"

Some Earth things just had no translation. "Never mind." I decided to change the subject. "Any luck on finding Linus?"

There was a collective shaking of heads. "I have a friend in town that is working on something. I am hoping he has a possible clue for us. We'll wait for a bit and then go. I'm not going to leave the ship just in case Johnny Triggerfinger is still out there waiting." I settled into a chair and began the wait until Jimmy came up with something.

"There is no record of him for any cargo coming or going. He either died in that bombing or went into hiding."

Jimmy had shown up several hours later and was explaining yet another dead end in our search for Linus. I hated to give up but it appeared our trail had gone stone cold and we were no closer to finding the package than when we left Olovane's asteroid. I thanked Jimmy for the attempt and he left the ship with a promise of meeting up again sometime in the future. I didn't think that was going to be possible as by all accounts our time had run out. The seven days allotted by SanDyer had just run down and he would no doubt be on his way to make good on his threat.

"Where to now, Argon?" asked Fig. I gave her a look that only thinly veiled my worry.

"I'll come up with something. I know there is something I am missing." I started for the crew quarters. "I need to think." To their credit no one tried to stop me though I knew they were all looking to me to find the missing thread. I was not the best container for their hope. About like trying to carry lava in a paper cup.

I found A1 sitting in the quarters looking at his dog-eared note from his daughter. He seemed very focused on it recently. That or I just never bothered to notice as we were usually quarreling when ever we came in close proximity.

"Looks like we have run out of time and destinations," I said.

"I figured it would come to that," he mumbled. "Sorry I got everyone involved in this mess. Just know that my intentions were good."

"What? Getting us rich? There might have been less dangerous ways to do it. A few tickets to the Galactic Lottery perhaps?"

He gave a slight smile. "Yeah, that'd have been better." I know our relationship had changed but it wasn't like him to just let that go. He seemed...defeated.

I had little left in my bag of tricks but I decided it couldn't hurt to farm the one lead we had started this mad adventure on - A1's story. "Listen, A1. I was thinking. Maybe there is some tiny detail that you may have missed about this thing. It could be the key to unlock this mystery."

"I don't know anything else. I told you what happened."

"Right. But you weren't too specific."

"What's there to be specific about? Brill told me to find Olovane. That was all he said. We found Olovane and that didn't help one bit."

"It doesn't make sense though," I explained. "He had to know you'd seek out Olovane and that the trail would run cold after that. He met Olovane. He must have been on his way to find Linus."

"Big assumption. We don't even know if Linus has anything to do with the package."

"It was the only thing Olovane had to offer. If Brill had the same info we had then he must have been on his way here. Where was it you found him?"

A1 scratched at his rough beard. "He was crashed on a moon. I picked up his distress call as I was passing by. Found him next to his ship, shot and dying."

"And then you killed his attacker?"

"Sort of."

"What does that mean?"

"I shot a couple of natives that were throwing rocks and spears at us."

"But you said he was shot. Doesn't sound like these natives had blaster technology," I pointed out.

"I don't know. I was trying to save the man! And these fool idiots were trying to bash our brains in with rocks. I don't think I even hit them. Brill shot one and my shots scared the rest of them off."

Something about this wasn't right. "What exactly did he say?"

A1 paused for a moment collecting his thoughts. Finally, "He was hurt bad and fading in and out. He said he knew about the Lost Package of Dehrholm Flatt and that he was on the way to find it." He appeared to be focusing on the memory. "He was out for a minute and I thought he might have passed but he suddenly jerked awake and said, 'Olovane! Find Olovane! He's the one!' and then he was gone."

"And then you located Olovane."

"Yeah. Took months and greasing a lot of palms but I found him. That's when I came to find you."

I looked at A1. He was a resourceful guy and had been around for a long time but to find a guy named Olovane on a secret Xydoc Zyn base deep in Farnok space...that would be some feat. "Where was it that you found Brill? What moon?"

"It was Ambroc 2."

"The hell you say? Ambroc 2?"

"What of it?"

I slapped my own head. "Ambroc is in this system! It's the fourth planet. You found Brill on a moon orbiting the planet next to where we are!"

"So?"

"SO? Doesn't that seem strange to you? A little coincidental, maybe?"

"Brill was headed here and crashed there. It was on the way." He seemed annoyed at my sudden revelation like I was thinking it was a grand discovery to find 4 in between 3 and 5.

"But what if he wasn't heading here? That he was heading right where you found him?"

"That's a lot of supposing."

I grinned at him. "Why, yes it is. We are going to Ambroc 2!" I ran for the Bridge. I had a feeling our answers were on that moon.

"WHY ARE YOU ASKING THESE FOOL questions," grunted Ord as I passed him another strange wrench. He was trying to fix the air handler in the Life Support mechanical room and seemed to be having little luck.

"Just curious I guess," I answered.

He slid out from under the huge unit and eyed me suspiciously. "You growing a stupid idea in that tiny brain of yours?"

"No," but it sounded more guilty than I actually felt. I knew Ord would pick up on it. And he did.

"Why, that's it! I told you if you ever went sniffin' after that cursed package I would knock the idea right out of your head." He was standing before I could move and the large wrench was raised in a swing that was sure to knock more than an idea out of my head. I figured a few teeth and maybe an eye.

I threw my arms up. "No, I swear! I'm not after it!" I yelled.

He hesitated. "Then what's with the questions?"

"There were a couple freight pushers back on Icym that were talking about it." I peeked at him and he lowered the tool but gave me an uneasy eye.

I had been on the Nir'don for almost three years and Ord had grown to be the best friend I had on the ship. The fact that he had been about to beat me with a large metal wrench showed in what good standing I was with the rest of the crew. It wouldn't be for another four years before I actually got any kind of respect. And that was only because of a lucky fluke.

But I had accomplished what I had set out to do: I was a crewman on an interstellar freighter and had broadened my horizons a hundred fold. Only having been on Earth and Blag for my youth there was a lot I was unaware of in the huge expanse of our Galaxy. And one thing that I found was that this mysterious Lost Package thing Ord had told me about in my early days onboard was much more prevalent than I imagined. Seemed almost every bar I would visit had someone talking about it. I didn't really have any desire to go looking for it, Ord had made sure to instill enough common sense and fear in me to make sure those thoughts would never seem a good idea.

"It was at 'Easy Nanceen's'. They were at the next table and one of them seemed positive he was onto it. He said the secret was Singularity. He felt somehow the whole thing boiled down to them."

He sat down on a main power hub case and looked at me. "That's how it starts, you know. Some fool hears something that sounds like it is legit and then the next thing you know off he goes never to be heard from again unless you come across him in some back alley gnawing on a mangy fur-puck, the poor sod."

"I swear I'm not going out after it, Ord," I gave my most open look and stretched out my arms as if I was hiding some alternative motivation up my sleeve. "Honest, man. I wouldn't give all this up for some stupid package!"

He considered me for a moment then shook his head. "So help me, Bosch. You leave for that adventure and I'll fucking find you and give you a package you'll never forget."

I nodded. "Understood. You don't need to worry."

"Oh, I worry alright." He bent back down and crawled under the unit. "What do you want to know?"

"Is there really a connection between the Package and Singularity?"

"That is a common thought. It is based on the fact that Flatt was hired by Singularity to deliver the Package but they never reported it missing or made a claim or completely filled out the manifest."

"So they knew what was in it then?" I offered.

"Some think so. It was also the time when the big shake up happened within the Company."

"What shake up?"

"Lord, Bosch, you ever watch the news on Blag?"

"I was a damn kid, Ord. What kid watches the news?"

"Fair enough," he agreed. "Well, Singularity was started by three brothers, the Craines. Ilfain, Tolos, and Pik. They were the brains behind the whole Company. I don't know what happened but they ended up angry at each other and two of them ended up leaving and only one brother remained, Tolos Craine. But sometime later, the two brothers disappeared and then Tolos left. He just walked away. It was right after Flatt was sent off with the Package. No one ever heard from any of them again."

"Wow. That's strange. No one ever was able to find any of them?"

"Nope." There was bang of metal on metal and then the wrench spun out from underneath the air handler. "Dammit, Bosch! That's a number two! I asked for a number four!"

"Right. Sorry." I quickly dug the wrench out of the tool box and handed to his clenching hand.

"So it's a dead end then?" I said.

"Afraid so. The only three people that would know what was in that Package are lost forever."

SEVERAL HOURS LATER WE WERE approaching the coordinates that A1 gave Doon as the crash site of Brill's ship. Uncomfortable as it was standing around on the Bridge with Fig I still wanted to keep a wary eye on the scanners. I couldn't shake the image of Rink SanDyer flying toward us at best speed with his entire armada close behind. Any second I expected a telltale ping on the scanner just before our ship explodes into a fiery ball of plasma, twisted metal, and body parts. Luckily that didn't happen.

"Yup, that's the spot," pointed A1 as we had landed and stepped out into the moist, hot air. Ambroc was a large planet that was devoid of any life but it had five moons that produced two habitable worlds; Ambroc 1 and 2. While Ambroc 1 had a much chillier climate - much of the planet was ice - this moon was balmy. The sweat stood out on my forehead immediately and the humidity did everything it could to keep it there.

Large reddish-brown plants stretched far above us and the small clearing we had landed in was only a small bald patch in a thick jungle of flora. It was only a few meters to the thick forest on all sides. I was glad I didn't suffer from claustrophobia.

I couldn't tell where A1 was pointing as the direction just led to what might be either a small path or just the separation of two trees. I could only assume he recognized it as a path he had taken months before.

I limited the group to A1, Doon and me. I wasn't sure what we were going to find. A1 could lead us to the wreckage and I could use Doon's back-up if things got dicey. Zyryn wanted to go but I didn't need her usual complications and distractions. Finally she relented but only if we took Bruce along. It was my turn to argue but in the end I also had to give in or we'd be there still.

"It's fuckin' hot," muttered Bruce. "Reminds me of those days I spent on Blag."

"You were on Blag?" I said a bit stunned.

"Yeah. Running cargo for the Klanx. God knows they love that blaganite shit."

"When was this?"

"Twenty years ago. It was before I got involved with the Zyn. It paid well but not the amount of adventure I was looking for. Plus, I tried that Blag crap and it only made me sneeze. Was glad to get the recruitment from the Zyn. Better pay and the benefits are pretty sweet as well...if you know what I mean." He gave me a heavy nudge and a wink. I tried not to think of what he might be suggesting as far as the "benefits" of working as a blood-thirsty space pirate.

"This is the life, I tell ya. Well, maybe not this baby-sitting slog but raiding ships in deep space? That's the ticket. I remember one time we pulled up on a Reen ship out near the Spanner Nebula. Luxury craft out star gazing on its way to Yanterra Prime. A fuckin' sitting duck! We had their engines disabled in minutes. Raiding party was inside the ship in even less. The security was for shit and we pulled in a huge score.

Plus all those tight little Reen chicks." He gave an unhealthy chuckle. "Let's just say that my own private *raiding party* wasn't having any trouble gettin' *in*, if you follow me!" Again with the nudge and wink.

As A1 led us through the thick growth I couldn't help but feel we were being watched if not outright followed. Bruce's continued talking did little to help me ascertain what it might be or where they were. He barely said three words on the voyage yet now he was Mister Social. It was grinding on my nerves.

He continued on with "So I had propositioned one of the fancier staterooms..."

"You mean appropriated? Unless of course you planned to have sex with the room."

"Duh. Of course I meant to have sex in the room," he explained.

"Never mind," I surrendered.

The feeling of others around us seemed to intensify but if anyone else noticed they didn't give a sign.

"So, I got this sweet room and gathered a bunch of Reen girls in there with me."

"The Reen have five different sexes. How do you know they were girls?"

"Cause they had what I needed, you ass!"

"I have a feeling you aren't too picky, Bruce. I imagine anything with a hole might suffice."

"Fuck you, Bosch. You're ruining the story," he argued. "Anyways, I had a whole bunch of them in there of all kinds of sexual natures. It was like a goddamn jigsaw puzzle, man! And I was right in the center!" He laughed at his own description, admiring the wittiness of it.

"And so what piece was Barry then?" I asked.

He stopped dead in his tracks and glared at me. "What you gettin' at, Bosch?"

"Nothing," I smirked. "You guys just seem really...close." I winked and he drew his gun. A1 and Doon spun around.

I raised my hands. "Ease up, Bruce. Just joking with you. No need to get all hot and bothered. I'm sure Barry has his own cherished memories of the night."

"Aw. Fuck you!" he shouted, dropped his gun and yanked a knife from his belt. "You and me are going to have a talk." He started toward me with violence in his eyes.

He was too close for me to draw my pistol and fire and A1 and Doon were behind me with no easy shot. I've been in a lot of fights but I didn't even enjoy trying to defend against a pissed of brute with a stabbing on his mind. Easy way to lose a finger, ear, or your life. I stepped back and tried to anticipate his lunge. It was all about timing and that was not my strong suit. I feared this was going to turn out badly.

Then something rushed out of the bushes to my right and hit Bruce. It was blur and then gone but had been in the path just long enough to remove Bruce's knife. And his hand. And most of his arm. A thick shot of blood signaled its departure. "The Fuck?" he said.

A1 shouted, "Run!" and I didn't ask for clarification. He went deeper into the forest and Doon and I followed close behind. As we turned in a bend of the thin path I glanced back over my shoulder to see Bruce stagger forward and fall face first into the matted ground. His other arm was missing and a deep rip across his chest. I managed to pass Doon and A1.

"Shouldn't we be running toward the ship?" I panted.

'No," replied A1. "They are coming from that direction. We have to get to the next clearing."

I had no option but to let A1 chose our path and I focused on the path and keeping my pace. I tried to also watch the thick foliage along the perimeter of the trail but the floor of the path required my full attention. There were fallen trees, roots, and vines crisscrossing the ground and the very last thing I needed was to trip. No sooner had that thought and the horrid outcome flashed across my imagination then I heard a grunt and thud behind me. Doon had tripped.

I stopped and A1 shot by me. I spun and saw Doon scrambling for footing while somewhere close behind there was the distinct rustle of branches. A lot of branches!

"Take my hand if you want to live!" I shouted. His palm slapped into mine and he was upright, his feet moving before they landed. We ran.

"Really, Argon," he gasped as he raced alongside me. "Movie quotes?"

I almost laughed realizing what I had said when something hit me from behind and I fell just as we entered the clearing. I saw a rusted wreck of a ship then the ground. I rolled, came up with gun in hand, and fired just as something was leaping at me. I caught a glimpse of fur, scale, and teeth and then a cloud of bone and blood. Behind it a clot of creatures filled the path, boiling into the clearing. I didn't stay to greet them instead getting myself to the crashed ship.

I pumped my legs and saw A1 and Doon at the hatch of the ship waving me on. Doon was aiming his gun past me and released a volley of shots designed to scare what was chasing me more then hit them. Judging from the grunts behind me they were not deterred from their dinner.

"Run like you mean it, son!" yelled A1. I so wanted to slap him right then.

Just as I got to the hatch something swiped at my leg and I felt a sudden numbness. Doon fired a shot and I collapsed inside the ship. The heavy hatch clanged shut and then my head felt like it was full of helium. I mumbled, "This sucks ass," and then I was out.

I awoke with a start, as is often the case when one blacks out. A sudden loss of time and circumstance keeping your mind firmly planted in the past.

"Easy, Argon." It was Doon. He was leaning over me, his boyish grin stretched across his face with just a slight stain of worry weakening its infectiousness. "You are okay. Dr. Won here says you'll walk again but your dancing career is gone."

"Mom will be so disappointed," I said more as a habitual smart ass reply than a conscious retort. "What happened?"

A1 was watching out of a portal nearby and fired a shot at something outside. "Those damn things ended up catching up to you and one of them took a swipe at your leg. A bit of a gash but we got you patched up. Your friend Doon here managed to blow its head off or it might have gotten its teeth in you and while that might have given us a little more time, we wouldn't have your sparkling personality to enjoy."

"Funny," I said and tested my leg. It was stiff and sore. I tried to stand but it would have no part of trying to support me. "Looks like I am not doing anymore running either."

"If we can get you back to the ship we can get that patched up better and you should be able to walk," said Doon. "We already called back to the ship and told them to stay put. No sense in them coming all the way out here and risk getting attacked."

"Good call," I admitted.

"I just hope they mind it. Fig was pretty upset and I know how stubborn she can be. I wouldn't be surprised if she just went ahead and started out alone to get here."

The thought gave me worry. "Tell me you convinced her, Doon! She can't do that!"

"I know, I know. Settle down. I didn't tell her you were hurt or she would be on her way right now, devil creatures be damned."

"A1, what are those fucking things?" I asked

"I don't know. I didn't see them last time though I heard them when I was leaving. That's why I had to leave Flashburn Brill's body behind. Couldn't drag him back to my ship with those monsters rushing after me."

"Are they still out there?" A sudden shot by A1 answered my question.

"Well, there's one less of them out there now."

"What are we going to do?" asked Doon. I could see the concern on his face. I imagined it mirrored my own. Trying to stand once again I managed to shift enough weight to my other leg to stand. I stumbled to a port and looked out. Something hit the portal just as my face drew close. "Fuck!"

"They can't get in through those," remarked A1. "Too small. But there are some openings in the hull that they could get squeeze through. I am really hoping they don't find them."

"We can't just wait it out," I said. "How many are there? Maybe we can just pick them off from in here." I moved toward the portal again. I cautiously eased my face up to the opening and looked out. I saw them milling about just beyond the ship. There were ugly things reminding me of a cross between an alligator and a bear. It looked like there were about a dozen of them. I could nail that many with just my gun. "I think we can kill them all from here."

"There are more," answered A1.

"What?"

"There are more on the other side and a lot more in the forest. They surround us. You can see the six I've killed laying out there. When you kill one they scatter and later come back with more. I've no idea how many of the damn things are out there. Plus I don't like the idea of waiting for them to find a way in here because then it is going to get interesting."

"Well, shit. We can't wait it out and we can't kill them all. What are we going to do?"

"Maybe we could have the Sononi Heart fly over and drop down a line and we could climb up to it," suggested Doon.

"Not bad, Doon, but I don't know if the Heart could hold steady enough. Plus I don't see an overhead hatch anywhere. There is likely one in here somewhere but I don't want to chance leaving this compartment. A1 said the hull is breached. They could be right outside any hatch we open."

As if on cue something heavy banged against the interior hatch leading into the ship from our compartment. "Holy hell. That's not good." I walked over to the hatch and looked for something to brace it. Something banged again and I could hear a scratching and grunting on the other side. "Yeah, they're inside all right. This might come down to how long we can hold them off."

"Then that's what we do," agreed A1. "Hopefully they run out of numbers before we run out of ammo."

And just like that the hatch broke open and one of the creatures burst forward. "Again...fuck!"

The compartment erupted in noise and the thing blew apart hit by over eager marksmen intent on making sure it didn't get past the entrance. After several shots it was obviously dead but was now lying across the threshold barring the hatch from closing. There was noise from further in the ship signaling the arrival of more of the beasts. With an entrance to their meal they were not running off as easily when one of their lot was killed. I feared they might overrun us by shear numbers.

"Back up!" I shouted. "Get against the far wall and keep them from getting in here!"

Our only bit of luck was the fact that the opening was small enough to only let one of the creatures push through at a time. They were tough and didn't die easily. Soon the entrance was jammed with carcasses and it was harder to tell which ones were dead and which were alive as the arriving ones were causing the corpses to shake and twitch as the fresh beasts pushed forward.

"I'm almost out!" yelled Doon over the din.

"Me too!" echoed A1.

The constant noise prevented me from determining how many more might be coming our way. It seemed like they were slowing their assault but I wasn't sure if it was lack of numbers or the fact that the entrance was completely clogged with carrion. And then I heard a different noise that chilled my blood and signaled our death knell: a banging on the hatch next to us. The creatures had discovered another way in and were about to burst in through an alternate entrance. We were about to be caught in a crossfire of fang and claw. A1 and Doon both looked at me with a sudden dire realization on their faces.

"A1! You and Doon focus on the opening. I'll move to fight off the new threat!" I shifted my back to the original threat and brought up my pistol to blast the life out of the next creature forcing its way into our compartment. Just as the hatch opened I heard Doon shout, "I'm out!"

This was just not going to be my day.

CHAPTER 20

I had readied myself to blast into the new horde that was about to burst into the room but never fired a shot. The hatch pounded once, twice and then swung inward. My gun clicked empty and then I stopped pulling the trigger. A man came through the hatchway with a pistol in each hand. He gave me the slightest of glances and then made for the far opening. His rounds kicked up gore and sparks as he hit both animal and door frame. As he approached the carcass filled opening he finally stopped firing and we were greeted with beautiful silence. The monsters were all dead or gone.

"I guess we owe you a debt, sir," offered A1.

The stranger turned and eyed us suspiciously. I noticed he did not lower his guns completely. "Who are you?" he asked.

"My name is Argon Bosch. These are my companions Doon and A1. Thanks for saving our asses from those...things" I motioned toward the bloody mass behind him.

"They are crykons. Ill tempered and mean spirited. My friends managed to scare off the rest or we would have been overrun for sure."

"Your friends?"

A short, young man rushed in the hatchway our benefactor had used. He was dressed in simple animal pelts, crykon from the look of them, and hurried over to the stranger. They exchanged words in a language I was completely unfamiliar with. I noticed a tension in A1's manner and his eyes narrowed in on the native. It dawned on me that this was likely to be the natives that had tried to bean him with stones.

After their brief conversation the native rushed off again. "One of your friends, I take it."

"Yes. The indigenous people that live here were kind enough to take me in when I showed up here. That is after they pelted me with rocks."

I picked up a common theme. "You live here with them then?"

"Yes, I have for quite some time. But of more importance is why you are here? This isn't a place where people come to vacation."

I pointed to A1. "He was here before and he brought us here to investigate this crash site. A...friend of ours died here."

"I did find a body here several months ago. My friends told me of a crashed ship and a fight. I had assumed the man that left had killed the other."

A1 shook his head. "No sir. He had crashed already when I got his distress call. And he was already dying when I found him. I would have taken him with me but your *friends* tried their rock greeting with me and I found it none the welcome I am accustomed to. I high tailed it out of here before they crushed my skull."

"Understood. Well, I have already buried your friend. But I am curious about one thing."

"What's that?" I asked.

"If you knew he was here why did you need to bring two ships?"

"Excuse me?" said A1.

"I tracked two ships landing near this wreck."

"Listen, friend. We just had one ship. The other one must be..."

"Olovane," said A1.

The stranger's eyes grew large and his demeanor switched instantly to panic.

"He's light years away," I reminded him. "Plus he didn't have a ship, remember?"

"Olovane," whispered the stranger and he set his guns down on the ground. He seemed resigned to some sad, unavoidable fate. I finally realized he and A1 were no longer looking at me but past me.

I spun around and there he was, standing in the hatchway, rifle pointed threateningly at us. I also recognized his outfit and the scorch mark at his waist. "It was you!" I exclaimed. "You were trying to kill me on D'Moc!"

"An unfortunate circumstance but necessary I assure you," he admitted.

"Unfortunate my ass! What the hell are you doing here?"

"Trying to finally finish up a job that has lingered for far too long."

I turned to the stranger. "OK. Let me guess. This makes you Linus."

"Correct." His stature shrunk and he no longer seemed the confident warrior that had saved our lives from the crykons. Now he just looked like an old man, defeated, and tired. "My brother is here to kill us all."

"But why?" questioned Doon. "I don't understand."

"You're not alone, buddy," I agreed. "We left you alone on your asteroid, Olovane. Why in the hell are you trying to kill us? What did we do to you?"

"Your ceaseless searching for that cursed Package has drawn you into our private matter and while I have no malice towards you, I simply cannot let you wander off with the information you possess."

"What information? We don't know what the hell is going on," I explained.

The stranger moved forward, anger manifesting with each step. "He doesn't want you to know what sins he has committed in his righteous   furor."

Olovane made a motion with his rifle for the stranger to stop. "What would you understand of these things? You are a traitor to your family and a failure to your wife."

Somewhere in my head a long forgotten neuron fired and a realization took hold. The bizarre mixture of memories, experiences, and supposition finally merged into the vague notion I had had scratching at my consciousness since we left Olovane's asteroid home. I spun around to face our mysterious savior. "Tolos?"

"He is Tolos but he has long ceased to be my brother," announced Olovane. "His anger has destroyed everything."

"Oh, you should be so pure of heart to judge me?" argued Linus, who I had realized was actually Tolos, one of the Craine Brothers that founded Singularity. "Has anyone ever been so quick to blindly seek their own form of justice? I call it hate and malice to be so single minded in your quest to destroy me. You have no right to stand before me now and call me sinner, you murderous reprobate!"

"The fact that I can stand before you is a miracle of itself given the horrid state you left me."

"I can see this is a tearful reunion and all," A1 interrupted. "But could someone explain what the hell all this is about?"

"I am not required to explain myself to you. You have no stake in this," said Olovane.

"I would have to disagree, robot, seeing as you plan to kill us."

"I will admit that is a sad circumstance but necessary. Too much has already happened that I cannot undo the course I have set. In the end, know that you have managed to do me a great favor in locating my brother. He has proven difficult to uncover."

Linus moved forward again causing Olovane to point his rifle more directly. "Ilfane you evil bastard! You destroyed the entire town of Adarenah just in hopes to kill me. Who does that? There were families, innocent people just living their lives and you killed them all!"

I turned to Olovane stunned. Had he really bombed out an entire village to get back at his brother? "Is this true, Olovane...I mean Ilfane?"

"No, it is not," he replied.

"Liar!" yelled Linus.

"It was the Xydoc Zyn, you sanctimonious idiot. I told them what you had done and they took it upon themselves to bomb Adarenah. I did not condone their actions in any way."

"Did you even try and stop them?"

"I was unaware of the length they were willing to take. They said they would find you, everything else I had no knowledge of. But it was you that set this in motion, Tolos. The fate of those people falls on you and you alone. I am here to collect justice." And with that he fired and shot Linus in the chest, throwing him backward into the wall. He crumpled to the ground.

"Olovane!" I shouted. "Your brother."

He swung the rifle on me as I moved forward. "Sorry, Argon. I fear your clever tenacious behavior has unveiled more than I can let you leave with."

"Olovane, don't." I raised my hands in surrender. "You don't need to kill us. We don't know as much as you might think."

"I wish I could believe that. You have unwittingly uncovered the secret of the Lost Package and I cannot have you furthering that search."

"You're wrong. We don't know where it is and I am happy to just let it go."

"Well, I'm not!" exclaimed A1. "If we have the clues and means of finding it then that's what we're going to do and you ain't stopping us, robot."

"Oh, but I am, you sad old man. You show the same unflappable spirit of your friend Brill. That's why I had to stop him before he continued. I attacked his ship as he sped toward D'Moc. I had hoped that would be the end of it but then he happened to survive the crash and you found him. It would be over if not for you and your meddling. I sincerely hope this ends with you." He raised his rifle at A1 and I jumped. He swung the rifle more quickly than I would have imagined and fired. It caught me in the side and I flew backward landing next to Linus. He immediately drew on A1 and Doon.

A small grunt next to me made me turn and I saw that Linus was not dead though his chest was pumping out more blood than he could afford to lose. His hand came up and fired and I saw Olovane stumble back. He tried to right himself and return the fire but Linus got off two more shots blasting his mechanical arm from its socket. Olovane swung his head around realizing his fate. He tried to raise his other hand to beckon mercy but his cybernetic face would not mirror the emotion he was undoubtedly feeling.

"Tolos...I'm sorry." And then Linus blew his head to bits.

"Holy shit," remarked Doon.

I moved to Linus and looked to see if there was anything I could do but he was already fading away. "Linus, er...Tolos, how can I help?"

"It is done. I have stopped my brother at last."

A1 and Doon walked over and hunched down next to us. "Are you okay, AB?" asked Doon.

"Do you mean to tell me that Olovane and Linus are actually Ilfane and Tolos Craine?" asked A1. "The Singularity Brothers?"

I pulled up my jacket and shirt to look at my wound expecting a wound to rival Linus'. A nasty scorch marked my side and was not bleeding though I knew it would be yet another painful injury and scar for me to carry as a souvenir.

"I'm fine, Doon. And yes, A1, these are the Craine Brothers. Two of them at least." I turned back to Linus, "But he isn't doing too hot. Li...Tolos, what was Olovane talking about?"

"He had stolen the love of my life..."

"We heard all of that, already," interrupted A1. "What about the Lost Package?"

Linus' face grew even sadder. "In many ways, he was correct. I have done horrible things and he is right to have sought vengeance for himself and my younger brother. As for the Lost Package...there were two."

"I don't understand," I said. "Olovane told us about your wife and how your brothers fell in love with her. He said that you ended up losing her and blamed your brothers but he sounded legitimately remorseful at what had happened."

"He did not tell you what I did? I took my revenge on them. They had started this infernal thing with their fleshly desires and covetous ways but I would take that from them." His eyes closed and he coughed, a bloody foam spraying from his lips. He was silent for several moments and I thought he might have passed but then his eyes flew wide and he gripped my jacket. "But I stopped them! I took that from them. They would never look upon another woman with lust, they would never know a woman's caress. I stole that from them like they stole it from me." He coughed again and closed his eyes. Finally they fluttered open and he spoke in only a whisper. "I did something horrible."

"What did you do, Linus?" asked Doon.

"While they slept I drugged them. Then I took them to a surgeon I had paid off with shares in our company. He then operated on them by my instructions. In the end there was only the essence of them left with nothing else left in their lives but to think about what they had done and the sorrow of their regrets."

"My God, man. What did you do?" repeated A1.

"I had the surgeon remove their brains and place them in special life supporting cases. Then I contacted two delivery pilots known for their discretion. I packaged each one up and sent them in opposite directions to remote planets with instructions to simply leave the packages where they landed." He faded off again. We waited.

"I think he's gone," said Doon.

"Dead as dead," Echoed A1. "He's gone and we are no closer to that damn package than when we started! Curse our damn fool luck!"

Never had I seen A1 as angry as this. He stood and paced the room pausing every so often to give something a swift kick. He cursed through all the words he knew and then started again.

"I think he's mad," offered Doon.

"You think?" A sudden cough from Linus announced his return to the living but I doubted it would be but for few words if any.

"Neither arrived at their actual destinations though the manifests had false ones recorded along with other false information. One pilot was reported as captured by the Xydoc Zyn. Ilfane's packaged brain. They gave him a rudimentary body and placed him in a listening post. It looks like he's since gotten something a little more mobile." He gave a wet chuckle and gasped. "My younger brother...I don't know what happened to him. The pilot was Dehrholm Flatt. My brother *was* the Lost Package." His voice was only a breath at this point. I leaned in close, my ear at his mouth. He uttered a final gasp, "Find my brother...Pik."

And then he died.

"Confound it!" railed A1, shaking his fists. "This is the end of the trail. All of this for nothing. Nothing! It's all lost."

"At least we know what it was," suggested Doon.

A1 gave him an angry scowl. "That helps nothing, you fool. We had to find the *Package*! It was the *Package* that mattered!"

I sat up, a surprised look on my face. "We're not done yet, A1."

"What are you talking about? He's dead."

"I know where the package landed."

"Where?" they both asked at once.

"Alongago City."

"What's there?"

"A freak show."

CHAPTER 21

When we got back to the Heart there were a lot of tales to tell. Barry was suspicious of Bruce's fate but when I suggested he go look for the body he declined, especially after seeing the claw marks across my leg. I couldn't waste any time so my first stop was the Bridge to set the coordinates for our next destination. Our time had run out and I knew SanDyer was on his way to find us. We had one more day's travel ahead of us and I got Doon to pilot the ship to Alongago City at our best speed. There were a lot of loose threads hanging over my head from this insane quest but I felt many of them would tie themselves together once we arrived. I was just hoping that we lived long enough to get there and find them.

At Fig's insistence I followed her to the Med Bay for a much needed patch-up. My leg was hurting badly and the nerves in my side were waking up and I knew they weren't going to be happy with that blaster burn.

She did a proper bandaging of my leg in complete silence, never looking me in the eye. It was the perfect time to try and finally talk things out but I wasn't going to intrude in her quiet thoughts. Maybe she didn't want to talk at all. Lord knows I hadn't given her any reason to ever want to talk to me again. And then...

"I'm glad you got back in one piece," she said pulling a glob of some nasty paste from a jar.

"Really?"

She looked at me with a stern stare. Then worked at putting the smelly salve on my side. It helped sooth the growing pain brewing just under the char. "Do you even want to live?" she asked, surprising me with her sudden directness. "Because if you do, you are failing at it."

I was silent, not knowing what to say. The question kicked an emotion I had managed to bury - helpless surrender. Finally, "I don't know how to answer that, Fig. But I think I might actually not care."

"I never thought I'd hear you say that. You have always been so...strong and determined. But I know something has changed you. And I'll be honest, Argon, it's not for the better." She finished with the application of the stinky goo and put her hands on her hips.

"There was a time when I thought we had something. Something real. I've known you for as long as I can remember and I have loved you almost as long. Yet I look at you now and I don't recognize you." She walked across the small room and found a towel to wipe her hands on. She laid it carefully down on the counter and placed the lid back on the salve container. She was obviously thinking of what to say next and for once I just stayed quiet and let her.

She looked back at me wearing a sad little smile. "When you left I didn't know what to do anymore. You hurt me terribly. So much that I was lost for years. You were a part of me that suddenly was gone. It took me a long time to realize that it wasn't me. And that if you could just turn around and walk off like that, never even looking back, that I had been steering my life towards a mirage. I'm stronger now but being around you is not what I thought it would be like. When Doon asked me to come and help you I told him no. He begged me and I still said no. For the first time in over a decade I was afraid. I didn't want to see you. I didn't know what would happen or how I would feel. My nightmare wasn't that you'd still not care about me but that you would. That somehow, despite my better judgment, I would fall right back into being in love with you. I didn't want that anymore and I hated myself for even considering it a possibility. I don't want this," she motioned to herself and me. "I am happy without you. I don't need you anymore." She looked at me to see gauge my reactions but I had none. I sat there and just took it. I knew this was something she needed to say, something she had always needed to say. And as much as it hurt, as much as I wanted to try and explain away my fault in any of it, I still just sat there and let her talk. This seemed to give her pause.

"Are you even listening to me or have you already dismissed me?"

I shook my head. "No, I *am* listening. Maybe I'm listening for the first time since we met."

She tilted her head trying to read me. She was clearly puzzled by my reaction. "I am being honest with you, Argon. I only ask for honesty in return." I nodded agreement.

"I don't know what all has happened to you but you aren't the Argon I knew. You say you don't care, have surrendered. Given up. And I can see that now. I wasn't sure what it was when I got off my ship and saw you but that was it. It made me angry. So angry that I had to hit you."

"Why?"

"Because seeing you like that after all that happened made me mad that you had ever been something important in my life. I wondered why I ever cared for such a used up, waste of a man. It made me feel weak and stupid and I hated you right then for making me feel bad about myself again. So while you didn't bring back my old feelings, you actually negated them and that was even worse."

"I'm sorry," I offered.

"Why? Why are you sorry *now*?"

"Because you have never been anything but nice to me. No matter what I've done - and I have done a lot - you never wavered. You are right, I left. Me. To be able to affect you after all this time in such a bad way and all...it is wrong."

"What happened to you?" she asked almost pleading for some truth that would explain the contrast of the man she loved versus the man she now only finds sad.

"I'm not sure. I try and sort it out in my head but I can't figure it out. I think about my life and all I see are regrets for as far back as I can remember. I try not to think about it but they just follow me around like ghosts. Ghosts of Bad Decisions Past. I'm Scrooge getting woken up by some ethereal phantasm telling me how I've fucked up my life. It sucks but I can't escape it and I can't fight it because deep down I know it is true."

"Don't say that."

"Why? You asked for honesty and that's what I'm giving you." She looked even more frustrated. "That's how I feel! Really!" I threw up my hands.

"There are too many good things that happened for you to discount it all with a shrug," she said. "You do a great disservice to both Doon and I to simply jumble us in amongst your discarded life. There was good in there! And if you can't see it then you are lost and I don't know how to save...help you." She was angry again and let slip something important. Save me? Is that what she thought this was? Is that why she finally relented and came along with Doon? You don't try and save someone you don't care for.

She wanted to save me and I bet so did Doon. And here I was trying to save them. I thought I was being noble but they had set out on this crazy mission with only the idea of saving me to keep them going. I shook my head.

"What?" she asked.

"It's just that..." The ship abruptly stopped and I fell off the table. Fig tumbled forward and landed next to me. "What fresh hell is this now?" I mumbled.

"The ship's dead in space," she remarked.

My first thought was that SanDyer was attacking the ship and had disabled our engines but I hadn't heard any blasts or felt the impact of a close explosion. No, this was something else. "Head for the Bridge. I'm going to the Engine Room and see if there is something broken." She raced off without a word.

I awkwardly hopped and skipped through the ship on my bum leg trying not to put too much weight on it. The confines were too narrow to accommodate my floundering and I ended up tripping on a raised hatchway. I crashed forward but managed to get my bad leg underneath me and I was surprised it held. I discovered my leg wasn't hurt as bad as I thought. After that I made better time and was almost immediately in the engine compartment.

I called Fig on the comm system, "What happened?"

"Loss of power on the gravity-well drive. If we have to use the regular engine it will be a long time before we get to our destination.

"What caused it? Is there any clue?"

"Just dropped out. No explanation. Check the drive."

"I'm on it!" I shouted and moved toward the drive controls. The main panel was open and I could smell the burnt components from across the room. When I looked in I saw that several power couplings were fused to the panel. Something had caused them to overload and arc between plugs. It was a huge mess and not something that I could fix quickly. We were dead in space and sitting ducks for Rink SanDyer and his band of bloodthirsty pirates to find us. On a journey that managed to thwart us at every turn this was the one that would end it.

I relayed the information to Doon. "This is going to take quite a few hours to fix. Tell A1 to come down here and help me."

"He's not up here," she replied.

"Where the hell is he? Sleeping?"

"Nobody's seen him since we left. Doon's going to go find him."

I turned at a noise and there he was coming down the ladder into the compartment. "Never mind. He just showed up." I looked at him. "Where you been?"

"Just broodin' over this whole mess. Figured I'd come down and try and help with the engines."

"How'd you know what was wrong if you weren't on the Bridge?"

He looked at me with the look I had grown accustomed to: annoyance. "Well, let's just say I've been around long enough to know it wasn't anything in the galley, alright?"

"Right."

"Let's get to work," he suggested and I grabbed the tool kit from the wall.

"No! Hand me the one that isn't burnt all to hell!" I shouted. A1 fumbled around in the parts box again. It was now the fourth time he had handed me the wrong part. I began to suspect that A1's melon was growing sour. There were times during our voyage where I noticed him lost in thought, a million miles away. He had logged more light years in space than I ever would. He'd had his own ship and had crewed under Captain Galcursed. He was no stranger to ship repair and I would have imagined he could replace these parts by himself in the dark in half the time. "Stay focused, you old coot. We don't have any time to fart around." He just glared at me.

"I know this scientist guy and he once built a time machine out of a shoe box, some old wire, and a light bulb. He disarmed a bomb and saved a planet with a klegal wrench!" He just shrugged at me. "Wish he was here right now," I mumbled.

"What's your point, Bosch?"

"My point is you're not trying very hard."

"I'm doing the best I can," he argued.

"Really? The *best*? Somehow I doubt that. You are slowing us down and we need to get moving. SanDyer can show up anytime and he won't be here to ask questions."

"Fuck that pirate!" he cursed. "He shows up now and I'll kill the son of a bitch with a klegal wrench myself!"

He was suddenly riled up and spitting fire. I figured I'd never understand this old senile bastard. "Throttle back there, Captain Smackdown. Before you go off saving the galaxy with a simple hand tool maybe we should get this ship running so we can get back on our way. We've already wasted 5 hours on this."

He rubbed his eyes. "Sorry, son. This whole stupid thing is wearing on me. There's just too much riding on me finding that package."

"You? *You* need to find it? What about *us*? Hell, I need to find it more than anyone."

He gave me an odd look. "Why?"

"Because those are my friends up there on the Bridge and I'll be damned if I'm not going to get them out of this. Zyryn told me that she was told by her father to kill us even if we found the Package."

"What?"

"Yeah. It's all a sham. SanDyer is a damn pirate and being fashioned out of pure evil devil shit I was a fool to ever think we could trust him. Zyryn hates him more than we do and she will help us escape if I find the Package for her."

"No. I need the Package!" he shouted. His eyes narrowed and his voice dropped an octave. "That Package is mine."

"Hey now. Didn't you hear what I just said? Have you lost your sense *and* your hearing?"

His face was stone and his glare intense. "Listen, Bosch. I'll pay you all for the trouble but the Package is mine. I came up with this plan."

"Right. And thanks for that by the way, you ass. Your so called "Plan" was nothing more than playing bumper pool across the Galaxy hoping you'd run into it by accident. I got us there and if that's the golden ticket that's going to save my friends, then that's what I'm going to do with it. If Zyryn doesn't get it we are all good as dead. Seriously. You won't get two planets out before she rams a futon torpedo up your exhaust vent."

"A what?"

"Futon torpedo...I think it's from an old Terran TV show. Forget it. You'll be dead. You won't be rich, you won't be celebrating. You'll just be dead and being broke and alive is still better than dead."

He looked at me with that hard look and for a minute I thought he was going to try and fight me. Then his eyes softened and he dug in the parts box and handed me a good power coupler. He didn't speak the rest of the time we spent working on the engine. But it still took us another three hours.

"Alongago City," I announced. I had taken the controls on the Bridge once we entered the system. I knew where I wanted to start looking and it was best I just flew us in. Everyone was packed onto the Bridge to try and spot something. I welcomed the extra eyes but I doubted there would be a huge neon sign. I came in low as I approached the city. I imagined the flight control people were pitching a fit about then but I didn't care.

"Over there!" yelled Doon with a burst of excitement. "Look!"

I followed his excited pointing hand. It was a huge neon sign that flashed "Packages."

"Well, son of a..." I heard A1 whisper next to me.

"Oh for the love of crap. Really?" I rolled my eyes at him. "You really think there is going to be a sign?"

"I...we..."

"No. Look again and stop being so stupid." As we drew closer the lower part of the sign became visible. "Send them here! The USPS will get them there!" it read. Just the local United Space Parcel Syndicate staking their territory. It looked to be their central hub for the city. What I was looking for wasn't actually in the city but on the outskirts. It had been a long time but I soon had my bearings and turned the ship into a gentle arc to the east.

A few minutes later we were out of the city and over an older, more run down area that looked almost abandoned. I scanned the landscape trying to find the spot. The sun was getting low in the sky and I would be losing my light soon. I feared my chances of seeing it in the night would be almost impossible. I glimpsed a clearing amongst the large trees that were crowding in on the once inhabited outskirts and brought the ship in even closer. There were several ramshackle buildings crowded together and I recognized the layout. This was it.

"We're here," I said and brought the Heart in for a landing just outside the settlement. It was tight with the trees and vines strung between them but I managed to set her down without incident. I shut down the engine and stood. "Let's get to looking."

They followed me toward the hatch. "I think I should stay on board," said Fig.

I was puzzled. "Why? I think we'll probably be here awhile."

"I'm not leaving my ship unattended in a strange place."

I motioned toward the sprawling metropolis we had just flown over. "There's a huge city right over there!"

"It doesn't look like there is anyone here though and that kind of freaks me out. Where is everyone?"

I shrugged. "I don't know and I don't care. Stay if you want. It's going to get dark soon so would you leave the landing lights on?" She nodded. I looked at the rest of them. "Let's go then."

Zyryn put out her hand and stopped Barry. "You stay here with her."

"The fuck?" he barked.

"Just do it, Barry. I'm not leaving this ship with just her on it." He grumbled something and started back. Zyryn just looked at me and smiled giving me a little wink.

I popped the hatch and we headed outside.

"The Grand Wheastoviac's Cavalcade of Freaks," read Doon eyeing the large banner above our heads. It was weathered and torn but enough of the bold type could still be read. I was back.

"What is this place?" asked Zyryn.

"It's an old Freakshow," I explained. "I was here a long time ago and I think this is near where Dehrholm Flatt's ship went down. We need to look around and see what we can find. It's going to be dark in a bit so we should split up and try and find anything we can. Just be careful."

"I don't think we should split up, Argon," Zyryn said. She came up close to me.

"There's not a lot of time. We have to split up. Now start looking around and everyone keep your comms open and yell if you find something." She shuffled off discouraged. A1 walked over.

"I don't know what we are looking for. A crashed ship? Bones? What do you know about this place?"

"It's a hunch, A1. I think the answer is here."

"You think?" You got us all the way out here on a hunch?"

I turned on him and poked him in the chest with my finger. "It's the only fucking hunch we have, old man, so why don't you at least try and find something before the Xydoc Zyn show up and just nuke the whole site from orbit and be done with us? Huh? Think you could just *try*?"

He turned and walked away.

Fuck.

I hadn't realized until just then how tense and anxious I was. I had played a hunch and it would likely be my last. This was it. If we didn't get some answers here and now we were all doomed and I was the one who had to make the guess. I wasn't one for praying but I felt something like that go through my head right then.

I wandered through the empty paths between building and tent. It appeared to have been empty for a long time. The exhibits were all looted and dilapidated. The trees were so much taller than when I was there before. They rimmed the encampment like huge sentinels safeguarding my memories of a time long forgotten. I slowly made my way along the foot-worn paths, a cloud of dust rising around my boots. It was eerily quiet given the noises that accompanied my crowding nostalgia. 15 years ago this had been full of life and excited shouts; kids and parents taking in the multitude of sights, sounds, and smells. A congested midway of innocent thrills with a dark underbelly of corruption and fraud. The air full of the over sweetness of fruit turning spoiled. Then something familiar called out from a faded painting across the side of a small structure: Winston.

I stopped in my tracks and just looked at it feeling strange crash of memory new and old colliding from different directions. The only words left on the facade were "Winston" and "Brain." My memory filled in the rest and I stood there suddenly missing him for the first time since I left the Jackleg. My one employee who had been with me for almost 15 years. And in all that time I never knew the story of his brothers and the woman they all three loved. I never cared to ask him anything. His elaborate story he had presented to me as we left Alongago City was unbelievable for a reason - it never happened. I knew it then and I never bothered to challenge him on it. I just didn't care and that seems to have been my recipe for life. Never really care; never really get to know anyone else because my own life is just so damn important that no one else's matters. My God, had I really been that way even then? Had I ever been anything but? I thought back to my father, the day I last saw him alive and I was shocked to recognize that same Argon Bosch back then. His life left an empty husk after the loss of my mother. Alone, living on an alien planet, and I couldn't be bothered to show him a single care. Nothing mattered but me. Selfish. Self-important. Self centered. Even then it was all about me. Always about me.

A surprisingly familiar roar interrupted my thoughts. At the same time I heard Fig's voice crackle in my ear. "Argo...wa...out! ...ere's...hip...land..." And then there was nothing.

"Fig! Fig, come in! Anyone?"

Doon's voice buzzed over the comm. "What is it, Argon?"

"Doon! Get back to the ship. I think Fig's in trouble!"

"On my way!"

The sound I heard had been a ship landing but it also had a strange familiarity that I couldn't place. I instinctively pulled my sidearm and spun around to race back to the ship. I was surprised to see A1 standing there. His gun in hand and aimed at *me*.

"What are you doing, A1? I think Fig's in trouble. Something is going down and we have to get to the ship. And don't point that thing at me, you idiot."

"I'm sorry but you need to drop your gun, Argon." His face was a confused mask. He was sad but deliberate in his stance. "Please. Drop it." I could see regret in his eyes but a determination that let me know this was no ruse. I set my gun down.

"You better have something good to tell me, A1, 'cause I am getting pretty fucking angry right about now." I raised my hands slightly. He just looked at me seemingly unsure what to do next.

"What do you want to do now? Are we just going to stand here?"

"No. We wait."

"For what?"

He still looked confused and unsure and I thought I might be able to make a grab for my gun but I didn't think I would be able to bring myself to fire on him. Then I thought of Fig and her possible peril and I knew I'd have to do whatever was necessary. I needed to push the issue, keep him off balance and addled.

"So why are we standing here? Who could you possibly be waiting for?"

Then his eyes got big. A thin, unsteady smile started pulling up at the corners. The gun wavered in his hand and slowly started to return to his side. I was about to make my move when I noticed there was a tear forming in the corner of his eye, readying itself to roll down his leathery cheek. I froze and suddenly realized that he wasn't looking at me any longer. He was looking at something behind me.

"Abigail," he whispered.

"What? Your daughter?" I turned around and saw a person walking towards us. The sun was below the trees now and I squinted in the descending gloom. It was an older woman with long hair hanging down across her shoulders. Then a last fragmented beam of light from the failing sun slipped through a break in the trees and illuminated her. The warm light caught the highlights of her long hair and it seemed to catch fire in its brilliance. A fiery mane surrounding a beautiful face and I froze, my heart suddenly pounding in my throat. Trixie.

The impossible improbability of such a thing was comical in its sudden revelation. A ridiculous crisscrossing of circumstances that was astronomical in its reality. If it were in a movie I would have walked out appalled by the unimaginative laziness of the writer's plot device. A classic deus ex machina.

I mean, how could this get anymore implausible?

I heard a slight scuff of a footfall behind me and then heard Zyryn's voice.

"Mother?"

CHAPTER 22

If there was a group of four more stunned individuals in the entire universe I could not imagine what their circumstances could be.

A1 stood enraptured by the sight of his long lost daughter, Abigail Wun, whom he thought had been killed by the Xydoc Zyn decades earlier during a skirmish on a cargo freighter she had signed on. To add to his emotional avalanche, she had basically disowned him over an argument over her choice of profession almost a year previously. The unexpressed sorrow and regret he had carried all this time could be clearly seen etched across his weathered features.

Zyryn SanDyer, the daughter of the Lord of Pirates, was dumbstruck seeing her mother who had abandoned her as a small child to find safety away from Rink SanDyer. Her hope: to one day reunite and start a life with her daughter far from the madness of the toxic lifestyle she had been brought up under. She had finally been able to contact Zyryn and they had planned to escape together using the profits of the Lost Package to grubstake their future. An uneasy hope stirred on her face and I could see the resemblance between mother and daughter. Subconsciously I believe that it was this maternal similarity that had caused such a strong reaction when we had first met.

I was transfixed by the sight of the woman I only knew as Trixie, a girl I had fallen in love with as a young man only to have her torn away from my innocent dreams by a tragedy ending in her reported death. Crushed and rendered empty, my heart had scarred over preventing it from ever feeling such open surrender. She had been both my first and truest love but one that would never have lasted being born of youthful exuberance and misunderstood emotions. Such was the fate of most young loves that hung together with a rosy eye and an idealistic heart. There was no room in reality for such things or in the cynicism of age. Yet at the time it was as timeless and infinite as the stars themselves.

And stuck right in the middle of this was Abigail "Trixie" Wun. The confusion and shock froze her face into a rigid mask of exasperation. She could not begin to piece together the impossible circumstances that had occurred to create such a coalition of memories. To see three figures from her past grouped together caused instantaneous tears to spring to her eyes. I would never pretend to understand how she must have felt. With years of time to nurse her feelings both joyous and regretful she would have hung onto torn strands of dreams birthed in desperation and hope. And here she was faced with an outcome she could never have imagined. Her father, her daughter, and I gathered right before her. She could only have one question.

"How?" she asked.

A1 was the only one able to break free of his stupor as he walked slowly and hesitantly toward her as if she was a frightened wild animal who might spook if he drew too close.

"It's okay, Abby. It's alright now. Everything is going to be okay. Everything," he continued to ramble afraid to stop talking in case the spell was broken. "God. It is so great to see you after all these years." She simply stood, transfixed by his approach. "Abby, I've missed you so."

Her tears continued and she squeezed her eyes tight for a second. "Dad?" A1 nodded, tears now in his eyes. "Dad, I'm sorry."

He shook his head furiously. "No! No, my sweet angel. You have no reason to be sorry. It's my stupid, stubborn ways that pushed you away. I'm so sorry, Abby. So goddamn sorry for all these lost years." And then he hugged her and they clung to each other reaching past the years to find the time when they hadn't known this loss.

Zyryn started to move forward and I put out a hand to halt her. When she looked at me I slowly shook my head hoping she would wait and give them their moment. To my surprise she granted them their solitude. After a time they parted and looked at each other before Abigail looked past A1 and at Zyryn. She motioned her forward and A1 stepped aside to let mother and daughter embrace. He looked back at me with an incredulous look unable to understand how this was happening. He motioned to Zyryn and shrugged. I mirrored his gesture while offering my own toothy grin. He smiled and then looked back at Abigail.

"How the hell did this happen?"

She released Zyryn and kissed her forehead before looking back at A1. "It was Rink. After the Xydoc Zyn boarded our ship they stole me away with them as they retreated back to their own ship. I met Rink and he took an interest in me. He was actually nice to me at the start but after I gave birth to Zyryn he grew bitter about not having a son and turned cruel. I knew I had to escape before he eventually killed me. I couldn't bring Zyryn as she was only three at the time. I vowed I would return but too many things happened and getting word to her was nearly impossible. Finally I managed to infiltrate the Zyn with a friend I had made. He was able to join them and watch over Zyryn and let me know how she was doing. Through him I was able to get word to her about my plan for us to escape together."

Zyryn looked at me then at her. "It was Bob."

Abigail nodded. "Yes.'

Zyryn looked at her, an odd look in her eyes, "Father killed him."

Abigail's joyous face fell slightly. "I feared that would happen. Poor Bob, he was a good friend. I owe him a debt I can now never repay."

I walked closer to her and she stepped away from Zyryn and towards me. "I certainly didn't expect to see you here, Argon," she smiled. "It looks like you are still wearing that stupid head-rag thing I used to wear."

"And why would you ever expect to see me?" I said. "The fact that you recognize me and remember my name is enough to bewilder me. And I happen to like this 'head-rag thing' by the way."

She gave me a huge, tight hug and then a kiss on the cheek. "How could I ever forget you?" Her eyes twinkled and I was, for a moment, back under that tree on Blag. "You were never anything but kind to me. You gave me a home when I had none."

"I was in love with you," I whispered. I was shocked by my use of a past tense. It was not until that very moment that I realized that I didn't still love her; that what I thought I'd been carrying around with me was only an echo of a feeling I once had. I had grown used to the feeling and had long since lost its original source.

She gently placed her hand on my face and drew her fingers across my cheek. "I left my father feeling angry and bitter and thought I would never return. I felt lost onboard the ship with nothing to tie me down. No place to call home. But when I returned to Blag you were there, anxious for my return and so full of emotion that I was caught up in it and thought you were the place I was looking for. And," she looked at me so intently that I had to look away, "I think I really did love you then." She lifted my chin until I looked at her again. "You gave me what I needed Argon and I still love you for that." Then it was her turn to look away. "And I am glad that you didn't hang onto that. It was our moment but it wasn't to last."

"Of course not," I said, a bit more bravado in my voice than I intended. She glanced up quickly and I thought I saw a hint of disappointment in her eyes before she recovered from my such abrupt dismissal of our tryst. I backtracked, "I..no...I mean that after I heard about your 'death' I was brokenhearted and everything but I eventually moved on."

She smiled and drew close to me. "You don't need to say anymore." She put her lips to my ear and whispered something that let me know we understood each other both then and now. I felt my eyes begin to sting.

"I hate to break up this family reunion but I have some business to finish," came a voice from behind me. I spun around and found two men standing there, one with a hefty gun trained on us and the other one holding something I wasn't sure I would ever see again.

Winston.

"Garren Jot," I said recognizing the tall, thin man holding Winston. I glanced at the other man with the gun. "And your lackey, Mr. Nydak of course."

Again the Great Mysterious Nexus of the Universe had drawn in yet another piece of my life. The coincidence of having Jot show up here, the very place we first met when he killed Winston's previous "owner," Plood. He spared my life then only to have me run aground of his various nefarious schemes over the years. His ever-present minion, the large mountain of a man known only as Mr. Nydak, stood vigilant at his side training his gun at us with every intention of doing harm. I'd had the misfortune of dealing with Nydak on eight separate occasions, each one making me hate him even more. Seeing Winston in Jot's hands dawned the realization that the engine roar I had heard previously was familiar because it was my ship! Jot had stolen the Spud and Winston from the Jackleg office when I first met A1. Something about all of this smacked up against my brain as just odd. How was it that the person that had stolen my ship and employee would be showing up at the ass-end of the galaxy just as we find the truth of the Lost Package? He would have to have been informed of our progress...

I spun on A1. "You rat bastard!"

He looked at me with a surprised look but it quickly faded into guilt. "I...I..."

"Shove it, you traitorous old fool! You sold us out to Jot!"

Zyryn looked at A1 and then me. "What do you mean? What the hell is going on? Who is that tall asshole and why does he have a brain in a jar?"

I ignored her questions as any attempt to answer them would only result in even more questions and I doubted Jot was in the mood for my lengthy introductions. I focused my anger at A1. "How the fuck could you do this? How long, A1? How long have you been working for him?"

He shook his head. "You don't understand...I had to! He..."

I cut him off. "Anything you say is worthless, you stupid rusty old doorknob. You sold me out." Abigail looked at me with confused concern and then to her father.

"What did you do?" she asked. "What did you promise him?"

Garren Jot waved a hand as if to quiet all of the speculation and anger. "He promised me the Lost Package of Dehrholm Flatt in exchange for you, my dear. I contacted him and let him know that I had found your little hidey-hole and I would reveal it for a price. Your loving father agreed and now here we are." Another grand sweeping gesture. "I have done my part, Mr. Wun, now it is your turn to fulfill our bargain."

"Jot, you fool," I called out. "The Package is in your hand."

"What are you talking about, Bosch?"

"Winston. He's the Package. His brother sent him into exile and Flatt crashed here by mistake. Flatt died but I suspect that Plood found the wreckage and was able to salvage Winston from it and then designed a whole sideshow act around his unique abilities." I laughed at the irony. "You had the Package right in front of you when you shot Plood 15 years ago, you dolt!"

"Shut your hole!" threatened Nydak raising his gun to point it right at me. "You don't talk to Mr. Jot that way." He looked at the rest of us. "Nobody does," he added taking a step forward.

Jot waved him back. "Relax, Mr. Nydak. After all of the talk and legend I assumed that the actual truth would be less than...climactic." He smiled at me. "Argon Bosch we have had enough run-ins that you should know I always have a plan. The real goal here was not to possess some useless folklore trinket. Oh no. My true design was to motivate the desperately sad Mr. Wun to act as an unwitting lure to draw out my actual prize."

"And what the hell is this prize?" I asked.

"It should be here any moment," he revealed, his confidence oozing over his manner like thick oil. In all my misadventures birthed by Jot I always managed to narrowly avoid what I believed to be his intentions but now I was not so sure. He was a master puppeteer, pulling strings and orchestrating the Play with the real story only known by him. My last minute escapes could have just as soon been his real goals all along. Despite my exposure to him I never really knew what he was after. Maybe I was being played just like A1. I glanced over at him and I saw that same defeated man I had witnessed onboard the Heart. Abigail was looking at him with a deep sadness and she moved toward him to try and comfort him.

"Just stop right there, missy," warned Nydak.

"Don't point that gun at her," growled A1. His sorrow vanishing in anger. "You try and harm her and I'll rip your throat out." I had no doubt he meant it.

Nydak just laughed. "You dried up old turd. I'd crush you before you could touch me."

"Now is not the time, Mr. Nydak," started Jot. "My other pawn has already set the final act into motion. She has unknowingly brought my prize to me."

Abigail shook her head. "You've had me captive for the months. I couldn't have…"

Jot smirked. "Not you, silly. My sister."

"Huh?" I said. What other bizarre revelations were at hand I wondered.

"Zyryn," he called. "Come greet your brother."

She glared at him. "You are no brother of mine."

"Oh dear sister, you have no idea of the promiscuity of our father. I sometimes think he would fuck a Hranish Frill-back if it would stay still long enough. I, like you, was cast aside when he managed to find a new obsession to capture his attention." Zyryn looked uncomfortable. I suddenly felt that I had been played again. Jot continued, "I managed to navigate this little group just where I needed to draw you out so that you could deliver Rink SanDyer to me."

"What?" she gasped. "You wanted him here? Why?"

"To kill him of course. Isn't that what you wanted? For him to be dead? Haven't you dreamed of him dying after the way he treated you all these years? Well, sis, I plan on making that happen. You did notify him where you were, didn't you?"

She looked confused. "Yes. I…I let him know as soon as Argon told us where the Package was."

"Oh come on." I threw my arms in the air in surrender to this whole insane mess.

"And he is on his way as we speak. Just like when A1 called me to let me know. But SanDyer was further away and he would need to take a smaller ship to arrive in time. Oh, his fleet will be following but they will arrive too late."

"You can't...' Zyryn started.

"Really, Zyryn? You've dreamed of this! But you are my half-sister and after he dies you can take control of the Xydoc Zyn. Together we can create an invisible empire that will secretly control the entire Galaxy!" Already I could hear the megalomaniac tone rise in his voice. "This is all I need to complete my plans - an army of soulless mercenaries that can enforce the deals I need to make and instill in those I have yet to intimidate a necessity for loyalty. The Galaxy will be ours once you take our place as the new Master of the Zyn. Join me, sister!" He actually held out his hand as if she would take it as they run off toward the sunset.

An engine roar broke the moment and in a minute a small vessel had landed between two ramshackle buildings. There was little surprise when a defiant Rink SanDyer and three of his thugs strode up toward us. There wasn't much light now and the large moon illuminated the dust kicked up by the four of them as they approached. I noticed Nydak had his gun trained on them and not me. My pistol still lay where I had dropped it and I tried to calculate the chances of me reaching it before I was cut down by Nydak or one of the pirates accompanying SanDyer. Sadly I couldn't reach a suitable conclusion that didn't end up with me and most of my friends dead.

"Welcome...dad!" greeted Jot. "Glad you could make it."

To his credit SanDyer never broke stride as he drew close. "Who is this ass, Zyryn?"

"Aw...you don't even remember me, father?"

Rink slowed and then stopped. His guards had yet to even unholster their weapons being so wrapped up in their self-confidence from being a member of the Xydoc Zyn. He squinted in the dusk. "Garren?" The utterance of his name seemed to temporarily take the posture from Jot. "What the hell are you doing?" He did not utter either from being shocked by recognition or through the sheer force of SanDyer's will. "Never mind. Zyryn, where's this damn Package you were suppose to get me? You have managed to get it, right?" he chastised. "You called me here to pick it up before these morons sped off with it so you'd better have it."

Zyryn looked at her father and I could tell she was upset. She didn't answer and her lack of response only made SanDyer more impatient and angry.

"Can you not do anything right?" he stretched out both arms and shrugged. "I should have followed my first instinct and tossed you out the nearest hatch."

Abigail spun on him, her face flushed. "Don't you talk to our daughter that way!"

SanDyer suddenly realized who the woman was next to Zyryn and his face registered the surprise. "Abby? What the fuck is going on here?"

She turned toward him and started forward. "Leave her alone, Rink. She is going with me now. I had a hard enough time getting away from you and now when I am finally reunited with my daughter after all these years you suddenly drop in and think you can further berate her? Oh no," she shook her head and finger. "Look at what has happened to her in your care: she has been scarred and lost an eye. Is this what you do to your own daughter? I know you wanted a son but it looks like you already had at least one and here he is wanting to kill you! Are you just so indifferent and unfeeling that you can't love another person?"

"I'm a fucking pirate, Abby. Shit, have you forgotten that little bit about me?"

"No I haven't. I've spent the last twenty five years remembering that and hiding in fear of you finding me. Every night I would go to sleep thinking about Zyryn and wondering if that night would be the one where you would find me and kill me while I slept."

"You left *me*, remember? I had no desire to go after you. And as for your daughter...she did that crazy shit to herself."

Abigail turned to her daughter. "Zyryn?"

I stepped forward. "She did it out of frustration after he killed her lover, making up some story about her being attacked and raped..."

"Did she tell you that, Bosch?" interrupted SanDyer. "Ha. I never did anything like that. She got it in her head that I wanted a son and that she was too *pretty* to be an effective pirate..."

"Father!" Zyryn shouted.

"Go ahead and tell them, Zyryn," he coaxed. "Tell them how you killed your lover after you found him talking to another girl."

"Father," she pleaded. "No."

"Fact was, she actually scared me she was so brutal," he continued. "*Me*. The King of Pirates, the Most Feared Man in the Galaxy! She killed more people in raids than any of my men. She enjoyed it too much."

"No Father," she begged. "I wanted you to love me."

"He never will," shouted Jot. "He will never love you and he just wants you to run his errands and make him richer. Kill him and take his place!"

"What are you on about, Garren?" asked SanDyer. "You want me dead so you can take over?" he laughed. "At least you've got some ambition, I'll say that."

There was a lot of talk of killing and I was suddenly worried. Jot wasn't one to back down and Rink SanDyer was certainly not a man to threaten. Of all us standing there in the gloom, only they had weapons. Or so I wish that had been true.

Zyryn was very agitated and she had the look of a cornered animal, one that didn't know which way to turn or what action to take. Then I saw some resolution spark in her face and I knew right there that she had decided to take action. It just wasn't the action I had figured on.

There was a flourish of movement and she produced a knife from some place on her person. She spun it in her palm and I thought she was going to throw it but I saw that it ended its roulette with the handle firmly clutched in her hand versus the blade in her fingertips. She wasn't going to throw it. There could only be one thing she could do with it and that insane possibility had only enough time to blossom in my brain leaving me no time to act.

There is that moment in a movie where everything slows down to increase tension or to magnify a dramatic action. Then there are the people who talk about how they were in a life and death moment and they recount how everything happened in slow motion. That had never happened to me until just at that moment. I knew what Zyryn was about to do and it unfolded in long, stretched out seconds. But unlike the movies, I couldn't move any faster. I was stuck in some kind of horrible amber, sidelined in my own life and forced to spectate every detail of a truly terrible moment.

The sudden appearance of Zyryn's knife meant something entirely different to Jot. He thought his argument had clarified Zyryn's desire to kill her father and join him in overthrowing the Xydoc Zyn. He drew his firearm and leveled it at SanDyer.

SanDyer's men as well as Nydak also aimed their weapons to help protect their respective bosses. It was going to be a full-on firefight and we were right in the crossfire. But just as trigger fingers began to tighten and gun sights were aimed it happened and everything stopped. Zyryn plunged the knife into Abigail's chest.

I mentioned how time had slowed for this ballet of horror but just at that crescendo all time just stopped. I saw the shock on every single face. Every face except Zyryn's. She beamed a satisfied sense of accomplishment. She was perversely pleased and that made me rage. I don't know what crazy-inhibiting fuse had blown in her head but I wanted nothing right then but to get to her and strangle the life from her.

Abigail crumpled like Zyryn's knife had cut through her strings not her heart. A1 screamed something that carried such sadness that its impact was practically physical to everyone that heard it. He fell to his knees and scooped up Abby's lifeless body. Tears already stained his weathered face from the reunion with his lost daughter only moments before so the new tears that followed those tracks were literally washing away the joy with sorrow.

I used the sudden stunned paralysis to dive for my gun. Nydak saw my move and hip fired at me but the shot went wild and blasted into one of the abandoned buildings. My fingers found the butt of my pistol and I rolled behind an old carnival food stand. I could hear Zyryn shouting. "Father! Father! I killed her for you! She broke your heart and I killed her!" There was a maniacal lilt to her voice and I suspected that she had to be clinically insane. She had led me along like a fool with some grand scheme to finally prove her love for her father and vindicating her worth in some mad ploy to capture his approval.

Another shot from Nydak tore through the stand I was using for shielding and made me second guess its effectiveness. The third shot, inches from my face, convinced me. I scrambled for a barrier that had been placed to prevent vehicle traffic onto the street and just made it before another shot smacked into it. For now it held and I was granted a momentary reprieve to gather my bearings and devise a plan. Unfortunately I could not see Zyryn from my new shelter so I couldn't shoot her though I might have waited, still seeing the more satisfactory image in my mind of my hands on her throat.

"Father!" Zyryn was screaming. SanDyer either was too stunned to speak or was running for cover from Jot's eventual attack. "FATHER!" she continued to wail. Finally other blasts started coming from across the street as SanDyer's minions joined in and decided to try and take down Jot before he engaged them. Unfortunately for me, I had no shelter from them and if they decided to just go ahead and kill me now, I would have little cover. I needed to move...again.

Jot's voiced boomed over the weapon fire. "Zyryn, you stupid girl. You have thrown it all away. He still won't love you, don't you know that? He only cares for himself."

I chanced a look hoping that Nydak was too busy with the Zyn to focus on me. I peeked over the barrier and saw SanDyer running past me toward Zyryn. He was low and he fired a few shots toward Jot and Nydak. The Zyn mercenaries that had accompanied him kept a steady stream of shots aimed at Jot and Nydak forcing them to stay behind cover. I could have fired on him but I would have been killed immediately by the Zyn.

"What have you done?" he asked Zyryn as he squatted next to Abigail. "Why would you do this?" I couldn't tell if he was sad or just confused by her death.

"For you," she pleaded. "To show you that I choose you. Always you." She was crying in desperation, aching for the slightest hint that he would accept her.

"Zyryn, you are a fool. Don't you know...?"

I really wish I could have heard the rest of that statement. And I know that Zyryn will always be haunted by what he was going to say. But neither of us will ever know because right at that moment A1 pulled the knife from Abigail's chest and swung it in a fierce, hard arc right for Zyryn. SanDyer caught the movement out of the corner of his eye and sprung forward intercepting the knife's trajectory. I don't know if it was deliberate or reflexive as the movement appeared awkward and desperate but Rink SanDyer took the knife right in his neck and fell backward dead as a stone.

"Told you," coughed A1.

Zyryn screamed and backed away from her father's corpse, repulsed at the startling reality. This caused the Zyn to suddenly refocus their actions and turn their attention to Zyryn and A1. In the confusion and shock, one of them peppered the area with gunfire. It was impossible for me to tell if he hit anything but both A1 and Zyryn lay motionless. Once their senses recovered the three pirates ran for Zyryn and their fallen leader. The one that had loosed his fire on A1 and Zyryn hesitated in his sprint, seemingly concerned at the outcome of his panicked barrage of gunfire upon them. Nydak was able to pick him off easily as they scrambled across the road. The remaining two reached Zyryn and I saw that although she had been hit, she was alive. A1 remained upsettingly still. Nydak attempted to hit them but his angle was not sufficient to get in a well place shot. One of the pirates shouldered Zyryn so she could stand and they started back toward the ship they had landed in. It was obvious from their struggled escape and bloody trail that Zyryn's right leg and foot had been hit. The Zyn laid down covering fire but I saw my opportunity and took it. My blast took him out and it was all the excuse Nydak needed to renew his attack. Despite his efforts they made it to the vessel.

"I won't forget this, Jot!" Zyryn yelled out. The two of them boarded the craft and began their ascent. I was sad she wasn't dead. I stood up and Nydak, the eternal bastard, took a shot at me.

"Stop shooting, you ass!" I shouted. "I need to get to my friends."

"Throw down your gun, Bosch," he replied. All business that guy.

I didn't care at this point and I let it drop and ran to A1 and Abigail. I feared the worst and was filled with remorse when I found my trepidation was grounded. There was a huge pool of blood around Abigail and her eyes looked up at me lifeless. A1 fared little better, the severity of his wounds giving me the impression he was already dead. Hence my startled reaction when his eyes opened and he looked at me.

"Well, this isn't what I expected," he said.

I knelt down next to him and Abigail and carefully reached over and closed her eyes. "I'm sorry, A1. I'm sorry about a lot of things." I continued to look down at Abigail and I felt the heat of the tears stinging my eyes. I pulled off my head covering and placed it across her face.

He reached up and grabbed my arm. I put my other hand on top of his. "I am the one who is sorry, Argon. I betrayed you. I was shooting my mouth off about the Package and he must have found out because a couple weeks later his boys picked me up. He said he could trade me something special for the Package." He hacked on a wet cough and bit of blood caught on his lips. "Turns out he knew my Abby was still alive. Told me he would kill her if I didn't get the Package. I've been keeping him posted on our progress all along. I even had to sabotage the ship a couple times to buy him time to find us. He..." another nasty cough. "He even had me sidetrack us into the Blanket in order to run us across SanDyer's ship. The crazy son of a bitch had this whole thing mapped out from the get-go."

I patted his hand and then it fell away as his remaining strength left him. His eyes closed. "You know, your little joke about your name really was pretty funny," I whispered.

For a moment I thought he was gone. Then he let out a sigh and spoke, eyes still shut. "Really?"

"Fuck no."

He managed to cough out a horse laugh and a fine spray of blood. "You are such an asshole." Then his face grew more serious. "She really loves you, you know."

"Your daughter was a very special and wonderful woman."

"No, you idiot, not her! It's in the name of the ship." His words dying into a whisper. "Don't let her get away too." His hand rose up and I went to grab it thinking he was trying to take mine but he reached out and took his daughter's. He smiled and then he slipped away to join her on some distant plane. Looking at them together I choked on the failed stifling of a sob. I turned to stand and looked right into the barrel of Nydak's gun.

"Fuck!"

"You forget about us, Bosch?" he asked.

"Not enough." I stood up and brushed at the dirt on my knees.

"We still have some shit to settle, you and me."

"Right. How many times have you tried to kill me now?"

"Seven."

I came up quick, my head hitting him beneath the jaw. He fell backward and lost his gun. I turned quickly and dove for mine. I got my grip and rolled bringing up the barrel to Nydak's prone form. "Make it eight, asshole." I was proud of my little moment then I noticed Jot aiming his gun right at me.

"Not so quick Mr. Bosch. Maybe you'd like to put that back where you dropped it and stand up."

"Of course, Garren. I'll lay it right here for a minute until I can snatch it back up and shoot you in your smug-ass face."

"Always the attitude with you," he murmured in mock annoyance. "I've known you for a long time and you always have such contempt for me. I would think you'd go a bit easier on me given that I saved your life from that cheap swindler Plood all those years ago. But, no. You just have to keep getting in my way."

"In *your* way? Hell, three times you hired me to be a pawn in some elaborate scheme. Four other times I just happen to run afoul of your plans. We'd *both* be better off if you just left me alone!"

He picked some bit of lint off his jacket sleeve. "You are like that old, loose scab - I just can't seem to let you be. But I need to just get rid of you once and for all. This day has been far too troubling and disappointing. If I can salvage anything it will be seeing you removed from any further involvement in my plans. Mr. Nydak here can see to it. But I do have a question you can answer for me before you...go."

"Oh, by all means. What can I answer for you?"

He grinned and said, "How old is Zyryn?"

"What kind of stupid question is that?"

"I am just wondering. Now that she is going to be the head of the Xydoc Zyn I am curious if she even has a stake in that title. Abigail said Rink SanDyer became bitter after Zyryn was born because, as she put it, he wanted a son. Well, he had a son years before - me - and I can attest to the fact that he didn't care one bit about me either. Maybe he was bitter because he found out that Zyryn wasn't his daughter at all."

"Then who..." I stopped as I realized the point he was trying to make. It went off in my head like a bomb. "No."

He only grinned wider. "Sad, the only two people that know the truth are lying over there. Dead. And the one real clue to her identity is just about to join them."

"You motherfucker!"

"Now, now...I'm not the incestuous one here," he laughed. "Mr. Nydak, if you please."

I was completely helpless and Nydak aimed his gun right at my...

His head exploded right in front of me. Nydak's body sagged and plopped on the ground and some of his head had splashed on Jot's face.

I spun around and saw Doon running toward me, his gun still leveled in our direction. Jot took one look and sprinted around the side of the building.

"Need some help?" asked Doon as they closed in on me.

"Yeah! We need to go get Jot." Then I heard that familiar engine roar again. I knew instantly what was happening. "He's got the Spud! He's going to fly out of here and get away."

Doon stopped in his tracks. "I doubt that."

Then I saw the Spud rise over the buildings and turn toward the sky. In a moment he was going to be streaking into space and I'd have to worry about him coming after me all over again. Having him constantly on my mind, wondering when he would make his move, worried more than the nightmarish scenario he suggested. Well...almost.

Two rockets arced across the sky and impacted my old ship. It vaporized immediately leaving nothing in its place but some dust and my eternal thanks. I turned and scanned the sky for the source of the missiles and saw the Sononi Heart holding fast hovering above the spot she had landed. Fig. She dipped a wing and then started toward our location to pick us up. It made me think of what A1 had said.

I looked at Doon and asked, "You are half Obarnee. I know *sononi* is an Obarnee word. It means 'malfunctioning,' right?"

He looked at me and then back at the ship as it started to land in the road. He shook his head in disgust. "You still haven't figured it out? And here I used to think you were a pretty sharp guy. Must be the age."

"What?"

"You are using a literal translation. In slang it means *broken*."

"All this time we have been flying around in the Broken Heart," I mumbled more to myself than to Doon. He only continued to shake his head.

I looked down at the ground and saw something I had managed to momentarily forget: a small container that housed what appeared to be a human brain. "Nice to see you again, Argon," it said. "Been pretty busy I assume. But now that all the excitement has died down do you think you might be able to pick me up before some mangy creature comes along and gives me a piss?"

I snatched him up immediately. "Winston!"

"Easy, easy. Sudden movements like that can cause me to bang around in here. Lord knows something could come loose and then where would I be?"

"I've got a great story to tell you, my old friend," I almost shouted in excitement. "You won't believe it!"

"Frankly I find it hard to believe you took this long to come looking for me," he said not bothering to cover his annoyance.

"Oh that's not true, Winston. There have been people looking for you for a *long* time!"

I saw Fig come walking from the ship. Doon looked at her then at me and winked. I handed Winston over and headed for Fig. "Doon, this is Winston. Winston, Doon."

"Hi Winston."

"Doon, is it? Think you could locate me a good, stiff drink?"

"But you don't even have a mouth."

"Bloody hell. Another pragmatist."

I started picking up my pace as I drew closer to Fig. Finally I started to run. "Don't worry," she said. "I took care of Barry as soon as he got on board." I didn't say anything and just kept running. She stopped and asked, "Are you OK, Argon?" I reached down as I was heading toward her and scooped up my pistol. I leveled my arm, took aim, and pulled the trigger. That stupid, fucking space monkey never saw what hit him. She looked around surprised and saw his little hat flutter down behind her near the gangway of the ship. She turned back to me and smiled. I took her in my arms and kissed her before she could say anything more.

And to my surprise, she kissed me back.

EPILOGUE

"**A**nd so then there you were, sitting on the ground right at my feet like nothing had happened," I finished. I was sitting in the front office of the Jackleg Courier Service office with Winston at his usual station behind a bank of monitors beneath the Company logo.

"That's quite a story, Argon."

"It is one hell of a story," I corrected. "They could make a movie out of it!"

"Nobody would believe it," he asserted.

"Maybe I should write a book first. A memoir. Then..."

"Nobody would read it."

"You seem awfully sure of that," I said.

"Who would care about some lowly delivery pilot running about the Galaxy like a fool, trying to find a misplaced parcel?"

"I don't know. It has some interesting elements in it. There's some romance. Some mystery, maybe a laugh or two." I found I was a little offended by his quick dismissal.

"The only comedy is that you think people would give a single damn about it," he acknowledged. "Besides, there isn't nearly enough of me in there. I'm clearly the most charismatic of this sad pair. Maybe I'll write a novel about my adventures while you were off screwing a half-blind pirate who may or may not be your..."

"Don't say it!" I warned. "We will never mention that possibility again. Ever. To anyone. Ever."

Winston laughed, a sound I rarely heard from his little speaker. It was so unexpected that I had to laugh myself. And so there we were, Winston and me, laughing.

We had been returned to the suddenly welcome grounds of the Jackleg Courier Service office just two days prior by Fig after the rather shorter direct route from Alongago City. It was surprising that a journey that had taken so long and felt like we had circumnavigated the entirety of the Galaxy could be completed in a matter of just a couple days.

During our trip I had the opportunity to spend the majority of my time in Fig's company and I was glad for it. I won't say it was all just roses and chocolates as there was a lot of heavy baggage we needed to sort through. I had made a mess of things in the worst possible way and it wasn't something that would right itself in this short span. In my self-obsessed depression I had hurt her deeply and my behavior while she joined me on this quest had been abhorrent and unforgivable. I looked back and felt shame in how I had acted and wondered why she would ever care about me again. But to wonder such things was to commit an injustice to Fig's character and discount her ability to see beyond the immediate. It also was a testament to my own lack of understanding Fig. After knowing her for all of her life I still didn't know who she was. For some reason I still don't comprehend, she still had feelings for me and that gave me hope for a future that included her.

We made a short detour to drop Doon off at his home. I had not forgotten about him and realized that I owed an equally strong apology to him for my actions. He was easier to convince and more anxious to forgive but that had always been his way. And it is in that simple statement that I realized that he was the one person that I had most disappointed. While he quickly shrugged it off, I could not forgive myself for the anguish and hurt I had forced on him and how I had single handedly managed to wedge him in between Fig and me during this journey. He was in so many ways my little brother and I had taken his allegiance for granted. We sat and talked for several hours on one of the days on the return trip and I actually let him do most of the talking for once. He said some things that were uncomfortable to hear but needed to be said. When it was all done we hugged and he said he loved me. I found that my respect for him had grown and that I truly admired his loyalty and conviction. His friendship was a gift in the truest form. I also learned that he was married and had three children. The shame I felt upon learning this was deeply felt for I had never even bothered to ask him about his life during our whole ordeal. He had risked not ever seeing his family to come to my aid and that was a debt I would never be able to repay.

Finally I was back, and Winston and I had walked up to the door of our little office during the first light of day with the Sononi Heart rising up over our heads and curving off into the deep blue sky.

"Think we'll see her again?" he asked.

I smiled. "Yes. We will," and I turned and opened up the door and walked into my home.

That day was spent trying to catch up on the mess of our absence. I had left in a rush two weeks before and there were some over-due packages still sitting by the door waiting to be delivered. There were also several messages left on our message recorder. One man had sworn for three solid minutes before the machine had cut him off. He didn't even bother to leave a call back number or his name. I was certain that he would call again. There was also a mess where the packages sat as one of them must have contained some foodstuffs and they had spoiled, leaked, and otherwise fouled the office. It would be some time before we would be able to make the situation right given that we were without a ship. Winston busied himself with trying to communicate with the customers about their packages. I did my best at trying to negotiate a new ship for me to fly but our funds were at an all time low once Winston had manage to settle our restitution with the clients. Finally, near the end of the second day we had the deliveries brokered out to another company and the clients as happy as we could hope for. Winston and I settled in for the coming night and decided to try and figure out how to get a ship the next day.

"Winston?"

"No, I told you already, I don't have any money," he rattled off before I could say anything further.

"No, that's not what I was going to say."

"Well, what is it then?"

"As you know, I did a lot of thinking about my life on this trip..."

"How would I know that? I was chained to a wall and tortured daily while you skipped through space with your head buried between..."

"Hey! I wasn't...And you weren't chained to a wall."

"I was on a high shelf! I could have fallen off."

"And tortured?"

"No food or drink!"

I shook my head. "You are floating in water," I pointed out.

"Water? I am floating in my own waste! I'm encased in a toilet!" he complained.

"I'm sorry," I said. "Whatever the condition, it couldn't have been fun. I was worried about you. Seriously."

"Oh come on now," he moaned. "It's me you are talking to. *You* worried about *me*? When would that happen?"

Normally he would have been right. "A lot happened on this trip. And it has really made me think about what a jerk I have been to everyone. And that includes you."

"That must have been some trip! Was there a head injury involved?"

"Maybe," I said scratching at my head. I wasn't sure if I had been hit in the head during the journey or not.

"Why don't you actually tell me what happened and I'll be the judge of any changes of heart that might have arisen from your various trials and tribulations," he suggested.

"Alright, I will."

"And don't leave out any of the sex bits."

"I will only censor out what my modesty calls for."

"I am already bored to tears," he complained.

I gave him a look and then started with the tale. "I left here and went to Galder's as you might remember..."

"Like I said, it is quite a story," Winston repeated after he stopped laughing. "But one thing I am curious about."

"And what's that?"

"What was Abby doing all that time after she left Rink up until Jot found her?"

"She didn't really say. Why?"

"Well...I know it sounds strange but Linus' wife was named Abigail and she had the most astounding red hair. You don't think...?"

I looked at him, my eyes wide in surprise. "No. No, Winston. That is just too much of a coincidence. She couldn't have been..." I wouldn't even say it.

"Of course not, you idiot," he laughed. "Didn't your story have enough impossible coincidences in it already? Could you imagine if she was also Linus' wife? Hell, I would have spit in your eye myself and told you to get the fuck out of here."

I laughed again. "You had me," I confessed.

"Of course, Argon. You are an easy mark."

I stood and stretched. "I'm going to turn in and get some sleep. I need to find a damn ship tomorrow or we are not going to be able to keep this thing running."

"OK. I'll just stay here then and man the counter."

"Good night, Winston, and thanks."

"For what?"

"For being there this last 15 years. You're a good friend." I headed toward my room.

"Right. About that raise..."he started and I was through the door, a smile on my face.

The next morning I wandered into the kitchen next to my room and couldn't decide on what I wanted to eat. I wasn't really hungry and I dreaded what lay ahead. It looked like I was going to have to lease some pieced together death trap to try and get by until we could afford a new ship. The insurance I had on it didn't cover getting blown out the sky despite the fact that it had been stolen by some nefarious scoundrel. I asked for a review but I wouldn't be holding my breath for a better result. Given their glacial pace if the committee did rule in my favor it would have to be a posthumous award to some next of kin. Regardless, it was not going to be a pleasant day.

So I grabbed a couple pieces of Balasian spine-fruit and walked out to the reception room where Winston was always camped. I thought I heard the murmur of low voices as I opened the door. A client? Why would Winston even entertain them? We hadn't a ship to deliver anything so unless it was going to somewhere I could walk...

"Surprise!"

I almost fell over. Fig was standing there along with Doon. "What are you doing here?" I grinned. It was highly unexpected but at that moment I suddenly realized how much I had missed them in this short time.

"We have a surprise for you," said Doon. His notorious huge grin was threatening to take over his face.

"Well, it must be good one! What is it?"

Fig came over to me and gave me a hug. Then she took my arm. "Follow me." We headed out the door and into the large open area in front of the building. Then I saw it.

Sitting on the landing pad was a brand new Hanton Model 11XC-9! My ship, the reliable Space Spud, was an 11XC-7. This beautiful ship was a newer model and it gleamed! The lines of the ship were smooth and exciting with not a spec of rust or corrosion affecting the hull. There were small differences (besides the rust) that revealed it as a later model. The high tail fin was more swept back in design and the engine had a better aesthetic helping it look more like it was part of the ship and not just jammed into the end of the body like a giant suppository. The color was a close approximation to the brownish bronze of my original but, without the odd plating patches or burn marks, it looked so much better.

And painted carefully on the side of the craft was "Space Spud 2." I looked at Fig and Doon and managed to stutter out, "How?" while a tear of happiness rolled down my cheek.

"It was Doon," explained Fig. "He wanted to get this for you."

"I did!" he exclaimed. "I had to do some searching right after I got home and it took a bit but I found this one and I knew it had to be yours!"

"They stopped making the 11X ten years ago," I said. "The series 12 was the last line to be made. And there weren't that many as Hanton went out of business that year after struggling for decades."

"I know! But I found a guy who had one and he wanted to get rid of it. Said he hated the look of it but had bought it since they were known to be fast."

I nodded. "That's about all they had going for themselves." I quickly reverted to feeling guilty and a little embarrassed by their charity. "But I can't take this. Really."

Fig grabbed my arm again, hard. "Oh, you're taking it or we will beat you right here and now."

Doon nodded. "She's right. We can't return it and I will hold you down while she knocks the shit out of you if you mention not accepting it one more time."

I almost complained again but then I relented. I put up my hands in surrender. "You win."

"Good," smiled Fig.

"Did you both fly in the Spud? How will you get home?"

"I flew the Spud here. Doon brought his own ship. It's parked over there," she pointed.

I looked across the lot and saw a stunning ship of white with bold graphics along the side and underbelly. Then I noticed some people crossing towards us. "Is that...?"

"It is my family," announced Doon proudly. "I brought them to meet you."

The woman was beautiful and Obarnee. Her jet black hair was worn short and contrasted nicely against her bright yellow skin. The two boys and the one girl varied in shade and it was nice to see the oldest boy taking after Doon with his light hair and tall build. After the introductions were made his wife, Nirian, gave me a huge hug. She said how much she had looked forward to meeting me as Doon never had anything but wonderful things to say about me. That was so like Doon - even after I left him behind and cut all ties he still would only tell her I was a great friend.

"Nirian, kids...Doon here is the bravest man I have ever met and the most loyal friend anyone could ever hope for. He is one in a million and I am lucky to call him...my brother."

He grabbed me suddenly and almost crushed me in his embrace. "I love you," he said. I held him for a moment and relished the fact that despite everything I had done to destroy this possibility, he managed to still make it happen.

"You helped save me, Doon," I said quietly. "You and Fig." He hugged me again and then let me go.

"Dad," his daughter complained.

I looked down at her and smiled. I put my arm around Fig and Doon and said, "Let's go inside and talk. I think I have a couple tales I can share with the kids that they'll enjoy." Doon's children perked up at the promise of stories that might embarrass their father. "Have you kids ever seen a brain in a jar that can talk?" They laughed and said that was gross and couldn't be real. "Oh, he's real alright. His name is Winston and he just *loves* kids! In fact, the thing he really loves is to be picked up and quickly spun in circles!" We walked back toward the Jackleg the three kids racing ahead for the door...

I looked at Doon. "How long can you stay?"

"Oh, we have to leave in a little while but I think Fig's going to go home later."

I turned and looked at her. "How will you get home if your ride leaves?"

She smiled that smile I realized I had missed for 15 years. The smile that I grew fond of when she was a little girl and then grew to love when we were adults. "I happen to know this guy that just got a brand new ship and is itching to take it for a spin. Maybe I can bum a ride from him tomorrow."

I laughed and thought how lucky I was walking along between the two people I loved the most in the Galaxy. I winked at Fig. "Or, maybe the day after."

I touched down near the housing community on Lorak 5, the one habitable moon orbiting the enormous gas giant Lorak. It always amazed me that planets would use some kind of numeric designation for their planet instead of naming it. Was it laziness or utter lack of imagination that would cause some committee to simply count out the number of planets or moons and then just arbitrarily assign them a number based off some overall name used by the most popular planet? I would think those living on this planet would have some issue with this. Even back on Earth we picked out names for all of the planets and moons throughout the solar system with the exception of our own moon which received the dubious distinction of being named "Moon."

The city of Trenjaban (thankfully not named Lorak 5 City 148) was small and surrounded by farmland. My package was being delivered to a Jaban Shoe who lived somewhere amongst the multitude of close packed houses centered in the city. I found the closest landing spot and was lucky to discover that Jaban's house was directly in front of the pad. I dropped down from the cockpit hatch and opened the side freight compartment on the ship. It wasn't a large package but I had doubled up on deliveries this round and had sensitive equipment packages that needed to be transported inside the ship. At the last moment, as I left the Jackleg, I had grabbed this little gem since I could drop it off on the way back and net a little more profit not having to make a separate trip. Genius.

I carried the box over to the house and rapped my knuckles against the frame of the door. A moment later the door swung open and a tall figure stood in the doorway. The indigenous people that live on Lorak 5 are a race known as Plondus. I hadn't met one before but at first glance they reminded me of some kind of hairless cat with but a single, large, multi-pupiled eye right in the center of their somewhat feline face. The one facing me had to be over seven feet tall and was only wearing some kind of long skirt. Judging from what I found to be a common norm in race sexuality, this specific Plondus was a female. And I made a mental note that Plondus were not shy.

"Hello. Do you speak Common?" I asked. A standard question

when delivering to more rural planets and one best to get straightened out from the beginning as almost every planet speaks Common to some degree and I can only barely speak a handful of other languages competently enough to get through a simple delivery. Thankfully Winston can speak almost anything and he is usually just a call away.

She nodded. "I speak some good."

"Fair enough. I have a delivery for Jaban Shoe." I held up the package. "It is from..." I looked at the manifest again. "A mister...Grontus Shoe. Are you Jaban?"

She gave a noise for what I assumed was a laugh but might have been a curse for all I knew. "No. No, no, no. Son be Jaban. Mother am me."

"Oh, sorry Mrs. Shoe. Is Jaban here?" I found myself speaking slowly and loudly using my freehand to gesticulate. She didn't seem to mind so I continued during our exchange.

"Here inside is Jaban." she turned and bellowed something unintelligible but I thought I picked out the son's name amongst the gibberish. I stood there, a polite smile frozen on my face as we waited for Jaban to appear. Normally I like to just drop and run but this one did require a signature and the special instructions specified that I leave the package with Jaban. Mrs. Shoe howled out some strange combination of sounds and then I heard the rapid pounding of feet upon the floor deep inside the house. Finally what I assumed to be Jaban came panting up to the door. He looked somewhat like his mother and like her, did not wear a shirt. His skin was a slightly darker pink, bordering more on a pale red. Perhaps that was a difference between the males and females of the race but it was far too early to formulate a theory.

Mrs. Shoe moaned out some more odd sounds and Jaban replied in kind. Then she turned and looked at me. "It be Jaban's beginning anniversary Uncle Grontus gift. He am excited much."

My head was starting to hurt from so many confusions of syntax so I asked her to sign my D-pad and I would be off. She did as young Jaban bounced around like some kind of unstable molecule. I thanked her and started back for the ship.

I called Winston on my personal comm. "Winston! Just finished the delivery on Lorak 5. Another happy customer."

"Wait. What are you doing on Lorak 5?"

"I happened to see there was a delivery out here when I was getting ready to leave and it was on my way back so I figured it would save me some time and make us some extra money. Pretty smart, huh?"

"But I don't understand. Your interior was full of all those packages for Mitech Industries. There wasn't any room for anything else." I could hear some annoyance in his tone and it bothered me that he still didn't want to give me any credit for taking the initiative. Why did he always think of me as some idiot?

"Do I need to remind you that I have an extra cargo compartment on the ship? You should know this. It isn't that different from the original Spud."

"That is a non-monitored compartment. It does not equalize pressure between trips. A sealed container can react poorly should it be opened suddenly. Didn't you notice the warning on the outside of the box?"

"What did it say?"

"Live cargo."

"Uh...what happens to that?" I could still hear Jaban laughing and excitedly asking his mom to get the box open. I was about to turn around when I heard a sickly, wet pop noise, a small scream, and the sound of Jaban crying. I decided it would be best if I just kept going.

"Never mind. I know what happens."

"Idiot," mumbled Winston.

ABOUT THE AUTHOR

Kirk Nelson lives in Scottsdale, Arizona with his wife and two cats.

When not writing (or working) he can often be found playing video or board games, drawing, creating videos, watching movies, and of course, reading.

This is the author's first novel.

Made in the USA
Middletown, DE
04 August 2022

70603824R00219